****

Monroe Doctrine

Volume III
****

By James Rosone and Miranda Watson

Published in conjunction with Front Line Publishing, Inc.

1

Copyright Notice

ISBN: 978-1-957634-08-1

Sun City Center, Florida, USA

Library of Congress Control Number: 2022903244

Table of Contents

Chapter One: This Is Bananas 5

Chapter Two: Baron Returns 19

Chapter Three: VX-9 54

Chapter Four: Recalibration 67

Chapter Five: In the Dead of Night 78

Chapter Six: A New Beginning 99

Chapter Seven: R2-D2 111

Chapter Eight: Kamikazes 118

Chapter Nine: Task Force Dupre 125

Chapter Ten: Weight of the World 146

Chapter Eleven: Island Hopping 152

Chapter Twelve: Battle Bots 161

Chapter Thirteen: The Gator Brigade 172

Chapter Fourteen: R&R 187

Chapter Fifteen: Bogotá Blues 192

Chapter Sixteen: Three Options 204

Chapter Seventeen: Big Picture 207

Chapter Eighteen: Escalation 218

Chapter Nineteen: King of Battle 227

Chapter Twenty: Oh Dark Thirty 249

Chapter Twenty-One: Operation Margaritaville 262

Chapter Twenty-Two: NATO–South 274

Chapter Twenty-Three: Airborne Leads the Way 293

Chapter Twenty-Four: The Enemy's Vote 312

Chapter Twenty-Five: Operation Market Garden Redux 323

Chapter Twenty-Six: Bumblehive 338

Chapter Twenty-Seven: Arc Light 358

Chapter Twenty-Eight: Giant Lawn Darts.. 363

Chapter Twenty-Nine: I Am the Future.. 371

From the Authors.. 386

Abbreviation Key 390

Chapter One

This Is Bananas

Montecristo National Park

El Salvador

Sergeant First Class Rusten Currie slapped the side of his neck a bit harder than he had intended to. Pulling his hand away, he saw some blood on his fingers. He wasn't sure if it was his or from the damn mosquito. The little bastards were almost the size of a nickel.

"I told you to start taking those garlic pills," said their medic, Mark Dawson, teasingly. "They work like magic at keeping those things away from you."

"Yeah, and they keep the women away from you too," Currie shot back angrily as he swatted at another one.

"Maybe that was the plan all along," chided Dawson with a grin.

"Ha, is that what you were trying to do, Dawson? Keep all the girls to yourself?" Currie countered.

Dawson laughed as he shook his head. "I'm just trying to help you not become an all-you-can-eat buffet for the local bugs of Central America. You're free to think what you will."

Slapping yet another mosquito, Currie grudgingly said, "You were right, Dawson. I should have accepted your offer of those garlic pills."

"What was that, Currie?" Dawson asked with a lifted eyebrow.

"You heard me. I'm not saying it again."

Dawson laughed. "I just wanted to hear you say it one more time."

"Say what one more time?" Currie pressed.

"That I was right."

5

Currie looked at his friend and spat a stream of chewing tobacco on the dirt near his foot, shaking his head.

"Damn, you two whine and fight like a married couple," Captain Thorne commented good-naturedly before turning serious again. "In five mikes, we're going to move to Checkpoint Gamma and either clear it or confirm what's there. Then we'll stand by and see what headquarters wants us to do next."

"You really think the Chinese built up some sort of massive military complex here like they did in Cuba?" Currie asked skeptically.

Thorne shrugged. "Ours is not to wonder why. Ours is but to do or die, gentlemen."

"Why can't we do normal Special Forces stuff—you know, like train up an insurgency either here or in Venezuela?" asked Currie. "I heard 1st Battalion's fully deployed down in the Amazon part of Venezuela."

"Yeah, and part of 2nd Battalion is here doing the same thing," Dawson added angrily. "Yet our company continues to draw the short stick for this crappy reconnaissance work."

"Hey, you all wanted to be part of a HALO team," Captain Thorne chided. "Reconnaissance work is like our primary function. We go in behind enemy lines, find important and valuable targets and either blow them up or set them up to be blown up. Now stop your whining and get with the program. We've got two more grid squares to recce before we can get out of here. Let's do our damn jobs and scoot."

The guys nodded at the short rebuke from their team leader. Currie realized this was something they should be talking about back on base, not out here in the field. They had broken field decorum a bit with their whining. Chief Miller shot them both a dirty look, letting them know they'd get an earful from him when they got back to base.

Master Sergeant Altenburg had a slight grin on his face as he shook his head. Currie had just made E-7 when the war had broken out; he wanted to be a team sergeant like Dawson and lead his own team, but that wasn't going to happen if he had to question everything. The fastest way to move up in the Army and Special Forces was to be damn good at your job and just do as you were told.

"All right, all right. I get it," said Currie. "I'm shutting up now. Sorry—I just needed to vent and get it off my chest." Currie finished off his protein bar and then buried the wrapper.

****

Four Hours Later

Dawson raised his hand, then lowered it as he took a knee. Currie could hear voices in the distance, speaking in Spanish and Chinese. He scurried up to Dawson, and Thorne made his way up to them as well.

"What do we have?" Currie whispered.

Dawson pointed off in the distance. "Looks like a joint patrol." He paused. "Yeah, it's a patrol. I count nine tangos."

Thorne grunted at the assessment. "Good catch, Dawson. Let's let them pass through the area and then look to backtrace where they may have come from. We need to see if they're operating out of some sort of larger facility or just a small camp."

"That's a good copy, sir." Dawson then pulled his map out and found their exact position. His finger traced the edge of the ridge they were skirting along. "I'm going to lead us along this section and see if there may be a camp in the base of this valley or along the top of the ridge section here. My gut says they're operating in one of these two locations."

Thorne nodded. "I like it. Let's do it. Currie, I want you to scout ahead of the rest of us, but move parallel to us along the top of the ridge. Let's minimize our coms—only make contact if you find something. We'll do likewise. Got it?"

Currie smiled; he liked this plan. He was a bit of a lone wolf. "Got it. I'll see you guys in a few hours."

****

Two hours later, Currie paused just long enough to eat a bite of his protein bar. The climb up the ridge had really sapped the energy right out of him. Aside from the initial patrol they'd spotted earlier, they hadn't seen any new groups of soldiers.

Moving through the jungle just below the top of the ridge, Currie did his best to listen for anything out of the ordinary.

Looking to his right, he saw a multicolored parrot gnawing on a banana. He smiled at the bird. It was beautiful and majestic. The red, blue, and green colors contrasted against the colors of the jungle in the most incredible way.

Suddenly, the bird stopped eating and took to the air. Currie instinctively dropped to the ground, ready to fire on whatever had scared it away.

Then he heard a soft, faint voice. Currie couldn't tell if it was far away or just muffled by the jungle. Scanning the area around him, he thought he spotted something that didn't belong.

Currie moved slowly to his right as he kept a handful of large trees and some thick bushes between him and the source of the noise. As he advanced, his eyes darted around, searching for what his ears told him was nothing good. His body snaked around a fallen log as he sought to go low, sensing he wasn't alone out here. When he slithered through a large bush, his eyes caught a glimpse of an object that clearly wasn't a natural part of the jungle.

Oh, wow. I need to call this in...

He depressed the talk button on his throat mic twice. The double chirp of the radio would let Thorne and the others know he needed to speak with them.

He waited for what felt like an eternity but was more likely sixty seconds. Time seemed to stop as he waited for the reply that would let him know they were ready to receive his message.

The longer he waited, the more concerned he became. *Did something happen to them? Are they still all right?*

Finally, he heard a two-chirp reply. Captain Thorne was ready.

Currie depressed the talk button. "Red Six, Red Two. I have a visual on a mobile radar truck, likely part of an HQ-9 system. Break. Along the top of the ridge appears to be a single-lane dirt road. Break. Do you want me to deploy my Black Hornet to get us an overview of the area?"

Currie waited for the reply, hoping he'd get the go-ahead to deploy the nanodrone—it was great for providing a quick overview of the battlespace without requiring him to leave his hide or overwatch position. The only drawback to the little drone was its battery life. Currie knew he had to get the images and situational awareness he wanted quickly and return home, or it could end up crashing because it ran out of juice. If the drone crashed in the wrong location, it could let an adversary know they were nearby.

"Red Two, that's a good copy. Deploy the Hornet and get us some eyes on the ridge. Break. We're deploying a Hornet down here. We think we've found a possible bunker complex. Over."

"That's a good copy. I'll get it linked up to Red Five. Out."

Currie pulled his patrol pack off his shoulders and grabbed for the Hornet's case. He unzipped it and turned the device on. Once it was synced with his secured phone app, he searched for Red Five's stealth phone. These were the newest piece of coms equipment the folks at DARPA had created for SOF units operating behind enemy lines when they needed to establish mobile hot spots without being detected. Moments after Currie activated the ghosted Bluetooth on the Hornet, the drone synced up with Red Five's network. Captain Thorne and the rest of the team would now be able to see what he was seeing.

Currie pulled the visor control unit over his eyes and activated the Hornet. As he gave it a little bit of juice, the drone gained altitude. The camera captured a good view of the radar truck, which had been parked on the side of the trail. Currie also saw half a dozen Chinese soldiers milling about near it.

Currie panned the drone in a slow 360-degree circle, taking everything in. As he looked further down the road, he saw what he thought were a few barrels sticking out through some tall grass and jungle vines. Once he'd gotten a good overview of the area around him, he angled the drone to head toward the mystery objects.

When the little drone got within maybe fifty meters, Currie knew what he was looking at. It was a PGZ-09: a self-propelled anti-aircraft artillery truck. They were equipped with two 35-millimeter cannons and four fire-and-forget infrared homing missiles.

Crap! How many more of these do they have up here?

His earpiece chirped. "Red Two, see if there are any additional PGZs on the ridge. Then get us a view of the rest of the area. We need to see how many potential hostiles are up there. Make sure to tag the grids of these vehicles. Break. We'll designate them for a follow-on strike once we've left the area."

Currie smiled at the idea of raining steel down on these bastards. They'd spent the last four days traversing the jungle in search of the Chinese SAM bastions. It appeared they finally found one.

Fifteen minutes later, Currie had surveyed a good chunk of the ridge. He'd managed to find two more PGZs and probably three dozen Chinese soldiers. They had set up a number of machine-gun positions and fortified positions around the vehicles. He also found a second radar site, further down the trail. Now they just had to figure out where the command-and-control center was and the various missile pods. Chances were, they'd be somewhere within a two-to-five-kilometer radius of the radar sites.

Retrieving his microdrone, Currie swapped out the spent battery with a fresh one and put the unit away. If he needed to use it again, it would be ready.

"Red Six, Red Two. I'm going to start moving toward RP Beta. How copy?"

A second later, Currie received a single chirp, letting him know they'd heard him and he was good to head to the rendezvous point. Once they linked up, the captain would probably break them down into three- or four-man teams to finish scouting the area. They had a lot of ground to cover now that they knew the enemy base was nearby.

It took Currie nearly an hour to slither and skirt his way down the ridge to the floor of the valley below. Thirty minutes after that, he finally reached the rally point. As he approached it, he felt he was being watched. He got a single chirp in his earpiece, then a soft voice announced, "We're here. I'm going to stand up, so don't shoot me." Currie recognized the voice of Dawson, his partner in crime.

Dawson stood. He was maybe twenty feet from him, and Currie hadn't even seen him. *Damn, he's good at that*, Currie thought.

Captain Thorne stood up not too far from Dawson and made his way toward them. He motioned for them to take a knee.

"Good job finding those radar units on the ridge," said Thorne. "You were right, they probably have the other ridge over there fixed with a couple of them and probably another PGZ or two up there as well. That means the C&C truck and base are probably nearby as well. I'm going to phone in what we've found so far.

"Once we've phoned in, you and Dawson are going to come with me. We're going to hike up to that hilltop over there. If you look at that group of trees right there"—Thorne pointed to a group of them that did seem a bit out of place—"I think those are cleverly disguised radio antennas. We're going to check it out and see what we can find. It's possible we stumbled upon something much larger than a SAM complex."

Dawson shot Currie a worried look. He didn't like this plan one bit.

"What about the rest of the team? Shouldn't we try and stay together since we know we're about to stumble into an enemy camp?" Dawson questioned.

Currie felt he should probably say something as well. "I think he's right, sir. We know we've got hostiles all around us. We should stay together as a group in case we bump into something."

Thorne shook his head. "No. Only the three of us are going to break off from the team to check that place out. The rest of the team will stick together and continue to search the area down here. Chief Miller and Master Sergeant Altenburg said they can handle it."

Something about this didn't feel right to Currie. But if Miller and Altenburg were cool with it, then who was he to speak against them? Those two guys had more time and experience in the SOF world than Currie and Dawson had combined. He'd defer to their judgment.

Taking a deep breath, Currie asked, "When do we leave?"

****

Lying with half his body tucked under a fallen log and the other half covered in leaves and underbrush, Currie tried to control his breathing and not make any unnecessary moves that might give away his position.

A tree branch snapped. Some leaves and underbrush got kicked. A boot stepped down just inches from Currie's face. He tightened the grip on his Mark I trench knife.

The old trench knife was a personal weapon his great-grandfather had carried in World War I, when he'd been part of the 1st Army Division. Then his grandfather had carried it when he had been in the 101st Airborne Division in World War II. His dad had then carried it during his three tours in Special Forces in Vietnam and Grenada. Currie had carried it with him during his deployments in Afghanistan, Iraq, and Syria. That knife had been with a Currie in a war for more than a hundred years.

The boot didn't move. It just stayed there for what felt like an eternity. Angling his head just slightly, Currie followed the boot of the man up to the rest of his body. He saw the man was wearing a woodland-color camouflage uniform. The soldier's face was painted green with a few stripes of black and brown to further break up the contours of his face. The man was wearing body armor, fully equipped with quick-load magazine pouches, hand grenades and a first aid kit. His hands were tightly holding his CS/LR-17 assault rifle as his eyes darted from one position to another, searching for enemy soldiers that he didn't realize were hiding in plain sight.

Ten minutes ago, they'd been using their microdrone to scout the area. That was when they'd spotted an enemy patrol moving in their direction. This wasn't some sort of small patrol, either. There was close to a company-sized element, kicking bushes and scouring the area.

Then they'd spotted two more patrols: one on the opposite ridgeline, and one in the valley below, both doing the same thing. These large units weren't out on a peaceful stroll through the jungle. They were searching for something. Presumably, they were searching for the Americans who had infiltrated their AOR.

Knowing that if they tried to withdraw from the area, they'd likely get spotted by the converging groups, they opted to try and hide in plain sight. Thorne sent a quick sitrep to their headquarters, letting them know they had found something substantial in this area. He also sent out an alert to Chief Miller in the valley below, telling the rest of the team that trouble was headed their way.

As Currie lay half under the fallen log with his trench knife in hand, he couldn't help but wonder if the ChiComs had somehow detected their radio transmissions. Technically, that shouldn't have been possible—not with the new high-tech coms units they were using. The encrypted microburst transmissions and frequency-hopping capability were supposed to allow them to stealthily communicate without being found. But as the Chinese soldier, standing inches from him, didn't move, Currie couldn't shake the sickening feeling that their coms weren't as impervious to detection as they had all thought.

Leaves, twigs and underbrush crunched nearby. Then he heard a new voice in Spanish, which was a language Currie happened to be fluent in.

"Comrade, we are at the location you gave us. It is possible they have moved on since their last transmission?" the Spanish-speaking soldier asked.

The Chinese soldier replied in terrible Spanish. "If they left, where do you think they could have gone? Do we have some possible tracks to follow or an idea of where they may have headed?"

"*Sí, señor*. We found some tracks that look to be leading down to the valley below," the Spanish-speaking soldier explained. "We believe they may have detected us and so they relocated down to the valley to try and evade us."

Damn! If Chief Miller doesn't get a move on, they may get trapped.

The Chinese soldier, who'd been standing practically on top of Currie, took off at a trot toward the valley floor.

When the patrol had left the area, Currie sat up and slowly raised his body up against a tree. He surveyed the area around him, looking for Thorne and Dawson. When he eventually spotted them, he quietly made his way over to them.

"Captain, we got a problem," said Currie. "The guy in charge of that patrol practically stepped on me. I heard one of the Spanish-speaking soldiers tell him they were 'at the location their radio transmission had originated from.' I think these guys have a way of being able to track our coms. I'm also pretty sure they know exactly where the rest of the team is located, and they're heading toward them right now."

Thorne looked at him, perplexed. Currie understood. They hadn't used their coms for very long; it was hard to fathom that the Chinese could have triangulated their positions, let alone done it that quickly.

"Get us your best guess on what our location is right now and where you think Chief Miller and the others are," Thorne directed. "I'm going to see if I can't get us some CAS. I think we're about to get hit and hit hard." Thorne pulled his patrol pack off his back and sat down against the base of a large tree.

Dawson took up a position observing the area around them. Currie got the captain the coordinates he was asking for. Then he got their little microdrone up and running. With the visor on and the controller in his right hand, Currie sent the drone down the ridge after the enemy soldiers who were trying to box their brothers in.

Currie could hear Thorne making contact with their higher-ups. He relayed what they had found and placed an immediate call in for help. Currie was doing his best not to eavesdrop, but it was hard. Thorne was having a heated debate with someone over what kind of help they could or would provide. He told them if they didn't work on getting them something and arranging an extraction ASAP, chances were, they wouldn't make it more than a few hours.

Currie finally caught up to the patrol. They weren't exactly working hard to maintain their noise discipline. They appeared to be more interested in speed and reaching a specific destination than they were in getting there quietly.

Damn! They've probably figured out where the rest of our guys are.

"What do you see, Currie?" Thorne asked. He'd apparently finished his call.

"I think they found Miller and the others. These guys are hauling ass through the jungle. They aren't concerned with being quiet. I think they're trying to get in position before they spring some sort of ambush."

Thorne cursed. "This is all about to go belly-up, isn't it?"

Currie snorted at the assessment. "Yeah, I'd say we have a few minutes before contact will be made. Did you send a warning over to Miller and them? Let them know what's coming their way?"

"Yeah, I told them to do their best to evade if they can, and if they can't, then hunker down while I work on getting us some CAS," Thorne explained, concern in his voice.

Dawson dropped to a knee next to them. "What's the call, sir? Are we going to help them out, or what are we doing?"

Judging by the pause in his response, Currie figured the captain was calculating what they could do. Currie knew their friends were about to get hit if they didn't do something, so he offered, "Sir, what if we cause a distraction? Maybe get them to reposition and come after us instead? The three of us could lead them further away from here and give Miller and the others a chance to escape."

"That's not a bad idea. What do you have in mind?" Thorne asked, almost relieved.

"We got one of those PGZs not far from us—just a couple hundred meters over there. What if we get close enough to use Dawson's SMAW on it?" Currie offered. "If we hit that thing, you can bet they're going to recall that unit that's heading toward Miller to come find us. Even if we miss, they'll send guys out to find us. They can't let that thing get nailed."

"It's not a bad idea. But if we're going to do this, we need to do it quick. Those guys are likely to be on Miller any minute now," Dawson added.

Suddenly their radio chirped.

"Red Six, Red One. Contact imminent. Will do our best to E&E back to RP Zeta. How copy?"

"Damn it! We're too late," Dawson muttered.

Shaking his head, Thorne replied, "That's a good copy, Red One. We've got some CAS roughly sixty mikes out. QRF is close to the same. We'll meet you at RP Zeta. See you there."

Thorne practically sank when the call ended. Currie could tell this decision was killing the man inside. No matter what he said or did, his team was about to make contact with the enemy, and he wouldn't be there to lead them. The best he could do was try to get them some air support, in an area that was essentially a well-laid trap for fighters and helicopters.

"Screw it. We need to take that PGZ out now more than ever," Dawson huffed angrily. "If we have some CAS inbound to the area, then we need to do our best to take some of those AA guns down or those flyboys are going to get smoked." He unslung the SMAW from his back and started to get it ready.

"I agree, sir," said Currie. "We need to head back up to the top of the ridge and take that bastard out. If we're able to, we should also try and take those two radar trucks and the other PGZ. It'll help the flyboys out."

Thorne looked at Dawson and Currie. "Let's do it!"

Chapter Two
Baron Returns

81st Fighter Squadron "Black Panthers"
Soto Cano Air Base
Honduras

Major Wilhelm "Baron" Richter was practically panting when he entered the squadron briefing room. He'd been on the other side of the base when the emergency briefing had been called. They were being scrambled for an emergency TIC or troops in contact mission.

As he grabbed an empty seat, Baron observed that a few others were breathing hard like him. The master sergeant from the intelligence office was showing them a map of the area he assumed they were going to be assaulting.

"As you can see, this area is pretty dense with tree cover down in the valleys. It thins out a lot along the ridgelines up here." The sergeant then pointed to a thin dirt line on the tops of the ridge. "This spot here is a trail where the radar trucks and AA guns are located."

The master sergeant then moved his finger down to two spots on the map. They looked to be roughly a kilometer apart from each other. "The ODA team is broken down into two groups. There's a nine-man team here. This is the group in contact right now. They're doing their best to withdraw to the evac point three kilometers away, over here. This other group is a three-man team. They're the command element that placed the call in for help. They told us they took out one of the PGZ-09 trucks on this ridge before they had to conduct a fighting withdrawal themselves."

The master sergeant paused for a second before continuing. "These guys are in a tough spot. They've been in contact with the enemy now for coming up on fifteen minutes. We don't know how many casualties they have, or if they'll be able to make it back to the evac site."

Before the briefer could continue, one of the pilots interjected, "Master Sergeant, what more can you tell us about these ridges? What threats are we facing?"

"That's a good question, sir. Prior to being discovered, the ODA team had identified four radar trucks. Two on this ridge, and two on this ridge. They're roughly eight kilometers apart, so the radars and gun trucks provide very good interlocking fields of fire. There may be other AA guns or SAMs out there, but this is what they've found so far."

The master sergeant brought up another slide with a couple of items annotated on it. Along the side of the slide was a picture of a PGZ-09 self-propelled anti-aircraft vehicle. The specs said it was armed with two 35mm autocannons and fire-and-forget infrared homing missiles.

Baron knew all about those little bastards. His A-10 had been shot down during the first day of the invasion of Cuba by a pair of these gun trucks.

"The ODA team said each ridge has two of these guns positioned on them. The three-man team took one of them out on this ridge, so I'd approach from this side," the master sergeant explained. "These trucks are serious threats. They'll blow you out of the sky if you're not careful. Most of our A-10 losses over Cuba can be attributed directly to these trucks."

A senior captain then asked, "If this ridgeline and the radar trucks are protected by these gun trucks and God only knows how many other SAM launchers in the area, how the hell are we going to get in there and give the team on the ground any sort of CAS without getting our squadron ripped apart?"

Their squadron commander, Lieutenant Colonel Leah "Casper" Moody, stood and walked to the lectern to answer this question. "That's easy, fellas," she began. "The British reactivated RAF Belize at the start of the war. They've allowed the Navy to base a squadron of F/A-18 Super Hornets there. These Hornets are fielding the Navy's first-ever squadron of Loyal Wingman drones. The combat drones and Hornets are already en route to the ODA's location as we speak. Once in range, the drones will carry out the SEAD mission targeting the enemy radars and hunt down the missile launcher sites. They'll clear the area of SAMs for us. They'll also loiter in the area while we make our CAS runs, in case more radars turn on.

"As to our mission, the A2 shop has pointed out this is a dense jungle area. As such, each of you is being equipped with four Mk 81s. We're going to be danger close to the guys on the ground, so I don't want us to carry anything larger than a two-hundred-and-fifty-pound bomb. As to your other hardpoints, you'll be carrying a pair of Hydra rocket pods. Our purpose isn't to go after and destroy the enemy base or SAM fortress in the area. Our only goal is to provide CAS to the Snake Eaters in the thick of it. A company of soldiers from the 101st is going in as the QRF to recover these guys. All the ODA has to do is reach this location here," she said as she pointed to an area on the map roughly three kilometers from the closest ridgeline with a pair of PGZ-09s on it.

"If the Navy doesn't take these gun trucks along this ridge out, then we need to. In the meantime, make good use of your guns and rockets. Use the 81s if you must, but make sure you know where the ODAs are in relation to where you're dropping them. Now, let's go get airborne. Those guys have been fighting the enemy now for almost twenty

21

minutes. They're going to need our help and we're still thirty-some minutes out. Dismissed."

Baron got up and made a beeline for the door. He got stuck waiting for a few others who had beaten him to it. Then he heard a voice call out, "Baron, hold up a second."

When he turned around, he saw the squadron commander. "Ma'am."

"Please, just call me Casper. Baron, you flew against these trucks. Any words of wisdom?"

Baron blushed slightly. "Yeah, I flew up against them. They shot me down too."

"I know. That's why I'm asking."

Baron snorted. "Well, I can tell you this—they sure can spit out a lot of rounds in a hurry. The targeting radar is damn good, too. It doesn't get spoofed easily. The missiles it fired do, so make sure to keep your flares ready. But those autocannons practically ripped my Warthog apart. I barely had time to eject before the plane blew up."

She nodded at the information but didn't say anything. She had started her career in the A-10s. A handful of years ago, she'd transitioned to the Tucanos as they'd started to get them formed up.

When the two of them walked out onto the flight line, she finally said, "I guess we'll see how good the Navy's Loyal Wingman drone program is, won't we?"

She turned and headed toward her aircraft before Baron could say anything. He hoped those drones were as good as everyone said they were. The last thing he wanted to do was get shot down a second time. At some point, the Air Force would stop giving him new planes and he'd find himself riding a desk—a death knell to any flyer.

"You ready for this, Baron? It's our first combat mission," announced his backseater, Lieutenant Lucas "Vodka" Smirnoff, excitedly.

"Yeah, no sweat," Baron replied. "Hey, do a quick check of the weapons before you climb in. I'm going to run through our checklist so we can get airborne."

Baron was still getting used to flying with a backseater. He'd spent his career in the A-10s, which didn't have one. It was different flying with a backseater—he had more than one person to think about when he dove in on the enemy.

Five minutes later, they were airborne and on their way to go save some Greenie Beanies.

****

The sound of gunfire continued to echo and ripple across the jungle. *BOOM...BOOM...BOOM!*

"Where the hell is that artillery coming from?" barked Captain Thorne angrily as a series of explosions rippled across the valley floor half a kilometer away from them.

"I don't know, but if those flyboys don't get here soon and silence it, they're going to wipe Miller and them out," Sergeant First Class Dawson replied angrily.

Currie was frustrated as hell with what had been going on the last half hour. Sure, they'd taken out one of the PGZ-09 AA trucks. But they hadn't been able to link up with their team yet.

"Sir, we need to try and link up with Miller and the others. Maybe we can get close enough to provide them with some covering fire or create a gap in the enemy lines for them to escape through," Currie proposed.

Thorne nodded in agreement. "Give me an ammo check. I need to know where we stand before we move to engage these guys. We've got the QRF team on the way. They should be here in less than twenty minutes at this point."

Currie checked his ammo. He still had four full mags. The one loaded in his rifle right now had thirteen rounds left. His drop bag had two empty ones. Pulling them out, he grabbed for a couple boxes of ammo to reload them before they headed out.

"Sir, what if we blow some trees down and create a new LZ, closer to our position?" Currie offered. "If we have the QRF land at the rally point, it'll take them at least thirty minutes to cover the ground to get to Miller's teams."

"I agree, sir," said Dawson. "I've got enough det cord to take out those trees over there and create a hole big enough for a single Chinook to land at a time."

Thorne didn't respond right away. He pulled out his map and looked at their current position and the original rally point. If they created a new LZ here, it would place the QRF two kilometers closer to where they needed to be.

"OK. Get it done," Thorne ordered. "As soon as you blow the charges, we're going to haul ass to see if we can maybe create a hole like Currie suggested."

A few minutes later, Dawson gave Currie and Thorne a thumbs-up, indicating that he was ready.

"Let's do it," Thorne said, just loud enough for Dawson to hear.

Bang!

As the trees fell, Thorne sent the pilots flying the QRF team to the new LZ location. Then the three of them raced toward the sounds of heavy gunfire and the shouts in Spanish, Chinese, and English.

****

2nd Battalion, 327th Infantry Regiment, 101st Airborne

"Five minutes! We're five minutes out!" shouted Lieutenant Branham, their platoon leader.

"Am I wrong to be this excited?" Private Ailes asked Specialist Sabo.

"Wrong, no…strange, yes," Sabo replied.

"Why is it strange?" asked PFC Fitzgerald. Fitz was another new replacement that had just joined their platoon around the same time as Ailes.

Sabo looked at his two new guys. "Think about it. We're being called in to bail out a Special Forces team that apparently bumped into something bigger than even they can handle. There's a very high likelihood we're about to be in a major gunfight in less than ten minutes—a gunfight that may result in some or all of us getting killed. So no, it's not wrong to be excited about what's about to happen, but I'd say it's strange to be excited about rushing into a battle that'll likely get a few of us killed."

"Yeah, I guess that makes sense. Do you think it's a good or bad thing they changed our LZ?" Fitz quizzed.

"Damn, you ask a lot of questions," Sabo said with a shake of his head. He sighed. "Who knows? I'm sure those SF guys know what they're doing. We'll be on the ground in five minutes. I'm sure we'll find out then."

Fitz bit his lip and just nodded. Then he turned to look out the back of the helicopter.

Was I ever that green? Sabo asked himself. He looked out the back of the helicopter like the others. The jungle landscape below was beautiful. They'd officially crossed over into El Salvador. This was going to be their first mission in the country. Sabo just hoped it went well and they all survived.

Looking up toward the pilots and the two side doors near the front of the helicopter, Sabo saw a couple of explosions erupt along the top of the ridge. He also saw multiple strings of red and green tracers zipping across the sky. A couple of missiles leapt out of the jungle into the air as they sought out the aircraft attacking them.

Oh man, this looks like a big soup sandwich we're about to land into. This isn't good...

"We're here! Prepare to get off ASAP!" shouted the crew chief over the roar of the engines as the Chinook slowed to a hover and descended directly into the jungle.

Looking out the back of the helicopter, Sabo wasn't sure there was a hole for them to even land in. Trees were everywhere.

Then the helicopter descended and passed the upper canopy layer. *Damn, this is a tight landing zone*, he thought to himself. Moments later, they descended past the next canopy layer, and then they were on the ground.

"Out! Everyone, out!" shouted Lieutenant Branham.

The platoon ran off the back ramp and immediately fanned out to establish a perimeter around the LZ.

As the soldiers exited the Chinook, the platoon's two AlphaDog quadpedal machines exited and took up a position near their operators.

The AlphaDogs were a much-improved version of the Boston Dynamics Big Dog and LS3. They were substantially quieter, smaller, lighter, more agile, and easier to fix and maintain and could operate for a much longer period before they needed to power down to recharge. The quadpedal pack mule could carry as much as four hundred pounds of water, munitions, and heavy weapons for a platoon, freeing the soldiers up to focus on the immediate tasks of killing the enemy.

As Sabo took a knee against the side of a large tree with his weapon at the ready, he could barely make out the sounds of gunfire. However, when the Chinook started to rise out of the artificially created landing zone, the sounds of war began to intensify.

"Specialist Sabo—you five, come with me!" shouted Staff Sergeant Peters. "We're going to start pushing this perimeter out further."

The next Chinook, carrying Second Platoon, descended into the hole the SF soldiers had created for them. The fighting in the distance was intense. They heard a lot of shouting.

Sabo and the guys advanced about fifty meters inside the jungle, toward the fighting. They eventually set up a loose perimeter while they waited for the rest of the platoon to move up and join them.

Lieutenant Branham took a knee next to Sabo and grabbed for his radio handset. While Sabo couldn't hear what was being said on the other end, he could hear what Branham was saying just fine.

"Warrior Six, Warrior One-Six. We're on the ground. We've taken a position fifty meters to the west of the LZ. Break. Do you want us to proceed and try to link up with the Red element?"

Sabo just looked off in the distance. He couldn't see too far away; the jungle was fairly thick with vegetation. More than that, it was also kind of dark. They probably had at least three more full hours of sunlight, but not a lot of that light managed to get through the double canopy layer.

"That's a good copy. The platoon will stand by for Warrior Two and Three before we move. Out," Branham said and then shook his head angrily.

27

"Sabo, I don't know if those Snake Eaters are going to hold out much longer on their own. The captain wants us to sit tight and wait for the rest of the company to join us before we move out."

Looking back at the LZ, Sabo asked, "Isn't Third Platoon next on deck? Then Fourth Platoon?"

"They are. But Fourth Platoon is going to get dropped off at the original LZ. Once we link up with the SF guys, we're to get everyone back to the original LZ. It's much larger and can accommodate three Chinooks at a time," the lieutenant explained. "Fourth Platoon is going to secure the area while the helicopters set down and wait for us."

Sabo snorted. "Well, let's hope we can get our guys out of there, then. God only knows how many enemy soldiers are in the area."

Before either of them could say anything else, a string of bullets zipped over their heads, causing them to duck.

"Contact front!" shouted Sergeant Lakers as he opened fire with their squad automatic weapon.

Ratatat, ratatat.

The heavy-caliber 7.62mm rounds cut through the underbrush, vines, and just about anything else that got in their way.

"Frag out!" shouted another soldier.

Crump!

Sabo raised his rifle to his shoulder and returned fire. His eyes darted from position to position as he looked for someone specific to shoot at. He hated firing his weapon for the sake of firing. He liked to know exactly where his bullets were going when he fired them.

"There you are," he said softly to himself as he centered the red targeting dot on a man's chest. He squeezed the trigger once, feeling the rifle bark and push back into his shoulder. Sabo couldn't see the actual bullet, but he watched the man stumble backwards a couple of steps from the hit.

Sabo smiled and congratulated himself for scoring a hit. But then he saw the man sort of shrug the hit off and resume shooting at Sabo's comrades.

What the hell? Sabo realized the enemy soldiers must be wearing body armor. *Why couldn't our battalion be the ones to get the new Sigs?* he bemoaned. Those slugs could punch right through body armor.

Returning his sights to the soldier he'd previously shot, Sabo placed the targeting reticle just below the man's neck and pulled the trigger in three quick, controlled pulls. He saw the soldier grasp at the wound as he stumbled briefly before falling to the ground. While Sabo couldn't see the man on the ground, he knew he was likely dead or about to die. He'd hit the man just above the chest plate of his body armor, a shot that would cause the man to bleed out in a minute or drown in his own blood.

"Ah! No, no, no!" Lieutenant Branham shouted somewhere to Sabo's right.

Turning to see what he was going on about, Sabo saw the third Chinook, the one carrying Third Platoon, on fire. It had somehow taken an RPG or missile hit to its rear engine. The thing was spitting out smoke and flame as the pilots fought to maintain control of it and set it down on the ground. It was still maybe fifty feet in the air.

Then an object flew through the trees and impacted against the cockpit. It exploded, blowing the Chinook into two pieces. Both sides were on fire as they fell the remaining distance to the ground.

Sabo saw a couple of soldiers desperately try and jump from the helicopter. Then the Chinook collapsed on the ground and exploded in fire and flames. Two soldiers somehow ran out of the burning wreckage, their bodies on fire as they flailed about like walking roman candles.

They were screaming in agony, begging for help from anyone that could provide it.

"This can't be happening!" Branham shouted. A torrent of obscenities spilled out of his mouth as he ran toward the wreckage.

Several soldiers from Second Platoon tried to help some of the survivors from the wreckage. Others tried to pull bodies from the flames if they could. Suddenly, a secondary explosion occurred, enveloping two soldiers from Second Platoon in fuel and flames.

"Everyone, move back. Clear the area!" shouted one of the nearby sergeants. No one wanted to give up on trying to pull survivors from the wreckage, but the sergeant was right. This thing was still dangerous, and all the ammunition the soldiers had on them was starting to cook off.

Then Sabo heard something he'd only heard about in Cuba but hadn't personally experienced. There was a loud shout in Chinese, then the shrieking blare of several whistles. In that moment, he knew exactly what was about to happen. He turned his back on the burning wreckage containing some of his friends and pointed his rifle in the direction he'd heard the whistles coming from.

****

81st Attack Squadron

"Damn, Baron! One of the Chinooks just went down," Vodka exclaimed, surprise and horror in his voice.

Baron stole a quick look to his left. Sure enough, some sort of missile had nailed the bird. It was belching flame and thick black smoke as it fell into the LZ.

Returning his gaze to his front, Baron leveled his aircraft out and pulled up on the stick to regain some altitude for another attack run.

The altimeter showed they'd just passed four thousand feet when their RWAR started blaring that they were being locked up by some sort of radar-guided missile. He couldn't tell if it was a MANPAD or something larger. Right now, he didn't care.

Baron banked the aircraft to the right as he lined up for a bomb run. He'd react to the threat once a missile had been fired and not until then. Baron was going to do his best to land one of his two-hundred-and-fifty-pound bombs on a cluster of enemy soldiers. Since he'd made contact with the SF soldiers on the ground, they'd been feeding him target after target to go after with either his machine guns or his Mk-81s.

The Tucano dove toward the ground at a steep angle. Baron tried to make sure he was staying within the box the SF guys said the Chinese were attacking them from because he had no way of seeing the enemy on the ground. They were buried somewhere under the double canopy of the jungle. Baron had to rely on the guys below to let him know where to drop these unguided bombs—not an easy thing to do, considering if he dropped it early, he could end up nailing his own people.

"We're still good. No missiles or guns shooting at us," Vodka called out, relief in his voice.

Baron sped toward the drop point and waited until he was sure he was over it before he pickled off one of the Mk-81s. Then he angled the aircraft to the left and applied more power to the engine as he looked to gain some altitude. It was maneuvers like this that made him feel like he was a World War II dive bomber.

Baron's great-grandfather had actually been a Stuka dive bomber during the war. When he was a young child, his grandfather used to regale him with stories of flying in the Luftwaffe. As a child, he didn't know the first thing about the Nazis or the atrocities their government had committed. All he knew was his great-grandad had been a pilot during the war and had the most amazing war stories to share with them.

His great-grandad had surrendered to the Americans at the end of the war. During his time in an American prison camp, he had assisted the US in understanding the German aerial tactics and provided details on some of the aircraft that were still in the works. He made a lot of contacts within the Army Air Corps. When he was able to immigrate to America at the end of 1947, he joined the newly created American Air Force to show his loyalty to his new homeland. He was fast-tracked into the new F-84 Thunderjet program, where he truly excelled in the new airframe. His six years of combat experience set him apart as a flyer. When the Korean War broke out, he immediately volunteered to serve. He went on to serve the duration of the war, earning numerous valor medals to go along with the ones he'd earned during the last Great War.

Baron's great-grandad served eight years in the Luftwaffe before going on to serve twenty-eight years in the US Air Force, ultimately retiring a brigadier general in 1968 after serving two of his last three years in Vietnam. Baron's grandfather also served in the Air Force, but he was killed when his jet was shot down over Laos in 1972. Baron's father continued the family tradition, attending the Air Force Academy in 1980 and serving until 2018, when he, too, retired a brigadier general. Baron had big shoes to fill and ninety years of flying history coursing through his veins.

"Missile, eight o'clock. Looks to be a MANPAD!" shouted Vodka urgently.

Reaching down, Baron moved the throttle to full power and then depressed the flare button. Red-hot flares dispensed from behind them, and Baron felt the aircraft jump forward as he gave the engines more power. He then changed directions, pulling up hard to the left and switching to angle the aircraft to the right while also shifting to dive down toward the jungle below.

We just passed forty-two hundred feet, he realized. They were dropping altitude like a rock as he sought to throw the aim of the missile off.

Baron's ears registered an explosion not too far away from them.

"Good job, Baron. It hit one of our flares!"

Smiling, Baron looked down to the jungle, where he'd dropped his last bomb. Black smoke drifted up from through the trees. *I sure hope that put a dent in the attackers.*

The radio chirped again. It was the SF soldiers on the ground, giving them a report of the bomb. Baron smiled when they said he'd dropped it right on top of the enemy. They were elated with the result. Reports like that made him feel good, like he was really having an influence on the war and saving lives. The grunts on the ground depended on pilots like Baron and his fellow flyers to have their sixes when they were in the thick of it. He really enjoyed this part of the job.

"Hey, I'm getting a call for help from another unit. I think it's that unit near where that Chinook went down. You want me to reply and grab the request?" his backseater asked.

Baron looked toward the ridge. A string of tracer fire flew off into the sky. Either the gunner was shooting at an aircraft in the clouds above them, or he had his sights set on something Baron couldn't readily see. In either case, Baron knew it had to be taken out. They were going to have more helicopters flying into the area.

"No, we need to take a pass, Vodka. Not sure if that PGZ-09 got missed or a new one just showed up, but on that ridge to our eight o'clock—another one just fired off a string of rounds. I want us to try and take it out. It's going to cause all sorts of problems for the helicopters if we don't handle it. Once we finish this thing off, I'm going to take us home to rearm once we've spent our ordnance."

"Sounds good, boss. Let's do it."

****

Soto Con Air Base
101st Airborne Division HQ

Major General Robert "Bob" Sink saw one of his brigade commanders talking animatedly with someone near the map table. Whatever was going on didn't appear to be going well.

Bob approached them. "How are my Screaming Eagles doing today, fellas?"

The colonel looked at him. "We've got a problem, sir. An ODA team ran into some trouble in this valley. They identified some radar and gun trucks along these ridges. The Air Force and Navy flew a SEAD mission and largely neutralized the SAM threat. However, one of the Chinooks carrying the QRF team to recover the ODAs went down here. It was an improvised LZ the ODA created for us to get the QRF closer to them. The third Chinook going in to use the LZ took a MANPAD and crashed."

The general scrunched his eyebrows. "So, what's the problem?" he asked. "Send some gunships and another flight of choppers to go fetch our guys out of there."

"It's not that simple, sir," said the S3 or operations officer. "We're less than an hour from nightfall, and the Air Force Super Tucanos in the area are reporting more AA trucks showing up and more MANPAD activity. They've already encountered some thirteen missiles themselves. They've lost one A-29, and two more took some damage. I think we need to let the gunships go in and clear the area out first before we send more transports in to fetch our guys."

"Sir, if we don't get more guys out there now, it's not just the ODA team that's going to be in trouble. It's the three platoons of the QRF as well," one of his brigade commanders explained.

"And, if we don't clear the area of the MANPAD and SAM threats, we may end up losing a lot more helicopters," the S3 explained. "We can't risk it. Let me send in the gunships and clear the area. Then we can send in a reinforced QRF to link up with our guys on the ground."

Bob looked at the map. He didn't like what he was seeing one bit. The last thing he wanted was to lose more helicopters. Then again, the thought of having a QRF team and an ODA team trapped and surrounded by the enemy all night wasn't a good alternative.

"Send the gunships in now," the general ordered. "See if the Air Force has a Specter on standby. We may need it if our guys end up stuck and having to wait until morning. Also, go ahead and send in the rest of the 327th's 2nd battalion. If they have to land a few klicks further away and hoof it in to link up with our guys on the ground, then so be it. In the meantime, make sure that QRF team links up with the ODAs on the ground. I don't want units scattered around the area. We need them to work together and hunker down until help arrives. Got it?"

"Yes, General. We're on it," the two officers echoed.

****

ODA 7322, Bravo Company

Captain Thorne knelt next to his second-in-command. "Chief, the QRF team is going to fire a flare once I give them the word. Help me spot it. We need to do our best to link up with them. We're running low on ammo. If we're going to be stuck here overnight, then we need to stick with them, or we're toast."

"Roger that."

Thorne depressed the talk button on the hand receiver. "Warrior Six, this is Red Six. Fire your flare."

Moments later, they saw a blue flare illuminate maybe five hundred meters to their right.

"Warrior Six, I see a blue flare. How copy?"

"Good copy, Red Six. That's us. Over."

"We're going to be approaching you from your four o'clock position. Challenge is Golden State. Counterchallenge is LA Lakers."

"Good copy. We're standing by," came the reply from the QRF commander.

"Let's get a move on, Chief. The Air Force bought us a reprieve. Let's not push our luck waiting around for the next assault," Thorne ordered as he headed toward their team medic. They had two urgent surgical patients. God only knew if they were going to get them back to a field hospital anytime soon.

The team did their best to move in the direction of the 101st troopers sent in to bail them out. It was ironic that the QRF team was now in need of being bailed out themselves.

It took them close to twenty minutes to cover the distance. It had already been getting dark, but as they approached their lines, it was practically pitch black.

Once they'd made it through their lines, a sergeant led them to the company CP and the casualty collection point.

"Where's your CO?" asked Captain Thorne as he approached the command post.

A lieutenant called out, "That'd be me, sir. It's good to finally link up with you guys. I'm sorry it doesn't appear like we'll be able to get you guys out of here before dawn."

As Thorne got closer, the young lieutenant motioned for the two of them to walk away from the others.

"Lieutenant, what's going on? Where's your captain?" Thorne asked now that it was just the two of them. While it was getting dark, Thorne could see the young man grimace at his question.

"Our CO was on the Chinook that was shot down. He was killed, along with nearly everyone in Third Platoon. Our XO was killed two hours ago, leaving me the only officer in the company left alive. I mean, Lieutenant Avery is still alive, but he's with Fourth Platoon. They left a couple of hours ago with the choppers to head back to Soto."

"Whoa, why didn't they just hoof it over here and link up with you guys?" Thorne asked, surprised a platoon of soldiers had flown back to the base.

"I don't know. It wasn't my call. I know they were three or four kilometers away. Maybe there was another enemy force between us and them and they didn't want to have three different units stranded in different locations," the young officer offered.

Looking at the man's name tape, Thorne said, "OK, Lieutenant Branham, I'm the ranking officer on scene, so I'm taking over. What's our ammo and water situation, and when is your higher headquarters planning on getting us out of here?"

Branham relayed the ammo and water situation. They were actually in better shape than Thorne would have thought—that was, until he learned this unit was still using M4s and hadn't transitioned to the new Sig Sauer infantry rifle. None of the extra ammo the AlphaDogs had packed was compatible with their weapons.

I'm going to need to see if the medevac they send can also drop some ammo for our rifles, or we're going to have to ditch them for the M4s from some of our dead, Thorne realized.

"OK, here's what I want to have happen," said Thorne, taking charge of the situation. "We're going to expand our perimeter on the right side by an extra fifty meters. I want this outcropping of trees included in our defense. Next, I want our claymores deployed along this section here. If we're going to have to hunker down for the evening, then we need to get those things set up. Then connect me through to your headquarters. I want to relay exactly where we are and what our coordinates are along our perimeter, and then I want to get some pre-positioned targets figured out for when the enemy decides they want to come back and finish us off."

The next twenty minutes went by in a blur as the two platoons of soldiers and the eight ODAs set about readying themselves for what would likely be a very long night.

Nearly thirty minutes later, half a dozen Apache gunships arrived on station. They went to work, going after the AA gun trucks and any other threats to the helicopters. They also used their thermals to help give the guys on the ground a better idea of what they were facing. If the pilots found a cluster of enemy soldiers, they engaged them with their chin guns, rocket pods, or one of their Hellfires.

As this was taking place, a single medevac helicopter was able to locate them and begin the process of lowering some crates of ammo for their 6.8mm Sig Sauer rifles and .338 Norma Magnum rounds for their two light-medium weapons, or Pigs as they were commonly called. After the chopper lowered the ammo, they placed an urgent surgical wounded man on.

The helicopter was able to loiter over their positions long enough for the two critical ODAs to get brought aboard along with five other Screaming Eagles. The remaining wounded would have to wait for another medevac. Once the helicopter left, the gunships quickly followed suit. An eerie silence then replaced the sound of helicopter blades and sporadic gunfire.

****

Lieutenant Branham walked up to Captain Thorne. He took a seat against a tree trunk next to the Special Forces captain as he took his helmet off. "Thank God we got the wounded out of here," he said. "I was concerned we'd end up losing them because we couldn't get them to a hospital."

"Yeah, that was a concern of mine," Thorne concurred. "They aren't out of the woods yet. They need to get stabilized at Soto and then flown to the next-level hospital. But at least we've given them a fighting chance now."

"You think the enemy will try to encircle us again?" the young officer asked.

"That depends. If I were them, I would. But I have no idea how many soldiers they have in the area. Maybe we got lucky, and we bumped into a company or battalion that happened to be on patrol in the area and this is the end of it. Then again, if they have a larger base nearby, then maybe they'll look to take advantage of the situation they have with us being stuck for the evening. I suppose we'll see over the next few hours," Thorne replied optimistically.

He and the rest of his ODA were reloading their spent magazines, getting themselves ready to contribute in the next fight. They had practically run out of ammo prior to that resupply. Big Army fielding units with a mixture of ammo wasn't exactly a brilliant idea.

****

32nd Field Artillery Regiment
Nine Kilometers from Montecristo Trifinio National Park

The Chinook dropped off the final M777 Howitzer for Charlie Battery. Now it was a matter of getting the guns anchored and positioned to start raining steel when the call came.

A handful of Black Hawks had sling-loaded some additional ammunition in for them. A few ground guides were helping them get the pallets of rounds and powder positioned near each of the guns. Once the shooting started, they didn't want to have to chase down more ammo.

While that was taking place, another group of Black Hawks landed nearby and offloaded a company of infantry. These guys were going to be the perimeter security for the soon-to-be firebase the Screaming Eagles were going to establish. This position had been selected because it was half a kilometer inside the Honduras border and could provide artillery fire across the entire Montecristo National Park. The six ODA teams scouring the park had found a sizable Chinese element within the national park, just as their intelligence elements and local human assets had said there would be.

Like Cuba, the Chinese Army wasn't going to try and fight the Americans toe-to-toe. They had established a handful of fortresses in geographically defensible positions throughout El Salvador. The areas were heavily protected with surface-to-air missile sites, mortar and artillery positions, and a lot of infantry. Until the Allies rooted them out, the Chinese would be a continual threat in the region.

Now that a Special Forces unit and a company of infantry had been trapped in the park, it only sped up the regiment's deployment to this border region. It was more important than ever to get the firebase established and operational. It was becoming increasingly difficult for any sort of air support to assist the grunts on the ground in the dense canopy cover—especially at night.

Knowing the division was going to have to clear this area out, an executive decision was made to start deploying the artillery regiment ASAP. They'd start by getting Charlie Battery deployed first. Then they'd get the rest of the battalion deployed to the two other locations. Once the three firebases were up and running, there wouldn't be an angle or part of the mountainous jungled park they couldn't hit. Then it would just be a matter of deploying more howitzers to each firebase and increasing their capability.

"Captain Wharton," called out a sergeant from the tactical operations center that had been hastily set up near the center of the base.

"Whatcha got, Sergeant?" Wharton replied as he walked toward the tent that was still being put together. All they had so far was a table with a map of the area and another one with a laptop, a couple of radios and a few lanterns on it.

"Sir, we just established contact with Red Six, the ODA team on the ground," the sergeant relayed. "A Captain Thorne said he's taken charge of the ground force. Apparently, a butter bar is the only officer left from the QRF. Anyway, the SF guy provided us with their ten-digit grid coordinates so we'd know exactly where they are. He's provided us with the grids for the rest of their perimeter. He wants to know if we can drop a few spotting rounds so they can start establishing some predetermined markers in case they get hit tonight."

Damn, that didn't take long, Wharton thought. *We haven't been on the ground for thirty minutes and they want us sending rounds downrange already.*

"Um. Sure. Get their positions plotted first in the computer. I want to make sure we know exactly where they are and that the safety parameters are put in. Then yeah—tell them we can allocate a few spotting rounds for them. I'll go let the gun chiefs know we'll have a fire mission shortly."

Wharton called out for the gun chiefs to rally on him. He needed to let them know their crews needed to be extra careful with these rounds. They were going to be firing into some dense jungle. Tree limbs had a way of throwing a round off target, and the last thing he wanted was for a 155mm high-explosive round to land too close to their own people because they screwed up the coordinates.

Ten minutes later, the first rounds were on the way.

****

Currie didn't like this one bit. They couldn't get a gunship to watch over them through the night because the Navy hadn't been able to suppress the enemy SAMs, at least not well enough that a lumbering AC-130J Ghostrider could just loiter above. They couldn't readily rely on close-air support from the Tucanos until daylight, largely for the same reason. That left them with a single battery of just six 155mm howitzers.

"Round out," a calm voice announced over the handset, breaking Currie's thoughts.

He depressed the talk button. "Round out," he replied.

"Hey, we got another spotting round coming in," Currie announced, loud enough for the guys nearby to hear him. "Stand by."

It felt odd talking this loud while still out on a mission. He had to remember that at this point, he wasn't a Special Forces operator. For better or worse, their team was operating now as infantry grunts. Albeit extremely highly trained infantry grunts, but regular grunts nonetheless.

"Splash."

"Splash out."

Seconds later, the whistling sound of the projectile broke the stillness of the early-morning hours. Currie heard a loud cracking followed by the sound of wood splitting as the nearly hundred-pound projectile crashed through the double canopy before impacting on the ground. The explosion lit the place up momentarily and the ground shook from the sudden impact.

"Damn, Currie," said Dawson. "Either you really know how to call in an artillery strike or that unit is freaking good." He slapped his friend on the shoulder.

Currie grunted at the praise. "Remember when Joy was in charge of calling in rounds?"

Dawson laughed at the mention of Staff Sergeant Joy. "Yeah, I remember all right. He damn nearly called in a barrage on us. It was a good call having you take things over."

"Yeah, well, everyone needs to be good enough to call it in. I think the kid'll learn. He just needs time."

"Let's hope he made it," Dawson said bluntly. "I still can't believe it took those bastards four hours to get us a medevac."

"It's neither here nor there. Let's just focus on living long enough to see the sunrise."

Time seemed to tick by slowly. Once they'd created a few predetermined artillery markers, the jungle became quiet again. The darkness returned quickly. Captain Thorne had half the soldiers don their night vision goggles while the other half caught a few hours of sleep. Until they spotted enemy soldiers, he was going to have half the soldiers get two hours of sleep at a time. It had been a long day for many of them, and sleep would help to recharge their bodies and their minds for whatever may be coming next.

Currie had just fallen asleep—or at least he *felt* like he had just fallen asleep—when someone tapped his shoulder to wake him up. He glanced at his watch and saw he'd actually been sleeping for almost an hour.

"We got movement. Captain wants everyone awake and on the line," Dawson whispered.

Grabbing his rifle, Currie made his way over to the fighting position he would be in. He was slightly behind the main line from the others. His job wasn't so much to fight as it was to call in artillery. They had an SF guy positioned on each side of the perimeter, ready to call in artillery on the predetermined positions. They'd established these known reference points in advance, so all they had to do was adjust fire from there to where they needed the rounds to land. It would save them a ton of time when the fighting started.

Once he reached his position, Currie put on his NVGs and started surveying the lines. When he didn't see anything, he took them off and grabbed a night vision spotting scope. "Where are you seeing the movement?" he asked.

"Look at that spot there," Dawson said as he pointed in a specific direction with an IR laser pointer. He only flashed it for a moment, just long enough for Currie to see where he was pointing.

"Ah, I see it. Yeah, it looks like maybe two or three guys. I can't really tell what they're doing, but my money says if we can see them, there are probably a lot more we can't."

Captain Thorne practically snuck up on them and knelt next to them. "Currie, I want you to get an artillery round on those guys' position. When it hits, it should light the area up and give us a good view of what's out there."

"I agree. I was going to suggest the same thing. Let me get on the horn with the gun bunnies," Currie answered as he reached for his map and the radio hand receiver.

****

Soto Cano Air Base
Honduras

Major General Sink finished off his second cup of black coffee in just two hours. He was looking over the map of where one of his companies was hunkered down. The ODA and QRF groups had finally linked up. He was happy about that—at least the combined force numbered nearly eighty soldiers. His biggest concern right now was the lack of support they were able to provide. If the enemy truly made a concerted attack, they could very likely overrun them.

"You should try and get some sleep, General," Colonel Roy Dowdy offered. "I'll wake you if things heat up."

"No. Thanks for the offer, but until our boys aren't surrounded behind enemy lines, I want to stay right here in case something happens."

Dowdy, his deputy, walked up to the map table and looked down at it. They had the location of the surrounded unit identified, along with the new firebase they'd just created. They had two other locations circled in yellow, indicating where the other two firebases would be set up once morning arrived. There were also a handful of red circles, denoting where the enemy was located. Those points covered many of the ridges and hilltops overlooking the national park.

"It's nearly three forty-five in the morning," commented General Sink. "How soon will those other firebases be operational? I have a feeling we're going to need them before the day's over with."

"The entire regiment should land at their respective locations within ninety minutes of sunup. They've assured me they'll be operational within twenty minutes after touching down," Colonel Dowdy explained.

"I was thinking about this location here," said General Sink, pointing. "It's about five klicks from our trapped unit. If we dropped the rest of the battalion here just before dawn, they could hoof it the short distance to link up with our guys. Thoughts?"

"We can do that. But I'd suggest we still drop another battalion at the original location and have the two units converge on our trapped unit," Colonel Dowdy offered. "Keep in mind, sir, while that other location is only five klicks, half that distance is up and over a nearby ridge. For all we know, it could be an enemy stronghold. We have to prepare for the fact that we could have two full battalions heavily engaged with the enemy by lunch."

Sink thought about that. He reached for his coffee mug, noting it was still empty. Walking over to the hot plate, he poured himself another cup. Then he turned around and looked at the plot table again. "I like that about you, Roy. You're not a yes-man. You tell it like it is, no matter the rank of the person before you. You're going to make a damn good division commander one day.

"But back to your point, Roy. I think you're right. We have to go into this action with the knowledge that we're likely to have both battalions heavily engaged by lunch. That's why it's important for us to get those other firebases up and running. We've got the rest of the 1st and 2nd Battalions ready to go in ninety minutes. Let's go ahead and send in the 1st Battalion, 506th with them as well. If either of those battalions makes contact, then I want 3rd Brigade to mount up and deploy to whichever battalion needs it. We're going to go ahead and get the bulk of the division deployed into this park and finish this fight. In for a penny, in for a pound, as they say."

Dowdy smiled at the phrase. "I agree, sir. Our mission objective is to clear this entire geographical area. We know the enemy is there since they trapped one of our units. We might as well as deploy the rest of the division and end this fight. Once it's secured, then we can move to the next one and hopefully bring an end to this campaign before it gets super ugly and drawn out. I have a feeling the big fight in this war is still awaiting us down in Venezuela."

****

Firebase Eagle

One of Captain Wharton's last acts before he was going to sack out for a couple of hours was naming their little base. The men had opted to call it Firebase Eagle in honor of their parent unit, the Screaming Eagles. Perhaps if he hadn't been awake for twenty-six straight hours, he might have come up with something wittier. However, all he wanted to do in life was curl up and grab a couple hours of shut-eye.

He was literally in the process of falling asleep when a soldier in the TOC shouted the words every redleg wants to hear. "Fire mission, fire mission!"

Those four words sent a jolt of adrenaline through Captain Wharton's body, instantly waking him up. Wharton jaunted over and asked, "What do we have?"

"Sir, Red Six says they've got movement along their lines. They want a single round to see what's out there," the soldier manning the radios said.

Wharton bobbed his head in agreement. His eyes searched for the coffee, hoping someone on the early morning shift might have gotten a pot going. He heard the generators still chugging away, so they had power.

"OK, send the fire mission to the FDC and let's get that round on the way," Wharton ordered. "Oh, someone go find the first sergeant for me as well."

A few minutes later, a single round fired, waking anyone who was still asleep. The first sergeant went around to all the gun chiefs, telling them to get their crews ready for a sustained fire mission.

The six howitzers at Firebase Eagle had a crew of four soldiers and a gun chief. A good five-man team could effectively shoot a standard two rounds per minute. A highly skilled crew could get off five rounds a minute. The guns themselves had an effective range of twenty-four kilometers. There were some different ammo types that could increase that to thirty or even forty kilometers, but they hadn't brought any of that kind of ammo with them.

Wharton walked over to the map table they had hanging from the side of the tent. It was near the radio operator and next to a table with a hot plate and a fresh pot of coffee.

"New fire mission," the young soldier announced excitedly.

The soldier next to him had his fire directional computer standing by, ready to input the new coordinates so they could be sent to the individual guns. This information would tell them how many powder bags to place in the breach and give them any last-minute elevation adjustments.

"Adjust fire from PD Tree," said the young soldier as he relayed what the grunts were telling him. "Up two hundred meters. Right fifty meters. Three rounds HE, fire for effect."

The FDC soldier typed the coordinates in, then double-checked them with the radio operator before he sent them to the guns.

Moments later, all six guns fired off a three-round fire mission, sending eighteen hundred pounds of high explosives eleven kilometers away.

"New fire mission. Adjust fire from PD Six. Down fifty meters. Left one hundred meters. Two rounds HE, fire for effect."

Less than two minutes later, twelve additional rounds fired. The ground and area around the firebase lit up with brilliant flashes of light each time a howitzer fired.

Wharton looked at the plots on the map as they were being called in. He wanted to see if he could get an idea of what was happening on the ground around the grunts. From what he could see, it looked like the enemy was trying to press them on two different sides. He shook his head—he could only imagine what those guys must be going through right now. It had to be scary as hell knowing they were cut off, surrounded in a jungle by God only knew how many Chinese and Salvadoran soldiers. Wharton was determined to make sure his crew did their part. Come hell or high water, they were going to provide as much artillery fire as they could.

Wharton went to find his first sergeant. "Top, make sure you're staying on top of our ammo guys," he directed. "When we drop down to one-third of our rounds, get a call in to Soto Cano for a resupply."

"You got it, sir."

****

Sergeant First Class Currie dropped his empty magazine and slapped a fresh one in place. When he turned to his right, he saw three or four Chinese soldiers jump into the American lines. A PLA soldier took the butt of his rifle and struck an American soldier's jaw, hurling him backward before firing three or four shots into him. Another PLA soldier plunged his bayonet into the side of a US soldier, and the young man howled in pain as he tried to push the enemy soldier away and pull the blade out of his side. The fighting at this point had devolved into a hand-to-hand brawling, with soldiers punching, clawing, and stabbing each other.

Currie leveled his rifle at the two ChiComs and fired. His first round hit one guy in the side of the neck before his second round blew the side of his face off. The next round hit the second enemy soldier in the side of the head, dropping the man instantly. Two of the Chinese soldiers then caught on that Currie was shooting at them and dove for cover. At this point, Currie knew if he didn't take these guys out soon, they would likely kill him. He pulled the pin on one of his grenades and tossed it in their direction.

Crump!

Currie came around the other side of the tree he'd been hiding behind, firing several quick rounds as he did. He managed to take out a guy who was about to fire an RPG at them.

Damn, that artillery needs to hit freaking right now, or we're done.

"Get down!" Dawson shouted at him.

Currie didn't hesitate and dove to his right just as a handful of tracers flew right over his head. When he rolled and came back up, he fired several rounds at the closest enemy soldier, hitting him multiple times.

Boom, boom, boom!

Dozens of explosions erupted three to five hundred meters from their positions, dispersing tens of thousands of tiny shards of red-hot metal in all directions. Currie heard all sorts of whizzing and snapping noises swirling around him.

Screams of agony spread up and down their lines. Some soldiers yelled out for a medic while others begged for their mothers. All around him, people were calling out for help in English, Spanish, and Chinese as the artillery fire shredded nearly everything around them. Currie wasn't sure if it was their own fire that had fallen short or if the enemy had somehow timed their own barrage to hit at the same time.

Currie jumped back into his fighting position and reached for the radio, only to see the hand receiver had been shredded.

Damn it!

Currie opened his patrol pack and found the spare hand receiver. This was the first time in his ten years in the military he'd actually needed to replace one. Once he had the radio running again, he reestablished coms with the lone firebase—their only support until the morning.

"Eagle One, Red Six. Good fire mission. Repeat last fire mission, only fire for effect six rounds, danger close," Currie shouted into the radio.

Gunfire had started to pick up, drowning out many of the cries from the wounded. The killing wasn't done yet, and the survivors of the artillery barrage were hell-bent on finishing what they had started.

A handful of friendly soldiers jumped into some of the fighting positions near Currie. "Captain Thorne sent us. Where do you need us?" asked a specialist whose face was covered in dirt, grime, and blood.

"Place two of your guys over there on the right," Currie replied. "Then you two take that position there. I'll do my best to help, but I need to keep calling in arty missions on these guys. We got another mission hitting soon, so stay alert."

More bullets and machine-gun rounds zipped across their lines as the enemy started to recover from the last strike.

While Currie waited on the next set of artillery rounds to hammer the enemy, he helped some of the wounded around him. Practically everywhere he looked, he saw injured soldiers.

****

101st Division HQ
Soto Cano Air Base

"It's happening, sir. The enemy is launching a major offensive against our guys," Colonel Dowdy announced.

General Sink shook his head in disgust. His boys were dying out there, and he couldn't do a damn thing about it. He looked at his watch and saw it was almost five in the morning. They had another hour or so until dawn. He cursed under his breath.

"Dowdy, send word down to the airfield. We're going in," General Sink bellowed. "We're not waiting for dawn. I want all units in the air and on their way to the landing zones immediately. Tell those flyboys to get airborne. I don't care what they have to do, those guys are going to need our help, or they're all dead."

Dowdy had a determined look on his face as he turned to grab an outstretched hand receiver.

"Colonel Davies, your mission is a go. Get your men to the LZ and relieve our boys ASAP. They're in the process of being overrun. They won't hold out much longer if you guys don't get there soon."

Dowdy turned back to the general and nodded. They'd done their part. Now it was on the individual units to execute their parts of the plan.

Chapter Three
VX-9

Air Test and Evaluation Squadron Nine
RAF Belize

At some point, you have to put your money where your mouth is and prove your concept actually works, Captain "Pappi" Lemoore reminded himself. He'd echoed those words just a few months ago during a visit to his squadron, the Vampires, by the National Security Advisor and congressional leaders shortly after the new president had been sworn in.

"Vampire Actual, China Lake. The Valkyries are airborne and moving into position now. We're ready to begin when you are," the calm, reassuring voice of Commander Holly Boyette announced.

Easy for you, Holly, thought Pappi. *You're tucked away nice and safe back at China Lake.*

"That's a good copy, China Lake," Pappi replied. "I'm heading in. Let's prove our naysayers wrong, shall we?" He spoke with all the bravado and confidence of a fighter pilot who'd flown combat missions in Kosovo, Afghanistan, Iraq, Libya, and Syria.

"Stay safe, Pappi, and know we have your back," Commander Boyette added before they turned to the business at hand.

Pappi smiled to himself; he knew Boyette was concerned for him. In a weird way, that made him feel giddy inside. If anyone knew they'd been having a secret relationship, it would likely result in him losing his command or her being reassigned. It was improper for a commanding officer to be having a romantic relationship with a subordinate. Not that either of them cared—they were both single and madly in love.

"Just cover my six. Things are about to get hairy up here. Out."

Pappi pulled up slightly on the EA-18G Growler, leveling himself out at an altitude of eighteen thousand feet. It was still dark. In a few hours, the predawn would push away the darkness and usher in the new day.

"You ready for this, Pappi?" asked Mango, his backseater.

"I'm about as ready as you can be when you're about to fly into a hornet's nest. Just make sure you stay on top of that jamming equipment. I managed to fly for twenty-eight years without being shot down. I'd like to keep that record going."

Mango chuckled and went about getting his own stuff ready. Their aircraft was a specialized version of an F/A-18 Super Hornet, tricked out in electronic warfare and jamming pods. Mango had one of the most important missions on the plane—jamming the enemy radars and any missiles fired at them.

"OK, Mango. I'm taking us in," Pappi announced. "Stay frosty and stay ready. We'll likely start encountering these SAMs in the next few minutes."

He turned the Growler toward El Salvador. They'd already topped off their tanks from a refueling aircraft over the Gulf. Now it was time to earn their pay and prove this decade-long multibillion-dollar program could work in combat and not just in a simulator.

Twenty minutes into their flight, they had crossed most of Belize and Honduras. At current speeds, they were five minutes out from where the American ground soldiers were encircled and duking it out on the ground. Pappi and Mango knew what was at stake. The guys on the ground couldn't get adequate air support or even a medevac until these damn SAMs had been cleared. Two A-29 Super Tucanos, a Chinook, two Apaches and a couple of Black Hawks had already been shot down the day before.

Pappi looked at his radar. *Nothing.* No sign of any enemy ground systems trying to engage him.

A few moments later, his RHAW lit up, and suddenly his ground radar showed a couple of systems attempting to acquire them. It was like they had crossed some magical line, and now the enemy wanted them dead.

"Pappi, China Lake. We see 'em. We're vectoring one of the Valkyries in now. Stand by," came the cool, calm voice of Commander Holly Boyette.

A new alarm abruptly blared in his helmet—the one letting him know a surface-to-air missile had been fired at them.

"I see it. I'm already on it!" Mango called out before Pappi had a chance to say anything.

Pappi looked at his altimeter—they were still cruising at eighteen thousand feet, plenty of room to maneuver and get out of the way of this missile. It was still six kilometers away but closing fast.

Pappi banked the aircraft hard to the left and took them into a steep dive as he sought to shake it. The g-forces rapidly climbed from three to nearly seven in seconds. Pulling up on the stick, Pappi shifted directions and angled them hard to the right as he increased power. They'd gone from eighteen thousand feet to six thousand feet in seconds—now they were gaining altitude once again.

"Two more missiles just launched."

Looking at his radar to get an idea of where the missiles were, Pappi saw the first one appeared to have lost them. It was now heading off in a completely different direction. The two new ones, however, they were barreling down on him fast.

"Hang in there, Pappi. Valkyrie One just hit a launcher site," Commander Boyette relayed. "Valkyrie Two has glide bombs inbound to the radar sites."

"One of those missiles is coming in pretty hot, Pappi," Mango called out, urgency in his voice.

Hitting the afterburner, Pappi pushed the aircraft hard as he rolled over onto its side and turned hard upwards. His altimeter showed them gaining altitude fast. Then his defensive system started spitting out chaff as the SAM closed the distance between them. As Pappi pulled out of the high-g turn, he yanked up on the stick and applied his air brakes, dumping most of his speed.

In seconds, the enemy missile flew through the first chaff cloud and zipped right past them. It completely missed. Pappi closed the air brakes and lit the afterburner up a second time to gain more speed. He also dove for the deck, wanting to use gravity to his advantage as he sought to grab as much additional speed as he could.

When his aircraft had dropped below three thousand feet, the sky in front of him lit up with bright red tracers. They looked like flickering red lasers crisscrossing the sky. Pappi banked from right to left, doing his best to weave through the hailstorm he'd inadvertently crossed into.

Pappi flipped a switch and activated his two AGM-88 HARMs. They were flying roughly five hundred and forty miles per hour at an altitude of twenty-five hundred feet, but once they left one valley, a new set of radars tried to acquire him. Worse, a new set of AA guns joined the fray, sending hundreds of rounds crisscrossing the valley in front of him.

"Oh, crap! They just nailed two of our Reaper drones," Mango called out as the two MQ-9 Reapers disappeared from their radar.

"Have we lost any Valkyries?" Pappi asked as the ground below continued to whip past them.

"No, it looks like—scratch that, I'm showing one of them just got zapped. Looks like it was an HQ-9 that got it."

That's not good. Damn, I need to take some of these AA guns out before we get nailed ourselves, Pappi thought.

As they dipped into another valley, Pappi spotted a PGZ-95 coming up quick. The tracked vehicles' quad-barreled 25mm autocannons were filling the air with bullets at a crazy rate of fire.

Pappi slid his aircraft to the right as he dodged a string of bullets, then locked the truck up with a HARM and depressed the pickle button. The missile activated and dropped from its hardpoint, its engine igniting fractions of a second later as the solid-fuel missile reached a top speed of 1,420 miles per hour in the blink of an eye, reaching its target before its laser proximity fuse detonated its high-explosive fragmentation warhead.

"Pull up! Pull up!" Mango screamed.

Pappi pulled back on the stick as he lit his afterburner for a third time, dumping fuel right into the jet engines. As he did this, the aircraft's defensive system identified the missile chasing them down as a heat-seeking MANPAD.

The missile saw the bright heat signature of the flares and went right for them. The explosion was just far enough behind them that they escaped the shrapnel radius.

Their aircraft continued to gain altitude and speed as they flew across the Salvadoran border into Honduras. Looking into the distance, Pappi caught a glimpse of six more MQ-9 Reaper drones on their way to the valley he'd just escaped from. The UCAVs were being directed in to hammer the remaining PGZ-95s and -09s they knew of. While they were engaging them, the three remaining XQ-58 Valkyries would continue to finish off the remaining HQ-9 radar trucks, missile launchers, and any other support systems Pappi's little foray into the lion's den had uncovered.

"Damn, that was good flying, old man," Mango blurted out rather loudly over their coms. "Wow, I don't care what they say about you, Pappi—you're a hell of a pilot, the way you just flew into the valley of death like that. I thought for certain we were dead at least half a dozen times, or we'd have to eject. That was incredible."

Pappi unfastened his face mask from his helmet. Sweat ran down his face as what they'd just lived through hit him. He felt his heart racing—his breathing was hard and labored.

I need to calm down or I'm going to pass out...that was way too close.

Looking at his radar screen, Pappi saw the search radars blinking out one after another. This included many of the PGZ-05 and -09s.

The Reapers must be getting them all.

Then it dawned on him his backseater had said something just a moment ago. He grunted as he recalled what he'd said and almost laughed. He knew what the younger pilots said about him—they thought he was getting old and slow. He'd managed to get zapped a couple of times in the simulators by some of the lieutenants and lieutenant commanders who had transferred to the unit. To be fair, the Navy tended to pull some of its best pilots from across its squadrons to become test pilots. Still, it did sting a bit to have some of the younger guys succeed in taking him out.

When they were in the air and not in a simulator, though, Pappi fared a lot better. He never could get fully used to the simulators—at least not the old versions they'd been using. The new ones, the ones being used with the XQ-58s—well, those were about as real as anything he'd ever seen, used, or read about.

"Thanks for the words of encouragement, Mango," Pappi remarked. "I'll be sure to note them in your next fitness report."

"You're welcome, Pappi. I'll be sure to note how reckless you were in endangering your electronic warfare officer's life in my award recommendation," Mango retorted as he laughed. Pappi joined the nervous laughter.

Their helmet radios crackled to life. "Vampire Actual, China Lake. That was a damn fine mission. How are things on your end?" asked Commander Boyette.

"I think we used up all nine of our cat lives, but other than that, I think we're OK. Bigger question is, did we take out the enemy SAMs and enough of those AA guns so our helicopters and Tucanos will be able to help our guys on the ground?" asked Pappi. Although he was flying this mission, he was also the squadron commander, so he was effectively the top naval test pilot in charge of this experimental UCAV program.

Commander Boyette didn't respond right away. She was probably collecting the data for him before she did. This might have been a high-priority SEAD mission, but it was also only the second time the Loyal Wingman program had been used in combat.

"We lost three of the four Valkyries and six of the eight Reapers involved in the attack," Commander Boyette relayed. "We did succeed in destroying five HQ-9 mobile radar sites, two previously unknown fixed radar sites, eight missile launcher sites, and fourteen AA gun trucks. Command is calling this an incredibly successful mission. They'd like you to return to base and rearm for a follow-up mission. The 101st is sending in a large helicopter mission as we speak. They'll likely be carrying out helicopter operations throughout the day, so any additional SEAD missions we can provide would be greatly appreciated." He knew she could have told him to wait until he landed, but not knowing for another hour would have driven him nuts.

"Tell me they have another unit providing them SEAD and it's not just us," he shot back.

"They do. The Air Force has a Viper squadron going in right now. Talk with you more when you're on the ground. China Lake out."

Pappi reached down and grabbed for some water. He drank the entire pouch down in a few gulps. When he landed, he wanted to change flights suits and drink a couple more liters.

****

Captain Thorne moved along the western part of his lines. Rays of sunlight were starting to pierce their way through the jungle canopy. It helped that a lot of new holes had been punched through it over the last few hours' worth of artillery strikes and precision guided bombs. Still, virtually everywhere he looked, he saw bodies. Some were wounded, moaning softly. Some called out for help, some begged to be put out of their misery, some called out to their loved ones, while a few were making peace with their maker.

Thorne saw a few Screaming Eagle soldiers from the original QRF group sitting with their backs against a tree. A handful of the newly arrived Air Force pararescuemen or PJs were tending to their wounds while they waited for the next medevac to arrive.

Twenty minutes ago, an Air Force Pave Hawk had finally been able to make it to their position. They'd brought four of the highly trained rescue men and a combat surgeon with them. The helicopter had also been able to retrieve eight of their most urgently wounded soldiers.

Someone from the division headquarters at Soto Cano Air Base told Thorne they had a company's worth of soldiers from the famed Red Currahee or 506th regiment on their way to his position to relieve them. They asked if he could create a clearing large enough for a Black Hawk to land. If not, they'd do their best to rappel in. Thorne wasn't sure if they could make a clearing or not. It all depended on how much det cord or C-4 they still had left.

Pushing that task aside for a moment, he looked past their lines and saw the person he was looking for. Sergeant First Class Russ Currie was out beyond their perimeter with their team medic, checking on the enemy soldiers that littered the ground around them. Unfortunately, this was a task that had to be done. It wasn't acceptable to just leave wounded soldiers out there—they had to be disarmed so they couldn't kill more of the American soldiers, and if it was possible to treat them, they had to be given medical attention.

This was a dirty job, and while Thorne and his team had no love lost for the enemy, they weren't barbarians either. If a PLA soldier didn't appear to be beyond help and their medic could treat him, then they did, and they took the individual prisoner to be interrogated later. When an enemy soldier was past the point of treatment, they'd usually mercy-kill them so they wouldn't suffer in agony.

Captain Thorne walked over to Currie and Franklin, the team medic. The guy they were tending to had a horrendous wound to his gut. Parts of his intestines had been ripped open and were spilled out on the ground. The medic shook his head as he looked at Thorne and Currie before he made his way to the next wounded man.

Currie sighed and then blew some air out his lips. The PLA soldier wasn't conscious. His eyes were closed, and his lips moved ever so slightly between ragged breaths. Currie pointed his pistol at the man's head and fired a single shot.

The sound of the gun made Thorne jump for some reason. The others around them didn't really pay it any attention. They knew what Currie and the Special Forces medic were doing. Some looked at them with disgust, some with pity, but they all seemed relieved they weren't the one out there pulling this duty.

"Why did you guys volunteer for this, Currie?" Thorne asked. "You could have assigned it to one of the regular Army guys."

Currie stepped around a small crater in the dirt that had been created by a 155mm howitzer round. "Most of these guys left alive and functional enough to do this job are just kids, sir. Their remaining NCOs are either dead or wounded." Currie paused for a second. "Sir, I couldn't order a nineteen-year-old to come out here and do this. I wasn't going to condemn one or more of these kids to the kind of nightmares that'll likely haunt me. They've seen and done enough in these last eighteen hours to last a lifetime."

Thorne hadn't thought about that, but he knew Currie was right. He suddenly had an even higher opinion of the Special Forces sergeant than he had just a few minutes ago.

"How many do you estimate we've had to put down versus treat and take prisoner?"

"If I had to guess, I'd say we've been able to save and treat maybe eighteen. Mercy kills, probably twice that number. The rest were already dead. But this is just our side of the line. I don't know what the other teams have done."

Thorne shook his head. This wasn't how his team was supposed to be used. This wasn't something they trained for or specialized in. They were just supposed to move through the national park and identify radar vehicles and AA guns and see if they could locate the enemy base of operations.

Currie stopped in his tracks for a moment. He reached for his CamelBak hose and took a drink. "Sir, when that new unit arrives, are we getting out of here or sticking around?"

Thorne saw the tired look in the man's eyes. He'd soldier on if Thorne told him to, but the captain could see the man was physically and emotionally spent. "I was told it was my discretion. I'm voting that we leave. Nearly everyone on the team has been nicked or wounded. Two of our guys are dead. It's time for us to get out of Dodge."

"That's a good call, sir," Currie replied, obviously relieved. "Oh, and this is all the remaining det cord I have—I think it's enough to take down a few trees if that's what you were looking for." He pulled the items from his patrol pack.

Shortly thereafter, a number of A-29 Super Tucanos began carrying out a series of attacks throughout the valley around their positions. They were later joined by a handful of Apache gunships as they scoured the ridges and valleys for any potential threats to the Black Hawks that were on the way.

Fortunately for Captain Thorne and Lieutenant Branham, the sole surviving officer from the Screaming Eagles, they had been able to clear quite a few trees in an area not too far from their lines. They'd had to resort to using a few RPGs and a SMAW round against a couple of tree bases, but they'd gotten the job done, clearing a hole in the jungle large enough for a Black Hawk to land.

When they heard the rhythmic thumping of the helicopters starting to arrive, one of the Screaming Eagles tossed a purple smoke grenade into the newly created LZ. Moments later, the first Black Hawk descended. The PJs and remaining medics ran the wounded forward and waited until the eleven newly arrived soldiers got off. They piled the wounded on, and the bird took off. They repeated this process three more times, until they had all the wounded aboard and on their way out of there.

Captain Thorne and Lieutenant Branham talked with Captain Kush, the CO for the unit taking their place. They relayed what had transpired over the last sixteen hours and where they thought the enemy had likely retreated to. Thorne had one of their Black Hornet microdrones follow them back to a cave that likely led to a mountain fortress. The Chinese had clearly built this area up to allow them to move large numbers of soldiers from one ridge and valley to another via tunnels and passageways out of sight of American satellites or surveillance aircraft.

When the handoff had been completed, the remainder of the QRF boarded the next set of helicopters and left. Thorne and his five remaining operators waited for the last bird to land. When it did, the last of the Red Currahee soldiers got off and they got on.

It wasn't until they were in the air that Thorne saw how thoroughly torn up this part of the jungle had been by the last eighteen hours of fighting. Shoot, the artillery unit had provided nearly four straight hours of continuous artillery fire around their perimeter. During one of the final human wave assaults, the newly fielded *Kennedy* strike group that operated a hundred miles off the coast of El Salvador had sent in a squadron of F/A-18 Super Hornets to carry out a massive air strike for the beleaguered defenders. To support the attack, the Navy had fielded its brand-new Loyal Wingman program for the first time. Coupled with a wave of Reaper drones, they had successfully eliminated most of the enemy air defenses in the region and saved Thorne and their motley crew from being completely overrun.

When the helicopter had turned away from the national park they'd fought so hard in, Thorne looked over to see his guys. All of them were asleep except Currie, who was looking out the door like Thorne, seemingly lost in thought. In forty-five minutes, they would arrive at Soto Cano. As soon as Thorne could slip away to get a shower, he would. Then he'd pass out for the next couple of days before finding out what kind of mission the brass had for them next.

Chapter Four
Recalibration

Zhongnanhai
Beijing, China

President Yao Jintao looked down the table at his military advisors before settling his gaze on Dr. Xi Zemin. He stared at Xi longer and perhaps a bit more intensely than he did anyone else. It was, after all, his machine that had guided them to where they were now. It was his machine that would lead them to either an eventual victory or an utter defeat that could result in the dismantling of the entire country.

Yao could tell his inner circle was nervous about this meeting. It was still dark outside, only being five twenty in the morning. When he'd thought up this meeting yesterday, he had intentionally given them all little notice other than to inform them they had better not be late. Worse, Yao hadn't given them any heads-up on what he wanted to talk about or if they should have something ready to brief him with. Meetings like this were usually the kind one didn't come home from to kiss one's wife or children—one might simply not come home at all.

Yao let them squirm a bit longer as the stewards finished pouring everyone a glass of tea and left some breakfast pastries and fruit for them to nibble on. The tension in the room was thick and palpable. Even the stewards seemed to know something bad was about to happen. Once their duties were complete, they hurriedly vacated the room.

The silence once they had left was incredible. Yao could almost sense the fear and unease oozing from each of them, with the exception of General Luo Ronghuan, the head of the PLA Air Force, and General

Gao Weiping, the head of the Strategic Support Force. Those two knew something the others didn't but soon would find out.

Yao coughed sightly as he placed his tea down on the table. After clearing his throat, he began. "I called you all here this morning because we have something important to discuss. We need to review the current direction of the war and how it has been progressing. First, our naval losses have been unacceptable—our entire Indian Ocean task force has been destroyed. Even now, NATO is preparing to retake the Indonesian islands of Belitung and the Riau Islands.

"We fought a tough campaign to capture these islands to give us control of who can enter the South China Sea. If NATO is able to wrestle them away from us, it could make holding our island bases substantially tougher. Worse, it'll open the entire southern half of the country up to further attacks."

Fleet Admiral Wei Huang shook his head angrily in disagreement at the accusation that his force had failed to live up to expectations. "Mr. President, we have implemented the strategies and plans given to us by Dr. Xi's computer," he declared. "My own planners on several occasions had warned that some of these plans either were unworkable or would lead to unacceptable losses. On each occasion we brought them up, we were told to just follow what the computer had put together. If the Navy has failed, it has not been the fault of my men and officers, but the fault of the machine ordering us to implement strategies that could not succeed."

Several admirals and the head of the PLA ground force voiced similar concerns. They all felt Jade Dragon was in charge of the military and not the generals and admirals. In private, Yao would probably admit they were right. But that would also mean the AI was essentially in charge of the country and even his own position was redundant. That was a scary thought.

Generals Lua and Gao kept their poker faces on. They were the only two not agreeing with the others.

Yao turned to look at his overall PLA commander, who was essentially the equivalent of the American Chairman of the Joint Chiefs. "General Li Zuocheng, Taiwan surrendered to our forces a little more than two and a half months ago. What is the delay in getting Taiwan ready to repel a potential American invasion? Why is most of the country still without drinkable water, power, and basic life support functions needed to keep the people happy and subdued? We need the population to come to our side and work with us—not form militias and insurgencies."

General Li tried to maintain a stoic expression. "Mr. President, during the campaign to subdue the island, Jade Dragon recommended a series of missile attacks that devastated parts of the country's infrastructure. These are not things that can be readily put back together. They require months of work, which is only being made harder because of a lack of power. Now insurgency groups are springing up, which is slowing construction projects down further. The problem with Dr. Xi's AI, Jade Dragon, Mr. President, is it only sees a problem that needs to be solved. What it doesn't see is the human cost to some of its proposed solutions. It also does not take into account the second- and third-order effects of some of these decisions."

The general paused for a second, almost like he was trying to decide if he should say something further. "Our forces are doing the best they can, but when the AI hands us a new set of objectives and we have no say in how we are to implement them, it ties our hands. The battle against the Japanese and Korean fleet in the Yellow Sea is a perfect example.

Did we defeat the enemy? Yes, but at the cost of the destruction of our northern fleet. We now no longer have a fleet that can pose a continued threat to the American, Korean, or Japanese fleets.

"The same thing happened in the Indian Ocean, when Jade Dragon recommended we attempt to block the Bab al-Mandab Strait near Perim Island. That entire campaign cost us a huge portion of the southern fleet—a fleet of warships we no longer have available to protect the South China Sea or our Indonesian islands with."

"So, what are you saying, General? That Jade Dragon has outlived its usefulness?" Dr. Xi responded defensively.

The general turned to the doctor. "I'm not saying that at all. I *do* believe that maybe there is a better use for Jade Dragon than micromanaging the military and our tactical decisions."

"The war is going fine," Dr. Xi countered. "We are fighting a host of nations on our own and still winning. As it stands, we have achieved nearly half of our overall objectives. Taiwan is firmly in our hands. By this time next year, we should have most if not all of the Russian Far East under our control. At that point, we'll have met our military objectives and we can sue for peace."

General Li countered with something unexpected. "I want to quote you something, Dr. Xi. In February of 2002, the American Secretary of Defense said during a press briefing, 'I classify unknowns into one of the following two types: known unknowns (expected or foreseeable conditions), which can be reasonably anticipated but not quantified based on past experience as exemplified by case histories. Then unknown unknowns (unexpected or unforeseeable conditions), which pose a potentially greater risk, simply because they cannot be anticipated based on past experience or investigation. Known unknowns result from recognized but poorly understood phenomena. On the other hand, unknown unknowns are phenomena which cannot be expected because there has been no prior experience or theoretical basis for expecting the phenomena.'

"I repeat this to you because while Jade Dragon has performed exceptionally well in certain areas, when it comes to fighting a war with real-world consequences, it is beginning to encounter a series of unknown unknowns, and it is failing to recognize them or understand how to overcome them."

Yao sat there, almost stunned by what General Li had explained. *Perhaps I should keep him around a bit longer*, he thought. *Li, you just unknowingly saved yourself with that observation.*

"That is a good point, General Li. Dr. Xi, do you believe there is some truth to what the general has just shared?" asked Yao. "Perhaps there are still things Jade Dragon needs to continue learning if it is to be fully successful in fighting a war."

The scientist had a perplexed look on his face. *The bastard is so used to being right, he can't fathom being wrong*, thought Yao.

Xi looked at Yao for a second before conceding, "I would not call Jade Dragon a child, but its thinking process can sometimes be akin to one. The machine is always learning—learning from its mistakes and then learning from the mistakes of our adversaries. It is also discovering more based on our successes and theirs. All of this is helping to shape JD's 'brain,' and ultimately, his cognitive abilities." One of the generals shot Xi a disapproving look when he referred to the AI by "he" instead of "it." Xi continued, unhindered. "If I can, I would like to point out something else that has not been taken into consideration."

Yao bowed his head for him to continue.

Dr. Xi seemed determined. "Our military losses have been severe up to this point—I will concede that. But they have not been without cause. We have achieved all of our military objectives thus far. While our losses have been brutal, they are nothing in comparison to what we have inflicted on the West. They are only now coming to grips with their own losses. Even now, the Americans are discovering that once their current inventory of F-22 Raptors runs out, there are no replacement aircraft coming. It's the same with their submarines and destroyers. It will take them *years* to replace those losses, and trillions of dollars—money their government can't afford because of the pandemic we released on them and the rest of the West prior to the war.

"When we look at our economy, JD knew this war was coming and when. It knew what our immediate losses would be. It anticipated them. Six months prior to the start of the war, it purchased in advance all the materials our factories would need to function for a year without outside supplies. It also began a rapid arms buildup transition, moving our factories to a war footing months before the West. As we speak, our shipyards are producing one destroyer, six corvettes, four frigates, and four submarines a week. Our factories are building over one hundred fighter jets and two hundred helicopters a week, along with twenty cargo aircraft, two refueling aircraft, and literally hundreds of drones. That will only increase over time. The armies of the West cannot hope to catch up to us. By the time they get done expending themselves in the Caribbean, they won't have an army or navy left to challenge us with in the Pacific," Dr. Xi explained. He leaned back, sitting up even taller before he added, "I know the situation appears tough right now. I get that. But JD has war-gamed this all out. We need to trust the AI, at least a little longer."

Yao sat there thinking about all of this for a minute. He had brought up a good point. They were only five months into this war. *The losses, though...they are unsustainable in the eyes of the people*, he realized. Maybe if the losses became more severe, he could assuage the people by eliminating some of the generals and explaining that it was their failures that had led to these casualties.

That could be a way of eliminating more of the old guard...I think this could work.

"OK, we've been talking long enough. I want everyone to continue with their existing tasks and missions. I am going to retire to my office and have some breakfast. Dismissed," Yao said as he got up and left the room without looking at any of them further.

The guards standing at the door opened it for him. He gave them a slight shake of the head, letting them know his previous plans had changed. They were not to execute everyone in the room—at least not yet.

****

Yao walked into his presidential office. His secretary stood, and he barked to her that he wanted breakfast for four brought to his office immediately. He told her to make sure it was a full breakfast, not a light affair. He was ravenously hungry, and he was sure his guests were as well.

Minutes after entering the expansive room, he heard a knock at the door. One of his security guards opened it slightly. "Sir, your guests have arrived."

Without speaking, Yao motioned for him to let them in.

Generals Gao and Lua and Dr. Xi walked in. Yao pointed to the dining table near one of the office windows. Some cups of tea had just been poured.

"Breakfast will be brought up for us shortly. Please, take your seats. We have some urgent business that needs to be discussed," Yao explained as he took his own seat.

"Thank you for inviting us to breakfast, Mr. President," General Gao replied as he reached for his tea.

"General, please tell me the status of the Dragonflies. Are they ready for combat?" Yao asked. He was gambling a lot on this particular program working.

Gao smiled at the mention of their secret project, and so did Dr. Xi, who had been instrumental in the testing process with JD.

"I believe they are ready. But once we release them, Mr. President, there will be no going back," Gao explained. "Our secret will be out of the bag, and the West will begin to work on a counter to them. We need to unleash them where they will be able to do the most damage possible."

Yao turned to Xi. "Once the West encounters them, what are the most likely ways they will look to defeat them? Where are the Dragonflies' vulnerabilities?"

Dr. Xi looked like he was calculating for a moment. Then he responded, "In the short term, the West will likely resort to using shotguns with bird shot. It'll work at shooting them down, but it won't stop them or address the larger problem of how to stop a swarm. To handle that, I believe they will look to employ some sort of electronic device aimed at disabling the drones or interrupting the signals controlling them."

"What are the more extreme ways the West, in particular the Americans, may try to counter them?"

"If I had to guess, Mr. President, I would say the Americans will likely go after the satellite networks and probably the GPS system," Dr. Xi explained. "I'd like to think they wouldn't, but unless they were able to come up with some other sort of technology that could either jam or disable the Dragonflies, I don't see them having a lot of other choices."

Yao thought about that. Their détente with the West when it came to the world's GPS and satellite infrastructure had held so far. He hated the idea of losing them.

The Chinese President turned to General Gao. "Let's assume the Americans go that route," he proposed. "Let's also assume we go after theirs. How soon until we can get a new network operational, at least over China?"

"We'd need to wait a few weeks once this started," Gao posited. "We'd want to wait until the shooting had stopped. Then I think we could get a new network reestablished over China with a few rocket launches. It would also depend on the severity of the debris field created in orbit. Depending on how bad that got, there is a chance we might not be *able* to reestablish our network, at least not until it had been cleaned up a bit first.

"Fortunately, the DragonLink satellites are small. It's conceivable they could last longer in a large debris field or possibly not get damaged by it. Another advantage is that each rocket could carry nearly a hundred of them. We'd likely have our territories reestablished with just one or two rockets. The bigger challenge is figuring out how fast the Americans would be able to take it down a second time." Gao paused for a second before adding, "I think if we planned on having to do this a few times, we might be able to get the Americans to give up. They can only destroy so many of our satellites before they run out of antisatellite munitions—"

"Not if they were to use directed-energy weapons," Xi interrupted. "Then they could conceivably keep taking them out with impunity."

"Then how do we make them stop going after our satellites?" Yao pressed.

75

"Easy. We don't go after theirs," replied General Gao. "We make it clear the satellite network is still off-limits. I know it has made things harder on our own forces, and yes, it's led to a lot of our people being killed, but it's also allowed JD to maintain his grasp on what's going on around the world and allowed our own hackers to cause a lot of chaos and problems within the West. If the Americans go after our network because of the Dragonflies, then chances are, it'll be a local attack and not a global one. Meaning, they'll look to zap the satellites covering Central and South America but largely look to leave the rest of our network alone."

Yao shook his head in frustration. On the one hand, he really hated the idea of leaving the West's satellite network and GPS alone. It was a huge strategic and tactical advantage that the West was making full use of. He wished he could take it away from them to help level the playing field, but making sure Jade Dragon had global access to what was going on appeared to be paying its own dividends, even if it lent a strategic advantage to the West in this war.

"So, when do we release this new weapon of war on the West?" Yao finally asked.

The generals smiled. "Let's just say when the Americans launch their invasion of Venezuela, we will have a surprise ready to greet them," Gao replied.

A devilish grin spread across Yao's face at the idea of tens of thousands of American Marines landing along the shores of Venezuela only to be greeted by a swarm of killer drones. It would be a quiet surprise, one that would ensure that by the time the Americans kicked them out of the Caribbean, the Yankees would no longer have the capability to wage war beyond their borders for years if not a decade to come. They would finally be reduced to a territorial army, unable to stop China from achieving its true greatness.

"Very well. Continue with the drone programs," Yao ordered. "And, Xi, let's move forward with Operation Terracotta—I think it's time we give JD a real body." The West and the Americans had no idea what was about to be unleashed on them.

Chapter Five
In the Dead of Night

Soto Cano Air Base
Honduras

Rusten Currie had just finished typing up his final after-action report from their previous mission. He'd been procrastinating for days. Finally, Captain Thorne had told him he'd run out of time and had to turn it in by the end of the day. Currie had been holding out on writing it primarily because he didn't want to relive the events of that day. It was battles like this one that he wanted to stuff down in the back recesses of his lizard brain and forget about. In his mind, there was nothing honorable or worthy of remembering.

When he reviewed the final report, Currie did feel he'd covered everything. Every little gory detail had been included for posterity's sake. He'd also made sure to highlight the valorous acts of several of his team members, to include Captain Thorne. Currie had stayed up into the wee hours of the morning, making a point of writing up nine specific soldiers for valor medals. Five were for guys from his ODA, the other four for the 101st guys who'd come to bail them out. He didn't list what medal they should be given—he figured once the report had been read, the officers would render a decision on what should be awarded.

After completing his labor, Currie collapsed into his bed, falling into a dreamless sleep.

Sometime later, he woke in a cold sweat to the thundering sound of a jet engine. Currie swung his feet around and placed them on the ground. He grabbed for a shirt and used it to wipe the sweat from his face before putting it on.

Currie looked around. Some of the guys were still asleep, their bodies absorbing as much rest as they could. He knew he should doze off, but it wasn't in the cards, at least not right now. He exited the room and walked over to the latrines to relieve himself.

Looking off toward the airfield, Currie saw it was abuzz with activity. Air Force cargo planes were constantly arriving. They'd land and offload some vehicles or palletized equipment and then leave to head back and pick up another load. He saw a couple of UPS and FedEx aircraft as well. Yesterday, he'd seen a Southwest plane land. It had disembarked a hundred and fifty soldiers and some cargo before it too had left, presumably to return with another load.

Currie stood there with his hands on his hips and just shook his head at the entire operation. It truly was incredible when he thought about it. Just four weeks ago, when they'd arrived at this backwater counterdrug base, it had still been relatively small. During their three-week jaunt in the jungle, the place had transformed itself into a massive sprawling facility. Thousands of soldiers had arrived each day—it was incredible to see.

"Couldn't sleep?" asked his medic buddy, Mark Dawson.

"Nah. You?"

Dawson just shrugged. "Me and the guys are going to go into town later today—see if we can find a bar to get wasted in and maybe try some local food or even get laid if we're lucky. You want to tag along?"

Currie thought about the offer. He really should. He needed to cut loose and blow off some steam. If he didn't, the memories of this last battle would eat him alive.

"Hell yeah. Count me in."

Dawson smiled. "Awesome. Now, let's go rouse the guys and get a solid run in this morning. We've been slacking the last couple of days and that needs to end."

The seven remaining members of their ODA team went on a solid five-mile run. They ran through several CrossFit regimens and really got the blood flowing. By 0900 hours, they'd gotten themselves fed, showered, and ready for whatever was going to be thrown at them next.
****

48 Hours Later

Currie walked into the hangar his team had been told to report to for a briefing. Captain Thorne was already there. He and Chief Miller waved to get their attention and motioned for them to come over by them.

As he walked through the hangar, Currie saw some faces he hadn't seen in years. It quickly became apparent that the large group in the hangar was one of the three squadrons from Delta Force, also known as the Unit or JSOC. A handful of pilots from the 160th were present, along with a contingent from the Rangers, likely the security detail for the mission.

"What exactly did you just volunteer us for, sir?" was all Currie managed to whisper before a loud booming voice got everyone's attention.

A colonel by the name of Imhoff stood at the front of the room and announced, "This is it, gentlemen. We've got a lead on Major General Cai Yingting. He's the military commander for the PLA Forces in El Salvador and he's also the second-in-command for all PLA forces in our hemisphere. Intelligence has learned that he's going to be smuggled out of the country tonight."

As Colonel Imhoff talked, the operators all gathered around two large TV monitors that had some map images brought up on them. On the side of the map was a picture of the PLA general.

"Our source says the general is going to be smuggled across the Honduras border, where they'll make their way some sixty miles to the Nicaraguan border," the colonel explained. "Capturing this guy is a priority one mission. Any asset you can think up is being made available to us to apprehend him. This guy needs to be brought in alive. Dead men can't talk, and we need this guy to sing, so do what you have to, but don't kill him, if at all possible."

"Sir, what's our order of battle going to be?" asked a lieutenant colonel from Delta.

"That's a good question. Our source indicates the general is likely going to be smuggled across the border at this location here," Imhoff said as he pointed to a location on the map labeled Puente La Amistad. "Since the start of the fighting, there has been a massive surge of refugees trying to flee the fighting into Honduras. The source has said this is the border crossing they'll be using.

"To complicate things, in addition to our source on the ground telling us this is the location the general is going to cross from, we've also picked up a single piece of signals intelligence asking a Chinese Special Forces team be at this location here." A new map location appeared. It showed a bend in the Río Goascorán that looked shallow enough to wade across. "We're not sure if this might have been intentionally broadcast to throw us off, but we obviously can't be in two places at once. Chief Warrant Officer Miller and Captain Thorne have volunteered their ODA to provide overwatch of this location. Should the general cross at this position instead of trying to intermix with the refugees, then Thorne's ODA will be in position to interdict them."

Raising a hand, Chief Miller said, "Colonel, we're down four operators from our last mission. What additional support units will be accompanying us?"

That's a good question, Currie thought.

"Chief, we're going to send a platoon of Rangers with your team. We think it'll likely be a bust we're sending you on, but we need to make sure. Should your ODA and the Rangers run into trouble, we have four Apaches on standby. There will also be a single Reaper in your AO and an AC-130 gunship, should things really go south."

Imhoff went on for another ten minutes before he handed off the briefing to a couple of others. They spent close to an hour going over the main objective, details about the border crossing, and how they were going to identify the general and neutralize any possible security that might be with him.

From Currie's standpoint, this mission looked like it would be better handled by a small four-man team with a surveillance group than a squadron of Delta operators.

When the briefing was finished, Captain Thorne had the team head back to their location to load up. They spent an hour going over their weapons, ammo, and kits to make sure they had everything they needed for this mission. Once they'd double-checked each other's kits and weapons, they headed over to the hangar to link up with their Ranger contingent.

Sergeant First Class Currie approached Captain Thorne. "Sir, how are we going to work this out with these Rangers?"

Thorne grunted. "I was just thinking the same thing, Russ. We don't normally operate with a security detachment. We usually *are* the security detachment. I suppose we'll figure it out once we link up with them."

****

Bravo Company, 3rd Rangers

Sergeant First Class Amos Dekker looked his guys over and nodded in approval. The platoon was ready. Now they'd hang tight and wait for the ODA team they were going to provide security for to arrive.

When he saw Captain Meacham walk toward them, he asked, "Sir, what's up with us pulling security for an ODA team? Why don't we just execute the mission and leave them out of it?"

Meacham just shrugged. "I asked the same question to the colonel. He told me the J2 believes there's a PLA Special Forces team escorting the general or at least meeting him at the RV point. They want this guy alive, but they also want overwhelming firepower present in case it turns into a shooting match. The ODA gets the general, we get the SF team."

Just then, the eight-man Special Forces team entered the hangar and headed toward them. Their chief warrant officer introduced himself and the rest of the team. They talked for a few minutes, sizing each other up and seeing where they'd all been up to this point in the war. Dekker felt a little better when he learned this particular ODA had been involved in a few major pitch battles. It meant they likely knew how to do more than reconnaissance work and blowing up targets behind enemy lines. It wasn't that he had anything against the ODAs—they just weren't Delta or Rangers. Direct-action missions weren't a specialty of theirs.

Someone from the S3 brought a handful of maps for them to look at, along with some recent aerial photographs of the area.

Captain Meacham commented, "Looking at these pictures and this map, we've got a little island in the center of this river with roughly thirty feet of water on the Salvadoran side and twenty feet of water on the

Honduran side. This village is only four or five hundred meters from the crossing. How do you think we should deploy our guys?"

"I've been thinking about this as well," Captain Thorne replied. "They really aren't giving us a whole lot of time to prepare. Ideally, we'd get in a hide position at least twenty-four hours in advance. As it is, I think we're going to get lucky and have maybe three to five hours."

Thorne began explaining what he thought might work best. As Dekker stood to the side and listened to what the ODA captain was saying, he found himself nodding along. This guy really knew his stuff. In the span of a couple of minutes, he'd outlined a pretty solid plan for how their two forces would interact and handle this snatch-and-grab.

The ODA guys were going to spread themselves out on the island itself and look to grab the Chinese general when his escorts brought him across it. The Rangers would be broken down into three groups—two on the Honduran side, opposite the island in the river, and one on the Salvadoran side of the border. Should the Greenie Beanies run into trouble, the Rangers would be in a good position to render aid, and if a firefight should break out, they'd be in an excellent position to neutralize the threat.

An hour went by as the two groups talked about the mission and what kind of opposition they might face. It was likely the general would be traveling with a security team of two to five people so as to draw minimal attention. He'd also probably have a larger security team nearby. Then again, if a Chinese Special Forces team really was being sent to collect him, then that would certainly complicate things.

"Everyone, listen up!" bellowed Colonel Imhoff loudly. "We're going to load everyone up in the choppers in twenty minutes. We've got forty minutes of light left. This means you all should be landing near your objectives just after sunset. That'll give you plenty of time to get your bearings, find your hide locations and settle in for the night.

"Remember, our source says the general and his escorts are going to wait until around 0300 hours to attempt the border crossing. He may try and cross sooner, or he may wait until daylight. He might even wait another day. So stay frosty and keep your heads on a swivel. The noose is tightening around Venezuela—if this guy is going to link up with their forces there, then he has to get out of El Salvador ASAP."

Time went by in a blur, and before he knew it, Dekker was calling out to his guys to start loading up in the Black Hawks. Minutes later, the small air armada was headed south. As the helicopters flew over the sprawling American base, Dekker marveled at how large it had grown. Before the war, he'd participated in a couple of counterdrug operations out of this base. Soto Cano Air Base had been used by the US military since the mid-1950s for various purposes. The base was a Honduran facility, not an American one. It was also home to US Southern Command's Joint Task Force–Bravo (JTF-B). The JTF's role was to help provide regional security assistance and help the central American governments counter the growing influence and role of transnational narco cartels.

The group of helicopters turned southeast as they hugged the terrain. Normally, they'd fly high, but with the proliferation of Chinese MANPADs across El Salvador, the pilots were doing their best to mitigate the likelihood of getting shot down by just flying low and fast.

Dekker felt reasonably confident the war in El Salvador would come to an end pretty soon. The Salvadoran Army wasn't a very large force. It had been virtually wiped out during a couple of major battles during the first five days of the invasion. Similarly, the Chinese didn't have nearly the same number of soldiers here as they did in Cuba or were rumored to have in Venezuela. They'd largely anchored themselves in a couple of major pockets, knowing the Americans would have to expend a lot of resources and soldiers to root them out—resources and soldiers that wouldn't be available later on for the pending Venezuela campaign.

It took them nearly forty minutes to reach the objective. The pilot made a few false landings to throw off any observers who might have been trying to track them. Then the pilot swooped into the real LZ and hovered just long enough for Dekker and his squad to get off. Once on the ground, the helicopter took off and headed toward its next fake landing zone before it'd return to Soto Cano.

On the ground, Dekker's squad had fanned out into a circle. They listened to the helicopter conduct more fake landings in the distance while they allowed their eyes to adjust to the darkness.

Flipping his night vision goggles down, Dekker surveyed the area around them. He did a quick coms check with the rest of the platoon and Meacham. Then they made contact with the ODA team on the island. They were in the process of getting themselves ready to observe the river, watching for anyone that might try and wade across it.

When twenty minutes had passed and they hadn't heard a peep from the surrounding area, Dekker had his squad start to move out toward their observation points. They'd establish their hide positions and settle in for a long night of observation. If all went well, the Delta Squadron to their north would nab the PLA general and they'd get picked up in the morning. After a rip-roaring ten weeks in Cuba and now three weeks into a six-week rotation with B Squadron, Dekker was looking forward to a quiet evening of observing an empty river.

****

Sergeant First Class Currie was propped up against a fallen tree near the water. Something had caught his attention near the water's edge. He flipped the lens cover off the thermal spotting scope and scanned the area. Sure enough, he saw a heat signature. It looked to be a single figure. He couldn't see further back to know if there were more people because there was a slight rise in the terrain that blocked him.

Depressing the talk button on his mic, he let it chirp twice, signaling Captain Thorne he'd seen something.

A minute later, Chief Smith sidled up next to him, then Thorne joined them. "What do you have, Currie?" asked Smith.

Currie passed the thermal lens over to him and pointed to where he'd seen the figure. After observing him for a minute, they determined that the person on the opposite bank was doing something very similar to what they were doing. He had a similar type of scope out and appeared to be scanning the area in a very methodical way. Fortunately for the Americans, their new uniforms and IR reduction blankets greatly reduced their thermal signatures. It wouldn't eliminate them entirely, but it would make it significantly harder to detect them.

"Look, a second guy is joining him. What's he doing?" asked Thorne.

The new figure appeared to be unpacking something. A moment later, the second figure appeared to hurl something into the air. When they saw that, they knew immediately what it was. He'd just launched some sort of drone. Whoever these guys were, they were scouting this area for something.

Thorne sent a very brief message telling the team to stay still and quiet since their area was likely being observed by a surveillance drone. They needed these guys to think the place was clear so they'd move on. Thorne also sent an activity report to the headquarters team at Soto Cano.

They needed to know the general might actually be crossing at their location and not that border crossing as originally thought.

Thorne made sure the Rangers knew what was up. They in turn reported some movement on the Salvadoran side of the border. A couple of beat-up-looking cars had just arrived, and a total of six figures had gotten out of the vehicle and headed toward the river. On the Honduran side, a two-man spotter team the Rangers had set up nearby reported that a convoy of five vehicles had just arrived—it was probably the Special Forces unit that was supposed to pick the general up.

Another ten minutes went by when a group of people appeared near the edge of the river on the Salvadoran side. Several individuals armed with rifles waded into the river. It wasn't terribly deep—the water only seemed to come up to their bellies. The lead individuals made their way toward the island in the center of the river. When they were halfway across, another group started to make their way into the water. There were two individuals on either flank, one in the lead, one in the rear and then two people in the center. One of them was presumably the general they were after.

The general and his seven escorts crossed the river and made their way onto the island. This was where Thorne and his people planned to abduct him.

As Currie examined the group through his night vision goggles, he noticed that one of the men in the center was not holding a rifle, and his body armor wasn't fully kitted out like the rest of the Chinese Special Forces soldiers.

He spoke very quietly into his throat mike. "Captain, one of these monkeys doesn't look like the others. Man in the center, three o'clock— can you confirm this is the general?"

"Wait one," Thorne replied.

There was a pause. "Confirmed, one of these monkeys isn't the same. Let's do this."

Currie had his M17 9mm silenced pistol in his hand, aimed at the soldier closest to him. It had taken the operators a few minutes to identify roughly where on the island the Chinese soldiers were going to guide the general so that the eight-man team could position themselves appropriately.

As the group of soldiers walked past Currie, he leveled the M17 at the target he'd been assigned and gently squeezed the trigger. His pistol spat a single 147-grain jacked hollow-point projectile across the thirty feet of distance between him and the soldier nearest the general. The man's head snapped back, and before the body could fall to the ground, Currie had already pivoted to the next soldier and fired another round at his head. While Currie fired both of his shots, the others on his team fired their own guns.

Once the guards surrounding the Chinese general collapsed to the ground around him, Dawson stood and fired a tranquilizer round from the specialized pistol they'd been given for this operation. The tranquilizer zipped across the space between Dawson and the general, hitting the man squarely in the chest. In a fraction of a second, the guy stumbled a single step forward and then collapsed. The entire ambush had taken less than five seconds. All seven guards had been neutralized and the general knocked unconscious.

A smile of satisfaction spread across Currie's face at how fast and seamlessly this entire thing had gone down. Then the tranquility of the early morning was shattered by an urgent call over the radio. One of the Ranger teams said the Chinese soldiers must have realized something had happened—they appeared to be preparing to assault the island.

Half of the Chinese Special Forces soldiers took up a defensive perimeter near the edge of the river, while four soldiers moved rapidly across the river on the Honduran side toward Currie and the now-unconscious general. As those four soldiers advanced on Currie's position, the two-man Ranger team further away reported another group of vehicles racing toward them—there were two SUVs and what appeared to be a small truck. The scout team said they'd be on their position within a minute or two.

Currie heard a short message over their coms. The Ranger platoon leader said they were going to engage the hostiles and end this before it had a chance of getting out of control. Captain Thorne then placed a quick call to Soto Cano, letting them know they had the general in custody and were about to be attacked by a larger force. He requested immediate assistance and an evac.

****

Sergeant First Class Amos Dekker raised his Sig Sauer rifle at the Chinese soldier closest to him and prepared to fire. He'd just placed his targeting reticle on the man's chest when he heard Captain Meacham fire the first shots. Dekker squeezed his trigger and felt the rifle kick into his shoulder as the 6.8mm projectile slammed into the enemy soldier's chest plate. The Army's newest upgraded ammo punched a hole right through the chest plate as a gush of blood erupted out the newly created hole in the man's chest.

In that instant, all hell broke loose as the two squads of Rangers opened fire on the Chinese Special Forces operators. Half of the PLA soldiers were dropped where they stood, dead before they had a chance to react. The remaining enemy operators reacted to the ambush and started fighting back.

One of the Chinese soldiers rolled to one side and came out of his roll into a kneeling position; he leveled his Special Forces version of the Norinco QJY-88 GPMG and fired. The light machine gun spat out dozens of 5.8mm bullets at the Rangers, causing them to duck or move to find a new position to shoot from.

Dekker heard the crump of a grenade going off nearby. One of his soldiers shouted out in pain. Looking to where he'd heard the voice coming from, Dekker saw their platoon medic rushing toward their wounded man. A string of red tracer fire crisscrossed the air around the medic. Dekker saw the medic get thrown backwards and then to the side as he took a few rounds from whatever had just shot him.

Dekker pointed his own rifle in the direction of the tracer fire, then sighted in on a single soldier standing behind the hood of one of the vehicles maybe a hundred meters away. The man had a machine gun set up with the bipod resting on the hood of the vehicle and fired relentlessly at Dekker's guys.

Dekker pulled the trigger, holding it down for no more than two seconds at a time. Since the rifle was in full-auto mode, a third of the bullets in his magazine were fired at the machine gunner. Dekker's first pull of the trigger buried a handful of rounds into the side of the car and the hood, and the second pull landed most of the rounds into the chest and upper body of the shooter, throwing him backwards.

Damn, I like these new rounds a lot more than the ones on the old rifles we had.

Dropping down to avoid being seen, Dekker dropped the spent magazine and replaced it with a fresh one. He then scurried over to a nearby tree and took up a different firing position. By now, most of the Chinese soldiers had been killed. There were still two of them left alive, near as Dekker could tell. They'd consolidated their position together as they fought their way back to their vehicles.

Then the new vehicles arrived not too far away. The drivers were smart enough to stop the vehicles away from the direct fighting so the occupants inside wouldn't get smoked before they had a chance to get out. Dekker saw four soldiers climb out of the first two vehicles, and then the truck unloaded probably twelve more.

Two of the new arrivals had some sort of cylindrical tubes they'd carried off the vehicle. They aimed them in the air in the general direction of the Dekker's guys and fired. Not sure what this new thing was, Dekker looked away and lined his rifle up on the enemy soldiers, who were spreading themselves out and starting to shoot at them.

"Dekker, we've got a gunship sixty seconds out. See if your squad can keep their heads down long enough for them to get on station," Captain Meacham called out over the radio.

Sergeant Dekker turned to yell at his guys and told his Pig operator to start slinging some lead. His other machine gunner was already laying into the new arrivals.

A handful of the Chinese soldiers appeared to have broken off from the main group and were trying to flank the American positions. One of the guys in their group was carrying some sort of rotary-barreled grenade gun launcher—he started firing 35mm fragmentation grenades at his squad's positions, forcing Dekker's men to duck for cover to avoid getting shredded by the shrapnel filling the air around them. It was during these few critical moments while they had their heads down that the Chinese Special Forces soldiers flanked Dekker's squad and rapidly advanced across the distance between their two groups. When Dekker raised his head to look for a new target, he couldn't believe how fast these soldiers had moved in on them.

He had just pulled the trigger, sending a handful of rounds into the chest of one enemy soldier, when he heard some sort of unique buzzing noise. Dekker looked up just in time to see something dart down at a rapid speed from the darkness of the morning sky and slam into the ground thirty feet from him—right in between his Pig operator and his assistant machine gunner.

In the blink of an eye, a bright flash occurred, and a shock wave threw Dekker backward, head over heels. He lay on the ground after being tossed like a rag doll, struggling to open his eyes. When he did, he saw blades of grass and a few leaves on fire as they floated back down to the ground.

What happened? he wondered. But he couldn't make sense of what had just occurred. He tried to move his body, but everything felt so heavy. His eyelids suddenly seemed heavy too, so he closed them for a moment. Then the blackness enveloped him, and suddenly everything didn't seem to matter so much.

****

Currie watched in horror as two diamond-shaped black objects swooped down from somewhere in the sky. They slammed into the ground near the two squads of Rangers and erupted into a massive explosion. The overpressure hurled the Rangers outward, virtually taking the entire squad out.

"What the hell was that?!" shouted Sergeant Dawson as he sent another barrage of bullets at the advancing Chinese Special Forces.

"I have no idea, but those two things just took half our guys out," shouted one of the other sergeants.

Just then, the ODA team heard a loud tearing noise come from high above them. The finger of God reached down from the heavens in the form of a red light that seemed to run itself across the Chinese attackers' positions. Intermixed with the tracer fire from a General Dynamics 25mm GAU-12 Equalizer five-barreled rotary cannon, a 40mm L/60 Bofors cannon landed high-explosive rounds amongst the Chinese soldiers.

Not to be outdone, the single 105mm howitzer on the Spooky II aircraft cut loose a couple of rounds into the enemy vehicles, destroying them and killing anyone that might have hung back from the main attack to guard the vehicles or observe what was going on. The gunship above them had fired a sustained twenty-second barrage on the attackers, completely decimating them. Once the shooting from the gunship had stopped, the remaining members of the ODA team and the Rangers likewise stopped shooting.

Once the gunfire had ended, the sounds of the wounded carried across the air. Currie heard voices crying out in agony, speaking in English and Chinese.

Thump, thump, thump, thump.

Helicopters approached. The first choppers to arrive on the scene were a pair of Apache attack helicopters. They searched the surrounding area and made sure they didn't have any additional vehicles or groups heading toward them. Then Currie saw a group of CH-47 Chinooks arrive, along with a pair of Pave Hawk helicopters.

The Chinooks landed, unloading part of the B Squadron from Delta, followed by the Pave Hawk helicopters. These stayed on the ground for a moment as the Air Force PJs started treating the wounded. They'd get them stabilized and then loaded up on the Air Force helicopters, which would race them back to the field hospital at Soto Cano.

A handful of Delta operators had made their way over to the island in the middle of the river, where the ODAs were holding the Chinese general. They did a more thorough search of the Chinese Special Forces team members, collecting any and all pocket litter, maps, phones, or other electronic devices. They wanted to know everything they could about the group sent to protect their new detainee.

One of the Chinooks that was loitering nearby came and settled down on the little island. The ODA team loaded up on it along with their prized prisoner. When the helicopter got airborne, Currie could see two one-meter-wide circular black holes where those unknown objects had impacted next to the Rangers' positions.

Currie had no idea how many of the Rangers had survived the blasts. All he knew was if that Air Force gunship hadn't shown up when it had, chances were, he and his team would have been in for a world of hurt.

That second group of Chinese soldiers that had shown up appeared to be equipped with some new weapons they hadn't encountered yet. Reliving the attack in his head, Currie hoped it wasn't a sign of things to come. He wasn't sure they were ready to fight this kind of war just yet.

****

Soto Cano Airbase
Honduras

Standing in the brightly lit room, the two CIA men looked down at the body of Major General Cai Yingting as his chest rose and fell in steady breaths.

Carson Ngo turned to his partner, "Smith." "So, this is him?"

"Biometrics confirm it. We got him."

"He's gotten a little pudgy since the last time I saw him," Carson remarked.

"That was how many years ago?" Smith prodded.

"It feels like a lifetime ago…" Carson lamented.

"He's still out from the tranquilizer. Do you want us to try and wake him or let him come to naturally?" Smith inquired.

Carson nodded slowly. "Yeah, use the salt, but be gentle. He's a general…and an old friend…"

How in the hell did you manage to engineer your own capture, Cai? Carson wondered.

Not saying anything, Smith walked over to the sleeping man and broke a smelling salt. He waved it around the man's nose. The general woke hastily, coming to his senses.

The Chinese general looked up at Carson Ngo, and a slight smile began to spread across his face. "It's been a long time, Carson," he said in Mandarin.

Carson held his chin up a bit. "Too long, Cai—much too long," he responded, speaking in perfect Mandarin himself. The two then moved toward each other and gave each other a sturdy bear hug—the kind you give to a family member or close friend you haven't seen in a very long time.

Smith stood silently in the back of the room. His job now was to observe and assist if necessary.

"Come, let us sit and drink some tea," Carson said, easing them back into English. "We have much to talk about, Cai." He wanted to conduct as much of this conversation in English as he could, knowing it would be listened to by a lot of senior officials.

Cai moved to the table and took a seat. As Carson sat down, Smith brought them a tray with a set of cups, water, bags of Cai's favorite tea and all the trimmings, just the way he liked them. With their tea in hand, they got down to business.

"I want to defect," the Chinese general said, very matter of fact. "I want political asylum and I want to be placed in your witness protection program, Carson."

Canting his head slightly, Carson countered, "Cai, you are a rising star in the PLA Ground Force. Why would you want to give all of that up and live the life of a fugitive? At best, if we were to grant you this, you'd be stuck working some sort of manual or menial job not befitting a man of your rank, stature, or education. Cai...you are brilliant. You rose above your peers in the army because of that brilliance. Why are you throwing all of that away? Why did you arrange to get captured, and more importantly, how in the hell did you manage to pull that off without getting yourself killed in the process?"

Cai looked at Carson, not saying anything for a moment. Instead, he took a couple of sips of his tea.

Finally, he spoke. "When I was in winter survival training near the Russian border, do you know how they taught us to kill a wolf?" he asked rhetorically. "You take your knife, cut one of your fingers or thumb and spread the blood across the blade. If you have to squeeze more out, then you do it, but you make sure you *cover* the blade with blood. Then you anchor the knife down in the ground with the blade pointed straight in the air, climb a nearby tree, and wait. The wolf will smell that blood from miles away. His nose will lead him straight to it. With his hunger for blood good and worked up, he'll begin to lick it. Before the wolf even realizes it, the blade has already cut his tongue. But his taste for blood is so strong he can't taste the difference anymore. He just wants more blood. In a short period, the wolf will eventually grow tired from the loss of blood. When he is weak, then you can climb down from your tree and kill him with ease. The meat from that wolf will feed you for a week."

Cai took another sip of his tea before he continued. "You asked me why I am throwing away my career and forsaking my country"—he turned away briefly, using one of his fingers to wipe away a tear that was starting to form—"why I have forsaken my family, why I have in all likelihood killed my wife...my two sons. Because right now, I don't know if my country is the wolf or the blade. But what I am certain of...is that Jade Dragon is that person sitting in the tree, waiting for us to grow weak before it climbs down and kills us all."

Chapter Six

A New Beginning

February 2025

US Embassy

Havana, Cuba

President Maria Delgado listened to the CIA station chief and her Secretary of State as they talked about the man they were recommending become the new leader of Cuba.

"Why this particular man? What makes him so special over the others?" she pressed. She'd had her eye on another man, a person who'd been a leading human rights activist in the country.

The CIA station chief, a man who only went by the name "Bob," leaned forward. "Madam President, I understand you have another person in mind. That candidate is not necessarily a *bad* choice. However, we firmly believe Mr. Esteban Ochoa will be a better option long-term for both Cuba and America. While he may not have been an outspoken firebrand speaking against the former regime, he worked quietly within it for the betterment of his community. During his time as the port manager in Mariel, he managed to secure higher wages for his workers and the local community.

"When the government wouldn't agree to pay those higher wages, he worked with the Chinese firm overseeing the port modernization to cover the difference. They did, and they also supplied Mariel and his workers with more food rations and better health care. Mr. Ochoa found ways to work within the confines of the communist regime to take care of his people and improve their lives. These are the kinds of character traits we want in the leader of a country."

The President canted her head to the side, sensing there was more to this story. "What else aren't you telling me about Mr. Ochoa? We have a group of candidates to choose from—why push him over some of the others?"

Secretary of State Hayden Albridge interceded, "We want to back Mr. Ochoa because he's a pragmatic man of the people. He's a realist; he understands what can and can't be done. If we throw our weight behind him, the political party he's forming will likely win majority control of the new parliament. That means he'll likely become president once the elections are held." Albridge turned to Bob. "I think you should show the President the file you showed me the other day," he directed.

Maria lifted an eyebrow as Bob pulled a folder out and handed it to her.

"Madam President, it's the routine practice of the Agency to ascertain as much as we can about key political, military, and business leaders. Aside from the standard information we collect, we do our best to entrap them in various compromising situations along the way. This creates leverage we're then able to use further down the road, should we need it," Bob explained nonchalantly. "In this case, while Mr. Ochoa was the port manager in Mariel, a position that allowed him to oversee all the military equipment being transported into Cuba, my lead agent on the ground here was able to catch Mr. Ochoa in a compromising situation— a situation we may be able to use to influence him toward more favorable decisions."

Maria looked at the images. There were a handful of pictures of Mr. Ochoa with an exceptionally beautiful naked woman. They were clearly having sex. It was obvious this woman wasn't Mr. Ochoa's wife; she was much younger and more athletic. There was a note in the file that said they also had a video recording with sound to go along with the pictures.

Delgado shook her head. "I take it these haven't been shown to Mr. Ochoa or his wife yet?"

Bob almost laughed at the question. "No, of course not. The kompromat will be held in reserve in case there's a time or situation when it might be needed."

Maria shook her head in disgust at what the Agency had done. This was the dirty side of politics she despised. She wondered what kind of kompromat the Agency had on her, her husband, or her kids. She wouldn't put it past them to have developed a comprehensive package to be used against her at the right moment in her presidency.

"You guys really think Mr. Ochoa is the right guy we should throw our support behind? He'll be a good, honest leader for the people of Cuba?" Maria asked hesitantly as she placed the folder on the table.

Secretary Albridge spoke before the Agency man could. "Madam President, the next three to five years are going to be crucial to the long-term success of Cuba. We believe Mr. Ochoa is in the best position to work with us and help transition Cuba away from communism and a planned economy to a market-based economy. We don't want to make the same mistakes we made in Iraq with de-Baathification. We want this to be as smooth a transition as possible."

Delgado remembered all too well how screwed up things had gotten in Iraq when the US had detained all former Baath Party members instead of trying to get them to buy into a new government and use their connections in a positive way. She wanted to make sure that didn't happen in Cuba either. Finally, she nodded.

"I want to meet this Mr. Ochoa. If our government is going to back him, then I'd like to talk with him and get to know him a bit."

****

Later that night, Mr. Esteban Ochoa was brought to the American embassy. After going through some security checks, he was eventually led to the ambassador's private study.

President Maria Delgado saw the port manager walk into the office and smiled warmly at him. He was five foot eleven inches tall and had a thin build, likely from years of poor nutrition. He had kind of a typical look for most Cubans she'd seen up to this point.

Delgado motioned for him to take a seat at the couches near the desk. Once they were situated, he spoke first. "Madam President, it is an honor to meet with you. I want to thank you personally for intervening in Cuba. I fear if you had not, then our country would have just become an extension of Mainland China."

They exchanged some pleasantries for a few minutes before they got down to business.

"Mr. Ochoa, I wanted to meet with you because my advisors believe we should back your political party in the upcoming elections. How would you feel about that?"

President Delgado observed him as he took in the information. He seemed to be calculating whether her support would benefit him or not. Finally, he broke the silence. "Madam President, I appreciate the gesture. What might work best is if the American government does not try to get involved. Having a foreign power picking the winners and losers might not help us in gaining the kind of long-term political support needed to govern the country legitimately."

Maria smiled at the bluntness of the man. *Yeah, I can see myself working with this guy.*

"Mr. Ochoa, I can appreciate your position. My country wants to make sure that some of your newly formed political parties succeed above others. We have just spent a great deal of blood and treasure removing the communist regime and the Chinese from your country. We are not going to allow a similar government to form in its place. Is that understood?"

The Cuban nodded knowingly. A new Workers Party, which was just a rebranded Communist Party, looked like it might be gaining some steam, at least in the rural areas of the country.

"Madam President, perhaps if I could bring up a policy proposal that you act upon, showing I have some political clout with you? Or maybe my political party could receive an influx of donations? Something along those lines might be all that's needed for me and my political party to win the coming election," Mr. Ochoa offered.

Delgado bit her lower lip at the idea. He knew how to go about getting what he wanted without making it look like he was taking a bribe.

She leaned forward. "Here's what I want to have happen, Mr. Ochoa. The State Department is going to do as you asked and we're going to subtly back you and your party in this election. The Agency"—she pointed to Bob—"is going to make sure that in the end, you ultimately win. But I have some nonnegotiable items on my end that will need to be met."

Ochoa didn't smile but nodded.

"Once the election is over and you have come to power, there are some property rights issues that need to be addressed and put to rest. When Fidel came to power, he stole a lot of land and property from many Americans—the Cuban exiles living in the US need to be allowed to return to Cuba and have their full citizenship restored if they choose to return. As restitution, they shall have their property, businesses and finances returned to them. My government will provide your country with an infusion of cash to make sure you can cover this, but it needs to happen so the healing process can take place.

"Once in power, you need to fully embrace market reforms and open up to the West. I will remove all embargos against your nation and fully allow for commerce and financial dealings to occur. I will remove all tourist restrictions previously placed on the island so Americans can once against flock to Cuba. This will help bring an immediate economic stimulus to your country. You will also need to expedite the sale of as many state-owned businesses as possible. I'm going to dispatch a team of experts from our commerce department, who will help you in this process and begin the modernization of Cuba.

"Land reform will be another big piece that will need to take place. I can tell you right now, many Americans are going to be interested in purchasing land here. They'll want to settle in Cuba and bring their families over and set up businesses when this war with China is over—"

Mr. Ochoa interrupted her to ask, "What about the military? Right now, many of them are in prison camps doing nothing. What do you want us to do with them?"

Secretary of State Aldridge interjected, "You will campaign on a message of negotiating a release of all captured Cuban military personnel. You will also campaign to have them reinstated into the new Cuban Army, where they will swear a new oath of allegiance to Cuba and the new constitution your government will be writing and ratifying. When you win, these will be easy political victories we can help you achieve right off the bat."

President Delgado nodded her head, adding, "I agree. Once you win, this could be one of your first official acts. While they are in captivity right now, we'll work with them on developing discipline, physical fitness, and other basic soldiering skills our military police can teach. Then we'll transition the soldiers into becoming a new Cuban Army. If we're able to, we might even integrate them into the NATO force gearing up to fight in Venezuela. If nothing else, the English-speaking ones could be used as translators embedded with our forces."

Esteban Ochoa spent the next two hours talking privately with the Americans. They had big dreams for Cuba, and bigger dreams for a world without China at the center of it. Ochoa told them he wasn't sure that was possible, but he was eager to see the Americans try.

****

When Mr. Ochoa left, Secretary Albridge announced, "Madam President, it's time to head down to the basement. We have a SCIF down there where we can conduct our next meeting."

Maria Delgado hadn't originally wanted to head to Cuba. She was much more comfortable in D.C., but her advisors had said a visit to the front to see the soldiers and meet with some of the Cuban people and politicians would be a good PR move as well. The US had sustained some terrible losses subduing the island these last four months. Her hope was that visiting Cuba to press the flesh with her soldiers would go a long way toward endearing her to the rank-and-file members who were doing the fighting and dying.

When Delgado walked into the secured room, she saw that Mr. Blain Wilson had gotten things ready for her. Major General Gary Bridges, the Special Forces Commander for US Southern Command, was already present, along with the division commander for some of the other units still present on the island.

As soon as everyone had taken their seats, the meeting began. Reconstruction efforts across the country were going strong. A few regime holdouts and some pockets of Chinese resistance still popped up every now and then. Dozens of airfields were being rebuilt, and new ones were taking shape as the military continued to prepare for the eventual invasion of Venezuela.

General Bridges stirred things up. "Ma'am, we're two months into the occupation duty of Cuba. What no one has come out and asked yet is exactly *when* we're going to invade Venezuela and remove the Chinese completely from our sphere of influence."

A couple of the more senior generals on the video teleconference back in D.C. stared daggers into the two-star general for asking such a question.

President Delgado caught the awkward looks between her military commanders and just smiled. She liked keeping them off-balance and unsure of what to do.

Delgado looked down at a calendar and then back to General Bridges. "We're coming to the end of February. If we decided June first was the jump-off point, how ready would our current forces be?"

One of the generals back in D.C. replied before Bridges could say anything. "At current pace of deployment, we should have III Corps's entire force deployed along the Colombia-Venezuelan border in the north of the country and the XVIII Airborne Corps deployed in the south well in advance of June 1. We're talking eight full divisions, along with fourteen support brigades. That's a total of one hundred and thirty-eight thousand soldiers and another thirty thousand airmen ready to liberate the country when you give the word go."

"What other forces are we planning on invading with, because surely that's not all?" Maria asked, skeptical of the low numbers.

"It's not. The Marine Second and Fourth Divisions are going to open a new front by capturing the port city of Cumana along the northeastern part of the country," replied Admiral Thiel, the Chairman of the Joint Chiefs. "This will essentially open three fronts on different sides of the country once the Marines have secured the port and the airports in the local area. This is also where our NATO allies, the British, French, and Spanish forces will begin to bring their own soldiers ashore to assist us."

"Will NATO have cleared some of those islands from the PLA, or are we bypassing them for the time being?" asked President Delgado with a raised eyebrow.

"It's not that we're bypassing them entirely," assured General Bridges. "We're deploying a Marine Raider battalion along with a reactivated Marine regiment to support a British and French force they're dispatching to take down the HQ-9 SAM sites and antiship missile batteries. Once they're neutralized, the forces on those islands are essentially irrelevant. We can circle back and retake the islands at a later date."

"What about local support inside Venezuela?" Maria asked, looking at Bridges.

"Yes, ma'am. We're already on that. I've got a battalion from 7th Group already in-country working on developing and growing an insurgency force inside Venezuela. Actually, we have three separate forces we're training there. I've also got a battalion from 1st Group deployed to keep tabs on the Chinese units moving around inside the country and mapping our best approaches once the invasion starts. They're also working on developing an insurgency in the northwestern part of the country, where the Chinese forces are largely located."

Maria smiled at that news. It sounded like the Special Forces teams were ahead of the ball game in Venezuela, at least. "General Bridges, as your SOF teams get these insurgency groups trained up, how soon are they going to start carrying out operations?" she asked. "Are we getting enough supplies and weapons brought in to support them?"

Bridges let out a deep breath. "In the south, we're moving a lot of the weapons we're arming these groups with through Venezuela's shared borders with Brazil and Guyana. This is mostly through the Amazon, so it's some really rough terrain. We're trying our best to make use of some remote airstrips to ferry in as much as we can directly into Venezuela and then let the teams disperse it as they see fit. The CIA's actually been pretty helpful in this area.

"As to how soon can they start carrying out attacks...soon. The initial goal was to identify some cell or insurgent leaders, get them trained up and then have them start recruiting more people to join. Once they got some new recruits, they'd be taken to our training camps and we'd begin the process of building up small units or cells. It's kind of a long process, but we should be ready to start sowing some serious chaos within the country within the next thirty to forty-five days."

"That sounds good, General Bridges," the President replied.

She turned to General Stavridis. "What about El Salvador? How close are we to having things wrapped up down there?"

Stavridis cleared his throat. "Madam President, we're still working up a third invasion point closer to the capital, utilizing the XVIII Airborne Corps. We hope to have that figured out over the coming month. We're in the process of deploying the 42nd Infantry Division to replace them so we can shift them down to Colombia. The Guard units will work on stabilizing the country and finishing off any remaining holdout units."

President Delgado leaned forward in her chair. "Thank you, General. I know I haven't given you a firm invasion date, and it's made it hard to plan as a result. Let's go ahead and change that. Let's plan on the invasion starting around the first of June. We can keep that date somewhat fluid and adjust it as the opportunity presents itself or as the situation may dictate, but this will at least give you a date to work toward.

"Now, if there are no more pressing matters—I have a dinner to prepare for. You have your marching orders—let's get to it and prepare to kick the Chinese out of the Americas."

****

Blain grabbed his folder and was about to join the President when "Bob" asked if he could stay behind in the SCIF for a moment. "What's up?" Blain asked, knowing he didn't have a lot of time.

"I know you need to stay with the President, but this is important, Mr. Wilson. I wouldn't ask you for your time if it wasn't," Bob asserted. There was a serious look of concern, almost fear in his eyes. "We've recently come into some unique intelligence on Jade Dragon and what's been going on within the PLA ground forces and within China."

Blain glanced at his watch, then got the attention of one of the Marine guards outside the SCIF. "Sergeant, please pass a message to the President's detail leader that I need to stay behind and handle something," he relayed." I won't be joining them for the dinner tonight."

"Yes, sir. Right away." The Marine spoke into his radio and headed toward a door that would lead him further into the embassy.

Then Blain turned to Bob. "OK. You've got my attention. Let's talk."

The more Bob explained, the more Blain's stomach began to churn. A Chinese defector—the PLA general that had been captured in Central America—was all but confirming some of the more extreme fears of his about this AI.

When Bob was done bringing him up to speed, Blain was still left with so many questions. He wanted to know where the AI was being housed, how it was powered, and whether it was air-gapped or directly piped into the internet.

"Bob, I want you to bring this guy and his handler to 'The Point' and put them under lock and key while you continue his debrief. I'm not about to bring this to the President until we have more information. She's going to ask a lot of questions—questions *your* people are going to have answers for."

The CIA man nodded.

"Oh, and Bob…this should go without saying, but no more Idahos," Blain said coldly, referring to the awful debacle that had occurred with Ma "Daniel" Yong. "I want a *real* security detail on them, their building, and 'The Point,'" Blain ordered.

If this PLA general is as valuable as it seems, then I'll be damned if they lose him, too, thought Blain.

Chapter Seven

R2-D2

Space Delta 9

Groom Lake

Lieutenant Colonel Ian "Racer" Ryan pulled back on the throttle of his Archangel as it zoomed past angels seventy. He was rapidly approaching hypersonic altitude.

"Racer, tighten up your position. You're starting to stray a bit," called out the voice of Colonel Hewitt, commander of the 1st Orbital Space Squadron, which was the first Space Force combat squadron of the new service branch.

Looking down at the map, Racer saw he *was* starting to drift from the others. "R2, keep us in formation." The technical name for the AI was ARTUμ. When the entire program was transferred over to the Space Force and became the branch's first combat fighter-spaceplane, they of course called it R2-D2, in honor of Star Wars lore.

"Yes, Lieutenant Colonel. You need to activate my flight controls first," the aircraft's AI responded, speaking into his helmet with the voice of Morgan Freeman.

Damn it! I forgot to switch flight controls over once we broke sixty thousand feet. I'm going to get my ass chewed out again when we land.

Racer tapped a button, switching the aircraft over from manual control to AI control. These were the kinds of mistakes that had nearly washed him out of the sixth-generation fighter program. Changing his mindset had proved to be difficult. It was one thing for him to utilize the autopilot on his aircraft—allowing the onboard AI to actually fly the plane for him and take over many of the functions he used to perform

111

was a completely different story. Every time the AI would turn or pull up on the aircraft, Racer's hands would instinctively grab for the controls.

The Archangel or F/S-36 was substantially more complicated than any aircraft Racer had flown or even heard about in the Air Force. This fighter-spaceplane was designed to operate at the fringes of what was aeronautically possible in a manned aircraft. Its dual turbo and scramjet engines allowed it to have an operational altitude of up to ninety thousand feet, placing it in the lower mesosphere of Earth's atmosphere. It was a quasi-fighter/spaceplane if there ever was one.

The Archangel flew with an AI-assisted copilot, offloading many of the complicated tasks a pilot normally had to handle. The AI could handle tasks like navigation, threat detection, and target acquisition while the pilot handled the tasks of deploying its weapons, communications, and flying the aircraft. When flying in super-cruise mode, the AI was supposed to fly the plane while the pilot focused on the navigation and other functions. As the AI learned more from its human pilot, the two would be able to function seamlessly between roles, leveraging each other's abilities while the AI continued to get better. It was believed that one day, these planes would fly themselves and carry out missions without a human in the loop.

"All right, Guardians, this is it," announced Colonel Hewitt. "I want a tight formation when we go to hypersonic. Once we reach Cuba, you're to break off into your Guardian elements and go after your individual targets. Let's prove the naysayers wrong and show them that our unit and aircraft are ready to fight this war."

Why did I leave the Air Force and cross over into the Space Force? Racer asked himself. He scoffed privately at their call sign. *Guardians...this isn't* Guardians of the Galaxy, *guys.*

When their aircraft had reached eighty-five thousand feet or eighty-five angels, the aircraft would transition from one propulsion system to what was called a combined-cycle propulsion. The Archangel essentially operated a turbojet and ramjet engines mounted in an over-under position. Near the air intake was a splitter that directed the airflow into either the turbojet engine or the ramjet. The turbojet got them up to a cruising speed of Mach 3.2, at which point the engine would switch over to the scramjet. The second engine then accelerated them to a super-cruise speed of Mach 6, which was sustainable for hours. The aircraft did have a maximum speed of Mach 10 but could hold that speed for a duration of no more than five minutes before it'd need at least a thirty-minute cool-down period; the friction generated on the wings and the body of the aircraft at that speed was incredible. Once they solved the friction problem, the Archangel likely would cruise at Mach 10.

As it was, in super-cruise mode, the Archangel could cover a distance of 4,600 miles per hour of flight time—meaning they were roughly fifty minutes of flight time from their base in Groom Lake, Nevada, to Caracas, Venezuela. They could essentially travel from Paris to Los Angeles in one hour and twenty-two minutes. Of course, if they traveled at their max speed for at least five of those minutes, they'd be able to cut that time to under an hour.

Twenty-two minutes into their high-speed flight, the Guardians passed Cuba. A minute later, Racer's radio crackled to life in his helmet. "You ready for this, Racer?" It was the voice of his wingman, Major Steven "Scuba" Johnston. He was another F-22 pilot who'd crossed over to the Space Force to fly this plane. He'd been a senior captain at the time, so the bump to major was an added bonus for him.

"Ready as I'll ever be," Racer replied. "I just hope these new weapons actually work."

"Yeah, I guess we'll find out shortly, won't we?" replied Scuba confidently.

Their two aircraft broke off from the rest of the squadron as they headed toward their individual targets. Racer and Scuba were going to carry out a strike on Isla Margarita—intelligence had identified a battery of YJ-18C or CH-SS-NX-13 antiship cruise missiles deployed around the island. The missiles had a range of 290 nautical miles and packed a 660-pound warhead; these threats had to be neutralized prior to any amphibious assault or ground operations that might require naval support.

Given the horrific aircraft losses the Air Force and Navy had sustained during the Cuba and El Salvador campaigns, it had been determined that this would be a good mission to test the Space Force's new aircraft and weapons. Their incredible altitude and speeds meant they should be impervious to the Chinese SAMs below.

"Lieutenant Colonel, we are five minutes out from our target," announced Racer's R2.

When the pilots had been given the option of choosing a voice for their R2, Racer had chosen Morgan Freeman's. He wasn't sure why, but it just felt right to him. Racer thought Freeman was an amazing actor, and having his voice as the sound of his R2 made him smile. It somehow also made him feel safer and less alone in his aircraft. Flying at altitudes of eighty thousand feet was placing him at the edges of space—he was practically flying in blackness at these altitudes, something completely different than when he flew in the Raptor.

"R2, identify our four targets and coordinate them with Scuba's R2."

"Yes, Lieutenant Colonel. Deconflicting targets with Scuba."

Activating the weapons bay, Racer turned the targeting computer on for each of the four Thor's Hammers his internal weapons bay held. These tungsten rods weren't explosive on their own, but when dropped from this height, they would reach incredible speeds before plummeting into their target. When the ten-foot-long, two-foot-around projectile slammed into the ground, it would hit with the force of a five-thousand-pound bomb, only it would throw off no shrapnel or flame—just an enormous concussive shock wave that would flatten everything around it and penetrate deep into the earth below. They were the newest innovation in kinetic weapons.

The weapons bay held two rotary launcher systems in a tandem layout. The first rotary launcher held four Thor's Hammers, while the rear rotary launcher held four AIM-260 JATM beyond-visual-range air-to-air missiles. With a range of 220 kilometers and the ability to reach speeds of Mach 5, the missiles could engage enemy aircraft or satellites with ease.

"Shall I turn on the directed-energy weapons?" R2 inquired since Racer had the weapons display open.

Racer thought about that for a second. He wasn't really sure they needed them. If a threat did materialize, he felt reasonably comfortable he'd have more than enough time to warm them up before they'd need to be used. *Still...it couldn't hurt.*

"Yes, R2. Go ahead and turn them on and leave them in standby mode."

"Very well. I have deconflicted our target package with Scuba's R2. We are ready to engage our designated targets at your command."

Racer followed protocol and double-checked that the targets R2 had identified were in fact part of the approved list of military targets before switching the aircraft flight mode over to the AI. Apparently, the

DoD wasn't fully on board with allowing an AI to identify its own targets and engage them autonomously—in the American aircraft, the pilot still had to be the one to release the weapons. Racer wondered if the rumors about the Chinese were true—were they really allowing AI to be in full control of their weapons systems?

"We are nearing the target," R2 announced.

The readout on the targeting display showed he was sixty seconds out. At twenty seconds, the weapons bay door would open, and the Hammers could switch over from his aircraft's external power to their own internal power systems.

Racer did a quick check of the radar and threat board—a host of enemy radars were active across Venezuela. It reminded him of what he'd seen that first day over Cuba when he'd been shot down. He'd never seen so many surface-to-air missile systems in his life. Judging by what his computer was telling him was down there, it was a much thicker layer of SAMs than what they'd encountered even in Cuba.

No wonder the brass was so willing to let us use this experimental weapons system here, Racer realized. *Our guys would take some serious losses trying to thin that mess out.*

Approaching the drop zone, Racer selected the first Hammer and released it. He cycled through the remaining three, sending them on their way.

If this attack proved successful, then Space Force might have just found a way to negate the Chinese tactical and strategic advantage over the Allies' airpower. It might very well tip the balance of the war back in the Allies' favor and away from the AI that up till now had been running roughshod over the West.

With his weapons released, Racer closed the bomb bay doors and reassumed flight controls from R2. "OK, Scuba. It's time for us to turn back for home," he told his wingman.

"That's a good copy, Racer. I sure hope this works," Scuba remarked. "That looked like it'd be a nightmare to have to fly through."

"You aren't joking," Racer replied. "I flew through a hornet's nest like that over Cuba, and I wouldn't wish it on anyone. Let's head back to base and get out of here before the Chinese get lucky and somehow detect us."

The two aircraft angled back over the Caribbean and headed for home.

Chapter Eight
Kamikazes

Soto Cano Air Base

Honduras

Sergeant First Class Amos Dekker started awake when he felt some warm water run down his left leg. His left hand immediately grabbed for the source of the water. As his grip tightened around someone's wrist, he heard a woman yelp.

"It's OK, Sergeant," said a soft voice, beckoning to him from the darkness. "You're all right."

As he slowly opened his eyes, Dekker saw a female nurse with a yellow sponge in her hand. His left hand still tightly gripped her forearm. He immediately released her arm and felt terrible. He almost burst into tears. "I…I'm so sorry," he stammered.

"It's all right, Sergeant," the nurse replied in a soothing tone. "You didn't know what was going on and woke up with a start. You're safe now. No one is going to hurt you."

"What happened? Where am I?" Dekker probed.

Just then, a doctor in a white lab coat walked up with a clipboard in his hand.

"I can answer that question better than my nurse. Amy, why don't you tend to the next person on this list? I have a few things I have to go over with Sergeant Dekker now that he's awake," the doctor said reassuringly.

The nurse left quietly.

"Sergeant First Class Amos Dekker, I'm Major O'Leary," the doctor announced. "How are you feeling today? Can you wiggle your toes and legs, move your fingers and hands?"

Whoa, I hadn't even tried to do all of that, thought Dekker as a shiver of fear ran down his spine.

He wiggled his toes, then moved both his feet. Next, he wriggled his fingers, then his hands and arms. He looked at the doctor nervously, unsure if his performance had been satisfactory. O'Leary smiled and wrote something on his clipboard.

"This is good. We honestly weren't sure whether you'd have full mobility when you woke up. I'm glad there doesn't appear to be any lasting damage, at least not right off the bat," the doctor explained.

Dekker was still a bit groggy and at a loss for words.

Dr. O'Leary saw his confused expression. "Sergeant, you and your platoon were brought here three days ago, after a battle on a classified mission. Hell, *I* haven't even been made aware of what happened to you guys, other than a large explosion occurred near you. When you were brought in, you technically died once on the helicopter en route, but the PJs managed to bring you back. You flatlined two more times in the ER, but my team and I were able to pull you through.

"Once we got you stabilized, your body didn't respond to any stimulation at first. We tried tapping on your toes, feet, fingers, and hands. For all intents and purposes, you were looking like you'd been paralyzed from the neck down. We saw the same injury with half the other Rangers that came in with you."

Dekker was filled with sheer terror at this explanation. Dr. O'Leary must have seen his distress, because he leaned in and placed a hand on his shoulder. "Fear not, Sergeant. It now looks like you're going to recover just fine. Whatever blew up near you appeared to have stunned your body into some sort of temporary paralysis or given you guys one hell of a momentary traumatic brain injury."

Dekker shook his head.

"I know that a TBI may sound scary, but that's actually a good thing," the doctor continued. "It means whatever they hit you with eventually wears off, and if it's a TBI, well, we can treat that a lot easier than paralysis."

Dekker wasn't sure what to make of what he was being told. It was all happening so fast. One minute he was in a firefight with that Chinese Special Forces group, and the next thing he knew, he was getting a sponge bath from a nurse.

The doctor continued to speak. "Now, no one has told us doctors squat about your mission or what happened out there. I was kind of hoping you might be able to fill me in a little bit. It might help me in treating some of your fellow Rangers who are still here with you."

Dekker suddenly remembered his platoonmates. He'd forgotten all about them—he realized he didn't even know who was still alive and who had died. "Where are they? Did they all make it? What kind of shape are they in?" he asked, rattling off question after question.

Dr. O'Leary held out a hand to calm him. "They're doing OK. They all came in pretty much in the same shape and situation as you. Beat up, hurt, and paralyzed. Over the last few days, they've all been waking up and steadily returning to normal. What can you tell me about the last couple of minutes before you were knocked unconscious?"

Dekker looked off into space as he tried to recall what had happened on that last mission. "We were on a mission to abduct a Chinese general. My platoon was supposed to provide security for the area while an ODA team carried out the actual abduction. Toward the end, we got in a serious firefight with a Chinese Special Forces team that was trying to recover and protect the general."

Dekker paused for a second, trying to recreate in his mind those last few minutes before he'd been knocked unconscious. He wasn't sure if he was giving away classified information, but if it could help the doctors treat his platoonmates, he almost didn't care.

"One thing I remember—when that new group of Chinese soldiers showed up, one or two of them fired something into the air. All I remember was it was some sort of black tube-looking thingy. At first, I thought it was a new rocket or missile, but then I thought maybe it was some sort of high-tech scout drone or something."

The doctor listened intently as Dekker recounted what he could. "I don't know if it was a few minutes into the attack, or just moments after they fired that thing, but something swooped down from the sky and landed maybe fifty feet from us and exploded. I didn't have time to shout a warning or do basically anything. The last thing I remember was some large blast wave washing over me, throwing me across the ground… and then nothing."

Dekker felt his palms getting sweaty and his breathing more labored. He heard the heart rate monitor computer blare out some sort of alarm.

He closed his eyes and tried to place his mind back on that hammock on Ray Caye Island in Belize. He took a couple of slow, deep breaths, holding them in, then fully releasing them. When he opened his eyes, he felt immensely better. The alarm on the heart rate monitor had stopped.

"Impressive, Sergeant. Whoever taught you those breathing techniques really knew what they were doing," Dr. O'Leary commented.

"My mother used to be a yoga instructor when I was growing up," said Dekker. "Back to my guys, Doc. How are they? How many did we lose?" he pressed.

A sad expression washed over Dr. O'Leary's face. "Two of your guys came in with severe gun wounds. Sadly, both died. The other Rangers appeared to have the same type of concussive injury you had.

"I think what'd be best for you to do right now, Sergeant First Class, is to just lie back and rest. Let your mind and body continue to recuperate. In another day, they'll make a decision on whether to send you back stateside or to one of the larger field hospitals in Cuba. In either case, they're going to want to run some brain scans to rule out a TBI before they let you return to duty."

The doctor then left to go attend to the other patients, leaving Dekker to lie there with more questions than answers. He felt he still didn't fully know what was going on. All he wanted to do was talk to someone in his unit and figure it all out.

****

Bravo Squadron

1st Special Forces Detachment Delta

Colonel Paul Imhoff looked at the aerial video of the attack for what must have been the fiftieth time in the last seventy-two hours. His people were still no closer to figuring out exactly what this thing was—they'd never seen this new kamikaze drone before.

What didn't make sense about it was *how* it blew up and what exactly it was made up of. Judging by the size of the drones and their explosiveness, they should have killed all the Rangers in the vicinity of the blast. But they didn't. The only guys that had died were the two that had been immediately next to the blasts.

"Still trying to figure out what's so special about that drone, sir?" asked a master sergeant as he took a seat next to him.

"I still don't get it," Colonel Imhoff replied. "If that thing had been encased in metal or wrapped in ball bearings or pellets of some sort, it should have dispersed enough shrapnel across the area to have severely injured if not killed the soldiers nearby. Instead, the overpressure from the explosion seems to have somehow just temporarily paralyzed them."

"We've been thinking about that as well, sir," said the master sergeant. "Near as we can tell, they may not have *wanted* to kill everyone with this drone. I mean, think about it—this group was sent in to retrieve the Chinese general, and they may not have known where he was in relationship to the different Ranger groups they were attacking. They may have just wanted to take everyone down before they moved in. You know, kind of like throwing a flash-bang into a room before you storm it."

"So, you think they probably have a high-kill version of this weapon and just didn't use it on our guys because they needed to recover the general?" Imhoff pressed. Now that he'd posed that alternate theory out loud, it was the only idea that made any reasonable sense.

"That's our thinking. Of course, I'd push the question to the guys at DARPA. Chances are, they've seen or thought of something like this before."

****

An hour later, Colonel Imhoff and a major from their Ranger company walked through the hospital ward with one of their administrative sergeants. He was carrying a board that held a series of medals on it.

When the trio reached Sergeant First Class Amos Dekker's bed, Colonel Imhoff presented him with a Purple Heart and a Bronze Star with "V" device. When the person tagging along had captured a couple of pictures, the group moved on to the next wounded Ranger from the mission.

When the nurse walked back to Dekker's bed and saw the medals pinned to his pillow, she asked, "Are these your first awards?" She fiddled around, as if she were trying to find a better way to display them for him.

Dekker smiled. "Nah, that's my third Purple Heart and my fourth Bronze Star. You stick around in these kinds of units long enough, you get thrown into a lot of crazy situations where they give you plenty of opportunities to get shot or blown up," he joked with her.

She laughed and refilled his glass of water.

"So what's the deal?" asked Dekker. "When am I getting out of here?"

"As a matter of fact, tomorrow morning you'll be flown back to Fort Benning, along with the rest of the guys in here with you."

Chapter Nine
Task Force Dupre

March 2025
Southern Caribbean
USS *Hue City*

The sun was still three hours away from cresting above the water of the southern Caribbean as the *Hue City* cut through the relatively calm seas. One of the stewards brought a fresh pot of coffee up from the galley and placed it on the hot plate in the CIC. Seeing the fresh brew, newly promoted Captain Michael Dupre grabbed his cup and made his way to the hot plate, grabbing one of the fresh sandwich halves the steward had brought up with him as well.

I'll have to thank the cooks for keeping the food and coffee going into the night for us, Dupre thought.

His task force had been patrolling some three hundred miles off the coast of Venezuela for close a month. A task force of Chinese and Venezuelan warships was hugging the shores, beckoning the Americans to charge in after them. It galled Dupre, like a prizefighter who is able to see the other opponent but not able to fight him just yet.

Following the end of major combat operations in Cuba, Captain Dupre had seen a handful of American, French, and British warships go in for the charge. A joint Allied task force led by a British commodore aboard the flagship HMS *Dauntless* had looked to sink the Chinese-led task force near Venezuela. The commodore had had three American *Arleigh Burkes*, a French *Aquitaine* and two *La Fayette*–class frigates with him, along with a lone Type 23 Duke-class frigate. When the task force had traveled within one hundred miles of the Venezuelan coast, though, all hell had broken loose on them.

First, there was a multiwave air attack by Chinese aircraft, firing antiship missiles from near the maximum effective range. Then, as that attack was getting underway, three waves of land-launched antiship missiles had attacked the fleet. While the task force had boasted a robust air and antimissile defense screen, the ships were just overwhelmed by the volume of missiles fired at them. As the ships' antimissile magazines ran dry, the defense had fallen on the close-in weapon systems or CIWS and RIM-66 systems to swat down the remaining threats.

The missile swarm attack had lasted less than thirty minutes. However, in that time, the *Arleigh Burke* destroyers *Thomas Hudner*, *McFaul*, and *Bainbridge* were sunk. The French frigate *Auvergne* and the *Surcouf* were also lost. The lone British Type 23 frigate, the *Montrose*, had finally succumbed to the attack when its CIWS guns had run out of bullets.

Whether it was fate or just dumb luck, the commodore's flagship, the *Dauntless*, had been the sole survivor, although it would take her crew nearly three hours to put out the flames from the missile that had hit its hangar deck. The helicopter in the hangar had been damaged and leaked several hundred liters of aviation fuel before it had ignited—the fuel had spread across the deck and managed to leak its way to the deck below, causing a massive fire that nearly sank the ship. When the *Dauntless* had finally limped into a friendly port, the commodore had taken his own life rather than live with the survivor's guilt of losing his entire task force.

Since that fateful day nearly seven weeks ago, the Allies had been skirting at the edge of the range of those land-attack antiship cruise missiles and supporting aircraft.

Captain Dupre's Tico, the *Hue City*, had been sent to Pascagoula, Mississippi, to undergo an emergency refit to its forward- and rear-mounted five-inch guns. The *Hue City* had been slated to have the upgrade in five months, but with the new war, the timeline had been moved forward. The tired old gun systems were swapped out for the Navy's newest advanced gun system, the Mod III 155mm howitzer. When utilizing the newly approved supercharged propellant, the cannon could throw a ninety-five-pound shell some sixty-five kilometers. If they used the rocket-assist shells, the range was extended to just about one hundred kilometers depending on the windage.

This update to the Tico's weapon system had breathed new life into what was otherwise a slowly dying breed of guided-missile cruisers in favor of the younger, smaller, and more capable Flight III *Arleigh Burkes*. While undergoing a six-week refit to their gun system, the ship's entire AEGIS Combat System and AN/SPY-1 radar system had received a massive overhaul and upgrade, essentially giving the ship the same capability as the new Flight III *Arleigh Burkes*.

Dupre hadn't thought the Ingalls shipyard could accomplish all this work within six weeks, but then a small army of technicians and contractors had arrived and gone to work with key members of his crew. Together they had ripped the ship apart and practically transformed her into a new warship. When they'd taken on their ammo, all but ten of their Tomahawk cruise missiles had been swapped out for additional Standard Missiles. In addition to the possibility of supporting ground operations with naval gun support, the *Hue City* was gearing up to be focused exclusively on air and missile defense.

When they'd left port and moved into the Gulf of Mexico, the ground war in Cuba had largely come to an end. Combat operations were in full swing in El Salvador, and it looked like the US was gearing up for round three with the Chinese in Venezuela. After he'd been promoted to captain, Dupre's little task force had now become official. He was made the commodore of a growing group of ships that would help lead the eventual ground invasion of Venezuela.

The Tico *Lake Champlain* and two *Arleigh Burkes*, the USS *Barry* and *Laboon*, had joined up with two British, one French and three Spanish frigates. In a couple of weeks, Dupre's task force would link up with a slate of five amphibious assault ships from the three foreign nations. Right now, his little force had to clear out the remaining naval threats before they escorted the more vulnerable troopships to get within range of recapturing some of the Caribbean islands the Chinese had helped the Venezuelans capture at the outset of the war.

Dupre turned to his tactical action officer, or TAO, Lieutenant Clarissa Price. "Have we heard any word from Space Command yet?"

"Nothing yet."

"Were you even able to detect their aircraft?" Dupre pressed.

Lieutenant Price shook her head. "Not really. I mean, we caught a glimpse of them here and there. But nothing we could actually lock onto or even track. Whatever those aircraft are, they're damn hard to find and fast as hell. We caught a glimpse of one over Cuba, then ten minutes later, they were practically over top of us. Incredible."

Dupre let out a soft whistle. "Let's hope the Chinese have as tough a time tracking them as we do."

"I wish we had access to our own satellites. We could spot those SAMs and antiship missile batteries and just nail them with our Tomahawks," Price lamented more to herself than anyone else.

Sighing, Dupre replied, "I hear you. I'm absolutely blown away by the electronic wizardry going on in space right now with all the spoofing and jamming of satellites. There may be some sort of agreement not to destroy each other's hardware, but they sure found a way to make it utterly useless to us, didn't they?"

"Ain't that the truth."

Dupre's ships were in a holding pattern. Space Command had sent in a squadron of their new fighter-spaceplanes ten hours ago, with some experimental weapon systems to clear out some of the ground-launched antiship missile systems. Once Space Command had neutralized the threats to his ships, they'd move to finish off the Chinese and Venezuelan warships once and for all. This would clear the waterways for the Allies to begin the next phase of the war—the final removal of the Chinese from the Americas.

One of the petty officers turned around and addressed Lieutenant Price. "Ma'am, we're receiving a message from Space Command. They're reporting their strike was a success. We're cleared to move in and engage the enemy naval vessels."

Captain Dupre smiled. Price turned to him, grinning. "Give the order, Lieutenant. It's time to start the hunt."

****

Nearly an hour after being given the all-clear to advance toward the Venezuelan coast, Dupre and his crew now had to figure out where the enemy fleet was. The Chinese were notorious for spoofing or jamming the satellite network.

"Any sign from the drones yet?" Captain Dupre asked Lieutenant Price. "Have they managed to locate the enemy fleet?"

After a tense all-nighter, the crew was growing exhausted. They'd been at general quarters for the better part of four hours.

"Not yet, Captain. I'm sure they'll find something soon. Do you want to hit the rack and we can come get you when we find something?" Price asked.

He was just about to agree with the idea when they received word that one of the British warships' scout drones had found the enemy fleet. "They're sailing off the coast of Isla Margarita," the communications specialist announced.

"Excellent," said Price. "Have they sent any details about how many ships are part of the fleet?"

The petty officer shook his head. "The drone was taken out, ma'am. They spotted three ships before it got nailed."

Price cursed softly under her breath. This would certainly interfere with the plan to get missile assignments generated and be the first ones to strike.

Damn, that was quick, Dupre thought. He looked at the digital map and did some calculations in his head. Isla Margarita was roughly two hundred miles away from their current position.

"Well, the Chinese know we're looking for them at this point. What kind of ships did the UAV spot before they shot it down?" Dupre exclaimed in frustration. He was hoping to keep the element of surprise on his side instead of the other way around.

Lieutenant Price had been on the battle net chatting with her counterpart on the British warship with the drone that had found the enemy fleet. She signaled for Dupre to join her at her workstation.

"Sir, the *Glasgow* says the drone spotted a *Renhai*-class cruiser and two *Luyang III*-class destroyers before it was taken out."

Crap, that's some serious firepower.

Dupre lifted his chin stoically. This was going to be a tougher fight than he might have first thought. Thus far, the US Navy hadn't encountered any of the Chinese guided-missile cruisers in the Caribbean. The *Renhai*-class ships were very similar to the Ticos, only about thirty-five to forty years newer. They were formidable opponents.

But what else do they have sailing with them? Dupre wondered.

"Price, see if the *Glasgow* has another drone they can send. We need to get a better idea of what we're facing. In the meantime, pass the word to the rest of the fleet about what we've found. I want them as prepared as possible. The closer we get to them, the higher the chance they'll engage us once they know our positions. They still have a reach advantage on us with their missiles."

"On it, Captain," Price replied. She immediately set to work alerting the fleet.

Dupre examined the current deployment of his ships; he had the Spanish frigates deploy in a much wider picket formation ahead of them. If the Chinese sent any drones of their own up, he wanted the Spanish warships to deal with them. Plus, they'd be the ships the Chinese would spot first and not his more capable Ticos or Flight III *Burkes*.

Two hours went by with the opposing fleets playing cat and mouse, each side jockeying to get into a better position to launch a surprise attack on the other.

Captain Dupre had made contact with the *Ford* strike group to coordinate a naval strike. He was sure his PLA counterpart was looking to do the same thing with their land-based fighters.

Which group will strike first? Dupre wondered. *Who will score first blood?*

****

Type 60 *Dingyuan* Battlecruiser

Senior Captain Chin Boa looked at the battle map on the main plot table in the center of the CIC. It displayed Isla Margarita near the center, his fleet of warships shown on the map as little blue icons. With the tap of a finger, he could bring up a detailed spec list of the ship he selected. To some, it might have seemed like a trivial feature, but Captain Chin found it exceptionally useful when managing a large group of warships.

His executive officer, Captain Lin, walked up next to him and leaned in close so only the two of them could hear. "Are you sure it is a wise idea to split our force up like this?" he asked softly.

"If we want to deal NATO another blow like we did a couple of months ago, then yes."

When a NATO UAV had spotted them several hours ago, Chin had divided his force up in hopes of deceiving them and laying a new trap. He wanted to use the island to his advantage. His plan was to give the enemy something to chase after—keep their focus on his secondary force while he snuck around the island from the opposite direction and attacked them from the rear.

"OK, I understand," his XO replied. "Still, I can't believe they took so many of our ground batteries out. That umbrella of protection has kept NATO at arm's reach for months, and it's what allowed us to wipe that last flotilla out." The aftereffects of this mystery strike against such a strategic asset were now being fully felt.

Senior Captain Chin only shrugged his shoulders. "It is neither here nor there, Captain. At some point, we would have to fight each other. Besides, this ship was not built to look mean or intimidate. It was built for war. Now, how much longer until our air support will be in a position to launch their attack? It is imperative we coordinate this, so everything hits them as close together as possible."

Lin tapped a key on his tablet, pulling some information up. "They should be launching their aircraft in twenty minutes. A recon force has already left. Once they spot the NATO fleet, they'll transmit their location and disposition to us and Captain Hong on the *Nanchang*."

Chin reached for his glass of tea and took a sip. Sending Captain Hong and his ship, the *Nanchang*, along with five of his ships and the two *Lupo*-class frigates of the Venezuelan Navy was a huge gamble. There was a high likelihood Hong's flotilla was going to be sunk. However, if they bought him the necessary time for the *Dingyuan* to get in behind the NATO fleet, it would be worth it. Sending a second enemy flotilla to the bottom might end any amphibious threat NATO still posed.

"Very well. Let me know when they have spotted them," said Captain Chin. "I am heading down to the mess to grab some breakfast. This is going to be a long day. When I return, I want you to head down and grab a big meal as well."

****

USS *Hue City*

"Captain, you have to see this," Lieutenant Price called out urgently. Her senior enlisted petty officer was standing next to her, the two of them looking intently at something on her screen.

"What do you have, Price?"

"Sir, we just received some footage and images from an Air Force RQ-170 Sentinel. It provided us with a good overview of the Chinese fleet. However, when it flew over the center of Isla Margarita to capture some footage of the island, it was apparently destroyed by what the Air Force is telling us was a directed-energy weapon."

Price and the chief were looking at a short video of three ships, one of which was obviously a lot larger than the other two.

"What is that?" Dupre asked as he pointed to the more substantial ship.

"We aren't sure. Chief thinks it might be that mystery Chinese battlecruiser we've heard about," Price offered.

Dupre's left eyebrow rose. They'd received intelligence about a new mystery Chinese warship that had supposedly launched just prior to the war. If this was indeed one of these novel ships, then it hadn't traveled through the Panama Canal before the conflict had heated up. That meant it would have had to travel around the tip of Chile and Argentina to get into the Caribbean.

"OK, before we go down the rabbit hole of what that ship might be and how we're going to deal with it, what are we looking at with that group to the northeast of Isla Margarita?" Dupre asked, refocusing their attention to the immediate threat.

Price nodded and minimized the screen with the mythical Chinese battlecruiser, bringing the requested information up in its place. "It looks to be anchored by a Type 54 destroyer, three frigates, two corvettes and two Venezuelan Navy *Lupo* frigates. I'd also wager they're probably coordinating with some air assets from land to assist them in attacking us as well."

Before anyone could say anything further, one of the petty officers manning the air-defense weapons called out, "Lieutenant Price! We've got contacts—multiple contacts."

"What do you have, Petty Officer Brady?" Captain Dupre asked as Lieutenant Price made her way over to the air-defense group.

"Sir, I'm showing twelve JH-7 aircraft forming up over Isla Margarita," Petty Officer Second Class Brady replied.

Lieutenant Price turned to Dupre with a look of concern on her face. "Sir, we may want to have the flotilla begin to disperse so our CIWS and RIMs can engage without hitting each other."

Dupre nodded. It was time to get his group ready for battle.

"How far out are we from that main group of warships?" asked Dupre. He wanted to start launching their own missiles sooner rather than later.

Chief Royal, who was manning the weapons section, looked over his shoulder as he replied, "We're in range of our Harpoons—we just have to get a solid lock on the enemy ships to feed some targeting data into the missiles."

Damn it! Dupre thought. *We can't get that targeting data if our UAVs keep getting shot down.* As frustrated as he was, he couldn't vent that frustration to his crew. As an officer, he had to complain up, not down.

"Oh, sweet," said Chief Royal as he stood behind of a couple of his junior sailors, pointing to one of their screens. "Sir, we're getting targeting data coming in right now. It looks like the *Glasgow* got another drone in position. I'm distributing the targets across the fleet's Harpoons right now. We'll be ready to fire in sixty seconds."

The new block II+ ER missiles had a range of one hundred and ninety-two miles, more than double what the older versions were capable of. Granted, these warheads were smaller, but they were supposed to be more damaging when they hit.

"Captain, we're showing another group of fighters heading toward us," PO2 Brady called out. "They're roughly two hundred and ten miles out and closing quick."

"What kind of aircraft are they?" asked Dupre.

There was a moment of silence before Lieutenant Price turned to him. "It's a group of thirty-six J-15s. They're moving at Mach 1.2, closing quickly on the maximum range of their Eagle Strike missiles."

Price had told the petty officer to move his screen to the big board. They all needed to see the air battle picture—things were about to heat up quickly.

"We're ready to fire our Harpoons, Captain," Chief Royal announced.

"Very well, Chief. Send the firing orders to the fleet," ordered Dupre. "I want those Chinese ships sent to the bottom. Lieutenant Price, prepare the ship for battle stations air defense. Find out if the *Ford* has any fighters they can vector our way. It'd be great if we could splash a few of those J-16s."

"That group of JH-7s have turned toward us," Brady called out. "They're increasing their speed to get in range of their Saccade missiles."

As the two groups of aircraft zeroed in on the fleet, the *Hue City*'s AN/SPY radar and AEGIS system began to prioritize targets for each of the ships to fire at. Once the AEGIS had fully slaved control of the *Laboon*, *Barry*, and *Lake Champlain*, the computer on the *Hue City* sent firing orders to the three ships.

The four American warships fired their SM-6 missiles at the two groups of inbound enemy aircraft. The AEGIS would only assign a single missile to each aircraft. If they managed to evade it, then so be it. The remainder of the SMs were held back to fire at the volley of antiship missiles they knew would be headed their way shortly.

Within a minute of the ships firing off fifty SM-6 missiles and another forty-eight Harpoons at the eight enemy warships, they had six missiles targeting each ship, knowing most of them would likely be shot down or intercepted before they found their marks. For a couple of minutes after firing off their missiles, the area around the NATO task force was shrouded in smoke and missile contrails. The sun had finally pushed away the darkness, ushering in a new dawn.

How many of these ships and sailors will still be alive in thirty minutes? Dupre wondered as the hundreds of missiles they had fired at each other began to find their marks.

"Those aircraft are firing," PO2 Brady announced, tension and a bit of fear evident in his voice.

Captain Dupre was sitting in his captain's chair, looking at the image of the larger battlespace. He had a group of twelve aircraft heading toward him from a 190-degree angle. A second group of thirty-six more capable aircraft were flying in from a 289-degree angle. Together, these groups had just unleashed a combined one hundred and ninety-two Saccade and Eagle Strike missiles at them.

Less than sixty seconds after the aircraft had fired their missiles, the Chinese warships fired their own barrage of eighty-eight Eagle Strike and Saccade missiles. In the span of roughly three minutes, a total of two hundred and eighty antiship missiles had been fired at the Americans. While this wasn't the first time Dupre's ship had been targeted by enemy antiship missiles, it was the first time he'd had more than two hundred of them fired at him.

Sitting in his chair, Dupre watched as the three tracks of missiles began to converge on his fleet. The incoming missiles were denoted as red arrows, but they were still too far out to know how many had been targeted at each individual ship. That would come later, as the missiles got closer and began to zero in on specific targets.

Closer to their ships but rapidly expanding outwards was the second wave of missiles the NATO warships had fired to go after the incoming threats. The British warship *Glasgow* was coordinating with the French and Spanish ships to engage the missiles fired at the fleet from the Chinese warships, while the American contingent went after the swarm of air-launched antiship missiles.

At the edge of the *Hue City*'s radar range, Dupre caught sight of sixteen F/A-18 Super Hornets angling in for an attack on the J-16s. The American fighters from the *Ford* were well outside the battle the *Hue* was managing, but it was nice to know they had help on the way from the *Ford*.

"Woo-hoo, the cavalry has arrived," Chief Royals announced excitedly. Another group of Super Hornets had just fired a barrage of Harpoons at the Chinese warships, adding more missiles to the mix.

What really improved the likelihood of sinking the enemy warships was hopefully not just throwing more missiles than their defensive system could handle, but also throwing missiles at them from multiple different directions and altitudes. If a RIM or CIWS system was engaging one target and then had to switch to a new target in the opposite direction, it took that system several seconds to traverse to face the new threat. With missiles traveling in excess of Mach 3, seconds equated to an eternity and could mean the difference between life and death.

As Dupre was starting to feel a little better at the news of the Super Hornets' arrival into the battle, his heart skipped a beat when a new track of missiles flew toward them from a different heading altogether.

"Where are those missiles coming from?" Dupre asked Price.

As his TAO, Price was largely responsible for coordinating the defense of the ship. She was one of the sharpest TAOs he'd ever served with, and he was glad as hell to have her with him in this fight.

PO2 Brady turned to him. "If I had to guess, Captain, I'd say they're coming from that mystery ship the Sentinel spotted before being shot down."

"Captain, I'd like to retask the *Laboon* to move in the direction of that mystery ship," Chief Royal requested. "If nothing else, they can help us get some targeting data on it."

"That's a good call, sir," Price agreed. "I can see if we can get the Hornets to help us out, but we can't fire on that thing if we don't have any targeting data."

"Fine, just make sure we aren't leaving the *Laboon* out on their own," Dupre responded. "Staying somewhat close together allows our defenses to interlock a lot better."

****

Type 60 *Dingyuan* Battlecruiser

Senior Captain Chin Boa watched the air defense monitors with more than a bit of concern as he monitored the volume of American Harpoon missiles still bearing down on his ships. The *Nanchang* had sustained several direct hits, but the captain of that ship had told Chin they should have the fires under control soon. Captain Chin had ordered his remaining ships to charge the NATO fleet at flank speed. They were going to try and close the distance between each other in hopes that they might get close enough to use some of their other weapon systems.

When they'd seen one of the American *Arleigh Burkes* breaking off from the pack to approach his ship, Captain Chin had prioritized the sinking of that warship. He'd ordered his two corvettes traveling with him to fire their four Saccades at the American destroyer and then fired six of his own Eagle Strike 12 missiles. The hypersonic missiles reached their maximum speed of Mach 3 within a minute of being fired.

The fourteen missiles had closed the distance between the warships at incredible speeds. The American destroyer had fired off two missiles

139

at each of his own. For Chin and the sailors with him, this was only the second time in their careers they had fired their weapons at an opposing force. It was terrifying and exhilarating, all at the same time.

The American warship had also fired ten of their Harpoon missiles at them. These inbound threats were going to be dealt with by their new directed-energy weapon system—it would be a true test of the new weapon.

Looking at the tactical display, Chin saw the American destroyer had managed to destroy eleven of the fourteen missiles they'd fired at it. He was honestly shocked and impressed. He'd need to add that to the after-action report. The Eagle Strike missiles were supposed to fare a lot better than that.

When three of the missiles slammed into the American warship, several of the sailors in the CIC let out hoots and hollers. Under any normal circumstance, Chin would have been furious at the lack of decorum and professionalism exhibited by these sailors…but they'd just scored three hits against an American warship, so he'd let it slide.

"Captain, the American ship is in flames," announced a sailor who was manning one of their stealth observation drones.

Chin got up from his chair and walked over to the drone operators. He looked down and saw the *Arleigh Burke* destroyer was engulfed in flames. One of the missiles had impacted against the rear hangar section of the ship, likely destroying the helicopter inside. Another missile looked like it had hit the forward section of the ship, near what Chin knew to be the AEGIS radar sections. The third missile had slammed into the ship, near the waterline, just below the flight deck of the ship.

Huge swaths of the ship were engulfed in flames and the rear half of the ship was already starting to slip under the water. Chin knew at this point the ship was lost. It would slip beneath the waves in minutes.

Returning his attention to the large screen in the CIC room, Chin looked at the inbound threats. They were closing in on their position fast. The officer in charge of the directed-energy weapon was pointing to something on the sailor's computer monitor. Moments later, one of the missiles that had been fired at them disappeared. Then a second, then a third. Before Chin could congratulate them, the CIWS systems opened fire.

"Brace for impact! Brace for impact!" came an automated voice over the ship's PA system.

Moments later, Chin felt the ship shake as a missile impacted against it. Then he felt a second impact.

Studying the damage control board, Chin saw a host of yellow lights blinking but no red lights. That was a good thing. Red lights were bad. Captain Chin glanced at a couple of the exterior cameras and saw smoke coming from the rear of the ship—that lined up with the yellow lights flashing along the rear half of the ship. When he looked back at the damage control board, the single yellow light near the center of the ship right above the waterline had stopped blinking. Upon further examination, Chin learned the missile had impacted against the side of the ship near the torpedo belt.

Like the Russian *Kirov*-class after which his ship had been modeled, the *Dingyuan* boasted a robust armor belt. It was believed the ship could survive multiple torpedo and missile hits and still stay afloat, but Captain Chin didn't want to test that theory. However, Chin *was* feeling pretty good about those features now that he had seen the armor belt shrug off an American Harpoon missile.

Moments later, the threats to the ship had ended. The American *Arleigh Burke* was destroyed and there were no more missiles being fired at them—at least not for the moment.

Chin directed his drone operator to get their stealth drone closer to the main NATO fleet, wanting a better view of what was going on. He'd already ordered his remaining ships further north of him to do their best to disengage and get behind Isla Margarita and out of danger. He only had three of his original eight ships from that group left. If they could return to fight another day, he'd like to try.

For now, it looked like NATO had finally broken the Chinese stranglehold on the southern Caribbean.

****

USS *Hue City*

Captain Dupre looked at the damage report readout of his little fleet. They'd managed to shoot down some two hundred and eighty-six missiles, a feat even he hadn't thought was possible. However, when they'd added in the missiles from the mysterious battlecruiser to what had already been fired at them, forty-six missiles had still managed to slip past their defenses.

The *Laboon* had taken three hits. She'd slipped beneath the waves within minutes, taking most of her crew with her. The *Barry* had taken four hits. They were still afloat but in a bad way. Her captain had said they could barely make five knots right now and had essentially no power to their weapon systems. The other Tico traveling with them, the *Lake Champlain*, had absorbed eight hits. Being the second-largest warship in the group, she'd become a magnet for missiles, just like the *Hue City* had. Dupre had thought the *Champ* was going to make it until a pair of Eagle Strikes had hit her almost simultaneously in the middle of the ship, nearly ripping her in half. Very few members of her crew had had time to abandon ship before the vessel had disappeared below the waves. An oil slick and flames were the only remnants to mark where she had once been.

The British warship *Glasgow* was ablaze. Dupre didn't think they'd make it, but the ship's captain said they weren't ready to give up on the *Glasgow* just yet. One of the French frigates had survived without a scratch. It had taken up a screening position between them and the mysterious battlecruiser. The other French frigate had taken two hits but was still afloat. All three Spanish frigates had been sunk.

The *Hue City* had taken three hits itself. A Saccade had nailed the bridge, killing his XO, who'd been manning it while Dupre remained in the CIC. The missile had trashed the bridge, essentially rendering it useless. A second Saccade had hit the helicopter hangar bay, ripping it apart and tearing the helicopter up. The aircrew and several of the mechanics had been killed in the blast. At least the second helicopter was still operational. Dupre had ordered it to get airborne and start search-and-rescue operations for any survivors from the ships that had sunk.

The third missile to have struck them hit in the forward VLS section. They were fortunate the entire section had already expended their missiles, or they might have had to worry about secondary explosions. As it was, the Eagle Strike missile had done considerable damage to the forward section of the ship, opening up a three-meter gash at the waterline. They weren't in any danger of sinking, but they wouldn't be able to travel quickly.

"Captain, we're receiving a message from the *Ford*," announced PO2 Brady. "They're asking if we need assistance in recovering our wounded and any survivors still in the water."

Dupre turned to the young man and nodded. He wasn't about to turn down help—not when most of his task force was still in danger.

"Lieutenant Price, where is the enemy fleet now? What's left of them?" Dupre asked, his stomach tied in knots at the thought of the Chinese raining more missiles down on them.

Lieutenant Price turned in her chair slightly to look at Dupre. Her eyes looked tired, and so did her body as her shoulders had slumped a bit since the height of the battle. "The only ships that appear to have survived, Captain, are that battlecruiser to the southwest of Isla Margarita and the two corvettes that had been traveling as escorts to her. I'm not definitively sure where they're headed, but they seem to be traveling in the direction of the port city of Cumana."

Dupre shook his head. "Did we even score a hit on that battlecruiser?"

Price shrugged. "I can't honestly say. A lot of missiles were thrown at it during the battle, but I have no idea if any of them actually scored a hit. When I spoke with the TAO on the *Ford*, they told me a flight of Super Hornets had tried to engage it when they were shot down. One of the pilots reported his wingman being hit by some sort of directed-energy weapon. He said his wingman was there one moment, and the next thing he saw was one of his wings being sliced clean off. It seems this new mysterious battlecruiser of theirs is employing some new advanced weapons or something."

Laser weapons…as if missile swarms weren't enough, thought Dupre in dread. *What else are the Chinese going to throw at us?*

"Send a message to the *Ford*. Tell them I'm ordering what's left of my task force to make best possible speed to Pascagoula for repairs," Dupre ordered. "Please ask if they can continue to assist in searching for survivors—right now, I need to focus on getting whatever ships can be salvaged out of the battlespace."

At no time in his naval career had Captain Michael Dupre felt as defeated as he did at that moment. His first major command as a commodore had resulted in nearly his entire fleet being destroyed. He now understood what that British commodore must have felt like leading up to his suicide. Dupre wouldn't end his own life, though. No, he'd look to get his ship repaired and back in the action as soon as he could.

Chapter Ten
Weight of the World

White House
Washington, D.C.

Blain Wilson opened his third Rip It in the last six hours and took a long couple of sips. He felt the sugar and caffeine course through his veins. To say the last eight weeks had been brutal on the new administration was an understatement. There was always a bit of disruption when administrations changed hands, especially if they were from opposite political parties. Throw in a major world war and the cleanup work left over from a second pandemic, and the new administration was really starting out on the wrong foot.

Blain had been one of the few holdovers asked to stay on by President Maria Delgado. She'd made a point during the campaign of trying to govern from a place of unity rather than one of "my side versus yours." In some ways, her strategy was working; in others it was creating a lot of friction. However, facing an existential threat that had NATO and the West on the ropes had created a lot of strange bedfellows.

"Whatcha working, sir?" asked Katrina Roets.

Katrina was one of the few people Blain had been able to save when the new administration had taken over. She was an obvious partisan and loyal to the previous president, but she was also damn good at her job, and right now he needed someone with the knowledge she possessed. She'd been running the Caribbean and South American desk of the National Security Council, so her knowledge of what was going on down there was invaluable.

"I'm still trying to evaluate Project Halo," Blain replied. "That DARPA, MIT, and SpaceX proposal about the GPS project they presented to us four weeks ago—I sent them back with about two dozen RFIs to answer before I'd even entertain it again or bring it up to the council."

Katrina furrowed her brow. "Let me guess—they finished answering your impossible-to-answer RFIs and now they want to talk about it."

Blain laughed. "I wouldn't call them impossible RFIs. Just thorough. But yeah, they finished answering them and then some. If I'm reading this right, they actually made some pretty big modifications to the satellites that appear to have improved them substantially."

"Are you serious about considering this, though?" Katrina pressed. "Once you go through with something like this, there isn't any coming back."

Blain sighed, a little louder than he'd intended. "Yes, we'd be crossing the proverbial Rubicon. But honestly, I'm not sure there's a more effective way to combat that damn AI than to cut off its access to the World Wide Web and the satellites above."

"Forget the AI. How are we going to handle the debris field that'll be created up there?" she asked, hands on her hips. "I've heard that once a Kessler syndrome or Kessler effect starts, it becomes a rapidly cascading problem that'll only worsen with time." She had been a strong advocate for not touching the satellite network if the Chinese were content with leaving it alone.

"I know the risks. That's why I sent them packing with some exhaustive RFIs. What they came back with actually demonstrates some pretty good theories on how to handle this, though. One idea is to resurrect Project Orion—an old broom project from the 1990s. It's actually not a bad idea. Their other idea is for us to deploy a new set of GPS satellites that would leverage a better encryption process, integrating blockchain technology. They'd place them in a geostationary orbit roughly twenty-two thousand miles above Earth's equator, giving them enhanced maneuvering and a robust self-defense capability."

Katrina shook her head. Blain knew the last administration would never have considered something like this. The previous president would have argued that the gains made from such an action wouldn't come close to the losses it would inflict on the world. Some things were just best left alone.

"Well, you know how I feel about this whole thing," Katrina asserted. "There has to be a better way to blind this AI and prevent it from just freely crawling across the web…*our* web."

Blain decided to change the subject. "Did you read that report from Space Force about their first-ever combat mission?" he asked.

"I sure did," Katrina replied, her voice softening. "Wow. That was impressive. I'll bet the President wants to start building a whole new fleet of those planes now. Maybe we found our answer to those Chinese SAMs." A lot of the people who were lucky enough to know about the secretive program were ecstatic about it. The only problem was they couldn't just go and share the news with everyone. Heck, not even everyone on the National Security Council knew about the program.

Blain didn't blame the new President for keeping some pieces of information close to the chest. Her administration was a lot more guarded with what they shared and talked about, both within the administration and with the press. Even in Blain's own office, he was now managing a couple of special access programs or SAPs his predecessor never would have allowed. Still, Blain knew the President personally, so he understood her intentions probably better than most.

Looking at the clock, Blain saw it was time for him to head to his standing meeting with the President. Every Tuesday and Friday he had a 3 p.m. meeting, just the two of them. On occasion, she might include her Chief of Staff or someone else, but these small private meetings were Blain and the President's way of staying on top of things.

****

Presidential Study

President Maria Delgado had been looking over a unique proposal when Blain walked in. She stood and gestured for him to take a seat opposite her. She liked meeting in her study as opposed to the Oval. It just felt more informal and cozier. Blain wasn't just her National Security Advisor; he was an old friend. And now more than ever, she needed friends she could trust.

"How are you, Blain? Are we working you too hard?" she asked jovially.

"Working too hard?" Blain replied with a chuckle. "I love what I do, so I wouldn't exactly call it work."

Maria joined the laughter. Everyone around her was so serious— few people felt confident enough to crack a joke or say something funny. It was frustrating at times.

"So, I talked with Colonel Hewitt last night about their first mission," Maria began. "I must say, I am truly impressed with what they've managed to cobble together in such a short time."

"It is impressive," Blain agreed. "He managed to find some very talented pilots who were in between aircraft and get them spun up on the program in a matter of months. Now we just need to find a way to get them involved in a *lot* more missions so they can have a true impact on the war."

"Speaking of making an impact in the war—someone told me that one way we could go after this super-AI, Jade Dragon, is to create series of disinformation projects and flood the internet with them. This way, the AI is being fed a competing narrative against what's really going on."

Blain held a hand up. "Madam President, that would not be a good idea," he countered. "We're already being hit ourselves by fake news attacks generated by this AI. If we start to churn out our own disinformation, we're going to run into a serious problem when it comes to how to identify real news and real information. Some people want to flood the waves with so much information the AI's brain won't know what's real and what isn't, but then neither will our own people—heck, we might end up spoofing our own intelligence apparatus. I think if we go down this route, we'd only be adding fuel to the fire and making the situation worse."

"I suppose you have another proposal for how to counter this AI, then?"

Blain nodded slightly. "I do. I was briefed an idea that might work. It would break our satellite détente; however, I believe they've answered my concerns about the ensuing Kessler event that would be sure to happen if we moved in this direction."

The President scrunched up her eyebrows. "What's a Kessler event? It sounds bad."

"Technically, it's horrible," Blain acknowledged. "It's the worst possible calamity that could hit space and our orbit."

"Then why on earth would we want to consider it?"

"Because it would all but blind Jade Dragon. It would greatly reduce its ability to collect information and monitor what's going on across the internet. To answer your question, a Kessler event is basically when a debris field forms in orbit. Because the fragments travel so fast, they continue to crash into anything that gets in their way, which creates a new debris field. Over time, this field becomes enormous. It gets so large, it makes it virtually impossible to place new satellites in space or get into a higher GEO because you have to navigate your way through the field."

"Blain, if that's the case, then that doesn't sound like something we want to entertain. We may be better off just dealing with the current situation rather than permanently banning ourselves from future space operations or even satellites."

"I would tend to agree with you, which is why I killed the proposal months ago...until the organizations proposing it had a better idea of how to combat the effects of what we'd be creating."

"Go on," President Delgado replied.

Blain spent the next half hour going over the basics of the proposal. By the time he was done, the President hadn't totally ruled it out. But she did have a list of new questions he hadn't thought of. When their meeting ended, Blain had the outline of a new RFI. Until a more effective way to remove the space debris was identified, this proposal would remain on the backburner.

Chapter Eleven
Island Hopping

March 15, 2025
Marine Special Operations Team 8211
Carriacou Island

Marine Raider Master Sergeant Donny Stotts was in the surf fifteen meters from shore. His team leader, Captain Coia, was just off his left shoulder. They were submerged in the shallows, the waves gently rocking them back and forth.

Marine Special Operations Team 8211 was now at one hundred percent strength after replacements had recently arrived from Camp Lejeune. Following the siege at Gitmo, the team had taken a beating. Then half of them had come down with a new strain of COVID-24, which had forced the entire battalion to stand down while they waited for it to burn itself out. A very high percentage of the US population had been vaccinated, but that didn't mean some of the new strains weren't still causing some problems. Now that the battalion was past that, the operators were eager to get back into the war.

During their battalion's absence, the Chinese and Venezuelan naval infantry and Marines moved rapidly to first capture Grenada. Then they'd leapfrogged and swiftly captured St. Vincent and the entire Grenadine chain of islands in the southeastern part of the Caribbean. With these islands under their control, they'd brought ashore several batteries of HQ-9 surface-to-air and antiship missile batteries.

Then, in the southwestern part of the Caribbean, the Chinese and Venezuelans captured the islands of Bonaire, Curaçao, and Aruba. Capturing these island chains would create a buffer off Venezuela's coast, which meant NATO would have to expend more resources trying to remove them if they wanted to remove the Chinese military presence in South America and depose the existing regime.

While Big Army was continuing to fight it out on Cuba and in El Salvador, an island-hopping campaign in the Caribbean had been handed down to the Marines—more specifically, Second Raider Battalion and the 24th Marine Regiment. When Space Command's new secret squirrel weapon had successfully neutralized some of the antiship batteries across Isla Margarita and the Grenadines, it had created the opening the Marines needed to slip their forces in and recapture the islands prior to a full-on seaborne invasion of the Venezuelan coast.

Master Sergeant Stotts stayed just below the surface of the water, breathing through his rebreather. He hoped the units at the other beaches and islands were in position and ready to go. Once the festivities started, chances were, the Chinese would alert all of their garrison that a major attack was underway. It was imperative that they hit all the objectives as close to the same time as possible. The sector of the island that Stotts and his men were hitting was called Gold Beach. They were the center; to their left was MSOT 8212 and to their right was 8213. The final team, 8214, was being held in reserve with the battalion command group about a kilometer offshore in rigid-hull inflatable boats, otherwise known as RHIBs.

To the north, the British Royal Marines would be hitting Canouan Island. The Commando Marines of the French Navy were assaulting Bequia, and the Special Boat Service, the United Kingdom's version of the US Navy SEALs, would attack the island of Mystique. The 2nd Battalion, 24th Marines and 4th Force Recon Company from 4th Marine Division would conduct a heliborne assault of Carriacou Island en masse. All of these attacks were to be conducted simultaneously, leveraging speed, surprise and maximum violence of action to take the PLA by surprise. However, Master Sergeant Stotts had been at this long enough to know that the enemy always got a vote, no matter how much planning had been put into a mission.

Captain Coia tapped Stotts on the leg. Stotts checked his watch and the luminous dials of his RESCO Bullfrog told him it was 0400 hours. It was time. Although spread across nearly fifty miles of ocean, elite combat troops from three NATO nations were about to execute the most daring seaborne invasion in modern history.

Stotts remembered Rogers' Rangers' fifteenth rule: *Don't sleep past dawn; dawn's when the French and Indians attack.* He hoped none of the Chinese had gone to Ranger school.

A quick scan to his left and right told him that his unit was ready. Knowing the entire team would follow his lead, he then made the first move. Stotts walked up a slight incline until his body was out of the water. Then he raised his rifle and had it at the ready in case he stumbled upon a roving patrol. The rest of his team had followed suit, advancing up the sand rapidly until they reached the edge of the beach. At that point, they dropped their Cobham rebreathers and covered them with sand.

Now that they were onshore and ready to move, each Marine unit launched a microdrone into the air; the little eyes in the sky were set to stay about fifty feet in front of the teams so as they advanced, they would give the operators a 180-degree full-color night vision picture of what was ahead of them. Once the small screen of drones was synced with the other MSOTs in the company, the collective image they gathered would be beamed to the battalion command post offshore. This would give the leadership element a full picture of the battlespace as it was unfolding in real time.

****

Lieutenant Colonel Gavin Blanco, commander of the 2nd Raider Battalion, was huddled next to the battalion S3, Major Booth. They were intently watching the drone feeds from the operators ashore, looking for any signs that the Chinese had been alerted to their presence. Behind him, Sergeant Jimenez sat with two radio handsets to his ears.

Blanco was always amazed how the kid was able to receive information from one radio, understand and memorize it, while at the same time relaying information that was completely unrelated over a second radio with no loss of fidelity in what he heard or sent. The kid was a savant when it came to military comms. Blanco glanced at Major Johnston, the battalion intelligence officer or S2. Johnston was intently monitoring the drone feeds, flipping between thermal and IR repeatedly. Blanco could see the lines on his forehead as Johnston looked from screen to screen.

"What is it, Two?" Blanco whispered tensely.

Johnston held up his left finger as his right hand continued to dance over the keys of his small workstation.

"Damn!" Johnston hissed.

Blanco crawled to Johnston and looked at his screen. Johnston pointed to the icon for MSOT 8213 and drew a line with his stylus to a small depression about twenty meters from their position. He tapped the screen to enlarge it and circled what looked like a tarp that was gently blowing in the wind. The live-motion feed switched from IR to full-color night vision, and it showed what was clearly a sniper's hide site. Blanco felt his chest tighten as he saw the team walking right toward the hide position.

"Tell 8213 sniper, eleven o'clock! All elements, go loud!"

As Blanco was relaying his commands, Sergeant Jimenez was already finishing the sentence for him over the net. Blanco had a flashback to his childhood, watching *M*A*S*H* with his grandfather and seeing the clerk, Radar, doing the same thing to Colonel Potter. This kid was amazing.

****

Stotts was about to hold up his hand to halt his element when to his right, all hell broke loose. The night sky was illuminated as green and red tracers flew back and forth in the predawn twilight, intermixed with explosions. Their entire right flank was going to hell in a handbasket.

The entire team hit the deck, rifles at the ready to unleash holy hell in front of them. The tactical visors attached to their advanced combat helmets automatically began linking the common operating picture for the team, populating probable enemy positions in relation to the SAM sites they had been sent to destroy and the associated antiship missile pods, with directions and distances to the targets. Despite the battle raging to their right, their experimental helmet visors were directing them to where they needed to go to disable the weapon systems their entire mission was centered around.

Looking over his left shoulder, Stotts saw Gunnery Sergeant Smolick, the team's comm chief, working on his terminal. It was a small laptop mounted on the front of his chest rig that he could just fold down and have immediate access to its tools. Stotts knew that he was pulling in the data feeds from the other teams and the battalion command post offshore. This would provide their unit with as much information as possible before shooting in their sector started.

Stotts waited for Smolick to give them the all-clear, signaling that they were ready to move out. Instead, he motioned for him to come take a look at his screen. He pointed to a couple of spots on the map where a likely enemy threat had been identified, probably a machine-gun position.

"Got it, Gunny. Good find," Stotts said. "Let's prepare to move out and hit these guys. We need to strike fast and take those sites out before the entire garrison gets deployed." He promptly left to pass along the info to the rest of their team.

The Marines took off, instinctively falling back on their training of how to assault a well-defended position. No sooner had they started their assault than the Chinese opened fire on them. The two bunkers were positioned just right, placing the Marines in a tough crossfire with little room to maneuver. Stotts and his team started tossing hand grenades like they were going out of style. The two grenadier grunts in their rank lobbed 40mm grenades at the enemy, causing further chaos and mayhem.

The Chinese seemed like they'd been caught off guard by the sudden appearance of so many Marines nearby. The gunners operating the machine guns in the bunkers were spraying wildly, crisscrossing their fire across the field but aiming too high. By the time the Chinese shooters strafed toward a group of Marines, they'd already dropped back to the ground. As more grenades started to pepper the Chinese positions, spraying shrapnel through the air, the gunners were being further thrown off.

As he ran forward, Master Sergeant Stotts saw one of his guys, Staff Sergeant Goldhammer, take a round to his chest and get flung to the side. Stotts hit the dirt again and turned back to look for Goldhammer—he just shrugged the hit off. Tracer rounds flew over his head where he'd just been moments earlier. They made brief eye contact and Goldhammer flashed Stotts a stoic expression and a thumbs-up, letting Stotts know he was OK.

Crump! Boom! Crump! Boom!

"Covering fire!" one of the fire team leaders shouted as his team prepared to close the final distance to the enemy gun bunker.

Corporal Fitzmier, their light-medium machine gunner, responded by delivering a murderous rate of fire to their immediate front. His Sig Sauer's .338 Norma Magnum bullets shredded everything they hit and kept the enemy's heads down.

"Moving!" called out another fire team as they leapt after the first team.

Stotts jumped to his own feet and followed after the two fire teams. They dashed forward nearly twenty feet, laying down fire of their own before they hit the deck. Miraculously, none of them had been hit.

Landing behind the next set of cover, Stotts yelled out, "Set!" This let the next elements further behind them know they were ready to lay down the covering fire so they could continue to bound forward.

Reaching a hand over, Stotts tapped Staff Sergeant Reyes on his helmet, and in turn Reyes shouted, "Covering!"

"Moving!" shouted Staff Sergeant LoCastro, the second element leader of the team. As the element sprang up to begin their rush, three PLA soldiers emerged from a concealed positions and fired.

Sergeant Reiken, who had been covering LoCastro's assault, had their lone Milkor MGL grenade gun. He pivoted toward the new threat and unloaded all six grenades at the attackers in less than three seconds. The six 40mm grenades, which traveled at two hundred fifty feet per second, found their targets in the blink of an eye, hitting earth and trees around the Chinese soldiers and showering them with shrapnel and flames before they knew what had happened. Their bodies were torn apart by the six rapid explosions, ending what could have been a terrible slaughter of the attacking Marines.

"Mako Five, Mako Six. Overhead shows ChiComs are running to the backside of the missile battery. Press now!" Captain Coia shouted over the team net to Master Sergeant Stotts.

"Six, Five. Good copy. Moving!" Stotts replied tersely.

Glancing down the line at the team, Stotts saw they were all sending massive amounts of lead into the enemy positions. He took a quick glance at the flexible wrist tablet affixed to his forearm. Captain Coia had pushed the enemy overlay to him so he could see where the enemy missiles were just beyond the copse of trees, fifteen meters to his front. He inhaled deeply, mentally preparing himself for the violence that was about to happen.

"All right, you gun apes, follow me!" he roared and then sprang to his feet and rushed forward.

****

"Sir!" Jimenez hissed, offering Lieutenant Colonel Blanco the radio mic. "It's the Brits—they're running into stiff resistance on their objective. So are the French Marines."

"How is this *our* problem?" Blanco shot back, not taking the receiver.

Jimenez diplomatically relayed Lieutenant Colonel Blanco's question to his French and Brit counterparts on the other end of the radio. Blanco watched as Jimenez listened to both handsets and was again amazed at how this twenty-something Marine was able to comprehend both messages at the same time.

"Sir, it seems that intel was wrong, and the bulk of the ChiCom defense forces in the Grenadines weren't here on Big Island but spread out across the whole island chain. The smaller islands have the missile batteries closer together, so the ChiComs are more concentrated there and putting up some mad resistance."

Blanco sighed and patched in to the USS *Bougainville*. They were carrying the newly reactivated 24th Marine Regiment. They were going to heliborne assault the Big Island with his Marines; however, it appeared like a FRAGO was in order.

After getting ahold of the CO, Blanco explained the situation. He said his Raiders could make do and secure the island, but the 24th should pivot from supporting his units to supporting their European allies, if at all possible. Once they secured those smaller islands, they could heliborne more units over to their island if they still needed the help.

In a matter of minutes, the heliborne force was redirected to support the French and British invasions, proving the undisputed versatility of the new *America*-class landing helicopter assault ships in what was swiftly becoming a war of mobility.

Chapter Twelve
Battle Bots

Army Infantry Center of Excellence
Fort Benning, Georgia

"What the hell is that?" asked Colonel Rafael Ribas, the officer in charge of the Maneuver Center of Excellence acquisition program.

"That, Colonel, is the future of the US infantry platoon," answered Lauren Heigl, a senior engineer. "He's called the Jackal XD500."

"Damn. You know that thing is a lot bigger than the Boston Dynamics quadpedal, right?"

"I'm sure, Colonel, and that's because the Jackal is a hell of a lot more than a pack mule like the other quadpedal I'm sure you've been shown."

Colonel Ribas had seen four other prototypes in the last week. This one clearly went outside the parameters of the request for proposal his group had submitted at the outset of the war. "Lauren, this looks neat and all, but you know the RFP was for a modular quadpedal that could support the infantry. This looks like it does a lot more than that," he explained as he waved his hand about.

The Jackal stood about four feet tall and was roughly six feet long. It was at least fifty percent larger than the other four entrants he'd looked at. The RFP was specifically looking for a smaller version of the previous units so they could be more airmobile.

"Colonel, the Army asked for a quadpedal that could support the infantry," Lauren confirmed. "This prototype will not only support the infantry—it'll provide them with more than just a pack mule with a remote-controlled gun on top. We've designed the Jackal with a one

161

hundred percent renewable energy power plant, large enough to accommodate a couple of modules that can be tailored to the specific needs of the mission." She proudly walked around the quadpedal robot, her left hand running gently across its sleek aluminum-alloy frame. Her red fingernails contrasted against the digital camouflage pattern on the outer body.

Before Colonel Ribas could say anything further about their robot exceeding the size specifications of the RFP, Lauren tapped a couple of times on her tablet and the Jackal came to life. The machine's eyes had a soft blue glow to them as it surveyed the room. Then it began to walk around the closed demonstration hangar, going through the RFP's required actions for consideration.

As the Jackal demonstrated its agility considering its size, one thing was abundantly clear—this thing was *quiet*. It deftly moved around the hangar like a predator stalking its prey. It jumped from one object to another with ease, then leapt through the air onto a rope ladder on the side of a twelve-foot wall and climbed up and over it. The one thing it couldn't do was crawl its way through the tunnel obstacle.

Despite the Jackal's inability to crawl through the cylindrical tube, Colonel Ribas did have to admit, it was hands down the quietest and most agile of the quadpedal robots he'd seen up to this point. It had also outperformed the other RFP submissions, showing a remarkable agility improvement over the Boston Dynamic robots the service was currently using.

"How'd you manage to make it so agile and quiet?" Colonel Ribas asked as he examined the machine up close.

Lauren shrugged as if it was no big deal. "Standard improvements in technology, plus that's proprietary knowledge," she replied with a flirtatious smirk.

Ribas grunted at the reply. He knelt down and looked at the machine's face. "These eyes. I suspect you have a mode that allows them to not glow like this?"

"There is. It also has a feature that allows the eyes to turn red if you want," she explained. "We figure in its normal operational mode on a base, we'd have it lit up with a light blue hue to let you know it was active and working. In the field, the lights would obviously be off to help keep it hidden. As to its quietness, that has everything to do with its electric engine, servos, and power plant. When we designed the Jackal, Colonel, we didn't try to reinvent the wheel. We looked to leverage as many commercial off-the-shelf items as we could while improving upon some of the critical servo components and joints."

Ribas shot her a quizzical look. "Boston Dynamics continues to use a gasoline engine, but you guys went with electric. Why?"

"Going renewable means the Jackal's range isn't limited by its reliance on a fuel source. So long as it can continue to charge its batteries, it can stay in the fight. Even in cloudy conditions, its solar panels will still be able to charge the system. It can also be plugged in externally if needed. Going electric also solved a lot of problems when it came to sound, and it meant the robot would have a much lower heat signature. We also saved a lot of space by not having a gas engine or fuel storage tanks. It did, however, mean we had to compromise some on size, but there are some very specific features we gained by making it the size it is.

"We think its increased capability will more than make up for the difference in size, especially once you see some of the modules we've created for it. Oh, and to boot, the Jackal is actually a hundred pounds lighter than all the other entrants you've tested up to this point—that's because we've made the entire thing out of aluminum alloys and composite plastics that are in fact stronger than steel."

When Lauren looked at the Jackal, she gave it a coy smile as she canted her head slightly and then approached it. As Colonel Ribas watched the interplay, he could swear the robotic machine was almost acting like a family pet in the way it reacted to her. It stopped what it had been doing and walked toward her. Then it stopped and sat like a regular dog would as it waited for her to stand next to it.

Lauren saw the look on the colonel's face and smiled. "This area here, Colonel," she announced as she ran her hands across the centerline of the drone, "is where the mission modules will sit. Whereas the Big Dog and the LS3 are essentially pack mules, we've designed the Jackal to be a multifunctional tool that can be used in a variety of different circumstances and environments. For example, we've designed an antidrone attachment to be used with the Jackal."

"Can it be deployed with airborne or SOF units?"

"You mean can it be rigged with a parachute and still function properly once it hits the ground? Yes. That was one of the requirements we built into it. You can throw it out of a helicopter or plane with a parachute, and it'll survive. We've tested that feature twenty-two times."

The colonel smiled. This thing would actually have a lot of versatility to it, more even than what was in the original RFP. Maybe he could adjust the original RFP so they wouldn't have to exclude the Jackal, or maybe he'd be able to issue a sole source contract for them.

"Tell me about these new modules you've built for it—I want to hear more about the antidrone capabilities," said Ribas.

Lauren walked toward a display table that had the module attachments sitting on them. A couple of technicians also stood behind each module.

"You know, you guys really need to come up with a better company name than the Institute for Human and Machine Cognition or IHMC if you want to become a serious player in the robotics world," Colonel Ribas offered. "Boston Dynamics has an easy name. Your products look light-years ahead of theirs, but the name...you have to come up with a better name."

"I hear they're working on that right now. I think they're waiting until we land our first major contract," Lauren said with a wink and a grin.

Ribas snorted. "I suspect there are a couple different versions of this little Frankenstein you've created, so why don't you tell me about each of them?" he replied, bringing it back to the task at hand.

"This, Colonel, is the sole reason why the US Army is going to agree to purchase a few hundred if not a thousand of our quadpedal robots," Lauren responded as she picked up one of the modules.

Colonel Ribas held his tongue at the comment but motioned for Lauren to keep talking. Not only was Lauren easy on the eyes, but she was incredibly smart—something he found very attractive in a woman.

"This, Colonel, is the XD500B antidrone or ray gun model, dubbed 'Fly Swatter.' It fits over the back center of the Jackal and looks like this when deployed." Footage of the Jackal with the module attached appeared on the TV monitor near the table. The video showed the quadpedal robot moving through the woods with a squad of soldiers.

Lauren continued, "When the unit is deployed, the hexagonal antenna deploys, scanning the spectral system of the known radio and electronic bands a drone or UAV is operating on. If your squad is using drones of their own, then you'd program in their frequency, so they'd be marked as friendly. However, once the electronic sensor and mini-radar unit have detected an unknown or hostile drone, it activates the self-defense system, which in this case is a directional shortwave microwave—"

"Whoa, hold up there, Lauren," Colonel Ribas interrupted in a disbelieving tone. "Are you saying this thing fires off some sort of ray gun at the enemy drones?"

Lauren paused for a moment before she replied, "That's exactly what I'm saying. And this doesn't just jam the enemy drones. It fries their electronics, rendering them useless. But before you get your panties in a wad, keep in mind this isn't some super-long-range ray gun device that's going to fry enemy soldiers, drones, missiles, helicopters, and aircraft for miles away. This is an incredibly short-range, directionally limited weapon."

Another engineer accompanying Lauren spoke. "If I may, Colonel—rather than reinventing the wheel, as you Yanks say, we looked to some existing weapon technology that's already out there and tried to figure out if we might be able to leverage it." The man's Australian accent was very obvious.

"OK, you've piqued my interest. Now tell me why this isn't a load of crap and a huge waste of my time," Ribas countered skeptically. The last thing he wanted to do was chase down immature technology that wasn't ready for prime time yet. His job was to acquire the latest and greatest technology and weapons to win the war they found themselves in—not finance a bunch of PhD pie-in-the-sky wizardry for the next war.

"Sure thing, mate. In the early 2010s, the Air Force research laboratory, more specifically the Directed Energy Directorate at Kirtland Air Force Base, had developed something called the Counter-electronics High Power Microwave Advanced Missile Project or CHAMPs. It's a highly classified program we were unable to gain entry to, but we looked at what they were doing and came to the conclusion we could miniaturize what they had created to make it work for our purposes."

"Does it actually work?" asked Colonel Ribas. He was surprised they knew about the CHAMPs program. Then again, the university they were affiliated with had strong ties to the Air Force. In a way, he was surprised CHAMPs hadn't been used in the Cuba campaign against the Chinese SAMs. He suspected the powers that be were saving it for the coming fight in Venezuela.

The Australian man smiled. "Oh, it works, Colonel. As a matter of fact, if an enemy drone or even a helicopter or low-flying aircraft comes within a two-kilometer radius of Jackal, this thing here fires a microwave burst that fries its electronics." The engineer pointed to a hexagonal panel mounted on a swiveling base plate.

"This piece here, this is the weapon. Because this thing works as a directional weapon, it just needs to be pointed at roughly a forty-five-degree angle toward the drone or drones it's being fired at to fry their electronics. We've tested this thing—it's been successful in zapping slow lumbering scout or surveillance drones as well as outright high-speed, highly maneuverable racing drones. The onboard targeting computer is able to distinguish which drone poses the most immediate threat and takes that drone out first. In our targeting tests, the Jackal was able to track and destroy more than thirty targets at the same time."

Colonel Ribas shook his head in amazement. "That is unbelievable. I'd like to see this module run through a few tests, but I think this alone would make purchasing these Jackals worth it. I read just the other day about an attack by Chinese Special Forces on one of our Army Ranger teams by some new types of kamikaze drone. God only knows what the Chinese have waiting for us in Venezuela."

Lauren and her partner nodded in agreement. They walked the colonel over to the next module, which they called the XD500C or "the Beast."

"This other module provides a squad or platoon with a level of firepower unheard of before," Lauren began. "When deployed, the rear housing unit opens to reveal a short rotary five-barreled .338 Norma Magnum gun. Unlike the Army's current .338 NM rifle, ours makes use of a liquid propellant, which cuts down on weight and increases the number of rounds it can carry. So instead of being limited to carrying maybe a thousand to fifteen hundred rounds in a continuous belt, it now carries a rotary drum with *just* the projectiles. When the round enters the chamber, a precise amount of liquid propellant is injected into the chamber and then is fired. This revolutionary way of firing means this module can carry some ten thousand projectiles in an easy-to-swap-out box. The liquid propellant is also easy to change out and is good to go for roughly ten thousand two hundred projectiles, so we'd recommend just changing it out at the same time you'd replace the projectile box."

Before the colonel could start to barrage her with questions, Lauren further explained, "Why this module is just as important as the drone module and likely has more functionality or use for the Army is this— on top of the gun is a sophisticated targeting computer that can track the heat signature or movement of individuals up to nearly a mile out. More than that, the computer knows precisely how many rounds to fire to score a hit on a moving target instead of wasting ammo. It can also be configured to go after incoming missiles, mortar, or artillery shells, giving the infantry soldiers an unparalleled ability to fight and defend themselves against threats for decades to come. Once you integrate the BlueForce tracker chips from the soldiers, you'll also reduce the likelihood of a friendly-fire situation."

Ribas interjected, "Lauren, maybe you can give me a situation in which you think this could be used."

Smiling at the opportunity, Lauren explained, "In Cuba or in El Salvador, if a squad or platoon suddenly found themselves in an ambush, all they'd have to do is tell the Jackal to take over. In its defensive mode, it'll anchor itself into a firing position and deploy both its targeting radar and its main gun, laying down an impressive volume of accurate suppressive fire. In an offensive mode, the unit can fire on the move as the squads advance or look to take out an enemy gun bunker or fortified position on its own without having to put the lives of US soldiers in harm's way. With ten thousand rounds of ammunition on board, this thing can rock and roll for quite some time."

Lauren then walked them over to the next module. "That brings us to the XD500D, 'the Sentinel.' This module is intended to turn the Jackal into a tank killer. Instead of the .338 NM rotary gun, it's equipped with a single-barreled 30mm liquid propellant antitank round. By using a liquid propellant, the Sentinel is able to carry three hundred and twenty projectiles. And before you ask me how it handles the recoil—when the gun is preparing to fire, the Jackal's quadpedal legs penetrate several inches into the ground and adjust its shock absorbers to mitigate the recoil. If we use the standard depleted-uranium-tipped projectiles, then the Sentinel should have the same hitting power as the A-10 Warthog's chin gun, only the Jackal will rely more on precision shots than volume hits like the A-10."

Colonel Ribas whistled. Lauren was talking his language: bullets, projectile speed, armor penetration, and killer robots.

Lauren cleared her throat. "Colonel, if you deployed five of these robots—two Fly Swatters, two Beasts, and a single Sentinel—with a company of soldiers, that unit would be able to fight so far above its weight class, it wouldn't be funny. A single company could hit with the same level of firepower as a battalion. They could operate with impunity against enemy drones, and they'd be able to lay down an impressive volume of fire while still staying on the move. In short, the Jackal is the ultimate infantry weapon. The only question our company would like to ask, Colonel, is how many units does the Army want? And the only question you should be asking us is how soon can we start delivering them?"

Colonel Ribas stifled a laugh at her bluntness. He liked that. He also knew she was right. They desperately needed this drone *now*—not in a year or two, but right now.

"OK, Lauren. What's this thing going to cost the Army? How many do you have on hand that can be deployed? And how fast can you produce them?"

Now it was Lauren's turn to smile. Her Australian counterpart handed her a tablet, presumably with the information he'd just requested on it.

"Like anything, Colonel, the cost of each unit goes down based on the number of units purchased. A single individual unit is nine million dollars. From ten to one hundred units, the price drops to seven million apiece. For orders above one hundred, the unit price levels out at five million. The antidrone module is a twenty-one-million-dollar upgrade, the Beast module is nine million, and the antitank module is seven million. As to units on hand, we have ten units with ten of each module. They can readily be swapped out, depending on the unit's mission."

She scrolled on the tablet for some different information. "As I said earlier, we control the entire acquisition and production line at our facility near Tampa. We can ramp up production to seventy units a month. We could probably double that number, but it would take us at least four or five months, so we'd need a firm contract in hand for at least five thousand units if you wanted us to double our factory capacity."

"Tell you what, Lauren—let's arrange a live-fire demonstration on Friday. I want to test all these modules. If they can do what you say they can do, I think you'll get your first DoD contract."

Chapter Thirteen
The Gator Brigade

April 1, 2025
116th Field Artillery Regiment
Camp Blanding, Florida

Newly promoted Staff Sergeant Rob Fortney stood in a loose formation with the rest of the Bravo Battery, 3rd Battalion, when their battalion commander took the stage. He didn't call them to attention; instead, he had them form a large semicircle around him.

"Morning, everyone. I know the rumor mill has been in overdrive about the future of our battalion now that all our units have returned from Cuba," Lieutenant Colonel Rathmore began.

Fortney looked around and saw a lot of uncertain looks on everyone's faces. All but one of the HIMARS trucks in his battery had been destroyed during an enemy counterbattery fire in the Keys. Then A Battery had lost half their HIMARS trucks during a Chinese counterattack outside of the port city of Mariel on the eighth day of the invasion. The two batteries had essentially merged after that, waiting until either replacement equipment and soldiers arrived or they were reclassed into something new.

"First, I want to put to bed the speculations that we're being converted to an infantry unit or will be filtered in as infantry replacements to 124th Infantry Battalion," Rathmore continued. Fortney heard audible sighs of relief from many of the artillerymen around him. "The few HIMARS trucks in the reserve depots are being slated for the active-duty units. However, our battalion has been selected to receive the Army's newest M1299 extended-range howitzer. Sticking to tradition, it's officially the M1299 Paladin now. It has the same basic chassis with an improved power plant for speed and maneuverability and an upgraded turret, featuring an autoloading system. What that means is instead of the standard gun crew of seven, it's been automated down to just the driver, gunner, and commander. It's essentially the same number of crewmen as we're used to operating with on the HIMARS."

A number of the soldiers around Fortney nodded in approval. This new artillery system was all the rage in the artillery world. The barrel was forty-nine percent longer than the previous Paladin version, but this bad boy could hit targets as far away as one hundred kilometers using a rocket-assisted shell. The standard range with the improved supercharged propellant was now sixty-five kilometers, double what the current Paladins could hit. If their unit wasn't going to receive any new HIMARS replacement trucks, then this was an exceptional transition.

"So, here's the deal with the new guns—there's going to be a bit of a reorganization," Rathmore announced. Fortney could feel the sudden tension in the room. "Our battalion is being disbanded and folded into 2nd Battalion as part of the 53rd Infantry Brigade combat team. A and B Batteries are now going to become Charlie and Delta Batteries of the 2nd Battalion, 116th Field Artillery Regiment. The transition is going to be immediate. Tomorrow morning, we have the official retirement ceremony for the battalion and the change of command to the new battalion. I'm going to be staying on as the battalion commander of the reorganized unit. Aside from that, not much else is going to change.

"On Wednesday, we begin orientation on the new guns. Monday, we conduct our first live fire. We'll spend the week learning the new system and getting qualified on it. The following week, our new equipment will be sent to the port to deploy with the rest of the brigade forming up in Colombia." Several of the guys hooted and hollered. They were eager to spend some time hanging out in the South American country. "Once we reconstitute with our equipment in Colombia, we'll likely conduct some maneuver and live fire training with the rest of the brigade. Most of their units have already left Cuba and headed to Colombia."

Fortney knew why there was so much enthusiasm about their new assignment: beautiful women, cheap booze, and amazing beaches. Of course, it also meant they'd be thrown right back into the meat grinder of the next campaign, but at least they'd have some time in Colombia before that happened.

Regaining everyone's attention, Lieutenant Colonel Rathmore put out some additional information and then dismissed everyone to their platoons. They had a lot of things to get ready for tomorrow's ceremony and then their new unit.

"So how about them apples, Fortney?" Specialist Tony Davis asked jovially. "Looks like we avoided the infantry." Davis had not been happy at the prospect of being reclassed to 11Bravo, the infantry MOS.

"I'm just glad we're staying in artillery," Fortney replied. "I heard the fighting amongst the infantry has been tough. Plus, this new gun system sounds awesome. Apparently, this new barrel and supercharged propellant can throw a ninety-five-pound projectile more than twice the distance of our standard M26 rockets. I mean, that's incredible if you ask me."

Fortney and his guys talked a bit more as they went about some of their tasks for the day.

The rest of the week went by in a blur. They were introduced to their new equipment, received the final batch of replacement soldiers, and prepared themselves for the following week of live-fire training and certification. A lot of the functions on the new system had been automated—this reduced both the number of soldiers it took to effectively operate the gun system and the training time to learn how to use it.

One of the cool new features Fortney liked about the upgraded Paladin was its ability to function in a GPS-denied area. No one knew how much longer the GPS system would stay operational, given the current world situation. Having a weapons platform that could work without it gave them a lot more options.

****

Sitting in the barracks dayroom one evening, Fortney was reading a book on his Kindle when he heard something on the news that caught his attention:

"In an unprecedented agreement, the leaders of the Democratic party have agreed to a historic overhaul of the Social Security program with Republican lawmakers in exchange for a massive one-time student loan forgiveness bailout. Lawmakers on both sides said they had put safeguards in place to make sure students could never be placed into this kind of debt in the future.

"University officials decried the reform, insisting that it would deny future students the ability to attend universities of their choice or pursue their passions. Similarly, AARP has decried the overhaul of the Social Security program, saying it would move the goalpost for millions of Americans who were set to start drawing their benefits. The administration insists these were needed structural changes that had to happen to shore the program up in light of a second COVID virus in four years.

"The nonpartisan Congressional Budget Office or CBO says these two economic overhauls will save the government more than six hundred billion annually, a necessary step in righting the federal government's finances as it seeks to ramp up defense spending to meet the demands of this new global war."

When the announcement concluded, Specialist Tony Davis took a long swig of his Mike's Hard Lemonade. "Oh man, my brother is going to be pissed," he commented.

The channel then returned to a new episode of *Shark Tank*, where one of the aspiring entrepreneurs had to make a choice between a licensing deal with Kevin O'Leary or a forty percent stake in his company with Mark Cuban.

Fortney placed his Kindle down. "Your brother is going to be mad about the deal they just struck in Washington?" he asked.

Davis nodded and then finished off the rest of his beverage. "Yeah, he's a lawyer in Tampa. He's been slaving away at an ambulance-chasing law firm for the last eight years to get his law degree paid off. He finally paid the last of his loans at the start of this last pandemic."

Fortney shrugged. "I know my sisters will both be happy. Sarah is a teacher over in Bartow, and Paulina, my oldest sibling, just finished her residency at Tampa General. She owes a fortune, so I'm sure she'll be excited about this."

A minute later, Lieutenant Colonel Rathmore walked into the dayroom wearing a Grunt Style T-shirt and some shorts. He had a bottle of water with him as he took a seat on one of the free chairs.

"Ah, *Shark Tank*. One of my favorite shows," he commented.

"Yeah, I like it too," Specialist Davis agreed. "I've gotten so many different business ideas from watching this show it's not even funny."

"Oh, yeah? That's cool. Tell me about one of them," said one of the other soldiers.

If they weren't a National Guard unit, it would be almost unheard of for a lieutenant colonel to sit in the dayroom and just watch an episode of *Shark Tank* with some of his gun crews. But the Guard was made up of citizen soldiers. They still wore ranks and maintained basic military discipline, but it wasn't uncommon for the enlisted and officers to interact a lot more freely than they did on active duty.

"Well, prior to the pandemic back in '20, I had an idea about a grocery delivery service," Davis started to explain.

"Ah, it sounds like you got beat on that idea," Fortney commented.

"Kind of. My idea wasn't so much a grocery delivery service to homes—mine was for assisted living care facilities and nursing homes," Davis explained. "When my grandma was living in one in New York, she used to complain to me about how the little store at the facility never carried what she wanted, and she didn't have a car, so she couldn't drive and get what she needed. That got me to thinking—what if I created a kiosk at the place, or we provided a tablet with our app on it to the facility and the residents could tell us what they wanted and we'd make a delivery, say two or three times a week?"

Colonel Rathmore put his water bottle down and sat up as he intently listened to the idea. His sudden attentiveness hadn't gone unnoticed by the others watching *Shark Tank*.

"So, what'd you do with the idea? Did you ever get it going?" another soldier asked.

"I tried to. We started development on the app and were trying to figure out our business model, but then COVID hit, and suddenly everything ground to a halt. I tried to get my partner to move forward on the idea with me—we were so close to having it done, and then he got diagnosed with cancer and died less than two months later."

"You couldn't keep it going without him?" Rathmore asked as he took a drink from his water.

Davis shrugged. "I tried. I just didn't have the technical chops to make it work on my own. I ended up going into the insurance business with my dad and my brother instead."

"Ah, that's too bad. That sounded like a good idea. I suppose if you're happy with your dad's business, then that's all that matters, right?" Rathmore offered.

When Davis was done explaining his business idea, Fortney saw his chance to ask their battalion commander a question in a nonformal environment. He might be in the National Guard now, but four years on active duty still made him feel awkward hanging out with his commander like this.

"Sir, maybe you can't tell us this or maybe you don't know, but what's this war about?" Fortney asked cautiously. "I mean, I don't think anyone knows or understands why we're fighting."

"We're fighting because the Chinese attacked us," chided one of the other soldiers angrily.

"I get that, but why did they attack us?" Fortney shot back. "What caused this war to start in the first place?" There was a bit more heat to his words than he probably intended.

Rathmore put his bottle of water down. All the guys in the dayroom were now looking to him to see what he'd say. He was their leader, their battalion commander, so his words carried some weight.

"Rob, you've asked a question a lot of people are also asking. I'd like to say it's something simple, but the truth is often much more complicated than that. Sometimes it's just a matter of the two toughest kids on the block getting into a shouting match that eventually turns into a fistfight.

"What I do know is this: the Chinese have unleashed a pandemic on the world that's responsible for the deaths of tens of millions worldwide. They've attacked our nation. What I want each and every one of you to remember is that, regardless of why or how this war started, it's here. We now have to do what's necessary to win this war. The defense of our nation, of our way of life and the kind of future our kids and families will live under, now rests on our shoulders. Know that I and the rest of the battalion leadership are here for you. We care for you, and we'll do everything we can to bring each and every one of you back home."

Everyone in the room nodded, though no one said anything.

Rathmore grabbed his water bottle and left the room, but not before telling them that tomorrow morning, a local IHOP was going to cater in breakfast for the battalion. It was their way of giving them a nice send-off before they left Camp Blanding. On Saturday, they'd start their five-day R&R before everyone had to report to MacDill AFB, where they'd board a flight to head down to Villavicencio, Colombia.

****

Phenix City, Alabama

It was Wednesday morning as Amos Dekker stretched his body under the covers of his king-sized bed. His Boll & Branch sheets always made him want to stay in bed longer—sometimes it was hard to return to the land of the living. Looking to his right, he saw that his wife, Lindsay, was still asleep. The clock on the side of their bed said 05:43 a.m. That meant they still had two hours and seventeen minutes until eight a.m., when her mother would be stopping by with their three little munchkins.

179

Lindsay's parents lived nearby, and they had decided to take the kids for the night. This way the two of them could have an evening alone together. Amos had been gone for nearly four months, and God only knew how long he'd be gone again once his unit redeployed. Amos was pretty sure the only reason they had come back to Benning was because of the high number of casualties they'd taken. Most of his platoon and company were still recovering from the blast of those drones just over a week ago.

Amos found it hard to believe that nine days ago, he'd been lying in ambush in Honduras in a heavy firefight, and now he was lying in his own bed. It felt like a lifetime ago; it also felt like it was just the other day. The longer he stayed in the Rangers, the harder it was making these strange adjustments between combat and the normalcy of daily life back home.

Not wanting to disturb Lindsay right away, Amos walked into the bathroom and began the process of getting ready. After a methodical shave, he climbed in the shower to allow the hot water to massage his aching muscles. While he was soaping up, his amazingly beautiful wife climbed in. He immediately felt himself rising to the occasion as the water ran down her body. Twenty minutes later, they turned the water off and started to get dried off and dressed.

Later, as he sat at the table in the kitchen listening to the morning news, Lindsay got a pot of coffee going.

"The FBI raided a home in Kentucky they believe was being used as some sort of safe house by Chinese Special Forces units," said a talking head from MSNBC. "A large gunfight ensued, leaving five agents dead and at least a dozen more injured. The FBI said they recovered two prisoners from the safe house, along with what they're hailing as a treasure trove of information. Twelve Chinese soldiers were reported killed during the shoot-out."

Huh, so that's what Alpha Company's been up to, Amos thought.

"Sources within the Department of Homeland Security have said this brings the number of Chinese soldiers captured or killed on US soil to over one hundred and forty-eight. The Director of DHS reports that his office, the FBI, and the rest of the interagency remain optimistic about finding and rooting out the remaining saboteur networks within the US."

"Wow, that's crazy," Amos remarked. "No wonder none of my friends from the other company have replied to my emails. They've been just as busy as we have."

Amos switched the channel over to BBC International. He liked getting his news from multiple different sources.

"Tensions continue to heat up between the Russian Federation and the People's Republic of China," announced the British news anchor. "The Russian President has accused the Chinese of intentionally unleashing the COVID-24 virus on the Russian Far East in an attempt to destabilize the region and wipe out the native Russians living there. Government sources have said one in four Russian citizens have died from the virus since its arrival. Meanwhile, Chinese immigrants living in the region are complaining of harsh treatment by the Russian government and pleading with their own government to intervene on their behalf.

"The Russian Ministry of Defense has reportedly deployed the 49th Army out of Stavropol and Maykop from their southern military district, and the entire 1st Guard Tank Army, along with 45th Guards Spetsnaz Brigade and the 76th Guards Air Assault Division, have been directed to their bases in the Far East. This is being seen as a major provocation by the Russians toward the Chinese.

"The Russian President released the following statement: 'The people of Russia have suffered enough at the hands of the Chinese. If they wish to avoid a conflict with Russia, then China needs to withdraw their forces from our borders and agree to pay monetary damages caused by the virus they knowingly unleashed on Russia. Their inoculation of their own citizens with a vaccine prior to the arrival of the COVID virus is tantamount to war and proof they knew this was coming.'

"Chinese President Yao Jintao denounced this overt act of aggression by the Russians and said that despite his nation's current war with NATO, China would repel any military incursion by the Russians."

"Whoa, I guess a lot has been going on back here at home since I've been gone," Amos said. "I think that little segment just gave me more news and information than I've had in the last three months." His wife brought him a cup of coffee, black and bitter, just the way he liked it.

"Yeah, I guess so," Lindsay replied as she sat down on his leg, blocking his view of the TV.

Moving his head around her body, he looked at the clock on the microwave. It read 7:28 a.m. "You know, that clock says we still have thirty-two minutes before we have visitors."

Lindsay had a mischievous look spread across her face as she placed her cup of coffee down.

Amos was in the process of forgetting about everything going on in the world around him when his alert phone suddenly chirped. He ignored the first two rings, but when the phone started vibrating in addition to chirping, he finally relented. The damn thing rang two more times before he finally reached over and growled at whoever was on the other end.

"Dekker. This had better be good."

"Dekker, this is Meacham. I know we're supposed to be off until Monday, but I need you to come in Friday morning. There's something new going on and they want our take on it," Captain Meacham explained.

Lindsay climbed off him and headed back to their bedroom to get cleaned up before the kids and her mother arrived.

"Got it. Any word on what it might be?"

"Something to do with drones, but they wouldn't tell me what else."

Amos grunted. "Fine, I'll see you Friday. Nothing personal, but the kids are due back at the house in the next ten minutes, and I need to get a few things ready."

Dekker hung up the phone and scurried off to the bedroom to get some pants back on and get ready to see his kids. It had been nearly four months since the entire family had had breakfast together and they planned on making this first breakfast a memorable one.

****

Friday morning had arrived, and Dekker approached the main gate. He had his ID card out, waiting for the guard to check it. Once he'd been scanned into the base, he headed off toward the Ranger training brigade building, like he'd been told.

When he pulled into the parking lot, Dekker noticed a handful of vans and some small trucks parked there as well. They weren't military—they appeared to be some sort of civilian group that was joining them.

When Dekker walked into the main training room, he saw Meacham waiting there for him along with some of the other senior

NCOs and officers. As the group of soldiers milled about, a colonel walked out to greet them. He was flanked by a handful of civilians. Dekker immediately recognized one of them and his heart skipped a beat.

Oh, this is going to be good.

"Good morning," the colonel announced. "My name is Colonel Rafael Ribas. I'm the officer in charge of the Maneuver Center of Excellence acquisition program. What some or most of you may not know is it's my department that acquires the fun toys your units get to use in the field. To that end, I wanted to introduce you to a new tool we're considering. We want your honest feedback on whether this is a viable and practical tool that will make a difference to your units in the field."

Colonel Ribas introduced the three civilians and who they worked for. The most recognizable person they saw was the owner of SpaceX, which meant whatever they were about to be shown was going to be pretty unconventional. To the entrepreneurial magnate's credit, he stepped aside and let the two other folks explain exactly what it was.

"My name is Lauren Heigl and this is my partner and senior engineer, Daniel Malloy. Our company, the Institute for Human and Machine Cognition or IHMC, is a subsidiary of SpaceX, hence why our owner is here with us. We had been looking to create a quadpedal worker to help with our eventual Mars mission. However, when the war broke out last year, we asked ourselves how we could help our country in its greatest hour of need. This is when we looked at our existing prototype, the Jackal, and reconfigured it to meet a request for proposal the Army submitted."

This announcement caused a lot of people to smile. They hadn't even seen what this new thing was, but they were already excited about it.

"To that end, I want to introduce you to the Jackal XD500 and then some of the modules that can accompany it. It's our opinion that this tool will revolutionize the future of warfare and give you all a competitive advantage in fighting the Chinese."

As Lauren was speaking, the Jackal made its debut, walking out of the building and to a testing field they were all facing. As the quadpedal machine approached, some people audibly gasped; some just looked on in shock. As Lauren spoke, Daniel ran the Jackal through a series of tests and demonstrations. Then they told the soldiers about the modules that could be added to the Jackal, making it far more than just a pack mule for the infantry. Daniel and three other assistants demonstrated how quickly the different modules could be swapped out on the machine.

The biggest piece of technology that caught the Rangers' attention was the antidrone module, the Fly Swatter, especially considering they'd just returned from a mission where they'd nearly been obliterated by a drone. A couple of standard drones were flown a couple hundred meters in front of the Jackal, and then suddenly they fell from the sky like a puppet string had been cut. Then a super-fast agile racing drone nosedived into the dirt. The soldiers sitting in the bleachers were simply amazed.

Nearing the end of the demonstration, the owner of SpaceX walked up to the front of the crowd and stood next to Lauren. He then took the mic from her. He made eye contact with Amos Dekker and pointed to him. "Excuse me for not recognizing your rank, Dekker, but if you'd had the Jackal with you on your last mission in any of its configurations, would it have made a profound impact for the good of your men and your mission?" he asked.

Damn, talk about being put on the spot, Amos thought. Nearly a dozen generals of different grades along with a slew of Special Forces officers all looked at him for his response.

Dekker stood. "If we'd had either this Jackal Fly Swatter or Jackal Beast—yes, it would have saved a number of people's lives, no question," he answered confidently. Then he sat down and hoped he hadn't shot himself in the foot by being honest.

The owner of SpaceX nodded and announced that if the military wanted him to produce these unmanned combat vehicles or UCVs, then he would retool his company's production lines to focus on building these tools of war.

The demonstration ended and everyone was welcomed inside the warehouse next door to look at the Jackals up close and ask any further technical questions they might have. It was clear to Dekker that the way wars were being fought was rapidly changing and getting a lot scarier. He couldn't help but feel like they were inching closer and closer to fielding Terminators like the ones from the movie franchise.

When Dekker showed up to work on Monday, Captain Meacham told him their company was going to run the Jackal through its paces there at Fort Benning while they took some much-needed downtime and waited to receive replacements to bring them back to one hundred percent. For the men of Bravo Company, this was a welcomed assignment—more time with their families and a chance to test something new that might actually change the outcome of the war.

Chapter Fourteen
R&R

La Libertad, El Salvador

The waves gently crashed against the seawall as the sun neared its zenith. Fishermen were starting to arrive at the pier, bringing the catches of the day to the large seafood market nearby. As the fish arrived, locals walked up to grab first pick of what had been caught.

Lieutenant Branham grabbed four of the privates in the platoon and motioned with his head for them to follow him as he walked up toward a group of fishermen. He then pulled out a few twenty-dollar bills and waved them in the air to get their attention. His tactic perhaps worked better than expected because he soon had the best catches of the day being shoved in his face. Despite his horrible Spanish, Branham managed to barter his way to nabbing a dozen of the largest sea bass most of them had ever seen. Once he had them in hand, he and his men returned to the rest of the platoon, holding them up with pride like they had just scored the deal of the century.

As they approached the set of tables and chairs the platoon had camped out on, Sergeant Lakers asked jovially, "What exactly are you going to do with all that fish, LT?"

"I know what he's going to do. He's going to get one of those little restaurants over there to cook us up some of the best sea bass any of you bastards have ever had," countered Staff Sergeant Peters with an approving smile.

"Hey, if we only have twenty-four hours to cool our heels in this little piece of paradise, then we're going to make the most of it—good food, good beers, and just enjoying the moment," Branham said to the cheers of his soldiers.

When Branham brought the fish to one of the local chefs, Sergeant Peters joined him near the cook station. He was clearly amused listening to Branham butcher his way through explaining how he wanted the fish he'd just brought over cooked.

"That was really nice of you to get lunch for everyone, LT," Peters commented, holding back any criticism of his poor Spanish skills.

"It's the least I can do for them. It's been a tough month. I don't suspect it'll get any easier going forward."

"Any word on when we're getting some replacements?" asked Peters. "We barely have enough guys to fill out two rifle squads, let alone a platoon."

Turning around so he could face the sea, Branham sighed deeply before turning to look at his de facto platoon sergeant. "Tomorrow, when the trucks come and pick us up to head back to San Luis Talpa, we're supposed to re-form back up with the entire battalion. We'll be moving as a unit back to Colombia to meet up with our new replacements. What happens beyond that is anyone's guess. But my gut tells me we'll likely do some R&R rotations back home before we start some sort of train-up prior to moving on Venezuela."

Peters nodded. He'd been in the Army long enough to know the game—hurry from one location to another, only to get there and end up sitting on their hands while they waited for someone to make the next decision. If it was one thing the Army was good at, it was "hurry up and wait."

"You know, if it's possible, sir, I'd like to rotate a few of the guys through the combat stress clinic if they have one once we get to wherever we're going. Two of the guys in particular look like they need the help.

I know they won't ask for it, but you can tell they're really struggling with what's going on."

"Let me guess—Private Ailes and Specialist Sabo?"

"For a butter bar, you're pretty perceptive," Peters joked. "What gave it away for you?"

"When I was in college, I majored in psychology. I'm actually two years into reading for my dissertation in clinical psychology. I've been doing a lot of research on post-traumatic stress disorder, studying how to identify it early on so it can be treated right away and not left unchecked."

Peters's left eyebrow rose. He hadn't really gotten to know Branham very well. He'd joined their company just a few weeks before the war had broken out, and it had been nonstop combat ever since. A lot of the bonds of friendship had been formed fast, centered around the desire to live. Not many of the NCOs had gotten to know the wave of new officers that had rotated into the company before the war.

Studying Branham, Peters offered, "Sir, it honestly sounds like Ailes, Sabo and the rest of the platoon might be better served talking with you than visiting the clinic. Like you, I know it's best to identify this stuff early on with the guys before it becomes a problem. I've seen many a good, solid soldier ruin their career, marriage, or life over not dealing with what's happened."

"How long have you been in the Army, Sergeant?" Branham asked. "No offense, but you look like you should be a first sergeant or master sergeant by now."

"I did a stint on active duty, then got out and was in the Guard for a few years," Peters explained. "I struggled with PTSD myself for a good while. Lost my first marriage to it before I finally sought some help. I eventually decided to go back to active duty again five years ago. Of course, I had to start over with time in grade as an E-5. All told, I have eleven years toward retirement and fifteen years toward time in service for pay. I have no doubt I'll be a first sergeant or sergeant major one day. I just need to do my time."

"I thought there was a little more to the story with you," Branham countered, smiling. "The soldiers think you're kind of a hardass. Now I think you're just trying to make sure they don't get themselves killed doing something stupid."

"I suppose I do come across as a hardass," Peters acknowledged with a shrug. "But like you said, these soldiers are just kids. I'm thirty-three—they're eighteen, maybe nineteen. They don't know what they don't know. If riding them hard during training or out on patrol keeps them alive long enough to learn, then I'm fine with them thinking I'm a crotchety old sergeant. These guys have their whole lives ahead of them. I just want to make sure they have the opportunity to live it."

Patting him on the shoulder, Branham said, "Peters, for what it's worth, I think you're a hell of a sergeant. I know I don't have as many years in the military as you, but you're a lot wiser than most of the NCOs I've met up to this point."

"Well, the feeling's mutual, sir," Peters responded, laughing good-naturedly. "You're probably one of the oldest butter bars I've met. For someone new to the Army, you've done a hell of a job leading. Especially during that crappy QRF mission to go fetch that ODA team— wow, what a cluster mess that turned out to be. I honestly didn't think any of us were going to make it out of that jungle. I think if it was just us and we didn't have those Special Forces guys with us to help us through, we'd likely have all died back there."

Branham nodded his head at the memory of that battle—one of a few they'd fought together. "That Captain Meacham, the team leader—

he actually put a few guys in our platoon in for some awards. I heard battalion had approved. I didn't want to mention anything yet, not until I knew it was official."

"Well, if you ask me, sir, I think everyone earned an award for that mission," Peters remarked. "By the way, did my own recommendations for promotions and awards get approved?" he asked.

"They did. I'm not sure if they'll be given when we re-form at the airport tomorrow, or if they'll present them when we get to Colombia," Branham replied. "You know, I heard that shop over there," he said, pointing to a small liquor store, "supposedly sells kegs. Why don't you walk over with me and we'll grab one for the guys? I'd rather they all get drunk and hang out together than go off and get in some sort of trouble on their own. I think we're good to occupy those tables for the rest of the day."

The rest of the day went by in a blur. The soldiers ate their fill of the best seafood and fresh grub they'd eaten in months. Some swam in the water, some lay out in the sun; most just sat around nursing a beer or two and talked.

Lieutenant Branham made it a point to talk privately with Ailes and Sabo. He wanted to make sure they were doing all right and offer them a few ways to help them cope with all that had been going on. For better or worse, this war appeared to just be getting started. They had a long time to go before things would return to normal. Branham might have only been a lieutenant, but he wanted to make sure he did all he could to take care of the soldiers placed in his care.

Chapter Fifteen
Bogotá Blues

Casa de Nariño
Bogotá, Colombia

Stepping off the Gulfstream, Blain Wilson found his ears and senses inundated with not just the sounds of a busy international airport but the thumping of helicopter blades and soldiers shouting various orders and commands. Leaving the cocoon of the Gulfstream and stepping onto the tarmac brought back a lot of memories of Iraq, perhaps more so here in Colombia than it had during his visits to Cuba. Maybe it was the rising temperature, maybe it was the sound of the helicopters—either way, it momentarily distracted him from the two military members calling out to him.

"Excuse me, Mr. Wilson, if you'll come this way," announced a captain, probably a protocol officer. He led Blain toward a waiting convoy of three up-armored Suburbans.

As they approached the vehicles, Blain saw the man he'd been hoping to see. "Gary, it's damn good to see you," he said. "How are things holding up?"

"Can't complain," General Gary Bridges replied, shaking Blain's hand. "How was the flight down?"

As soon as they piled into one of the SUVs, the convoy pulled out, headed toward the Colombian President's residence and working office. As the vehicles snaked their way around the airport toward one of the exits, General Bridges got Blain's attention. "Hey, heads-up. When you meet up with General Stavridis—he's been in a bit of a foul mood the last few days."

"Oh, what's going on?" Blain asked.

Blain and Gary had known each other for nearly thirty years. They'd served in Special Forces together before Blain had been injured in Iraq and forced into an early retirement.

"Let's just say we've been having a bit of trouble with some elements within our host nation. President Gustavo Márquez has been fighting an internal civil war with part of his government. There are elements within their Congress that have strong ties to various Chinese-owned firms, and there are others that don't want to turn Colombia into a battlefield. I hate to say it, but that failure to deploy those THAADs back in October really hurt us in the eyes of some of those politicians. As we drive to the meeting, you'll see some of the damage the capitol took from those ballistic missiles at the outset of the war. It really shook a lot of people up."

Blain sighed. He knew that that had been a political blunder from the previous administration. He had argued to move some THAAD and Patriot batteries to Colombia and Panama to help protect the most critical US allies in the region, but President Alton had gone with the Vice President's advice to keep the systems at home. During the first day of the war, the Chinese had hit several of the airfields the US had been using for counterdrug and surveillance operations in Colombia. For good measure, they'd also hit Bogotá with half a dozen missiles as a warning not to allow US forces to use their country.

"I know, Gary. You, Stavridis and I made the case," Blain reminded his friend. "Ultimately, we got overruled. Fortunately, we have a new President—one with some military experience that you and I happen to know personally."

"We sure do," General Bridges replied, grinning. "I haven't talked with her since she left the military, but I sure am glad she's in charge now."

"Putting all that aside, Gary, how are things shaping up?"

"I can only speak to the SOF side of the house. From our side of things, we're in better shape now than we were a few weeks ago. I'm finally able to pull nearly all my Green Berets and SEALs out of Cuba. I've had to leave a battalion and a SEAL team in El Salvador to continue with mop-up operations, but frankly, I need to get more of them in position down here before we kick off the invasion. They need to get cycled through some downtime as well. You can only run a team ragged like we've been doing for so many months."

Neither of them spoke for a few minutes. Blain knew all too well if they pushed people too hard, they were bound to break. They were barely four weeks away from the official invasion.

As they neared the presidential residency, there was a noticeable increase in security. The government had blocked all the roads for a full city block, making traffic a nightmare.

When they approached the entry control point, their convoy was waved through quickly. They drove down the deserted street until they came to the formal entrance to the residence. Once inside the building, Blain parted ways with Gary and headed to meet with President Gustavo Márquez and General Stavridis.

****

President Márquez seemed relieved—at least, that was the vibe Blain got when he finished conveying President Delgado's personal message to him. The two leaders had not met in person yet, something that had aggravated President Márquez, especially considering his country was being used as the springboard from which to invade Venezuela.

"Mr. Wilson, I do hope your president understands the precarious situation my country finds itself in," Márquez explained. "We are not only dealing with a political backlash for supporting you in this war and allowing your forces to base out of our country—we have now seen a resurgence of the FARC. We had hoped our peace deal with them back in 2017 would hold, but now it appears our Chinese friends across the border have reopened that wound. It's become a serious problem."

The Fuerzas Armadas Revolucionarias de Colombia or FARC was a Marxist revolutionary guerrilla group that had fought the Colombian government from 1964 until a peace accord had been reached to finally end the conflict. There had been a few small flare-ups since, but nothing like what had been taking place since the start of this new war between China and the West.

Blain leaned forward in his chair. "Mr. President, America understands the situation your country has been placed in. It is tragic that civilians end up getting caught up in these conflicts. President Delgado has asked me to convey the following: would you like our help in dealing with the FARC, and if so, how hard would you like us to press this action?"

President Márquez appeared to be weighing his options as he sat back in his chair. He reached for one of his signature cigars he was always seen smoking and relit it. He took a couple of puffs on it as he thought about the offer Blain had just presented. If Blain could read the facial expressions of the Colombian President's senior general, it appeared he wanted all the help he could get but didn't want to say something out of turn.

195

"You have presented an interesting proposal," said Márquez. "Right now, I am weighing the consequences of allowing your military to be unleashed on these domestic terrorists versus my own forces doing the job themselves. My biggest concern is that this could backfire on us if it is not handled correctly. I know the Chinese are funding them and they likely have Special Forces advisors and weaponry. The last thing we need is for the FARC movement to regain any semblance of public support. How do we convince the people that the FARC is being used as a propaganda tool by the Chinese to destabilize our country?" He held the cigar between his teeth as he waited for Blain's response.

Blain looked to his right. General Stavridis nodded. They had privately talked about this before the meeting and come up with a plan they thought Márquez would agree to and that President Delgado would authorize.

"These are tricky times we live in, Mr. President. Colombia is in a particularly tough bind. On the one hand, you have the Chinese trying to foment a popular uprising against your government while at the same time growing their influence and control over South and Central America. On the other hand, you have a growing NATO military presence in your country that not all your citizens are happy about. What if, instead of US forces leading the way in eradicating the FARC, General Stavridis provides your soldiers with unlimited intelligence and surveillance of these guerrilla forces? Furthermore, we could provide your forces with whatever kind of logistical support or weapons you may need. This way, the entire operation will have a Colombian face to it," Blain offered.

President Márquez smiled slightly. "I think that could work," he replied. "But what if we also had some of your Spanish-speaking Special Forces soldiers dress as Colombian Special Forces and assist our units directly in taking down the FARC leaders and some of the enemy base camps? It's not that I don't think my military isn't up to the task—your soldiers just happen to be substantially better-trained killers. Do you think something like that could be arranged?"

Blain grinned. "I don't see why not."

"Excellent. Then I think we have addressed the number one problem between our nations. Now onto the next most pressing matter. The Venezuelans and Chinese have been stepping up their air attacks the last four weeks. A few aircraft dart in fast at near treetop level to hit an airport or bomb a bridge, power plant, or distribution center. Many times, our aircraft don't know we've had a flight intrusion until it's too late or we don't have enough aircraft to cover down on everything.

"Also, and this is a big one—the Chinese have small units stationed all along the border. In many cases, these small units will blow up a bridge as far as forty kilometers inside our borders. They'll either do it with a small incursion of soldiers or hit us with artillery or mortar attacks. This has to stop, Mr. Wilson. I can't tell everyone and every business within forty kilometers of the border to move inland. Our army has limited capability in this area. I need your military to be more involved in this," President Márquez practically pled with Blain.

Turning to Stavridis, Blain asked, "General, any reason why your forces can't go after this?"

Sighing, the general countered with three letters: "ROE. I need the Pentagon to change the rules of engagement to allow us to get more aggressive in this area. As it stands, we can't return fire in more than ninety-five percent of these cross-border attacks. If you can get the ROE loosened up, we can put a quick stop to this."

Blain shook his head in frustration. "I'll handle this personally when we leave. Either they'll change the ROE before the end of the day,

197

or I'll call the President and have her demand they be changed. This is bull, and I'm not going to stand for it."

President Márquez seemed pleased by the response. He stood and offered his hand. "Mr. Wilson, thank you for flying down here to meet with me personally and convey your President's offer. Please tell her I am pleased with America's continued support and help. My nation looks forward to working with the United States to restore order and democracy to South America."

****

When the meeting ended, Blain followed General Stavridis back to his headquarters building. They had essentially set up US Southern Command's forward headquarters a couple of miles northwest of the international airport. It placed the headquarters near the airport and close to the capitol for coordination purposes. The US and NATO forces were intentionally trying to keep their footprint around the capitol as small as they could to minimize the likelihood of it becoming a primary target.

For the time being, the airport and surrounding areas were largely being used as a logistics hub to ferry in soldiers and material from the States before they'd be dispersed up to the DMZ or the rapidly growing southern front. NATO was looking at a three-pronged ground invasion once things officially got underway.

When it was just the two of them alone in the general's office, Stavridis cut to the chase. "Mr. Wilson, I know the President wants to start this invasion on June first, but here's the deal—until Isla Margarita and some of the surrounding islands are captured, we're not going to be able to open a second front as quickly as Chairman Thiel has indicated. Without the capture of Isla Margarita, it's going to be impossible to leverage the 4th Marine Division as he's outlined."

"Why am I only hearing about this *now*?" Blain pressed. "Have you brought this up to Admiral Thiel? Because he hasn't brought up any issues with this during our weekly updates."

Stavridis sighed. "I have. The Chairman believes the Navy and the Marines will be ready to invade by the fifteenth of June. But if you ask me, I think we should flip the timeline—have them invade first, draw off the enemy, particularly their air assets. Then we invade from Colombia while they're busy trying to beat back the capture of Isla Margarita. To stop us from capturing the island, the Chinese are going to have to leverage a large portion of their limited air assets. That means not only will they have to battle through our air and Marine aviation elements supporting the invasion, but they'll also have to deal with the naval ships. I've heard our Ticos and Burkes have been nearly stripped of their Tomahawks and geared up for anti-air support. When the Chinese attack, we'll be ready and wipe 'em out."

Pausing for a second, the general walked up to the map on the side of the wall and pointed. "Once the Marines have captured Isla Margarita with, say, the 2nd Marine Division, it then frees up the 4th Division to invade Cumana and Barcelona just to the south and west. The capture of those two cities will give them a number of ports to bring ashore their heavy equipment and form up a solid attack force to put pressure on the enemy from the east. The Marines, leveraging the SEALs, Raider and Recon battalions, will be able to carry out all sorts of hit-and-run attacks along the coast."

The general then changed positions and pointed at the western side of the country. "While that's happening, we continue with the original plan," he explained. "III Corps hits the enemy along the western part of the country, looking to grab Maracaibo. However, the key to all of this is going to be the SEALs' ability to capture the Puente General Rafael

Urdaneta bridge intact and hold it until a relief force is able to arrive from 1st Cavalry or the 4th Infantry Division and relieve them. If they can hold that bridge, then it'll make capturing the entire western portion of the country significantly easier. Grabbing the major ports in the area will also be a huge boon to future operations for us as well."

Stavridis then moved his hand down along the map as he continued to explain. "The 1st Infantry Division is going to drive south to El Vigía, at the base of the Andes mountain range. This will prevent the Chinese divisions from moving off the mountain and looking to invade Colombia or get into our rear area. While that's going on, the 29th Division will hit San Cristobal and move to the southeast, positioning themselves on the opposite side of the Andes again, trapping the Chinese divisions that decided to make that their line of defense."

As Blain listened to the proposed plan, he rubbed the bridge of his nose. Studying the map of the region on the wall, he saw exactly what the general was talking about. "Let me guess—down in the south, that's where you want to use the XVIII Airborne Corps?" asked Blain. "Have them go right up the gut and nail Caracas that way?"

Stavridis smiled. "Exactly. My plan is to have the 82nd drop battalions from here, all the way along Route 19 and then north along Route 2 all the way to Los Teques and the back door to the capital."

Blain furrowed his brow. "Walk me through that further," he said. "You can use the 82nd to grab some airfields or strategic points, but you'll need more than that."

"Yes, you're right," Stavridis agreed. The goal is to have the 82nd grab the airfields. Then I'm going to have the Air Force turn those fields into giant gas stations. While they're doing that, the entire 3rd Infantry Division is going to move along Route 19 until it connects with Route 2. I anticipate that taking close to ten to fourteen days. As they near the final leg, where the 82nd will be, that's when I'm going to land my knockout blow. I'm going to have the entire 101st Division heliborne all the way to the gates of Caracas itself. They'll land along La Cachino, which straddles the mountains and Highway 1 with Mamera to their left, completely cutting off any exit out of the city.

"At that point, they'll just have to hold those two mountain passes until the 3rd ID is able to catch up. While that's happening, the 4th Marines will be closing in from the east and the 1st Armored Division and 1st Cavalry Division will be closing from the west. To top it off, we'll have the 2nd Marines leave Isla Margarita and land at Maiquetía, which will completely encircle the capital."

Stavridis puffed out his chest, as if in admiration of his own plan. "I know we'll run into hiccups along the way, but I believe this plan I outlined to you is hands down the fastest way to end this war in Venezuela."

Blain concurred. Then he looked at the calendar. "General, I don't doubt that your plan would work, but we're ten weeks away from kicking this invasion off. I think we're too far down that path to change course on strategies," he asserted. "This is very different from what the Joint Chiefs presented the President with and what she approved. If you had doubts about the plan, then why didn't you bring them up during the planning stages?"

"I tried. Several times, Mr. Wilson." The general looked frustrated. "I'm supposed to be the theater commander. This is my combatant command. Instead of being allowed to plan the war as I see fit, I'm having to implement invasion plans being given to me by the Pentagon and the Joint Staff. I'm being micromanaged at every level by Washington. Even the Secretary of Defense and several of his own lackeys are getting involved in telling me how I should array some of my forces or what we can attack and can't attack. Hell, you've seen how screwed up the rules of engagement are, and we haven't even invaded yet. You should see the list of targets that are off-limits for the Air Force to hit right now. I mean, we should be carrying out all sorts of air strikes in preparation for this invasion, but we aren't. I'm being told to conserve my aircraft and cruise missiles until right before the invasion kicks off."

Blain knew there were some challenges brewing at the Pentagon between the administration's new people, who were steadily being confirmed, and the previous administration's holdovers. And then there was the permanent bureaucracy within the building. It was a constant tug-of-war between the three factions that didn't always align as one might think.

"General, I fly back to D.C. in three days. If I bring this up to the President and she agrees to override the current plan in favor of what you just proposed, would this shift our timeline?"

"Mr. Wilson, if you can get the President to allow me to run the war within my own COCOM, I can get things shifted around to keep the current timeline. I also believe that if we hit the enemy fast and hard like I just proposed, we may be able to end major combat operations before the end of the year. Then our military efforts can shift to support our allies in the Pacific."

After looking up at the ceiling for a moment, considering the situation, Blain finally made eye contact with Stavridis. "What does Gary think about this plan?"

The general almost seemed surprised by the question. "You can ask him yourself, but he'll tell you he thinks this is a far better plan than what D.C. is trying to have shoehorned into place."

"OK, you've made your case. Let me talk it over with the President, present your plan. Then I'll grill the Joint Staff on why they opted to send you a different proposal than what you had originally submitted. I'm not a big fan of Washington generals trying to manage a war they aren't actually involved in fighting, either."

Chapter Sixteen
Three Options

Venezuelan Military Base
South of Caracas

"I don't like these choices," asserted Adán Chávez, the Minister of Defense and General-in-Chief of the Venezuelan military.

President Javier Moros canted his head to one side as he looked at the two Chinese generals. "General Song Fu, do you share the same opinion as General Yu Zhongfu?" he pressed. "I find it hard to believe that generals of your caliber would have such a defeatist attitude."

General Song normally held a pretty solid poker face when he met with political leaders, but President Moros's comment had hit a nerve. They weren't fatalistic or spineless—they just happened to know what the bigger strategy was and how Venezuela fit into that strategy.

For better or worse, the strategic plan meant Venezuela might ultimately be sacrificed to achieve China's end goal, just as Cuba and El Salvador had gone down in flames. The tough part was having to keep that knowledge from the Venezuelans and even many of his own soldiers.

"Mr. President, General Yu and I are *not* being defeatist," General Song insisted hotly. "We are looking at all the options available to us right now. It is unfortunate that, after we invested many years and a great deal of money and effort in the Cuban and Salvadoran militaries, they were not able to hold out longer. Their rather sudden collapse has accelerated the time when the Americans and their European allies could launch an attack against your nation.

"I would like to note that China has already gone to great lengths to fight for and protect Venezuela against NATO. Our Navy has suffered some horrific losses protecting your shores. We've lost dozens of aircraft and thousands of soldiers as well. It is now apparent what the Americans and NATO are going to do next—they are gearing up to invade your country on or around June first. Now, we can let that happen and try to react to their moves, or we can preempt their invasion by launching a spoiler attack of our own and disrupt them before they are able to get things moving."

The Venezuelan President nodded; he seemed to agree. Then he asked, "How do you propose we launch this attack while still leaving enough forces in strategic positions to defend against NATO's invasion?"

"Yes, that is a good question, General Song," agreed Adán Chávez. "NATO will likely attack any amassing of our forces along our border. If they truly are only nine or ten weeks away from invading, then it is highly likely they will begin hitting our country with waves of cruise missiles and air strikes in the near future."

"We actually do *not* believe NATO will hit Venezuela with a large quantity of cruise missiles or air strikes," General Yu interjected. "Our analysis of their prewar stockpile compared to the number of strikes they have carried out since the end of October would lead us to believe the Americans are likely down to around fifteen percent of their prewar inventory. It will take them many months to produce more. We'll likely see precision air strikes carried out by their stealth aircraft, but no shock-and-awe campaign like we saw in Cuba."

President Moros seemed relieved by the response. "OK, so if going on the offense is the best defense we can muster, then when and where do we attack?"

General Song smiled. "Let me show you on the map what we are thinking."

Chapter Seventeen
Big Picture

III Corps HQ
Cartagena, Colombia

Newly promoted Lieutenant General Robert Sink looked at the map of the border region between Colombia and Venezuela. It was annotated with markers denoting what Venezuelan and Chinese forces were arrayed along the border and where. By and large, the border region was being guarded by a large number of small units, strung together to act more like a tripwire than a force to stop a large-scale invasion. Likewise, the Colombians had situated their own forces in a similar manner.

What galled General Sink the most right now was the current set of ROEs. The Chinese and Venezuelans would hurl mortar, rocket, and artillery fire across the border, and for the most part, his forces couldn't respond—not unless they were fired upon first. So instead of seeing the enemy getting ready to fire and shooting at them, they had to sit there and wait until the attack was underway and then they could respond. Since taking over command four days ago, Sink had found a way to work around some of this—when they spotted the enemy getting ready to attack, they'd tell the Colombians exactly where to fire their own artillery or mortars to take them out.

The previous commander of III Corps had been killed when his helicopter had been shot down during a visit to a forward Army base near the border. The powers that be had determined that General Robert Sink was the right man for the job, so they'd promoted him out of his division command to take over the corps. Now he found himself in charge of preparing to lead a corps and a few NATO brigades across the border to begin the liberation of Venezuela.

A knock on the door broke him out of his train of thought. His aide stuck his head in. "Sir, Colonel Swann from 7th Group is here to see you."

Sink motioned for the aide to send the colonel in.

Moments later, Colonel Zack Swann, the commander of 7th Special Forces Groups, walked in. "General, it's good to see you. You getting settled into your new position?"

Colonel Zack Swann had been a young infantry lieutenant in the 82nd Airborne when General Sink had been a major. Sink had written one of his recommendations to get into Special Forces.

"Ah, Zack. It's good to see a familiar face around here. Yes, I'm slowly getting settled in. Drinking from the proverbial fire hose. Oh, and, Zack, when it's just the two of us, call me Bob. We've known each other too long to be formal in private like this."

Zack smiled at that and nodded. He pulled a cigar holder out and offered one to Bob. They'd kept in touch throughout the years as their careers had crossed paths, and Zack knew Bob was an aficionado.

They lit their cigars and then looked at the map table. "Zack, I'm still getting brought up to speed on the corps and the overall invasion strategy and plan Stavridis gave me, not to mention some of the NATO allies participating with us. I have some immediate problems that need addressing, and from what I can see, these are going to be best handled by your command."

Zack puffed on his cigar before responding, "I've got all but one battalion in-country, finally. What specific problems are you seeing that we may be able to help with?"

"Actually, Zack, bring me up to speed on where all your guys are at right now first."

"Sure thing, Bob. I've got a full battalion deployed across the entire southern and southeastern portion of the country, growing our insurgency force and sowing general chaos and mayhem. I've got one company working with the Colombians to counter the FARC, which leaves me with two companies to support the coming invasion. I hate to say it, but my fourth battalion is largely just becoming a well to draw replacements from when we sustain casualties. I mean, I've kept one company available for other missions in the AOR should the need arise, but the other two are getting picked over as the casualties roll in."

Bob placed his cigar down on the nearby ashtray and reached for his cup of coffee. Now that he had a better understanding of where his Special Forces assets were, he started to formulate how he'd like to leverage them. He took a sip and pointed to one of the mountain ranges across the border. "I've got a problem in this area that screams Special Forces, but before I go into detail on that, let me give you a bit of an overview of the corps deployment and what's arrayed against me. I'd like your opinion on a few things once you're up to speed."

"No worries, Bob. But keep in mind that while my group's assigned to support III Corps and our insurgency operations in the south, 1st Group is assigned to XVIII Airborne Corps in the south. They're responsible for anything that has to deal directly with the Chinese forces until the invasion starts. They have the Chinese linguists and know their order of battle better than my guys," Zack explained, reminding Bob of the SOF breakdown in the country.

While 7th Group specialized in Central and South America, to include the language, 1st Special Forces specialized in Asia, with the bulk of their operators being fluent in Mandarin.

"Ah, yes. That's right. See? I'm still drinking from the fire hose," Bob joked. "Four days ago, I was in El Salvador trying to put that country back together. Now I'm gearing up to invade an entirely new country."

Zack laughed softly. "The Army sure does like change, my friend. But at least you've got a command staff to help get you up to speed. I mean, surely they know more about the grand strategy of what's coming next than I do. I'm just a simple Greenie Beanie."

Bob grunted. "You're right, I do. But I don't know them like I know you. You've always had a head for strategy. So shut up and listen to my little spiel and tell me what you think before I make a fool of myself and present it to my staff in a few hours."

Zack just smiled and motioned with his cigar for his friend to begin.

Bob cleared his throat. "As you can see, there is a static line of defenders in key strategic positions along the border. A lot of these positions appear to be lookout posts, but some of them are hardened positions meant to slow down an armored force or full-on ground invasion. Prior to the offensive, these positions will be hit pretty hard by artillery and precision air strikes." Bob pointed to several locations on the map table.

"This entire mountain range here is part of the Chorro El Indio National Park," Bob continued. "It's a mountainous region that stretches from San Cristobal to Barquisimeto, some one hundred and forty miles long. You have to hand it to the Chinese—they were smart when they planned out the defense of the country. Like Cuba and El Salvador, they appear to have turned a number of areas into those nasty air-defense fortresses. Depending on the system they turn on, they're able to engage aircraft up to three hundred miles away. This continues to cause havoc across much of Colombia, which has essentially had a no-fly zone across half their country. Aside from debilitating their economy, it's making logistics and troop movements for us challenging, to say the least."

Zack puffed away on his cigar as he listened and followed along, looking at the different points on the map table.

"God bless the Air Force," Bob commented. "They've been trying their darndest to take 'em out, but it's been taking a heavy toll on them. Just last week, we encountered some new sort of SAM system we hadn't seen before. It shot down a C-17 Globemaster near Cartagena, killing more than two hundred soldiers. This new SAM system appears to be located near the city of Pregonero—"

"A new SAM system?" Zack interrupted, surprised. "What do you mean?"

"I'm not totally sure about its specifics," Bob acknowledged. "My G2 brought it up to me during the daily intelligence brief last night. From what I've been told, this missile has an enormous range. The launch was first detected by our forces in Cúcuta. We didn't have any aircraft in the area, so it was odd to see a launch. It wasn't until the missile suddenly reappeared over northern Colombia, heading toward Cartagena, that we realized we're likely dealing with something new. By the time the missile reappeared on our radars, it was too late to intercept it or do anything about it. The damn missiles are apparently really, really hard to track and fast as hell."

Zack leaned forward as he looked at the area around Cúcuta. "I take it you know the location where this missile was launched from, and you want me to get some teams in the area to try and find it?"

Bob grinned. "See? I knew there was a reason they made you a colonel. We've narrowed down the launch site to a city located high in the Andes Mountains. What I need, Zack, is for you to get one or more ODA teams inserted near the area to find it."

"OK. First, this would be 1st Group's AOR as it's in the middle of the Chinese sector. But suppose they do find this site—are you wanting them to take it out or call a strike in to do that?"

Bob didn't say anything right away. Finally, he explained, "I was just made aware of a highly classified Space Force platform that is officially being made available to us for specific SAM-hunting missions. When the ODA finds the site, they'll call it in and stand by. That's all I've been told."

Zack snorted at the cloak-and-dagger approach. "You aren't able to share anything more?" he asked playfully.

Bob walked over to his desk and proceeded to unlock a drawer. He pulled out a folder and pointed to the chair opposite his desk. "This stays between us, Zack. Apparently, Space Force has some sort of new sixth-generation fighter-spaceplane. It delivers some sort of kinetic weapon from the edges of space. It's supposedly able to penetrate underground bunkers and hardened targets. But the real weapon is the aircraft. The Chinese can't track it, and even if they could, they can't shoot at it. It's ideal for SAM hunting."

Zack shook his head in amazement as he looked at some of the pictures and specs of the aircraft. "OK, I'll talk with my counterpart at 1st Group, but you should talk with General Tackaberry and get him to task his group with it. Personally, if we have aircraft and weapons like this at our disposal, I'd like to deploy a few more teams to go after some of these fortresses the Chinese have built. It sounds like this is the perfect platform to use against them. We hammer them with these kinetic weapons and reduce these fortresses to rubble. Should make things a lot easier on your divisions once the time comes to start capturing land."

"Agreed," Bob replied. "Oh, I've also just been chopped a squadron of SAS." Zack smiled. "They arrive tomorrow. If it's all the same, I'm going to assign them to your command. I'd like you to integrate them into your group's operations as you see fit. I've been told a squadron consists of sixty-five operators commanded by a major. They should help augment some of your units when they arrive tomorrow."

"Excellent, sir. Well, you've given me a lot to figure out, and it looks like you've done a good job of getting caught up. Let me know how else I can help—my office is just down the hall until things kick off."

****

Supreme Headquarters Allied Powers Europe
Mons, Belgium

General Lisa Yeager was now an hour into the weekly FEB meeting or Far East Briefing she had established some four months ago. As the SACEUR, or Supreme Allied Commander, Europe, General Yeager felt it was incredibly important to keep the leadership of the organization informed of what was going on and hold those responsible for certain parts of the operation accountable. She'd already relieved two colonels and one brigadier general for incompetence and failure to meet their goals.

"General Yeager," said the German briefer, an oberst or colonel. "I am proud to report that we are back on schedule in getting the secondary rail tracks laid and the additional supply bases built near the cities of Krasnoyarsk, Alzamay, and Irkutsk. We've also started construction on the new route connecting Bratsk as we seek to create a new northern rail track around Lake Baikal down to Chita. Now that the weather is turning warmer again, we are able to begin construction of the new rail routes further away from the Chinese border."

213

Yeager nodded approvingly. She'd fired the previous German commander when he'd failed to meet his original timeline—a timeline he had *insisted* could be met, only for him to come up with one excuse after another when he failed. She knew they were in a race against time. It wouldn't be long until the Chinese invaded Russia.

"Pardon my interruption, Oberst," interjected a British general, "but do we know if the paratrooper and mountain units have fully deployed to the region and are setting up their defensive positions? With spring finally arriving, we should expect the Chinese to start making their moves soon."

It was now mid-April, and the snow covering much of the Russian Far East was steadily melting away. While the ground was still wet and soggy, everyone knew it wouldn't be long before the sun and the warmer weather dried everything out. When that happened, the ground battle to seize the Far East would begin in earnest.

"They have, General," replied the German colonel. "The Italians have deployed the Alpine Brigade 'Taurinense' to Tarbagatay, a small village south of the city of Ulan-Ude. This is a key rail node for the Trans-Siberian Railway. The Alpine Brigade 'Julia' has deployed to the Petrovsk-Zabaykalsky area to protect the P-258 highway and the rail line. This is some rugged but critical terrain that has to be protected until we can complete a northern rail line bypassing the current line near the Russian-Mongolian-Chinese border."

Interjecting to ask her own question, General Yeager inquired, "Oberst, how are these two brigades going to defend this area and still be able to support each other? This is some pretty rough terrain."

Turning to face her, the colonel explained, "The brigades are building a series of outposts on different strategic positions along their lines. These outposts are going to be supported by a network of firebases.

If an outpost is attacked, then they'll be able to call on fire support from several different artillery bases. The Italians have also deployed the Airmobile Brigade 'Friuli' and the Cavalry Brigade 'Pozzuolo del Friuli' to act as a mobile reserve to plug holes in their lines or reinforce positions as needed."

At least the Italians seem to have found an area of the line they feel they can properly defend, thought Yeager.

The challenge with managing NATO was not only getting each member state to contribute troops when a need arose—it was figuring out how best to use the units they made available. Like the UN Peacekeeping units, the member nations didn't always offer up their best units. Then many appeared to have had a change of heart as the full scope of the Chinese threat became known.

The rest of the briefing went by rapidly as the other member states gave their own updates on their areas of responsibility. General Yeager listened to each briefer intently, but ultimately, she was most eager to hear the Russian update. The Russian delegation to NATO was sitting next to her, patiently waiting their turn to speak as they took all the information in.

It still felt odd having the Russians involved in a meeting like this— NATO's entire core mission had originally been to counter Russia. Now they had more or less added Russia to the fold. War had a way of making strange bedfellows.

General Alexander Solomatin cleared his throat as he prepared to present Russia's update. "General Yeager," Solomatin began, "I want to first thank each NATO member for coming to the aid of Russia. I know we have a unique history and have historically been adversaries, but perhaps this unfortunate war we find ourselves in against China will now give our nations a chance at a new future together."

Yeager observed several of the NATO members nod their heads. Even she had to agree with his comment.

"The biggest challenge we will have in defending against the Chinese is geography. It is also an advantage we have as the Chinese military will be dealing with the same challenges. This battle will be fought over a part of the world that has poor infrastructure and a tough climate to have to contend against. Part of the Russian strategy is to use this to our advantage as much as possible. To that end, we have successfully infiltrated elements of our Special Forces and reconnaissance units into Mongolia and northern China.

"As of right now, they are spotting a significant build-up in supply depots and military camps being constructed. While they have not detected large troop movements yet, these are precursor activities to such a move. Our intelligence assessment believes the Chinese will likely send large numbers of soldiers to these bases in the next few weeks. Once we see them move to capture Mongolia, we should expect them to cross our borders within weeks or days. At that point, it will be a matter of how effectively we can interrupt and bog down their supply lines and slow or stop their advances."

General Yeager interjected. "General Solomatin, where do you believe the biggest challenge is going to come from? Perhaps we may still have time to address this before the invasion."

"Aircraft, General," Solomatin replied. "Our intelligence believes the Chinese have one or more new drone aircraft they will be introducing once the war starts. We can build all the outposts and fire support bases we want. We can build a new northern rail line to keep Chita and the other major cities supplied. But if we can't control the skies, the Chinese will just bomb us into submission. If we can maintain air superiority, we can overcome their superior numbers."

The other members at the table all agreed. The advancements in air-defense systems had really proven to be a smart investment on the part of the Chinese and probably the Russians. If the Caribbean campaign had taught NATO one thing, it was that fourth- and fifth-generation fighters, including stealth aircraft, were not as invincible or all-powerful in the air as they had thought. This coming war in the East would likely be determined by who was able to wrestle control of the sky first.

A British air marshal then spoke up. "I believe we should have one squadron of our newest Tempest sixth-generation fighters available to deploy in the coming weeks. I think if we look to ramp up our own production of drone aircraft, we can better leverage them to support our ground forces, at least while we look to battle for control of the skies. It could be me, and perhaps I'm being overly optimistic, but I think if the Chinese do invade the Far East, they'll finally have bitten off more than they can chew. A nation can only sustain these levels of casualties for so long before the population begins to lose trust in and support for the government."

As the meeting concluded, General Yeager surmised they were about as ready as they were going to get for what was heading toward them. They still had units in transit to the Far East and many more preparing their fighting positions. Still, she hoped calmer heads would eventually prevail and the Chinese could be talked out of their death march and a war against the entire world they couldn't possibly hope to win.

Chapter Eighteen
Escalation

Fincantieri Bay Shipbuilding
Sturgeon Bay, Wisconsin

President Delgado looked at the nearly completed *Constellation*-class guided-missile frigate in a bit of awe. The ship had originally been designed and built for the Italian Navy. The US Navy had selected the Fincantieri shipbuilder over others because the ship had a proven track record of success in a handful of navies. Once the Navy took the base model of the ship and added in their own advanced weapons and technology, the frigate would be more than capable of meeting the Navy's mission for years to come.

"As you can see, Madam President, by leveraging the three shipyard facilities—in Marinette, in Green Bay, and right here in Sturgeon Bay—along with running a full twenty-four-seven operation, we were able to cut the original production time from forty-eights months to just eleven," explained the shipyard manager as he led the President and a few others on the tour of the facility. "This is going to allow us to fill in the enormous gap in ship orders from the Navy. We've also tripled the number of ships under construction from eight to twenty-four."

Maria thought about what he had said, and it kind of hit her—all those Navy orders were coming in because dozens of ships had sunk. Nearly fourteen thousand sailors had died over the last six months. It was hard to fathom these kinds of losses. Even when she had been in the Army during the Iraq War, they had never lost this many service members.

This trip to Green Bay and Sturgeon Bay had been the idea of Delgado's Chief of Staff. He had insisted that she tour more of the country and "press the flesh," so to speak, with the American people. He'd said it was "important for the people to see the President and for the President to be seen among the people."

At this point, nearly everyone in the country had received the COVID-24 vaccine, so the pandemic had largely burned out. Now, the country was left to pick up the pieces from the second pandemic virus and a surprise attack by the Chinese. The American people were reeling from one disaster after another over the last ten years. President Delgado's administration was supposed to bring the calm everyone had been seeking.

When the tour at the shipyard had concluded, the President traveled back to Green Bay for a luncheon with the local Chamber of Commerce. Several hundred people had gathered to hear her speak and have lunch with her.

After the photo op, she would board the plane and head to Detroit. She was going to tour a Ford plant that had been converted to manufacture military vehicles. Then she'd have dinner with the local Teamster group.

The next stop on the tour was Tuscaloosa, Mississippi, to tour another shipyard as they ramped up production of the *Arleigh Burke* Flight III among several other ship classes. Her four-day tour of the country would have her touring four states and eight plants critical to the war effort. However, what she'd rather be doing was touring some of the hospitals and medical facilities caring for those wounded in the war.

This wasn't how Maria Delgado had wanted to spend her presidency—leading a global war against China. She'd campaigned on an antiwar message, promising to bring American soldiers home from the myriad of foreign bases. She had wanted her presidency to be about rebuilding America and focusing all of its attention and money on solving domestic problems. Unfortunately, that was just not the hand she'd been dealt, and like the rest of the American people, she'd do the best she could, given the situation she found herself in.

****

President Delgado sat in the fortified limo that had been dubbed "The Beast" as her motorcade drove to Green Bay. She looked out the window and watched the countryside whip past them. Occasionally, she saw a small group of people standing along the side of the road, waving American flags. From time to time, she'd see someone holding up a poster that demanded an end to the war. Delgado wished it was that simple. The more the CIA and NSA unraveled of this super-AI, Jade Dragon, the clearer it became that this was a war that had been many years in the making.

Her National Security Advisor, Blain Wilson, interrupted these reflections. "Penny for your thoughts, Madam President?"

Delgado smiled tepidly. "I was just thinking how screwed up all this is—this whole war, computers, machine learning, AI..." She trailed off. "I remember reading an article a few years back about how IBM's AI Watson was able to diagnose heart disease better than a cardiologist, and how a New York hospital's AI had a higher accuracy rate of identifying breast cancer in patients than its human doctor counterparts."

She sighed. "How did we go from using AI and machine learning for good to engineering a military first strike against fellow nations and waging a world war, Blain?" she complained. "I just don't understand the depravity of humans. We have so many bigger challenges that need to be solved, yet we're going to squander the lives of millions and spend trillions of dollars on a war of conquest...it angers me, Blain," Maria finished. The frustration, tiredness and stress imposed by the job had been taking their toll on her.

Blain was a good trouper. He just sat there and listened. He didn't act like every other man would and try to solve her problem or offer up solutions. He was just present. Maria really liked that about him. He had been like that in the Army, too. Sure, he'd been a tough-as-nails Special Forces operator, but as a commander, he had known how to listen and really hear and understand what was going on.

I'm glad I kept him from the last administration...

"Oh, Blain, I meant to ask you—how did the call with the Chairman go?" she asked, suddenly remembering the broader picture. "Anything I need to know about?"

President Delgado had been giving a short speech at the shipyard when Admiral Thiel had tried to reach her. She had known there was a little bit of tension between him and the ground commanders, but the Joint Staff had its feathers ruffled when Blain informed her that the COCOM commander, General Stavridis, had shared his concerns with him about their plans.

"Ah, yes. It could have waited until our evening meeting, but I can tell you now," Blain replied. "He wanted me to pass along to you that it would appear that ground operations between Venezuela and Colombia are imminent. Aside from some SIGINT, our recon units across the border are reporting a lot of troop movements. Chinese and Venezuelan artillery and rocket forces have also started firing across the border with a lot more urgency than in times past."

Maria burst out laughing.

"What's so funny?" Blain asked.

"Seems like it was a bit more important than waiting four more hours for our evening meeting," she replied with a smirk.

"Well, there really wasn't a lot that you could do about it, so I didn't want to distract you from your next visit in Green Bay," he insisted.

Delgado knew he was right. The generals and field commanders knew what to do—she didn't need to micromanage them.

She made eye contact with her friend. "Blain, in this situation with Colombia and Venezuela—how would you respond if you were in my shoes?" she pressed. "What would you do?"

He slouched back in the seat, deep in thought. Finally, he replied, "Madam President, I was not elected to make those decisions. I'm not sure it's my place to say what I would do if I were in charge because I am *not* in charge."

Maria considered his response as the motorcade entered the city of Green Bay. "Fair enough. But I'd still like an answer," she insisted. "It's just the two of us."

"OK…if I were in charge, Madam President, I'd tell the Joint Chiefs their job is to support the combatant commanders with whatever resources and tools they need and not to micromanage the field commanders," he began. "I'd tell the field commanders the leash is off, do what you have to do to win this war and win it in haste. I'd use whatever executive power I had and maybe a little extra to make sure the economy was running at full speed to support the war effort, and I'd call on the American people to rally to the flag, to put aside their political differences and join the military effort to win this war and defeat this Chinese AI before it's too late and it enslaves us all. If I was in charge, that's what I'd do."

As he spoke, Maria could see a fire and passion in his eyes. She liked that about him. He was a straight shooter. Everything about him

222

was about what was best for the country as a whole, not one political party over another. She supposed that was why he was one of the few folks in Washington who was truly respected on both sides of the aisle.

"There was so much I wanted to get done domestically, Blain," bemoaned President Delgado. "I'm concerned if I unleash the military like you're suggesting, it may come back to bite me in the ass."

"I know. I understand," Blain acknowledged. "If you'd like, you could allow me and the Vice President to effectively manage this for you while you focus on the domestic front."

"That's not a bad idea. Let me run that past the VP and see what he thinks. I'd still need to be looped in daily or at least every other day as to what was going on. I am still, after all, the Commander in Chief."

The motorcade reached its final destination a few minutes later. The two of them got out of the vehicle and made their way into the building for another tour of an important shipyard. Then they'd attend another dinner and give another speech before heading off to Detroit to rinse and repeat.

****

Five Days Later

Blain sat in the Vice President's office, waiting eagerly to hear what he'd have to say.

Mike Madden hadn't been a politician before being elected VP, and he had no political aspirations beyond his current role. He'd come from the business world and was largely responsible for the President's business proposals and economic agenda. He had also been instrumental in garnering the senior vote—while Maria Delgado was fifty-three years old, Mike was seventy-one. He was along for the ride to help Maria as best he could, not position himself to run after she left office.

"Blain, I'll be straight with you—the military realm and defense are not something I'm familiar with. I'm sitting in this chair to help the President restore the American economy and improve the lives of the American worker. But Maria has asked me to work with you on this project, so that's what I'm going to do. That said, unless we're talking about business and the economy, this stuff is way outside my wheelhouse. The way I see it, I'm going to lend you political cover and authority, but I'd like you to lead this effort. I'll attend the meetings you tell me I need to, but I trust Maria and she trusts you. So, you tell me what to say or do and that's what we'll do."

"Thank you, Mr. Vice President, for your vote of confidence and trust. That really means a lot," Blain replied. "Then with your blessing, I'd like to give our military commanders the authority to execute the war as they see fit to win and defeat the enemy expeditiously. You and the President are right about the domestic front—we need to end this war promptly so we can refocus on rebuilding our country and recovering from a second pandemic in ten years."

"Amen to that. So, what are you thinking, Blain?"

"On the domestic side, I'd like your advice, sir, on how we get this economy retooled for war as quickly as possible to start cranking out the tools we need to win this thing," Blain explained. "In particular, we have an urgent need for aircraft, artillery, armored vehicles, and munitions for them all."

The Vice President grinned. "This is an area where I can certainly help. So, let's divide this task up. Tomorrow, during our first official meeting with everyone, I'm going to let them know that I'll be handling the economic side of this and you will be in charge of the military side."

"That sounds great, Mr. Vice President. I think we're going to make a great team."

****

When Blain Wilson left the Vice President's office, he placed a quick call to his assistant, telling him to arrange a call with General Stavridis as soon as possible. By the time he got back to his office, he was told the general was on the phone waiting for him.

He immediately picked up the receiver. "Kurt, it's Blain. You have a minute to talk?"

"I do. You caught me in a meeting with General Bridges, so Gary's on speakerphone, if that's OK?"

"Ah, even better. I just got done meeting with the Vice President about the President's proposal. We're a go," he announced. "He's going to effectively let me handle the military side of the house while he handles the economy and gets you the tools to fight and win. I want the gloves off. No more waiting around. You have full permission to initiate whatever offensive action you need to take. We're still a month and a half away from June first, but if you see an opportunity to strike now, then take it. The President wants this war over with in as short a time as possible, so short of nukes, let's see how fast we can finish this thing off."

"What about the Joint Staff and the Pentagon?" asked Stavridis. They'd been the bane of his existence up to this point.

"I have a meeting with them in two hours. The Vice President and I will be laying down the law on how this is going to work. They'll get in line, or they'll be replaced. The President is adamant about ending this war swiftly and making sure the field commanders are the ones in charge, not Washington."

"Blain, you're singing music to my ears," said General Gary Bridges. "Thank you for working your magic on that end. We won't let you or the President down. We'll put together a request for additional forces and get that sent to you in the next couple of hours."

Stavridis jumped back in. "If I've got your permission, Blain, I'm going to unleash III Corps ASAP. We've got Chinese troop movements headed our way and I'd rather punch them in the face before they have a chance to get organized and hit us first."

"You've got my permission and that of the President," Blain confirmed. "Go get 'em, Kurt. Send me that request in the next few hours, and I'll get you what you guys need. Let's show the Chinese why we're still the most lethal military in the world."

When Blain finished his call, he dialed up Admiral Thiel and told him to make sure the entire Joint Staff was present for his meeting at the Pentagon in two hours.

"The Vice President will be accompanying me as well," he explained. It was important to remind the Pentagon that they worked for the White House, not the other way around.

Chapter Nineteen
King of Battle

Charlie Battery, 2nd Battalion, 116th Field Artillery Regiment
30 Kilometers West of Cúcuta, Colombia

"Round up!" Specialist Tony Davis shouted.

Staff Sergeant Rob Fortney didn't hesitate. "Fire!" he shouted, sending the first official round from their gun toward the enemy.

"Firing!" Davis replied as he pushed down on the firing trigger.

Boom!

The cannon recoiled inside the turret. The entire vehicle rocked back slightly on its springs. The autoloader fed the next round into the chamber, preparing them to fire again.

"Round up!" shouted Davis, letting Fortney know they were ready to keep fighting.

"Fire!"

They sent their second round across the Colombian border to tear into some Chinese forces their forward observer unit had found.

"Check fire!" Fortney yelled as he saw the message flash across his screen.

"Check fire," Specialist Davis echoed. "Hey, what's up, Rob? We screw something up?" he asked, concern in his voice.

"I'm not sure, Tony. Let me find out," Fortney said as he grabbed for the radio.

A moment later, he explained what was going on. "Apparently, we pulverized the position, so they called off the rest of the fire mission. Oh, we also need to get ready to move out. The 53rd is advancing across the border, so let's get ready to move."

"Hey, that's awesome. Only took us a couple of rounds to beat those Chink bastards," Davis said excitedly.

"Dude—man, me and my wife are Asian. Why do you always have to use derogatory terms like that?" chided Private Xavier Cheng, their driver.

"Aw, come on. Not this 'I'm offended again' crap," moaned Davis. "You know we're fighting the Chinese, Xavier. It's nothing personal against you and your wife or family."

Cheng had joined Fortney and Davis's gun truck about a month ago. He was fresh from training and hated every minute of being in the Army. Had he not been drafted, he never would have joined. The fact that he had been integrated into a National Guard unit, a Florida redneck unit on top of it, really rubbed the San Francisco native wrong.

"Eh, cut it out, you two. We don't have time for this," Fortney cut in. "Xavier, make sure you have the new destination entered into the navigation system. Tony, get the truck ready to move. It looks like we're pulling out of here in five minutes."

When Davis climbed back in the track after securing their rear-firing anchors, Fortney gave the order for them to get moving. They'd link up with the rest of their battery around the small town of Caseteja. From there, they'd cross the Pamplonita River and proceed on into Venezuela.

Their brigade, the 53rd Infantry Brigade Combat Team, or Gator Brigade, was going to advance around the city of Ureña and head straight for San Cristobal with the 29th Infantry Division, their parent organization. From there, they'd continue toward the city of Barinas, some three hundred kilometers to the northeast. Meanwhile, the 1st Infantry Division would move through the mountains along Highway 1 to Highway 7, crossing through the city of Merida before they made it to

228

Barinas. The goal was for them to all meet in the middle of the country in the city of Barinas. Once there, they'd look to advance on Valencia and link up with the rest of III Corps as they prepared to approach Caracas from the west.

"I'm ready to go," Cheng said over the vehicle radio.

"Outstanding," said Fortney. "Let's move. Follow Alpha Two's ammo carrier. Oh, Tony—I want you up on your crew-served gun. Unless we're doing a fire mission, I want at least one person up on the gun at all times. We're about to cross over into Indian country, and we've lost enough people in this war so far. I'm not losing any more, you hear me?"

"Yeah, I hear you, Rob. Let me climb up there now," Davis replied grimly as he got into position.

Their battery commander was adamant about having someone from the gun and ammo crews manning their turret-mounted crew-served weapons when not conducting a fire mission. The stinging loss from their time in Key West was still fresh in their minds.

They'd driven maybe twenty minutes down some really shoddy dirt roads and snaked through a couple of villages that looked like they were from a different century when Fortney suddenly called out, "Vehicle, stop! We got a fire mission. Two rounds HE, coordinates coming in now."

Davis dropped back into the turret of the vehicle to get the gun ready. He read the targeting data and made sure the autoloader was prepped with a round ready to go and the proper propellant bags. He was still getting used to using the automated system.

"Guns ready, Staff Sergeant," Davis announced.

Boom! One of the nearby guns in their convoy fired its first round.

"Fire!" Fortney shouted.

BOOM.

"Reloading," came the quick reply from Davis as he observed the system load the round and grab the right number of propellant bags. Judging by the fact that it had grabbed four, these rounds were being lobbed well over fifty kilometers.

They fired their second round a few seconds later. Once they'd completed the fire mission, they got moving again. The vehicles in front of them lurched forward and they continued to snake their way through the single-lane dirt roads.

Once the fire mission had been completed, all the gun crews wanted to do was get moving. They all remembered what had happened at the outset of the war, when they'd been hit by a counterbattery barrage from the Chinese. That single attack had destroyed half their HIMARS vehicles and killed thirty percent of the soldiers in the battery. It had been a real blow to the unit and the Florida Army National Guard.

An hour later, they finally made it down to the river. An engineering unit had set up one of those heavy assault bridges the M104 Wolverine vehicles carried on top of them. The M104 was basically an Abrams tank chassis with a large piece of bridging equipment it could unfold across a river, tank ditch, or other obstacle the military needed to cross.

The engineers were doing a good job of keeping the traffic moving and not backing up too badly. There were two more bridges to help keep everyone rolling. The river below wasn't flowing particularly fast and it didn't look too deep, but why risk having units getting stuck or bogged down when they had a bridging system built for this very purpose?

While the battery waited their turn to get across the river, they received one more fire mission. They alerted the units around them that they were going to start firing—still, it caused a bit of a stir when they did.

Finally, their battery of vehicles was motioned to cross. The engineers probably wanted to get them out of the area in case there was some sort of Chinese or Venezuelan counterbattery fire.

As they continued to drive down the substandard roads to keep up with the faster-moving units, Private Cheng, who was sitting high in his chair so he could see through the driver's hatch, asked, "Staff Sergeant, is it normal for us to be firing on the move like this?"

Fortney held the bridge of his nose for a moment, holding in his frustration. He had to remember Cheng was fresh from training. He didn't have any real experience in the Army yet. He didn't understand how things worked.

Sitting in the commander's hatch, Fortney looked down at the young soldier as he drove along. "It depends, Xavier. Sometimes we'll stay in a fixed position and just stand by to lob rounds for the infantry. In this case, we're supporting a Stryker and armor battalion as our brigade looks to bypass a large city. These units are moving quickly, going around enemy strongholds as they come across them. When they spot something that needs to be hit, they give us a call. Because these guys are moving, we need to stay on the move with them. We don't want to fall too far behind them, or we'll be out of range of supporting them when they need it. We also don't want to be too far away from other units in case we run into trouble ourselves. As it is, each of the batteries only has a single MP platoon in their Guardian armored vehicles to provide security for us. If we bumped into an enemy armor or motorized unit, we'd be in trouble."

"Damn, I guess I hadn't thought about it like that," Cheng replied. "When we were training at Fort Sill, we trained on towed artillery—not the mobile stuff like this."

Fortney shrugged. "Yeah—you know, just a few months ago, we were a HIMARS unit. This entire system is new to me and Davis, too."

"Staff Sergeant, is it true you were awarded the Silver Star for shooting two Chinese Special Forces soldiers in the Keys?"

Fortney didn't say anything right away. He looked ahead of them for a minute. Finally, he responded, "Yeah. They did. That was the day our unit got hit by a counterbattery fire. They took half our vehicles out that day. My gun chief got killed. Shot in the head right in front of me by one of those Chinese bastards."

"Damn, that's what I heard. You shot him with a civilian revolver, a .38 Special you had in your pocket or something. When I heard that, it made me want to bring a pistol with me too in case I ran into a situation like that," Cheng replied with a bit of awe in his voice.

"Private Cheng, I truly hope we're never in a situation like that again. I don't want you to go through what me and Davis did. It was the worst day of my life—not something I'd wish on any of you, ever."

Fortney then swapped out with Specialist Davis on the gun and climbed back into the turret. He was having a hard time controlling his emotions right then and wanted a moment alone. Once he'd recovered, he joined Davis in his own turret.

Fortney surveyed the area around them. It was a surreal scene to watch. The convoy of armored vehicles continued to snake their way through the forested jungle and the occasional villages. Many of these smaller villages looked like something out of the eighteenth or nineteenth century.

The rest of the day moved by rapidly. They'd go a few hours without a fire mission, then they'd get slammed with half a dozen in a row. They stopped twice to take on more ammo from their field artillery ammunition supply vehicle. The FAASVs looked like giant armadillos. The armored ammo carrier would follow the M1299 Paladins and resupply them with rounds and ammo as needed.

While the Paladins could carry forty-six shells and the propellant bags to shoot them, the FAASVs could carry an additional ninety rounds. When the FAASVs got low on rounds, they could alert the higher-level supply units, who could either drop off a pallet of rounds or have a pallet airlifted by helicopter and brought out to them. It was one of many ways to keep the artillery mobile and able to keep supporting a fast-moving armored advance.

When the sun finally set for the day, they received word the units they were supporting were going to hold in place until morning. They needed to give the supply train a bit of time to catch up. They didn't want to make the same mistakes the Army had made in March of 2003, when they had overrun so many enemy units during the push to Baghdad that they'd left a lot of intact Iraqi Army units in their rear area, causing all sorts of problems with the supply units.

Fortney walked up to Specialist Davis. "Tomorrow, we're supposed to get back on the move again around 0600 hours. I need you to make sure I'm awake by 0530. I'll take the first shift with Private Cheng; we'll sack out until 0200 and then you can cover down until morning. Got it?"

Davis yawned and nodded. "You got it. Thanks for letting me go first to get some sleep. I'm toasted."

"No problem. We'll keep an eye on things. Tomorrow should be a busy day. We'll be skirting the city before we break out of the valley and get into the enemy's true rear area."

"Sounds like fun, Rob. I'm off to sleep now."

****

Bravo Company, 124th Infantry Battalion
La Llanada, Venezuela

Sergeant Jamie Roberts plopped down on the dirt next to Sergeant First Class Jeremiah "Ski" Grabowski, handing him MRE Menu #4. "Oh, my favorite. Spaghetti with beef sauce," Ski said as he pulled out his knife to cut it open.

"What a ballbuster of a day, Ski," Jamie said as she blew a stray hair out of her face and tore into her own MRE.

"Yeah, well, we survived, and so did everyone in our platoon."

"I still can't believe they sent you back to a front-line unit," said Jamie. "Hell—you were given the MOH. You'd think you earned a right to not have to get shot at again." She spoke between hurried bites, scarfing down her dinner like she hadn't eaten in weeks.

Ski didn't say anything for a moment as he chewed his food. "It's fine, Jamie. You know, back in World War II, there was a Marine named John Basilone—he was awarded the MOH for combat action in Guadalcanal. The Marines then sent him on a war bonds tour across the country. The jarhead actually requested to return to combat on several occasions. Eventually, they gave in and let him. He ultimately died on Iwo Jima, leading a platoon of Marines he trained prior to shipping out. When he was asked why he kept volunteering to return to combat and risk his life again, he told his superiors and the reporters that if him going back meant he was able to help to save the life of even one Marine, then it would be worth it."

Jamie scoffed at that. "Well, Ski, I'd be pissed if they did that to me."

Ski shrugged. "When they award you the MOH, Jamie, you get inducted into a sacred group of warriors. For me, I struggle with civilian life. I struggle with the peacetime military. I joined the Army back in the 2000s, before 9/11. When those terrorists attacked our country…something inside me changed. I knew in that very moment I wanted to be a warrior. I wanted to be that sheepdog that protects the flock.

"At the time, I was part of the 82nd Airborne. I had just gotten selected to attend Ranger selection. I was determined to become an Army Ranger. I learned during that training and my subsequent time in the regiment that I was damn good at being a soldier. Fighting wars is what I'm good at. Right now, our country's in a fight for its survival; I couldn't just sit back with my medals and not continue to do what I'm good at. I needed to return to our unit."

Now it was Jamie's turn to stay silent for a moment as she thought about what he'd just said. She was a bit of an anomaly herself—the first female National Guard infantry soldier. She'd help paved the way for other women to join the infantry in the National Guard, and now women were being allowed into the regular Army infantry so long as they could maintain the same standards as their male counterparts.

Like Ski, she was a beast of a soldier. When Ski had earned the MOH, she'd been awarded the Distinguished Service Cross; she was the first woman in the Army ever to receive it. Still, while many of the soldiers in their unit were glad to have Ski back, they were disappointed that his medal hadn't earned him the right to avoid combat and potentially getting killed.

Before either of them could say anything else, 1st Lieutenant Henry Hobbs walked over to them. "There you two are. You keeping him out of trouble, Jamie?"

"Ski, out of trouble?" she responded, laughing. "It's like his middle name. So, what's up, LT? You got us orders to go guard some bridge in the middle of nowhere…away from all of this?"

"Ha! Wouldn't that be nice? No such luck." Hobbs took a seat on the ground next to them, placing his rifle in his lap.

"So, tomorrow, they want our unit to skirt around the city and push to get on the other side of it," Lieutenant Hobbs explained. "The Virginia 116th Infantry Brigade is going to move in to secure the city and the surrounding area. They want us to stick tight with the North Carolina 30th Armored Brigade and hook around to the right of the city and get behind it. From there, we should be able to break out of this valley and into the wide-open plains behind it. There's one last enemy stronghold around the city of San Rafael del Piñal; a Chinese brigade is supposedly holed up in it. Beyond that, it's pretty much a clear path for a couple hundred kilometers before the next major Chinese positions."

"Awesome, sounds like a walk in the park," Ski declared nonchalantly.

The three of them laughed. "Yeah, well, we'll see," Hobbs replied. "It sounds like we got lucky down here in the south. We're not really running into a lot of Chinese units like III Corps is up north. The battle for the city of Maracaibo is apparently turning into quite the slugfest—at least that's what my friend in the S2 shop told me earlier. He said the 1st Armor Division has been duking it out with a couple of Chinese tank brigades the last couple of days."

Ski shook his head in amazement. "Did you ever think we'd be in a war where we'd have a tank brigade fighting another tank brigade or a division versus division again? We've spent the last two decades fighting insurgents in asymmetrical warfare. It's been a long time since we've fought a war with large conventional forces like this."

"Yeah, no joke. I just wish the Air Force was able to do more," Jamie chimed in.

Hobbs bobbed his head up and down in agreement as he finished off the last of his own MRE. "I hear they're trying. No one expected the Chinese air defenses to be nearly this good. Big Army is apparently making the adjustment by reactivating a number of artillery battalions and brigades. They want us to rely on artillery for support more so than air support like we have in the past."

"Makes sense to me," Ski replied. "So, tomorrow...are we expecting a bit more action than today? I don't think any of us even fired our weapons. Not that I'm complaining."

Hobbs blew some air out his lips. "I don't know. I frankly thought we would have run into more resistance or Chinese forces than we did. Maybe we did get lucky, and they're all hunkered down in the mountains—maybe they're on the opposite side of the valley once we cross over. I suppose we'll see once we get moving. Just do your best to stay alive and keep our people alive. Don't avoid a fight, but let's not try and play hero either."

"Agreed," Ski replied. "All right, if it's all the same to you folks, I'm going to try and sack out. You got first watch, Jamie. Wake me in three hours." He grabbed for his poncho and started to wrap himself up in it.

"Hey, no fair!" Jamie complained half-heartedly as she poked him. "I thought you had last watch, not first. I'm beat."

"Rank has its privileges. Now, leave me alone, Sergeant Roberts," Ski shot back with a wink.

"OK, I'm heading back to the CP. Just be ready to roll at 0500," Lieutenant Hobbs said, then got up to leave his two favorite NCOs alone.

****

ODA 7322, Bravo Company
Villavicencio, Colombia

"What the hell are we doing out here, Cap'n?" Currie complained now that it was just the four of them alone. "The war is up north, not down here."

"Quit your whining, Currie. Ours is not to wonder why, but to do or die," quipped Chief Miller, who jumped in before Thorne could reply.

"Currie, has it ever occurred to you that you complain a lot?" Dawson added, joining in on Miller's critique of his friend.

"Oh, not you too, Dawson."

Thorne shook his head in amusement. "Damn, Currie. I think you're the only one who isn't glad we're pulling duty down here. This is like easy peasy lemon squeezy. We aren't even having to do most of the fighting."

For the last several weeks their ODA team had been advising and training the Colombian Rapid Deployment Force or Fuerza de Despliegue Rápido, a.k.a. FUDRA. Since the start of the global war with China, Colombia had seen a sudden reemergence of the FARC in various regions of the country. Not only was the Colombian government trying to deal with the consequences of a second pandemic in five years, the FARC was threatening to tear the country apart. In response, the government was doing whatever it could to stop the reemergence of the FARC.

A Colombian Army captain walked up to them. "Sorry to interrupt, Captain Thorne. Everyone is ready. We can leave when you give the order."

"Excellent. Tell your men to load up," Thorne directed. "Oh, and, Captain—make sure the QRF team is ready. They need to leave the airfield ten minutes after us so if we need them, they won't be far off once we're on the ground."

"Yes, Captain. Which of you will be flying in my helicopter?"

"Sergeant Currie and I here will fly with you. Chief Smith and Sergeant Dawson will fly in the other helicopter," Thorne explained. The FUDRA captain nodded in agreement and left to go get his men ready.

A source the DEA or Drug Enforcement Agency was running told them the FARC had been using this particular rural farm as a base of operations to build improvised explosive devices and car bombs. In the span of two months, there had been over three hundred IED attacks against the police and government officials across Colombia. Just last week, a five-hundred-pound car bomb had ripped the face off the Ministry of Justice building in Bogotá. The attacks against the police and government buildings were becoming reminiscent of the drug wars of the 1980s and '90s with Pablo Escobar.

Once the Colombian officer was gone, Thorne turned to his guys. "Look, I know you all want to be up north fighting the Chinese—they're the ones that attacked our country. But if the Chinese are able to use the FARC to collapse the Colombian government, that destabilizes the entire region," he insisted. "These missions against the FARC are just as important as the missions against the Chinese; plus, there's a lot of intelligence saying we've got more than a dozen Chinese Special Forces units advising, training, and working with the FARC. While we're here to advise and train FUDRA, that doesn't mean we can't get our own hands dirty and do some of the fighting when needed. So, let's do our best to put this bomb-making factory out of commission and be home tonight for some steaks and beers."

Currie, Dawson, and Smith all smiled and started putting their body armor and weapons on. They'd head out to the waiting Black Hawk helicopters and load up in a few minutes.

The other eight members of their team were helping the remaining elements of the FUDRA intelligence group integrate the additional SIGINT and ISR resources that had been tasked with rooting out the FARC. It was these additional assets that were helping them to identify who the FARC leaders and members were and where they were hiding. Once they found a location of a FARC leader, one of the three four-man teams Thorne had broken them down into would assist the Colombians in taking them out.

When they walked out to the Black Hawk, the looks on the faces of the Colombian soldiers showed they were eager to hit this particular target. If all went according to plan, they'd put a real dent in the number of IED and car bomb attacks taking place in the region.
****

Moments after Sergeant First Class Rusten Currie had gotten himself strapped into the helicopter, it took off. As they left the base, they flew over part of the city of Villavicencio as they headed off toward the mountains of the Chingaza Natural National Park. The city below was beautiful. The people within it just wanted to go about their daily lives as the economy did its best to recover from the COVID-24 virus.

Now the city found itself at the crossroads of FARC territory and the government.

Currie couldn't help but admire the beauty of the mountains as he gazed off at the view. The lush greens of the trees were beautiful. In the distance, misty clouds hugged the sides of the mountain, bringing rain and moisture to the area.

In the last six months, Currie had seen parts of Cuba, Honduras and El Salvador. Now he was in Colombia and knew he'd eventually travel to Venezuela. He was confident they'd get pulled off this counterterrorism duty with the FUDRA and go back to fighting the Chinese directly—he just wasn't sure when.

"Stand by, we're five minutes out," the pilot alerted them.

The helicopter started a steep angle down from their higher-altitude perch. The pilots were going to angle them down to treetop level and approach the farm from there. It would hopefully give the defenders less time to realize they were being assaulted.

"That's the target," Thorne said to Currie, pointing as the pilot angled their helicopter in for the assault.

They landed in the field just as they had gone over in their pre-mission planning. The soldiers on board jumped off and fanned out. As the helicopter lifted off, the soldiers ran toward the buildings on the farm with their rifles raised, ready to fire on anyone that fired on them.

Currie and two of the FUDRA soldiers were heading toward a small shed a hundred meters away from the barn and the main house on the property. Captain Thorne and four other FUDRA soldiers would head toward the farmhouse to clear it while Chief Smith and Dawson took their teams to clear the barn and the other outbuilding.

They were on the ground for probably sixty seconds, with the helicopters barely a few hundred feet in the air, when all hell broke loose.

A lone figure emerged from the barn, whipping the door wide open. Then a pickup truck emerged with a twin-barreled 23mm machine gun mounted on the back. The driver of the vehicle rushed the enemy fighters toward the farmhouse and closer toward the retreating helicopters, while the gunner in the back laid into one of the unsuspecting Black Hawks.

The gun stitched the rear of the helicopter and the tail boom with a slew of rounds, causing a small explosion. Then clouds of black smoke billowed out of the helicopter as it spun out of control until it thudded down in the farm field.

Currie already had his rifle up and at the ready when the driver started heading toward the farmhouse. He cut loose a string of rounds into the windshield of the vehicle, hoping to hit the driver. Despite spidering it and pumping half a magazine in the direction of the driver, he somehow missed the guy.

Several more figures emerged from the barn where the vehicle had been hiding and started firing back at the FUDRA soldiers. Currie saw one of the guys in his group go down after taking a couple of rounds to his chest rig.

Damn, I hope those didn't penetrate the plate.

Currie ducked behind some cover as a string of rounds flew over his head. He was starting to have a bad feeling about this place. The last surveillance they'd received of the place hadn't indicated there'd be more than half a dozen people on the property.

His radio earpiece chirped to life. "I'm calling in the QRF," Thorne announced. "Something's off about this place. Currie, have your team focus on the barn and keeping those shooters' heads down. Dawson, have your team help my group clear this house. Smith, work with Currie's team to keep those shooters near the barn under control."

"Aren't you glad you had the QRF in the air before we landed now?" Chief Smith replied with a half chuckle. He'd argued before the mission that they should assault with the entire company of FUDRA, not just a platoon.

Crump, crump.

Two grenades went off near Currie and his three uninjured guys. Clumps of dirt and hot shrapnel flew through the air around them. Currie heard men cry out in pain for a medic. Then he could make out some shouting in Chinese.

"Oh crap, Captain! I think those are PLA SF over there," Currie said over their coms as he ran toward one of the wounded FUDRA guys. He grabbed for the man's first aid pouch and started applying some pressure on the wound. He then told the guy to keep the pressure on it and went back to shooting.

"It doesn't matter, Currie. Keep pressing them. The cavalry is on the way. Let's keep these guys fixed until then."

Popping his head up to see what was going on, Currie spotted the pickup truck he'd originally shot up. He couldn't see the driver, but he saw a red splatter across the windshield, so he knew the guy must have been taken out. The gunner in the back manning their makeshift anti-aircraft gun was also slumped over. One of the FUDRA soldiers had gotten him.

"Sergeant Currie, can you cover us while we try to flank the barn to the left?" called out one of the Colombian soldiers.

Currie felt stupid for not suggesting that himself. He was supposed to be advising these guys, not sitting on his duff watching. They needed his help right now.

"Yeah, go for it," he responded, slapping another magazine into place.

One of the Colombians popped up behind his cover and started firing at the Chinese soldiers. Currie joined in, sending a string of 6.8mm rounds in their direction. The other two FUDRA soldiers leapt to their feet and ran fast and hard for twenty feet to their left until they found a covered position to drop down behind. Once they'd gotten themselves ready, they started firing while Currie and their other comrade took off to join them.

I'm up, he sees me, I'm down, Currie kept saying to himself, mentally chiding the FUDRA officers for not remembering the most basic of infantry tactics.

An explosion not far away caught his attention. He looked back at the house and saw part of a wall and window had been blown out. Several Colombian soldiers rushed toward the breach in the house. One of them had a 40mm grenade launcher under the barrel of his M4. He fired one of the rounds while on the move. The fragmentation grenade exploded inside the hole in the house.

When the two soldiers had practically reached the edge of the opening, an object flew out, only to explode fractions of a second later. The grenade went off nearly at head level. The shrapnel from the blast nailed them both.

Shaking off what was going on at the farmhouse, Currie returned his attention to the barn and its defenders. Chief Smith and his group of soldiers had nearly gotten close enough to start lobbing their own grenades at the barn.

Lifting his rifle to his shoulder, Currie tried to zero in on one of the enemy soldiers. The guy was doing a damn good job of popping up from his position just long enough to zero in on them and fire off a couple of rounds and then duck back down. He'd move to a new position before he'd pop back up, just like what Currie and his ODA brothers were doing. These guys really knew their stuff.

Currie moved his rifle slightly to the left, making a guess about where he thought the enemy soldier would pop up next. Sure enough, he did, and Currie had his sight on the guy. He squeezed off a couple of rounds. The first round hit the guy's helmet, snapping his head backward a bit from the impact. His second and third rounds slammed into the side of the man's temple and cheek.

Currie ducked and crawled to another position as a handful of bullets flew right over where he'd just been. He'd kept his own head above cover nearly too long.

When he reached the new position, one of the Colombian soldiers fell backwards, almost on top of him as he clutched at his throat. Blood was gushing everywhere as he thrashed his legs about. Both of his hands grabbed at the gunshot wound, trying in vain to apply pressure. There was nothing Currie could do for the man—he was dead.

Moments later, the rhythmic *whomp, whomp* sound of helicopter blades echoed off in the distance. Their QRF team was nearly there.

Boom, BOOM!

One explosion nearby sounded like a grenade; Currie couldn't quite make out what the louder blast had been. He lifted his head above his covered position—there was only one shooter left near the barn.

"Currie, I need you to empty a mag in the direction of that PLA soldier," Chief Smith ordered. "I'm going to lob a flash-bang as close to him as I can and see if I can take this guy alive. He'd be a wellspring of intel if we could grab him."

"Good copy. Stand by," Currie replied.

Dropping his nearly empty magazine, Currie slapped a fresh one in place and darted to a new position.

245

"Firing," Currie said over their coms. He scootched up a bit and started shooting at the enemy soldier. He saw that he had a good clean shot to take the guy out but opted to send a bunch of rounds near his head and around him to cause him to duck for cover. As the guy dove to get out of the line of fire, Currie saw the flash-bang sail through the air—it practically landed on top of the guy.

Chief Smith and one of the Colombians were up on their feet, charging right for the Chinese soldier as the flash-bang went off. Smith was on top of him before the guy had a chance to even try and recover from its effects. Smith used the butt of his rifle and struck the man hard in the face, knocking him out. Then Smith and the Colombian soldier disarmed him before they zip-tied his hands and feet.

While that was happening, Currie and his lone FUDRA guy ran toward the barn. They helped to clear it quickly before they moved to clear the outbuilding that was their primary target.

By now, the QRF helicopters had landed. The additional soldiers helped secure the place and treat the wounded. They got the injured guys on the helicopters to be rushed back to the hospital while they lined up their dead and what appeared to be ten Chinese soldiers and eight FARC members.

"Hey, Currie, take a look at this," called out Captain Thorne from the barn.

Currie trotted over to find out what he was so excited about and let out a soft whistle when he saw what the captain was walking toward. "Damn, sir, this place really was a factory."

"Yeah, no joke. You said the shed you guys cleared was stacked with explosives?"

Currie nodded. "Yes, sir." Currie pulled out his pocket notebook and opened it up. "We counted eight crates of that new EP5 or explosive putty-5 the CIA told us to be on the lookout for. Oh, and as if that wasn't bad enough, we also counted a total of sixty antitank mines and more than two hundred antipersonnel mines."

"Hot damn, Currie. That's a hell of a find," Chief Smith exclaimed. "One of the FUDRA guys was telling me about how two police officers had gotten injured by one of those when it had been buried at night in front of the police station. Damn FARC is getting really bold in using these things."

"I think it's these Chinese Special Forces who are encouraging them to go that route. The ChiComs don't care if civilians get injured by the mines. They just want to sow fear and doubt in the people's minds that the government can't protect them," Thorne echoed before adding, "Make sure you document everything on that EP5 stuff. It's fifty percent more powerful than C-4. It looks like these guys had enough material on hand to crank out a few hundred IEDs and a handful of car bombs, if they wanted to."

Dawson motioned for them to come over by him. "Hey, if you look at this, I think they were teaching classes here. These are handouts, probably to some lesson plan. It's detailed enough for someone to continue using it as an instruction manual on how to build the IED. Look at this page here," Dawson said, showing them a couple of really detailed pages with pictures and diagrams walking a person through how to use a kitchen timer, a cell phone, an RC controller, or a command wire to detonate the IED. "I think these PLA soldiers were like us—sent here to train the locals on how to build the IEDs and how to use them most effectively against the government forces and our own. Once they've trained up a bomb-making cell, they probably give them a small stash of the EP5 and the mines to get them going."

Chief Smith shook his head in bewilderment. This was a much bigger find than they had first thought. This was far more than just an IED building factory or weapon cache; this was a damn Special Forces training camp for the FARC. "We got lucky today, gentlemen. Let's make sure we dust everything for prints."

Smith turned to Captain Thorne. "If you'll approve it, sir, I'd like to request a formal sensitive site exploitation team get out here ASAP. They can better exploit the site than we can and make sure we're not missing anything. Once we've gone over the CELLEX and DOMEX from the site, we might be able to locate some of the other Special Forces cells operating in the country."

"Yeah, I agree, Chief," Thorne replied. "Permission granted. Let's get an SSE team sent here ASAP. This was a big win, guys."

Chapter Twenty
Oh Dark Thirty

PLA 6th Armored Division
La Concepción, Venezuela

Captain Li Qiang's Type 96B tank was situated just behind a building on a side street near the edge of town. They had a good commanding position of the approach the Americans had to take to enter the city. He felt reasonably safe there. His tank company was hunkered down in the city with a battalion of infantry soldiers. Even the soldiers had been equipped with antitank guided-missile systems and MANPADs to help them ward off American helicopters and armored vehicles when they got in close. His tank battalion would do their best to make a valiant stand here against the Americans. They had good terrain to fight on and plenty of combined arms support.

The radio crackled to life, interrupting his private thoughts. "Captain Li, the scout drones are showing the Americans advancing toward your lines," explained the voice of his battalion commander. "You need to do your best to hold your position for as long as you can. Do not withdraw until you have gotten my permission. Is that understood?"

"Yes, sir. We will stop the Americans here," Li replied confidently. He truly felt they had the upper hand to do exactly that.

Forty-eight hours ago, the Americans had launched their invasion of Venezuela. Whether it was by luck or design, their invasion had taken place literally days before Li's own unit was set to cross the border and attack them. Now they were on the defense, reacting to the Americans' moves instead of the other way around. What surprised Li the most about the American attack was how fast their units had sliced through the Venezuelan units along the border—they ran them over like they weren't even there.

"Sergeant, we just got word from our scouts," Li explained to one of his NCOs. "The American unit should be approaching our position shortly. Stay ready; we will need to engage them rapidly."

"Yes, Captain. We'll be ready," the senior sergeant replied. He'd been a tanker twice as long as Li. He knew how to fight the tank and what needed to happen.

"Driver, when I tell you to move, you need to listen without question," Captain Li ordered. "I need you to keep moving our tank forward and back between shots or as often as I need you to do so. These American tankers are good. Once we start shooting they are going to be looking for us. Also, remember, after every third shot, you need to move us to our alternate firing location. Keep rotating us between them, is that understood?"

"Yes, Captain. I know the positions," the driver replied nervously. The prior day, they had identified multiple different firing positions their tank would rotate between. Li had been adamant about each of the tanks in his company making sure they had between three or four positions they could alternate to.

Then a voice came on over their company radio net. "Here they come," announced one of their scout units, just a little further ahead of the town. That unit would also be calling in artillery fire for them.

"Driver, move us forward into our first firing position," Li ordered. Moments later, the tank inched forward a bit. They moved the turret past the side of the street and the building they were hiding behind. Li's gunner began traversing the turret in the direction of where the enemy would be coming from.

Looking through the targeting scope, Li got his first good view of an American armored vehicle. There was a column of Stryker troop vehicles. A couple of them looked to be equipped with TOW missiles, while a couple more appeared to have a 30mm remote-controlled turreted gun system.

"Tank, one thousand, seven hundred meters, three o'clock!" shouted Li's gunner excitedly.

Captain Li moved his commander's independent thermal viewer and spotted the tank advancing ahead of the Stryker vehicles. The turret suddenly began angling right toward them.

Damn, how'd I miss that guy? Li asked himself. *Oh crap, he's going to fire on us!*

"Gunner, sabot tank!" he bellowed. His mind was now on autopilot as his training kicked in.

"Identified!" exclaimed gunner, eager to fire before they got hit.

"Fire!" screamed Li, hoping their round took that tank out before it was able to shoot at them.

Boom!

As the cannon recoiled inside the turret, the autoloader slammed the next sabot round into place.

"Send another round at that tank and then switch over to HEAT rounds for the Strykers," Li barked as his more experienced gunner fired their second round.

"Driver, back us up!"

BAM!

Debris and chunks of building rained down on their tank as the American tank fired their own round right at them.

"Did we get him?" asked his gunner.

The driver responded right away, "Yeah, yeah, you got him. There must have been another tank shooting at us. I'm going to move to another firing position."

Damn, that was close, Li thought as they prepared to do it all over again.

Spotting another target, Captain Li called out, "Stryker identified, two thousand, two hundred meters, load HEAT."

Sergeant Song repeated the command, letting him know the gun was ready.

Li let out a deep breath he hadn't realized he'd been holding in. "Fire!" he heard himself shout, louder than he'd meant to.

"Firing!" came the quick reply. The cannon belched flame and smoke as the projectile sailed across the distance between them.

Li watched with satisfaction as the HEAT round slammed into the front right side of the American Stryker, causing it to explode in a spectacular fireball.

"Stryker vehicle identified, two thousand meters. Load HEAT!" Li barked again as he moved his commander's sight over to the next vehicle he intended to hit.

"Round up," his gunner replied.

"Fire!"

BOOM!

The cannon recoiled, rocking them backward slightly until they shifted back into their firing position. When the breach opened so the autoloader could ram the next HEAT round inside, some of the smoke and fumes from the previous round wafted inside.

Li fired his cannon one more time and then ordered their driver to reposition their tank. When they arrived at the new location, there was nothing left to shoot at. What few American vehicles survived those first few minutes had popped their IR-inhibiting smoke canisters and were likely beating feet out of the kill zone they'd wandered into.

Li checked in with his platoon commanders. He was happy to hear that none of the tanks in his platoons had taken any damage. Their ambush had been so swift and violent, the American unit hadn't had time to react or fire back effectively. While he was elated by how well his unit had performed, Li also knew they had gotten lucky.

The Americans now knew a tank unit was in the city. Chances were, they'd send in some drones or helicopters to try and spot them. Whatever happened next, Li was sure his unit wouldn't come away nearly as unscathed as they had this time around.

****

2nd Battalion, 5th Cavalry Regiment "Lancers"
La Concepción, Venezuela

Staff Sergeant Odell Shinseki looked at the digital map of the city one more time. Their platoon of four tanks had been ordered to move toward the city to see if they could find the tanks that had shot up a Stryker company earlier in the day.

A handful of Apache gunships had gone in earlier, and they'd succeeded in destroying more than a handful of the enemy tanks and a few of their armored vehicles before they'd had to withdraw. Two helicopters had been shot down, and another two had taken some serious damage. It was now time to send in some American armor to root them out the old-fashioned way.

"I sure hope the captain knows what he's doing, breaking the platoons up like this," commented his gunner, Specialist Jake Thompson.

Private First Class Nick Giovanni added his two cents. "So long as we get to kill some of those Chink bastards, that's all I care about." Giovanni was their gunner. Both his parents, his grandfather, and two cousins had been killed by COVID-24, so he harbored a deep-seated hatred for the Chinese.

Shinseki responded to them all over their internal coms system. "This is a good plan, guys. The enemy has some artillery support, so spreading us out around the edges of the city minimizes our chances of getting collectively hammered by it. We're also a lot more likely to spot these guys and pick 'em off from a distance. So, stop the second-guessing and whining, because none of you have been doing this long enough to know what you're talking about.

"Driver, start moving us forward. Head to the point on the map I identified. Gunner, help me start scanning for targets. Loader, until I tell you to change rounds, you keep loading sabots. We're tank hunting, and my understanding is we're going up against Type 96B model tanks. These are good, sturdy tanks with thick armor. Now get to it, everyone," Shinseki barked at his crew. Unlike them, he'd been a tanker now for going on twelve years.

Ten minutes later, their tank and the three others from their platoon had gotten into position. They were approaching the city from the northwest, not too far off from where the Stryker unit had gotten smoked.

Creeping through some of the underbrush and foliage, Shinseki's tank edged near the rolling meadow that separated the forested area they had moved through and the city the enemy armor force had hunkered themselves down in. Sneaking through this area likely meant they'd catch the enemy by surprise, and hopefully take them out before they even had a chance to know what hit them.

"Vehicle, stop," Shinseki ordered. "Thompson, start scanning for targets. Those tanks have to be out there somewhere."

The two of them went to work, using their independent thermal viewers. Specialist Thompson scanned everything to the left of the barrel while Shinseki scanned everything to the right. One of them was bound to find a tank or an armored vehicle they could go after. A couple of minutes into their search, Shinseki found something.

"Thompson, I found them. Tank identified, two thousand, six hundred meters. Load sabot," Shinseki called out methodically.

"Got it. Tank identified, two thousand, six hundred meters. Load sabot," Specialist Thompson replied rapidly as he synced his gunner's thermal viewer with Staff Sergeant Shinseki's independent commander's thermal viewer.

"Damn, Staff Sergeant, how'd you find that thing?" asked Thompson in admiration. "He's so well hidden next to that structure." The enemy tank was practically inside a building, with just its barrel sticking out.

"There are no such things as perfect lines in nature, Thompson," Shinseki replied.

Private Giovanni did his part, moving the charging handle on the gun system, arming it. "Sabot up," he called out. They'd already been traveling with a sabot in the tube per his earlier instructions.

"Fire!"

"Firing!"

BOOM!

The cannon recoiled into the turret as it ejected the spent aft casing. It clinked on the floor below the cannon, some of the smoke and spent propellant from the sabot briefly leaking into the turret.

"Load sabot. We're going to put a second round into that tank," Shinseki called out as he watched the first round sail into the building the tank was hiding in and thud into something. It had kicked up a lot of dirt and created some smoke, but clearly, it hadn't slammed into the tank as he had hoped.

"Damn, it missed," called out Thompson angrily.

"Sabot up," Giovanni announced as he lifted the charging arm, which sent an electrical signal to Thompson and Shinseki, letting them know the gun was prepared to be fired again.

Looking through the scope, Shinseki saw the barrel on the PLA tank start to turn and traverse in their direction.

Oh damn, that's not good...

"Fire!" he shouted urgently, hoping this next round would score a direct hit.

The cannon fired. The round flew flat and true this time. The sabot sailed right back into the store, and this time there was a bright flash from an explosion. Seconds later, an enormous blast erupted from within the store the tank had been hiding in. A fire appeared to have broken out.

"Hot damn! We hit the bastard," Thompson shouted in excitement.

Before any of them could say or do anything else, something slammed into the front glacis plate of their armor and made the loudest thudding sound any of them had ever heard. The sudden hammer blow against the front of their turret had really rung their bells.

"Driver! Back us up and move to another firing position. Gunner, find that tank before he plugs us with another round," Shinseki roared.

The young crew of nineteen- and twenty-year-old soldiers had somehow cheated death, but if they didn't find that other tank fast, that luck might not hold.

"There he is!" Thompson shouted. "Tank identified, two thousand, eight hundred meters. Load sabot!"

Private Giovanni hit the ammo locker door lever with the side of his knee, opening it so he could grab for a sabot round. Once he'd pulled it free, he tapped on the lever again, closing the locker. He rammed the sabot round into the breach of the cannon and closed it. Then he lifted the arming handle, letting the computer know the gun was ready to fire.

Shinseki saw the gun was ready to shoot and didn't hesitate. "Fire!" he shouted in earnest.

"Firing," Thompson echoed as they sent their third sabot into the city in less than two minutes.

BOOM!

The cannon fired, even as their driver was moving them to another firing position. The sabot had crossed the distance in no time, slamming into the rear section of a Type 96B tank, which ripped its engine compartment apart. As the depleted uranium from the sabot round flaked off during its penetration, it caused the surrounding area inside the tank to catch fire. Moments later, the entire rear half of the tank was engulfed in flames.

As their driver moved them into a new firing position, Thompson shouted, "Missile! We have a missile coming toward us from our two o'clock."

"Activate the Trophy system. Driver, full reverse now!" Shinseki ordered.

The vehicle stopped moving forward and immediately went into reverse. They drove back maybe a hundred feet, pushing them a bit deeper into the forested area around them while the Trophy system went to work trying to jam the missiles locked onto them. If the system couldn't jam the missile, then the active defense would take over and fire a small number of explosively formed penetrators, almost like a shotgun blast, at the incoming missile.

Less than a minute after they had moved further back into the forest, the Trophy system fired. Fractions of a second later, the antitank missile racing toward them blew apart, showering the tank with shrapnel and debris.

"Damn, that was close, Staff Sergeant," Private Giovanni commented, saying aloud what they were all thinking.

"Yeah, it was," Shinseki acknowledged. "OK, let's put that out of our minds. We still have enemy tanks to kill. Driver, head to this new location I just sent you. It's time to kill us a few more tanks."

"Hooah," was the only reply the crew gave as the tank began to move again.

****

PLA 6th Armored Division

"Captain Li, they just took out Lieutenant Chung's tank. What do you want us to do now?" asked one of his other tank commanders.

Now it was just the two of them defending this side of the city. The last fifteen minutes had seen a lot of long-range shots exchanged between Li's company of tanks and an unknown number of American Abrams tanks. They'd managed to destroy five tanks, but unfortunately, it had come at a loss of fourteen of his own tanks.

Li was coming to the conclusion that their losses weren't the result of a defect in their tanks' capabilities so much as a lack of understanding of tank warfare. At every level of their command, there was a skill gap when it came to how to actually use and employ their force as efficiently and effectively as their American counterparts. His crews just didn't know how to handle and react to the evolving changes on the battlefield like their American counterparts.

Depressing the talk button on his radio, Li ordered, "Fall back to the final rally point. I'll inform the infantry commander that we are withdrawing. We'll look to link up with other elements of the battalion and maybe organize a counterattack when the Americans make their move into the city."

"That's a good copy, Captain. We did the best we could," came the immediate reply.

"Driver, move us to rally point Dragon," Li ordered. "Gunner, keep a sharp eye out for those Americans. I don't want to get blown up as we're withdrawing from the battlefield. Likewise, if you find us a target to shoot at, let me know. It'd be great if we could add another kill to our barrel."

Returning his gaze to the edge of the forest where the American tanks were, Captain Li spotted the columns of smoke from the tanks they had destroyed. He saw a couple more smoke trails but knew those had been scored by the artillery barrage that had just ended. His battalion commander had called in a withering barrage of rocket and regular artillery fire across the entire forest line. Judging by the smoke he saw, the artillery had gotten lucky and nailed four tanks. That meant they'd likely destroyed eight tanks in total. Still, at a loss of fourteen of their own, this wasn't a sustainable kill ratio.

The radio crackled. Li immediately recognized the voice of his battalion commander. "Captain Li, if you haven't ordered your unit to withdraw to rally point Dragon, please do so. We're going to withdraw as a unit to a position just south of the international airport. Once you reach the rally point, come see me personally so we can discuss our next moves. Got it?"

"Yes, sir. We're on our way now," Li replied, relieved that his commander had the good sense to order them to withdraw. He'd already given the order, but it was good to know his commander didn't have a death wish. They could look to fight another day.

****

2nd Battalion, 5th Cavalry Regiment "Lancers"

"Staff Sergeant, did I hear the captain right? We're going to drive into that city?" asked Private Giovanni.

"Yeah, dude. Someone has to provide the infantry with some support," Specialist Thompson explained.

"It's no big deal, Giovanni," Shinseki assured. "The fifty-caliber in my turret can be remotely fired, and we have our coax gun. As long as we have some infantry support, a tank traveling through a city isn't a death sentence."

The four tanks of their platoon were going to support a Stryker unit. Once the infantry started to deploy into the city, a Stryker equipped with their own remote-controlled gun turret moved forward with the infantry. This vehicle was then followed by one of the four Abrams. There was nothing more intimidating than a seventy-two-metric-ton main battle tank. Half the time, just having the tank around was enough to deter an adversary from trying to fight.

For the next two hours, the infantry advanced through the city with the support of their vehicles and Shinseki's platoon. They came across many of the Chinese tanks and other armored vehicles they'd destroyed early in the day, some with a charred body or two hanging from the sides. There were also a lot of dead Venezuelan and Chinese soldiers strewn about the city. Surprisingly, they ran into little resistance. Whatever enemy force had previously been in the city had vacated it, likely to take up a new defensive position further away.

By that evening, Shinseki's platoon had cleared La Concepción with the infantry. They had reformed up as a company on the opposite side of the city and waited to be refueled and reloaded with more tank rounds.

The next day, they'd link up with the rest of their battalion and head toward the international airport to support another infantry battalion as they sought to capture it. Once they had the airport in their hands, they'd have effectively cut off any remaining enemy forces still in Maracaibo. For now, they'd earned themselves a night off to sleep, clean their weapons and get ready for the next major assault.

Chapter Twenty-One
Operation Margaritaville

Task Force Margaritaville
Isla Margarita

Lieutenant General David Gilbert looked at the assembled naval and ground commanders sitting around the planning table. This was the final time they'd all meet on the USS *Mount Whitney* before they'd carry out the largest amphibious invasion since World War II. With the Cuba and Grenadine campaigns behind them and a lot of lessons learned from that quagmire, they were ready to tackle the next major challenge.

General Gilbert cleared his throat. "I want to tell each and every one of you how proud I am of what you've all accomplished up to this point. You have fought hard and lost much these last six and a half months. I'd like to say we've turned the corner in this war, and it'll get easier, but that wouldn't be true. We're about to enter the final phase of removing the PLA from the Americas, and with it, the dictatorship of the Venezuelan regime."

He turned to Captain Dupre. "Michael, is your task force ready to provide my Marines the needed naval support for the invasion and subsequent march inland?" he asked.

"We're ready, sir. These new guns on our Ticos have more than enough range to cover the entire island. We've got plenty of ammo and plenty more we can have transferred to us from the supply ships."

"Excellent, Michael. I know your task force took a beating a little while back. It's good to have your ships here for the invasion. Dave, is II MEF ready to hit the beaches?" Major General David Trout was the commander of the 2nd Marine Division, and it would be his division that'd lead the way in this coming invasion.

"We are, sir," General Trout confirmed confidently. "I've got some Marine Raider and SEAL teams to stir up trouble in the north prior to us launching the real invasion in the south.

"Once we're ready to initiate the assault, the landing ships will move us into position to assault Punta de Mangle. The latest intelligence we have from the Air Force and from our Raider and SEAL teams on the ground show this area of the island is sparsely defended. I believe the Chinese and Venezuelan garrison have fully accepted our ruse that we'll be hitting the island up north near the city of Altagracia. As of right now, it would appear we'll be facing only a minor token force in the area."

For the last four weeks, they'd had SEALs and Marine Raiders carrying out operations in the northern area of the island, pretending like they were mapping out the area for a seaborne invasion. They'd even "accidentally" lost some maps that had a detailed assessment of five northern beaches. All of this was designed to make the locals and the Chinese believe the real invasion was going to be in the north.

"What about the airport?" asked General Gilbert. "How fast will your guys be able to secure it?"

"Once the 2nd Battalion, 8th Marines secures the beachhead, the 3rd Battalion will heliborne in to capture the airport and establish a wide perimeter around it. Then the rest of the regiment, largely the 1st battalion along with our towed artillery and heavy mortars, will be brought ashore. While the 3rd grabs the airport and the 2nd pushes inland, the 1st Battalion will move eight kilometers to the southwest to capture Punta de Piedras. The port city has a series of piers we can use to offload more of our heavy equipment and supplies. By the end of the day, I should have most of the 6th Marines and all of the 8th on the ground. From there, it'll be a matter of expanding the perimeters until we make contact with the enemy," General Trout explained. The goal was to have two full regiments of Marines onshore with all their heavy equipment within the first forty-eight hours. The rest of the division would be brought ashore in various waves over the next five days.

General Gilbert nodded his head in approval. "I like the plan. Just make sure you can execute it effectively once it gets going. Oh, and I'm glad you picked 2-8 to lead the charge—Lieutenant Colonel Bonwit's a hell of a battalion commander. He did an outstanding job at Gitmo."

Gilbert turned to his G2. "Any change in the enemy disposition?"

The intelligence officer shook his head. "No, sir. We're still looking at two battalions of Chinese naval infantry scattered across the island. The bulk of that force has taken up residence in the foothills, near the northern beaches. Similarly, the Venezuelan force is a single battalion of Marines. They have a company stationed at the airport and a company near the beaches we'll be invading."

"All right, gentlemen. You know your objectives. Now it's time to head to your respective ships and commands. I want the ground invasion to begin at dawn on Wednesday, forty-eight hours from now. Good luck, God speed, and dismissed."

****

Task Force Dupre
USS *Hue City*

Captain Michael Dupre walked over to the hot plate to refill his cup of coffee. It was nearly four in the morning, and his squadron of ships was moving into position to support the pending ground invasion.

Following the previous naval battle in this same area a few months back, his ship had been hastily repaired and put back into action. With the loss of the *Lake Champlain*, the Navy had assigned the USS *Mobile Bay*, *Leyte Gulf*, and *Gettysburg* to join his growing task force. All three Ticos had been outfitted with the new 155mm gun system, which made them perfect for supporting the Marines. Four *Arleigh Burkes* had also been assigned to his task force. They'd also been retrofitted with the new naval gun system. At this point, he now commanded two thousand, four hundred and twenty-six sailors. Never in a million years had he thought he'd be in command of so many sailors and ships, but here he was.

When Dupre had taken a seat in his captain's chair, Lieutenant Clarissa Price got up from her seat at the tactical operations section and walked over to him. "Sir, the *Mobile Bay* and *Leyte Gulf* just reported they are in position and ready."

As part of the deception plan to keep the Chinese and Venezuelans focused on the northern beaches and half of the island, his task force was going to launch a barrage of cruise missiles at some defenses they'd built up north and then start a naval bombardment with their cannons. This would last for close to an hour to make the enemy believe the invasion was about to occur all across the northern half of the island. While that was taking place, the amphibious assault ships would move into position and start launching their AAVs and LCACs to grab the beach and establish a beachhead for the follow-on forces.

"Excellent, Lieutenant. Send the message to the *Mobile* and tell them to initiate their attack. It's time we get this show on the road," Dupre ordered, a grim look on his face.

With the order given, all he could do now was watch how things unfolded and adapt to any changes that arose. It was time to let the crews do their jobs.

****

USS *Iwo Jima*

2nd Battalion, 8th Marines

Lieutenant Colonel Mike Bonwit looked down at the well deck as the crew and his Marines got themselves ready to leave. The ship would start to take on some water to intentionally flood the well deck so the two LCACs would be able to exit the rear of the vehicle without a problem. The LCACs would bring ashore eight LAVs and two JLTVs, giving them some immediate firepower and light armored vehicles to push inland with. The rest of the well deck was loaded down with twenty of the Marines' newest amphibious combat vehicles or ACVs. These were the new vehicles phasing out the AAVs, which had been in continuous service for the Marines since 1972.

"You ready to load up, Mike?" asked Major Dave Balding.

Turning, Bonwit replied, "If I said no, Dave, would you lead them into battle for me while I sit back and have a cold beer and watch?"

"In a New York minute," Balding said with a laugh. "But you'd never miss out on being a part of an actual amphibious invasion. This is what we Marines live for."

The two snickered, breaking some of the tension. Balding had taken over as his new XO, and they were still learning to work with each other. After Gitmo, it had taken nearly a month to get his regiment back up to strength. By the time the Cuba campaign had ended, his regiment had sustained a total of sixty-two percent casualty rate—the highest in the Marines. They were eventually stood down for a couple of months to recoup and take on new replacements.

266

Bonwit turned serious. "Dave, I'd like to think we've covered everything leading up to this point. Still, my gut says the Chinese may have some tricks up their sleeves. We need to be ready to adapt to whatever they may throw at us."

His XO nodded in agreement. "We're Marines, Mike. Adapting and overcoming is exactly what we excel at. The men are ready for this. We'll do just fine. But it looks like it's time for us to load up before they flood the well."

A couple of the sailors managing the deck well were waving to them. One held up a hand with three fingers up, which meant they only had three minutes. If they wanted to climb into a vehicle for the ride to shore, now was the time.

Bonwit made his way over to one of the vehicles and climbed in. He had to admit, he really liked these new ACVs. Aside from being much newer, there was a bit more room in them and he felt a little less claustrophobic. The real beauty of these vehicles, though, was their speed in the water. They were twice as fast as the AAVs they'd replaced. They also had a V-shaped hull, which meant they could provide real protection against IEDs and mines.

Once his initial units had secured the beachhead, a group of three expeditionary fast transports would rush to the shore and begin offloading another forty ACVs and forty JLTVs for his battalion to use as they moved inland. The expeditionary fast transports were a new ship to the Navy, civilian catamarans that had been converted to military use. In the civilian world, they'd largely been used largely as ferries—in the military world, they were essentially being used in the same fashion, only instead of ferrying civilian vehicles, they were moving armored vehicles ashore for the Marines.

"Hang tight. We're moving," called out the vehicle commander to the Marines in the back.

Moments later, their vehicle lurched forward. The vehicle advanced toward the rear of the deck well, following the LCACs out the back and into the water.

"Here we go," the vehicle commander alerted them.

The ACV drove off the ramp and momentarily dipped below the water before popping up to the surface like a buoy. Once on the surface, the driver accelerated the vehicle to its max speed as they raced to get up on the beach before the enemy realized this was where they were landing. For the moment, the Navy was holding off on firing on the enemy in hopes of giving the grunts a little more time before they blew their cover.

While the vehicle moved across the relatively calm seas, Bonwit reflected that this was always the worst part of an operation like this—waiting as their vehicle motored along through the water at twelve knots. While it felt slow, they were traveling nearly twice as fast as the AAVs this vehicle had replaced. The prototype ACV had struggled to travel above the seven knots of the AAVs, but once they replaced the rear propeller with a new type of system developed in Sweden, it nearly doubled the vehicle's waterborne speed.

"How much longer to the shore?" Bonwit asked the vehicle commander.

"It looks like we're almost there. I'd say another ten minutes."

"Corporal, are you seeing any defenders yet?"

The vehicle commander did a quick scan of the beach using his specialized optical system. "Nothing so far, but we can only see the shore and a little way behind it," he replied. "They might have a spotting unit in a tower we haven't seen, or if we get closer someone may spot us. If we see something, I'm ready to engage with the fifty-cal."

Above the commander's hatch was a remote-controlled fifty-caliber machine gun. Some of the ACVs were equipped with Mark 19 grenade guns, but most of them were packing the fifties.

A few more minutes went by. Then the vehicle commander turned to Bonwit. "Sir, we're about to have company. It looks like they may have spotted us."

Just then, a series of illumination flares blossomed in the predawn twilight over the invading force. Once exposed, a new threat emerged. The sky started raining down 82mm mortar rounds. Geysers of water erupted as the explosive shells detonated on impact.

Bonwit heard shrapnel slapping the sides of their ACV. The vehicle commander started shooting the Browning M2 fifty-caliber machine gun at some targets he could see. The rhythmic thumping boom could be felt by everyone inside the vehicle. Then Bonwit heard a loud explosion as their vehicle was rocked by a large wave of water.

"What the hell was that?" Bonwit asked.

Not taking his eyes off the computer screen in front of him, the vehicle commander replied, "They just nailed one of the ACVs to our right. We're coming up on the shore right now. Do you want us to dismount you right away—"

"No, keep us going to phase line Apple," Bonwit interrupted. "Let's fight from the vehicle as long as we can and move inland."

Just then another ACV exploded nearby. After it emerged from the water, their vehicle wasn't as protected as it previously had been. Bonwit's ACV had only managed to get maybe a hundred feet away from the water when three of the four wheels on the right side got shredded by the impact of the ACV that blew up near them.

The corporal in charge of the vehicle yelled for everyone to dismount. He popped the vehicle's self-defense smoke canisters to give everyone some cover, but with their vehicle toasted, they needed to dismount and fight.

The squad of soldiers Bonwit was traveling with didn't waste any time in getting out of their stricken vehicle. They had the rear hatch opened in seconds. Some soldiers split to the right, while others split left.

When he emerged from their armored chariot, Bonwit saw several more ACVs that had been destroyed. Some were half-submerged in the water; others had made it partially off the beach and inland like his own. Many other ACVs had managed to get completely off the beach and were looking for targets to engage.

Seeing a flash and some flames belching to his right, in the direction of the airport, Bonwit grabbed for his pocket binos to try and figure out what it was. Meanwhile, his Marines ran toward covered positions. Others engaged the limited number of enemy soldiers and machine-gun positions they were encountering.

As he continued to look through the binos, Bonwit found an antitank gun nestled in what appeared to be a sand dune. The crew looked to be sniping at the vehicles that were bringing the Marines ashore.

Bonwit got ahold of the company CO who was nearest that faux sand dune and pointed out what he'd found. "Take that thing out before it kills more of my Marines," he directed hotly.

"Sir, over here," called out Lieutenant Sorenson, one of his staff officers. His job was mostly to make sure the administrative side of the battalion was kept in order.

Bonwit approached him. "You found us a location to get our HQ set up in or a new ride?" he pressed.

"We'll have a new ride soon," the lieutenant assured. "One of the LAVs that just landed is heading our way. I wanted to let you know the Charlie Company CO said his unit has made it ashore and they're pushing west to grab the port. Alpha Company lost three ACVs, but they're now back on the move in the direction of the airport. Bravo Company lost six ACVs to that damn antitank gun you found. They're also moving inland. They've reached phase line Apple 2 and are pressing on to Apple 3." He read some of the information off the notepad in his hand as he spoke.

Damn, my vehicle must have been one of the last ones ashore, Bonwit realized.

"Good job, Lieutenant. Send a message back to the *Iwo* that we've secured the beach. They can go ahead and send in the next wave."

"Yes, sir. Oh, there's our ride," Sorenson declared, pointing to one of the LAVs heading toward them. One of the staff NCOs waved to get the driver's attention.

Looking back toward the water, Bonwit saw several pairs of Bell AH-1Z Viper attack helicopters heading toward them. Some were breaking off to head toward the airport in support of Alpha Company while a couple pairs headed west to support Charlie Company as they moved on the port. Four of the helicopters continued to head toward Bravo Company, the unit Bonwit had chosen to travel with as they moved inland. Further behind the attack helicopters were twelve of the MV-22B Ospreys, ferrying in the assault force to seize the airport.

A pair of large explosions burst up from the ground in the direction of the airport. A few strings of tracer fire crisscrossed the sky. While Bonwit couldn't see specifically what aircraft were engaging the airport, he had a pretty good feeling it was some of their Harriers.

A Marine standing in the commander's hatch of the LAV that had just pulled up in front of them called out, "I heard you were looking for a ride, Colonel."

"I take it you're Tim, our Uber driver?" Bonwit replied jokingly.

The vehicle commander, a sergeant, chuckled and then motioned with his head for them to climb in the rear.

Once inside, the LAV got them moving again. The rest of the company was already a kilometer or two ahead of them. They were now advancing toward La Guardia to set up a blocking force to help protect the beachhead and the port they had just captured. Once Alpha Company and the elements from the 6th Marines had captured the airport, they'd move to the village of San Antonio and establish a blocking force, preventing a Venezuelan battalion in Porlamar from trying to retake the airport.

It didn't take them long to catch up to the rest of Bravo Company. Thus far, they'd encountered light resistance. A pair of Venezuelan APCs had engaged them, but the 25mm Bushmaster guns on the LAV-25s had cut them to shreds.

****

Now that the morning sun was up and their invasion was nearly an hour old, the Chinese clearly knew the force that landed on the southern side of the island was the main invasion—they started to shift their forces to the south in an attempt to throw them back into the sea.

The Navy began to hammer the Chinese positions with 155mm howitzer rounds. The four *Ticonderoga* cruisers and six *Arleigh Burkes* were really slinging some shells at the enemy. At one point, the ten ships were firing upwards of eighty-four 155mm rounds a minute at various targets across the island. They eventually had to slow their rate of fire— but still, they were landing some forty-two rounds a minute on the enemy when they spotted any sort of troop movement larger than a platoon. The near-continuous artillery bombardment was making it almost impossible for the enemy to move or reposition their forces.

In the meantime, the rest of the 6th Marines was able to land, along with their equipment. By the end of the day, close to one-third of the division would be ashore. Then they would start the painstaking task of rooting out the defenders.

Chapter Twenty-Two
NATO–South

May 5, 2025
VII Corps HQ
Tame, Colombia

"General Widmeyer, I have that report from the 2nd Yorkshire Regiment you asked for," announced Major General Oliver Norrie as he walked up to the map. "They're fully engaged with elements of the PLA's 112th mechanized infantry division just east of San Cristobal. The fighting's turned bloody fierce, just as you predicted it would be."

Oliver was the commander of the British 1st Division and the deputy commander for all NATO ground forces attached to the newly reactivated US VII Corps. The famed VII Corps had helped to drive Saddam Hussein out of Kuwait during the First Gulf War. The Corps had been revived to handle the influx of allied forces joining the war against China.

Lieutenant General Cooper Widmeyer had been tapped to lead the Corps since he had previously been a division commander and more recently served at NATO headquarters. He'd now lead the multinational Corps in what had been dubbed Sector Two—southwest Venezuela.

"That was fast. How are they holding up, Oliver?" asked Widmeyer.

"I think they'll do all right, but I'd like your permission to go ahead and shift the Duke of Lancaster Regiment over to help shore up their positions. The sheer volume of artillery fire those ChiCom champs are able to fire is downright scary. When I flew near their lines this morning,

I couldn't believe it. I don't think I've ever seen so much artillery fire in my life."

"You flew near their lines?" asked Widmeyer.

"Aye. I had a Lynx take me up so I could get an idea of what we're facing. Scary stuff, Cooper."

Lieutenant General Cooper Widmeyer shook his head in disbelief. "Please, don't do that again, Olly. You know the III Corps commander got killed a few weeks back doing exactly what you did," he chided. "I need your help corralling all these cats and dogs we're calling a corps."

"All right, I'll refrain from any more helicopter rides near the front," replied General Oliver Norrie with a laugh. Then his disposition turned more serious. "I do remember hearing about Lightfoot's death," he said. "Did you know the man well?"

"I knew of him, but our paths didn't really cross professionally," Widmeyer responded. "Shifting topics, what's the status of the French? Is the 27th finally deploying?"

Oliver nodded and highlighted their unit on the map board. "They have. They control the line from Abejales to Socopó, along Highway 5."

"It's a big stretch to protect, like sixty-seven kilometers. Are you confident they can hold that?" Widmeyer pressed. "I mean, at some point, you can bet on the PLA trying to break out of their defensive redoubt."

Oliver shrugged. "If they run into trouble, we can shift another brigade over from the British 1st."

"All right, Olly. Just try and keep them bottled up," Widmeyer directed. "Our goal isn't to try and root the PLA out of the mountains. We just want to keep them trapped while we capture the rest of the country. Once they see their cause is lost, hopefully they'll just throw in the towel."

"I hope you're right. This damn war's killed enough people already."

Just then, an aide rushed in, holding a piece of paper. "General, we've got a problem!" the major said in a huff.

"Whoa, calm down there. Take a breath and tell us what's going on," replied General Norrie calmly.

The British officer took a moment to catch his breath before passing along the information. "Sir, one of our recon drones caught sight of a Chinese unit on the move out of the mountains."

Widmeyer lifted an eyebrow at the news and motioned for the major to join them at the map table. It was a large touchscreen monitor with a digital display of their AOR on it. On the map was a digital representation of each division and brigade in the Corps, where they were located, and approximately where the Chinese units were located.

"Here, at this location," the major explained, pointing to the city of Barinitas. It sat on one of the few major highways leading into and out of the Andes Mountain range. It was also less than a hundred miles from the PLA's 38th Army headquarters.

Major General Oliver Norrie looked nervously to Lieutenant General Cooper Widmeyer. If the enemy made a concerted move there, they could reach Highway 5 and completely block their corps's advance on Barinas.

Pointing to a unit on the map, Widmeyer highlighted the 53rd Brigade. "Get on the horn with their commander and tell them they're to race to Barinas and establish a blocking position as fast as they can. We need to stop the Chinese from breaking out of the mountains."
****

Bravo Company, 124th Infantry Battalion

"Damn, my butt is killing me," complained Sergeant Jamie Roberts as she tried to shift into a better position.

Sergeant First Class Jeremiah "Ski" Grabowski laughed at her. "Ah, come on. Are you saying you don't like the new and improved all-leather jump seats?"

Jamie punched him playfully in the shoulder. "I miss my Tesla. Now *that* is a comfortable vehicle to be stuck riding in for a while."

"Damn, girl. You own a Tesla?" teased one of the other soldiers.

"Hell yeah. I bought that thing to celebrate my first big UFC win."

"Hey, wasn't that your only UFC win?" razzed another soldier.

Jamie laughed. "Well, one win is still more than any of you losers have. That fight won me twenty K for winning my match and another fifty K bonus for winning the best performance of the night."

While attending Central Florida University in Orlando, Jamie had fought a few amateur MMA fights and earned herself a slot on one of the UFC fight cards. Her goal wasn't to be a professional fighter; it was just a way of staying fit, paying for college, and proving she could do anything she put her mind to.

"Jamie, if you won your match, then why didn't you keep fighting and do more?" one of the other soldiers asked.

"Eh, I did, but only one more match. When I won, I was offered another match against a much better fighter. This time around they paid me forty K. But this new fighter...woo, she was no joke. I barely made it out of the first round. She ended up TKO'ing me two minutes into the second. After that fight, I decided I was done."

"Yeah, that was probably a smart move," said Lieutenant Hobbs, joining the conversation. "You can only do something like that for so long before your body just breaks down."

277

"Hey, LT, the captain's trying to reach you," the vehicle commander said and then handed him the hand receiver.

****

Lieutenant Henry Hobbs listened intently to the information. He saw the looks on the faces of the others with him. They were waiting for him to tell them what was going to happen next. Whatever it was, it didn't sound good.

When he finished the call, he handed the receiver back to the vehicle commander.

"OK, that was the captain. He said it looks like an element of the Chinese forces in the mountains is breaking camp to fight," Hobbs explained. "Apparently, a French recce unit much further ahead of us reported seeing a large movement of enemy vehicles looking to either block or engage our lead elements around Highway 5 and the city of Barinas."

"Oh man, that sounds like trouble, LT," said Ski, genuinely concerned. "I take it our company is being tasked with trying to get there ahead of the enemy and set up a blocking force of some sorts?"

"Exactly," Hobbs confirmed. "The only intel we have so far is coming from a French recce unit that parachuted in a week ago. Apparently, our drones keep getting shot down, so we're relying on what they're seeing, when there's likely a *lot* they're not."

"That's what I was thinking," said Ski with a nod.

"Here, take a look at this," Hobbs offered as he pulled out his map. "The French reported seeing a column of armor here, here, and here. The captain said since we're a couple of miles ahead of the main body, he wants us to pick a spot for the unit to settle into. I was thinking we could pick this spot. Make this our line in the sand."

278

Ski stared at the map for a moment, seemingly considering all the options. Lieutenant Hobbs realized that not knowing what kind of armor or how many units were headed their way made it hard to know if this was really a good spot or not, but he valued his NCO's opinion.

"LT, since we're infantry, what if we set up in these positions here?" Ski suggested. "Dig in and deploy our ATGMs. We've still got that platoon of Abrams tagging along. They could position their tanks here and here, with us protecting either flank. I think until we know more of what we're facing and how long we have to hold this position until reinforcements arrive, we shouldn't get too bold. For all we know, we could be facing a battalion, or we could be facing one or two brigades."

Looking at the map again, Hobbs rubbed at the stubble on his chin. "Yeah, that could work. This will also place that other town between us and where the French found that unit. The town will slow 'em down, giving us some additional time to wait on more reinforcements."

Ski smiled as he handed his map back. "Sounds like you got it all sorted, LT. Just another thirty minutes' drive till we're there."

****

81st Fighter Squadron "Black Panthers"
Venezuela

The sun had finally pushed away the darkness, bringing with it a new day of possibilities. However, at that exact moment, the only possibility Baron wanted to focus on was wrecking another enemy column of vehicles. Just below the canopy of his Super Tucano were the scratched-out markings of sixteen tanks and twenty-six other vehicles. He was proud of the kill markings that were taking up more and more space on the side of his aircraft. To him, it meant he was making a difference in this war.

Following the end of major combat operations in El Salvador, Baron's squadron had been redeployed to Colombia while an Air National Guard unit took their place. The higher-ups wanted more ground-attack birds in the area for when the invasion finally kicked off. Since the start of the fighting six days ago, his squadron had been constantly on the go.

"Panther Seven and Eight, this is Zoo Keeper. You are to proceed to Sector I6 and stand by for CAS mission," came the voice of the air battle manager, who was in one of the E-3 AWACS aircraft flying figure eights over Colombia.

"Zoo Keeper, Panther Seven, Eight. That's a good copy. Do you have a call sign for ground elements in I6 or any intel on type of enemy activity?"

Major Wilhelm "Baron" Richter had been chiding their intel shop for not doing a better job of getting them some sort of intelligence on the area they'd been flying the last three or four days.

"Uh, negative on the intel. Ground elements are any Gator or Hickory call sign. Do what you can to scout the area leading from Barinas on Highway 5 to Las Piedras. Out."

A moment of silence ensued as Baron and his partner Vader checked their maps to see where they were being vectored.

"Looks like they want us to follow that road leading up into the Andes," his wingman announced.

"Yeah, looks that way. When we get a bit closer to Barinas, I'm going to have Vodka establish coms with the ground element and let them know we'll be in the area. Maybe we'll find a few more tanks or other vehicles to blow up before our fuel runs dry."

"You just want to win the pool to see who can blow up the most enemy vehicles in a single week," Vader said jokingly.

"Hell yeah. Have you seen how large the pool's gotten? It's over two grand."

Every week, the pilots had to add fifty dollars to the pool to be entered for the week. To win the pot, a pilot had to blow up either ten tanks or twenty-five total vehicles in a week. A lot of pilots had come close, but thus far, no one had won, so the pool was becoming increasingly enticing.

They flew along at six thousand feet for twenty minutes, eventually making contact with the ground elements. That was when things turned serious. Apparently, they had some intel on a large vehicle movement headed toward them. The two aircrews lowered themselves down to a few hundred feet above the ground and started flying in the direction where the ground forces believed the enemy was.

****

Sergeant First Class Jeremiah "Ski" Grabowski got out of the Stryker vehicle, barking orders almost immediately. They'd made contact with the French unit and they were reporting a much larger force headed right for them. The enemy was still at least thirty kilometers away, which meant they didn't have a lot of time to get their positions ready.

"I want those Javelin crews set up over there," Ski ordered, pointing to the spot. "I want this Stryker relocated and hidden in that section of trees and underbrush. Mortar teams, I want you guys positioned right there. Dig yourselves some pits; if the enemy starts slinging lead your way, you'll need to be able to duck."

The platoon went to work getting their positions made ready. This was going to be a tough knock-down, drag-out fight until the rest of their forces got there. They needed to slow or stop the enemy just long enough for the rest of the battalion and brigade to arrive.

****

"Whoa, my RWAR is going crazy. What do you say we drop to the treetops and see if we can find the source of these radars?" Vader asked as he dove his Super Tucano for the ground.

"I was just about to suggest that," Baron replied. "You watch everything to your left, and I'll cover to our right. There may be some unmarked logging roads or farm roads they could be traveling down besides just the main highway. But stay frosty—if we find something, it's likely going to come up on us quick."

Once they dropped down to treetop levels, the radars trying to get a lock on them disappeared. Now they needed to figure out who was trying to lock onto them. As they flew less than a hundred feet above the ground, they practically buzzed the enemy column.

"Holy cow, Vader! That main road is clogged with vehicles!" shouted Baron, full of excitement at the suddenly target-rich environment they now found themselves in.

"Yeah, this logging trail I just found looks to be covered in vehicles as well," said Vader. "They all appear to be headed toward the Gator element around Barinas. I'm going to start engaging them."

"Vodka, call this in," Baron directed his backseater. "Give Zoo Keeper all the details and the grid locations. We need to get more help vectored into this area. Make sure they know about the SAMs too. I'm going weapons-free with Vader."

As soon as Vader fired his two Maverick missiles, streaks of red and green tracer fire started firing up through the trees after him. Baron had to remind himself to focus on his own targets.

Baron flipped his targeting pod on and soon found a tank, which he assigned one of his Mavericks to. Depressing the pickle button, he sent the missile on its way. Baron then moved the little TV camera on the pod a little further behind the first tank and found another one. He made sure the Maverick was locked onto that tank and fired.

With his two missiles expended, that left him with two Mk-20 Rockeye II cluster bombs. At this point, the enemy was on them. The ground below them was coming to life; some enemy vehicles must have been firing at them with their crew-served weapons. A few stray bullets came at them from infantry soldiers walking alongside the vehicles. Rounds seemingly flew at them from everywhere.

"We're starting to take hits, Hoss," his backseater announced in a slightly panicked voice.

Baron could feel and hear bullets hitting the bottom of his aircraft. Then he saw the first tank explode, then the second.

Flying toward the growing flames and black smoke, Baron lined the aircraft up just right and took them right over top of the road clogged with vehicles. The enemy ground fire was utterly intense. It was insane the number of bullets being fired at him and Vader. Once his plane flew over the final burning tank, Baron released the first cluster munition. At this point, his aircraft was traveling at a speed of three hundred and fifty miles per hour and had risen to an altitude of five hundred feet to give the cluster bomb a bit more time to spin and disperse its bomblets. Seconds after dropping the first Rockeye, he released the second one.

"Please tell me it's time to get out of here now that we've expended the last of our ordnance," Vodka said once the final Rockeye was away.

Baron turned the aircraft away, deftly dodging streams of enemy gunfire.

"I'm going to make one gun run as we head back across the column to return home. Then we're out of here. Just make sure our cameras are catching everything. We need to let the intel shop know what we're seeing."

Baron had turned the aircraft around and angled them to run right over the same column. It boggled his mind was how many vehicles were down there—the column seemed to stretch for miles on end.

Vader's voice came over the radio. "Baron, I'm going to follow to your right and make a gun run. Please tell me we're only making one run."

"That's a good copy—just a single gun run, then we're out of here."

Vader's voice was a bit rattled. Baron could tell he was terrified. He didn't blame him one bit; he was scared to death right now himself.

A swarm of tracer fire resumed shooting at him and now Vader. The two of them maneuvered their aircraft from side to side to throw the gunners off.

Once Baron spotted a juicy target, he pulled back on the trigger on his flight stick, sending a barrage of fifty-caliber bullets into a BMP. He released the trigger every couple of seconds and then held it down for a few seconds.

The craziest thing was that Baron and Vader were able to strafe this column for nearly six kilometers before they both ran out of ammo. They continued to fly low to the ground until they were at the outskirts of Barinas. They saw a small NATO element setting up a blocking position. Judging by the size of the force, it was clear to Baron and Vader there was no way they were going to stop them, let alone slow them down.

Baron got himself connected to the ground commander and relayed what they had just flown over. He also told the air battle manager on the E3 what they had seen and called in for as much air support to hit them as possible. It wasn't often they found this large of a concentration of enemy forces on the move. It was the kind of target-rich environment every ground-attack pilot only dreams of finding.

****

Charlie Battery, 2nd Battalion, 116th Field Artillery Regiment
30 Kilometers West of Cúcuta

Now that they had finished taking on more ammo, Specialist Tony Davis closed the rear hatch of the vehicle. "We're ready," he said to Staff Sergeant Rob Fortney, the gun chief.

"Great, just in time for a new fire mission. I'm pulling it up right…" Fortney called out before his voice trailed off in midsentence. "Oh, wow. This is a big fire mission, Tony. You may want to leave that door open."

"What do you mean by that?" Davis shot back. "We just took on forty-one more rounds."

"Yeah. Well, apparently, the FIST team spotted a large troop formation heading toward our guys. Until more air support can arrive, they're asking for all the artillery support they can get. We just got a twenty-round fire-for-effect mission for the entire battalion, not just our battery."

"Wait, what the—?" Davis asked, in shock. "That's like a three-hundred-and-twenty-round fire mission. Please tell me this is spread across a few grids, right?"

"Yeah, looks that way. It's spread across a six-grid section. Still, that's a lot of freaking artillery for a single mission. But come on, let's get this going." Fortney got the first set of coordinates plotted in the computer. It looked like each of the batteries and platoons was going after specific targets inside each grid.

Seconds later, the first howitzer started firing.

Boom!

It was quickly joined by many more. Then Davis lifted the firing arm, letting Fortney know the gun was ready.

"Fire!"

BOOM!

The howitzer sent the first round some forty-six kilometers from their position. The autoloader went to work grabbing the next high-explosive round, along with the correct number of supercharged propellant bags. Fortney fired the gun, sending their second round downrange as swiftly as the first.

With each round fired, the targeting computer would autoadjust the barrel or the turret just slightly. In some cases, it would even use a different powder bag to send the round a little further or maybe a little higher.

By the time they'd fired their twelfth round, an update to their initial fire mission flashed across Fortney's screen. When he read through it, his mouth practically hit the floor. The FIST team attached to their sister unit, the Florida Army National Guard 53rd Infantry Brigade Combat Team, had amended the original fire mission from twenty rounds to *eighty* rounds. They'd also called in four other missions, with each of them consisting of thirty to sixty rounds, fire for effect. This meant each gun was expected to fire a little more than four hundred rounds across a very large swath of territory.

"Davis, you aren't going to believe this."

"Let me guess—more huge fire missions?"

"Pretty much. Oh, Cheng—when this first mission is complete, I want you to move us over to this location—I'm sending the coordinates to your navigation computer. Got it?"

"Roger that, Staff Sergeant," Cheng replied, his voice a bit shaky. "I was starting to get nervous about that counterbattery fire you mentioned in the past."

"Yup, that's why we're moving," Fortney said with a nod. "Just stay alert. If you start to see things exploding around us, let me know. I may not notice it with the gun firing. I'll need you to haul ass out of here if that starts to happen, but just make sure you don't hit anyone as you're trying to race to safety."

"Good call. I'm on it."

Fortney sent their next firing location to their ammo platoon. They were going to need more than a few resupplies to get through the rest of this day. Whatever was going on near Barinas must be big, because the infantry grunts were clearly in trouble. Fortney had never seen a call for help like this before.

****

Ski jumped down into the hastily prepared foxhole with Lieutenant Hobbs, who'd just gotten off the radio with someone.

"Please tell me that was about getting us a resupply of ammo?" Ski asked, his hope of survival hanging on Hobbs's response.

"Yeah, it was. And yes, they're rushing us some ammo." The LT pointed to a clearing approximately three hundred meters behind them. "A handful of Chinooks are going to drop some additional reinforcements along with additional ammo for us. Oh, and it looks like the 150th Cavalry Regiment has finally arrived. We might actually have a chance at beating back those tanks."

Ski let out an audible sigh of relief at the news. Their situation had been growing increasingly graver by the minute while they tried to hold their current positions until the cavalry arrived.

"That's good, LT. Just have those forward observers from the FIST team stay on top of that artillery. Those fire-for-effect missions are about the only thing keeping the enemy from overrunning our positions right now."

"Speak of the devil," Hobbs muttered as the FIST team lead scurried over to their position.

"Lieutenant, I wanted to let you know our spotter drone found another unit gearing up to attack our left flank. I've already got an artillery strike called in, and I'm working with our Air Force TACP right now to try and get us a CAS mission, but it's going to get pretty hairy here in about five to ten minutes."

Damn it! We just can't seem to catch a break here, thought Ski. He was irate. They should have had a lot more air support available to them, but instead they had only part of an A-29 Super Tucano squadron for help. What they needed was an entire wing of A-10s, but those were harder to find than even the Tucanos these days.

When he heard the thumping sound of a Chinook getting closer, Ski grabbed his rifle. "I'm going to take a couple of guys with me and we're going to go meet the Chinooks and start bringing as much ammo up here as we can. Where do you want me to direct the new troops?"

"Send a platoon up here to help us and everyone else to the left flank," Hobbs directed. "It sounds like we're going to need the extra help there. I'm going to see if I can find the captain and try to get a few of those tanks to come up here and help us out once they arrive."

Running over to one of his machine-gun positions, Ski called out to the assistant gunner. "Come with me!" He then found two more soldiers and told them to join them. The four of them ran toward the clearing where the helicopters would be landing momentarily.

As they stood near the clearing, Ski saw two other soldiers nearby that he didn't recognize. One was on the radio while the other looked to be providing security. The soldier visibly relaxed when he saw Ski and his three other troopers.

Ski scrunched his eyebrows at the sight of the helicopters.

Those aren't Chinooks.

The helicopters approaching them had French flags painted on them. They were fairly large helicopters. One of the soldiers with Ski said, "I think those are French Super Cougars. Kind of like our CH-53 Super Stallions, only slightly smaller."

Flying with the four transport helicopters was a single Chinook flanked by six French-built Tiger attack helicopters. When the Cougar transport helicopters started to land, the Tigers broke off into teams of two and advanced toward the enemy front lines. They hadn't flown very far when they started firing some of their Hellfire missiles—they were already going after the enemy tanks.

When the French soldiers dismounted from the helicopters, one of them, presumably their leader, came running up toward Ski and his three other soldiers.

The officer studied Ski's uniform for a moment. "Sergeant, my name is Colonel Michel. I am commander of the 2nd Foreign Parachute Regiment. I need to speak with your commanding officer immediately."

"Uh, yes, sir. Can you have some of your soldiers assist mine in getting the supplies and ammo from that Chinook up to our positions?" Ski asked. "My men and I are dangerously low on ammo."

The French officer turned and saw the Chinook touching down. He also saw a group of wounded soldiers being prepared to board the helicopter once it was unloaded. Without saying a word to Ski, he barked some orders in French and a group of his own soldiers went to work on getting the munitions offloaded. Then they followed Grabowski's soldiers to help carry the ammo, food, and water where it was most needed.

As the two of them walked to find Lieutenant Hobbs, the French officer asked, "How many soldiers would you say your company has left to fight?"

Doing some quick math in his head, Ski replied, "I can't speak for the entire company. Our platoon, however, has forty-one out of forty-eight, so we're in decent shape. Just short ammo. The artillery barrage has really saved us."

The colonel didn't say anything; he just nodded.

"Sir, how bad does it look from the air? Do you know what we are facing?"

"If it wasn't bad, Sergeant, they wouldn't have sent my regiment. We're here because this position has to be held at all costs, even if it means we're overrun and wiped out."

Not the kind of answer I was looking for, Ski thought. *Then again, you don't send a regiment of French Foreign Legion to reinforce a position if it isn't vitally important.*

When they reached the fighting position that was acting as the command post, Ski made introductions. "Lieutenant, this is Colonel Michel, commander of the French Foreign Legion's parachute regiment."

Lieutenant Henry Hobbs's left eyebrow rose. Ski figured he'd never worked with or met anyone from the Foreign Legion.

Hobbs extended his hand as he stood up to greet Colonel Michel. "It's a pleasure, sir. How can I assist you?"

290

"Lieutenant, I will be brief as we do not have much time. The rest of my regiment will be arriving momentarily," Michel said as they turned to look back at the field. They could see a lot of helicopters landing just about anywhere they could to offload their human cargo. "There is at least one Chinese division and possibly a brigade headed toward Highway 5 and the city of Barinas. If the enemy is able to recapture this city, they will have effectively blocked VII Corps's advance. Worse, they will be in a position to threaten the paratroopers over in Zone C as they move to capture the capital."

The Frenchman pulled out a map he kept in a pocket on his body armor. "Your battalion is now under my command, along with the 150th Cavalry Regiment. Together, our units are going to hold the city of Barinitas and the surrounding area until the rest of the 29th and 36th Infantry Divisions are able to reach the city of Barinas and assist us in stopping the Chinese.

"I am not going to lie to you—we are greatly outnumbered. When I spoke with Lieutenant General Widmeyer from VII Corps, he told me every available air asset will be made available to help us—"

"Sorry to interrupt, sir," Hobbs said. "Did the general tell you by chance how long it may take for those other divisions to show up and relieve us?" He shared a nervous glance with Ski.

"Unfortunately, he did not," Colonel Michel responded. "He said he thought they'd be in position to assist us in forty-eight hours. Personally, as I flew over Highway 5 on my way to this position, I think that is being optimistic. As you know, that road is not the best and it is completely clogged with civilian and military traffic, on top of now having to deal with a string of IEDs. This is why my regiment was ordered in.

"We will fight to the death to hold this position if necessary, but I am confident the Chinese will give up after we beat them back a few times. Your team has already done a superb job with the artillery. Now, if you'll show me on my map where your platoon and company are currently located, I can go about getting my own units moved into position."

Chapter Twenty-Three
Airborne Leads the Way

82nd Airborne HQ
Yopal, Colombia

The sun had just broken above the horizon, and the colors of the new day began to change, painting the sky. The weather was perfect, or at least, at this time of day it was. By midday, things would really heat up.

Lieutenant General Don Tackaberry stood with his hands on his hips, studying the parking ramp intensely. It was filling up rapidly as more C-130s and Atlas C1s continued to land. The cargo planes were there to pick up the 1st Battalion, 505th Infantry Regiment and the 2nd Battalion, 16th Air Assault Brigade. These two American and British airborne units were going to lead the XVIII Airborne Corps assault into southern Venezuela or Zone C as they opened a third major front for the enemy to have to defend against.

Tackaberry watched as one of the British aircraft taxied toward a group of paratroopers standing near one of the hangars. The aircraft turned so its rear ramp would face the hangars before its engines came to a stop. Fuel trucks drove forward, and the airmen went to work on topping off the aircraft's tanks before the paratroopers would climb aboard.

The general turned to his division commanders. "General Franz, once the aircraft are in the air, how long until they reach the drop zone?"

"One hour and twenty minutes to K1. Then 2nd Battalion, 505th hits K2 an hour later," Major General Chris Franz replied.

"Then those airborne engineering units will land next, right?"

293

"That's right," Franz answered. "They'll get the airfields ready to start taking on aircraft and get the base turned into giant fuel stations for the 101st and their helicopters."

Brigadier General Giles Chiswell from the British 16 Air Assault Brigade smiled. "This is a brilliant idea, General. Turning these airfields into a long string of fuel bases is clever. We could very well capture the capital in less than two weeks—brilliant."

"I agree," said Brigadier General Jeannou Le Borgne from the French 11th Parachute Brigade. "I don't think an assault like this has ever been done before. Let's just hope our brothers-in-arms over in VII Corps are able to keep the Chinese forces bottled up in the mountains and the northwest. So long as the Chinese don't break out into the open and threaten our supply line, this should end the war."

Tackaberry turned to face his multinational airborne force. "Generals, when we pull this off, this is going to be written about in the history books and taught at military schools and beyond for generations."

General Franz snorted. "If we pull this off, General, they damn well better be talking about this at the Point for generations. This is the biggest airborne invasion since World War II, and more than that, no one has ever attempted to capture and then leapfrog air bases like we're doing. Having my guys grab the airfields so you can have the 101st and French land in the outskirts of Caracas without them knowing what's going on is borderline insanity."

"I'd feel better if we could have kept the 2nd Foreign Parachute Regiment with us for the big drop around Caracas," the French general lamented.

The British general nodded. "Agreed, Jeannou. But it sounds like they were desperately needed in Zone B. If the Chinese break out of that mountain redoubt they've built, it could throw our entire operation off."

294

"It's neither here nor there," Tackaberry commented. "Our plan wasn't relying on the Foreign Legion being a part of it, so we're still good to go."

Deep inside his gut, though, Tackaberry *was* concerned about the battle for Barinitas. If the Chinese broke out of that area and captured Barinas and Highway 5, they could sweep across the center of Venezuela and potentially cut his own airborne forces off. He didn't have a lot of brigades occupying the center of the country.

General Franz shrugged off the concern as he and his British and French counterparts grinned at each other. This was the kind of fight every paratrooper dreams about.

"OK, gentlemen, you all have your marching orders. Head back to your units and prepare to deploy with your brigades and divisions accordingly," Tackaberry ordered excitedly as he returned his gaze to the aircraft below.

****

Approaching K1—Elorza Airport

"Stand up."

"Hook up."

"Equipment check."

"Sound off," called out the jumpmaster. He stood near the rear door of the aircraft, which the Air Force crew chief had just opened up.

The jumpmaster completed his check of the doorway, making sure there was nothing sharp along it that could snag them on the way out. Sticking his head briefly out the door, he also got a good look at the target. They were approaching the airfield they were going to seize: K1.

One of the battalion's companies was going to parachute directly over top of the runway, while the other three companies would land to the southeast of the small town and converge on the airport, helping the first company capture it should they run into any opposition. If they didn't meet any resistance, then the battalion would move to secure the rest of the city and help clear the way for the 3rd Infantry Division, which would start their mad dash across the border around noon.

In the distance, the jumpmaster could see that their British counterparts had just started dropping their sticks a few kilometers behind them. They were responsible for securing several key bridges nearby before linking up with them at the airport.

Satisfied with what he saw, the jumpmaster motioned for everyone to get ready. When the pilot had them properly lined up and over the drop zone, he'd give them the signal.

The jump light turned from red to green. It was time to go.

Pointing out the door, the jumpmaster yelled, "Go, go, go!"

The soldiers raced right out the door. The entire row of paratroopers went out in less than a minute. Then the second row of paratroopers followed the first. Once they were all out, the jumpmaster and the first sergeant jumped out. They were the last ones off the plane.

****

Private Chad Heinz didn't have time to be scared. He just followed the person in front of him right out the door. Before he knew it, he was being jerked hard by the static line as it pulled his parachute out and it caught the air, filling it rapidly. It yanked his body hard as it slowed his rapid descent.

Heinz barely had time to see what was going on around him or even look at the airport or the small city before he was approaching the ground. His eyes registered that he was about to land, so he bent his legs slightly just like he'd been taught. This was only the ninth jump of his life. He'd completed the five obligatory training jumps in airborne school before getting assigned to the 82nd Airborne Division. Once in his unit, he had participated in one training jump at Fort Bragg, then one combat jump in Cuba and one training jump in Colombia. Still, he felt he was ready for whatever was going to be thrown at him.

Nearing the ground, he pulled the cord holding his drop bag and let it fall. It hit the ground moments before he did. Heinz did just as he'd been taught, tucking his knees in as he rolled to one side, allowing his body's inertia to reduce the impact. Once on the ground, he disconnected his parachute and rolled it up quickly. Next, he pulled his rifle out of its case and slapped a thirty-round magazine in place. He then moved to his drop bag and got his rucksack and patrol pack situated.

"Heinz! Grab your gear and follow me!" called out his squad leader, Staff Sergeant Jim Rodriguez.

"On it, Staff Sergeant!"

Heinz ran toward his squad leader. As he did, he saw his fire team leader moving toward him as well. The entire squad was making their way to Rodriguez, ready to execute whatever task he directed.

Looking around the airport, he thought they had gotten lucky. No one appeared to be shooting at them. There didn't appear to be any AA guns or military vehicles around the airport either. As a matter of fact, this airport seemed largely abandoned, aside from a few small civilian planes.

"Staff Sergeant, what do you want us to do?" asked one of the privates. Heinz wondered the same thing. *If there aren't any enemy soldiers around, what is there for us to do?*

"Hang on, guys. I'm trying to figure that out," was the only reply they got.

It was times like this that Heinz was glad he was just a lowly private. He wasn't responsible for anything other than showing up and doing what he was told to do. The life of a private was relatively easy aside from the stupid and mundane jobs he often got assigned.

After a pause, Staff Sergeant Rodriguez turned back to the group. "OK, we got some new orders," he announced. "Here's what we're going to do. Apparently, there's a bridge that connects this little town with Highway 19 on the opposite side of the Río Arauca. Our platoon's just been told to hoof it to the bridge, secure it, and set up a roadblock on the highway. We're not to let anyone use the bridge."

The privates all bobbed their heads in agreement. Their squad leader led the way, and the rest of them followed in tow.

When they moved out of the airfield, Staff Sergeant Rodriguez walked up to Heinz with a perturbed look on his face. "Hey, Private Heinz—keep your booger eater off the bang stick until you're ready to bring the hate. I don't want you to trip or get startled and accidentally fire a shot you didn't intend to shoot. Got it?"

Heinz felt his cheeks flush a little bit at the correction. He knew Rodriguez was right. Despite all the training he'd done up to this point, he was still nervous around firearms.

"Yes, Staff Sergeant. My mistake. It won't happen again," was the terse response he gave. Rodriguez nodded and then moved along to talk to his two fire team leaders.

As they advanced away from the airfield, the rest of their platoon steadily fell in with them. The bridge was barely a thousand meters from the single strip airport, so it wasn't a far walk.

As they continued their march, Heinz noticed a lot of locals come out to gawk at them. Many of the people seemed pleased they were there. He observed an occasional sour face, but by and large, the citizens appeared to be happy about their presence.

A couple of young kids came up to Heinz and some of the other soldiers in his squad.

"Are you Americans?" they asked. Heinz and his compatriots nodded.

Then the questions poured forth in rapid succession. The children wanted to know if they had any candy, if they had some extra food they could spare, what kind of rifle they were using, and most importantly, if they were there to get rid of the Chinese.

Man, am I glad I stuck with Spanish since middle school, Heinz thought happily as he understood everything the kids were saying to him.

He was surprised to hear so many questions from the kids, who ranged in age from about five to ten. Eventually, the children did move on.

When they reached the bridge, a single police car with two police officers had parked in a position that blocked off the road. When the soldiers had spotted the attempt at a police roadblock, their platoon sergeant called a halt and told the squads to fan out. He and the lieutenant were going to go talk to the cops and find out if this was going to be a problem.

They talked briefly. It looked like a friendly conversation. Neither of the police officers had their weapons drawn, probably a good decision on their part, considering they were looking at more than forty heavily armed paratroopers who were spoiling for a fight. The police eventually got back in their car and agreed to help them establish a roadblock on Highway 19. Their translator told them the police officers and the people in the city were no friends of the regime or the Chinese soldiers who had taken over their country.

When they reached the bridge, some of the soldiers from Third Squad examined it, making sure there weren't any explosives rigged to its supports. Then they set up a checkpoint on the side of the bridge that connected to the town and the airport. The rest of the platoon crossed the bridge and advanced a little further past it. Then they established a checkpoint at two different locations on Highway 19. The police used their car to help block the lane that typically had the most traffic.

Eventually, a squad of engineers who'd jumped in with them brought a few strands of concertina wire for them to unravel and string across the road. Its sharp razors would make it hard for anyone to move it or do anything to it without getting their hands cut up. The stuff was great for throwing up a quick roadblock when they didn't have anything else. With their checkpoint set up, now it was just a waiting game to see if they'd run into any enemy opposition while additional forces were flown in.

****

1st Battalion, 64th Armor Regiment
Arauca, Colombia

Staff Sergeant Rico Ramos stood in the commander's hatch of his M1A2 Abrams battle tank as they rolled across the bridge spanning the Río Arauca, which separated Colombia from Venezuela. He kept a keen lookout for anything out of the ordinary as his tank rumbled across the bridge.

For close to a month, observers had been watching the bridge day and night to see if the Venezuelan or Chinese soldiers would try and

300

place explosives on it. Oddly enough, they never attempted it. As a matter of fact, two weeks ago, what little military presence there had been along the border had picked up stakes and left. It appeared the enemy had chosen to withdraw inland and make a stand further back within the country somewhere. Aside from exchanging the occasional mortar rounds or sniper shots from time to time, they didn't appear to want to fight.

When their tank, Black Rider Two or simply BR Two, had made it across, Ramos breathed a sigh of relief. BR Two was the first tank from his platoon to reach the other side. Craning his neck to look behind him, he saw the others were on the bridge and nearly across it. In the front of his tank were two Stryker vehicles and two JLTVs. The two Strykers had set up in infantry carrier mode, to provide them with infantry support should they need it. One of the JLTVs was configured with a Mark 19 grenade gun, while the other was sporting the Browning M2 fifty-caliber machine gun. More support vehicles would join them once the platoon had fully gotten across. Then they'd lead the way for the battalion and brigade as they drove along Highway 19 until they linked up with a British and American paratrooper battalion in the small town of Elorza or K1.

The radio earpiece in Ramos's helmet crackled. "BR Two, BR One. The platoon's across. Begin leading the way. Oh, and maintain your spacing," ordered his platoon leader.

"That's a good copy, BR One. Out," Ramos acknowledged. Then he switched over to the channel their infantry support was using and passed along the message. He also told them that if they ran into any sign of trouble, rather than risking their own vehicles and men, they should let his tank handle it for them.

301

With his tank in the lead, the convoy rolled through the border town and into the Venezuelan countryside. Once they escaped the urban area, the surroundings became beautiful and peaceful. Everything was a very deep lush green. Some of the large fields appeared to be farms; others were just feral and left to their own devices. It reminded Ramos of south Florida.

They drove on the highway, which was more like a two-lane road that had needed a new layer of asphalt seven years ago. When the scout team reached the city of Guasdualito, they encountered their first sign of enemy resistance.

Near the fork in the road that would keep them on Highway 19 or lead them into the city, the recon units found what appeared to be two French-made AMX-30 main battle tanks. The tanks had been hidden along the approaches to the town and positioned to allow for a good field of fire along the highway. In the vicinity of the tanks were at least six Russian-made BTR-80s, likely there to provide the tanks with some infantry support.

Once the scouts ahead had reported what they'd found, Ramos passed along word to their lieutenant. He also shared his proposal for how to take these guys out. The idea was pretty straight forward; his tank and BR Three would snipe at the enemy vehicles, using their superior range. While they did that, BR One and Four would maneuver across an open field on the right flank and take out any hidden vehicles they might find on that side. As their tanks took out the enemy armor, the infantry in the Strykers would stand by to engage any remaining soldiers once the armored threat was gone. The goal of this engagement was to take the threats out rapidly so the rest of the battalion could keep moving. The lieutenant liked the plan and told Ramos to get it going.

Dropping back down into his commander's seat, Ramos closed the hatch above as they buttoned up the tank. "Blum, move us forward. We'll tell you when to stop," he ordered their driver, Specialist Andy Blum. "Harris, start scanning for those AMX tanks. I'll be damned if we're going to get knocked out of the fight by some French tank." The rest of his crew snickered at the French comment.

The tank moved down the road getting approximately five hundred meters past the infantry scouts before they spotted the first enemy tank. Once Ramos had ordered Blum to stop, he and Harris used their targeting optics to scan the area for additional vehicles before they moved forward to engage. They weren't in a hurry, so there was no need to bum-rush into the unknown. They'd take their time and do this right.

They spotted two of the three AMX vehicles, and then they found four of the BTR-80s. Judging by what they saw, it looked like the infantry soldiers had also built a handful of machine-gun positions to provide good fields of cover across the road and some of the nearby fields around the town.

"Harris, let's focus on that first AMX I tagged as Target One," Ramos directed. "Then we'll move rapidly from one target to the next."

"You got it, hoss," Harris replied. "I say we hit the first three with sabot. Then we can nail the rest of the vehicles with our HEAT rounds."

Sergeant Timothy Harris had been a sergeant for coming up on eighteen months. He'd likely make staff sergeant during the next board. Rico was trying to give him as much experience running the tank as he could, determining what type of tank rounds to use on what target and when. This way he'd be more prepared to take over his own crew when he got promoted.

"Sounds good, Harris. Lopez, make sure you keep up with the ammo and be prepared to swap out shells if Harris calls an audible. Got it?"

"Yes, Staff Sergeant," Lopez replied.

Private First Class Dwayne Lopez had been with their tank crew since the start of the war. However, this was the first time their battalion was going to see action. They'd missed out on Cuba, and El Salvador just wasn't good tank country, so their brigade had again missed out on the major fighting.

Harris peered through the targeting scope and settled on the first tank. He started calling out what he was seeing and what kind of round he wanted the loader to load.

Seconds later, the tank fired its first shot. The cannon belched flame and smoke briefly as it recoiled inside their turret. As it recoiled in, it spat the remnants of the rear shell casing to the floor. Harris had already called out the next target and the next round, and within seconds of the first one having been fired, their loader, Lopez, had the next sabot round already slammed into place and the cannon made ready to fire.

BR Four had joined in and was working its way through the BTR-80 vehicles. When Harris fired his second sabot round, BR Four fired its second round. They'd both scored hits.

By this time, the Venezuelans had started moving their vehicles to new positions. The last AMX tank did find them and fired. The round hit BR Four but ricocheted off their front plate, causing no harm to the occupants. Their second round hit Ramos's tank right in the hull, where their armor was the thickest. Aside from startling everyone inside, it didn't cause any damage. Seconds after they had taken the hit, the AMX was destroyed. Their sabot round must have hit when their ammo locker was open or they were reloading because when their sabot connected, the entire turret blew off the tank and flipped end over end a few times in the air.

"Driver, move forward slowly, no more than five miles per hour," Ramos directed, and their tank lurched forward. "Harris, if you spot any targets, you just take 'em out. I'm going topside to see what's going on around us."

Ramos liked to think of himself as Staff Sergeant Lafayette G. "War Daddy" Pool from the movie *Fury*. The movie was about a tank commander whose tank was disabled in the middle of a crossroads in the final days of World War II. They held off numerous German assaults until they were relieved by an infantry unit the next day.

Standing in the commander's hatch, Ramos unlocked the Ma Deuce, ready to slay bodies and stack souls should he have to. As their tank moved forward, BR One and Four fired off a couple of rounds. Off in the distance, Ramos could hear a couple of loud explosions, so he knew they'd hit something. Then he saw black smoke rising into the sky. Looking behind him, he saw the two Stryker vehicles and JLTVs were moving forward, following his tank and Black Rider Three.

Ramos's tank had driven forward a few hundred meters when the main gun fired one more time. Harris explained that he'd found another BTR off in the distance, so he'd fired. Ramos was glad to see his gunner taking the initiative to just act when he saw a threat—he'd need to do that when he became a tank commander himself.

As they approached the town, one of the machine-gun bunkers started firing at them. Ramos ducked down a bit as a string of bullets hit the front armor of the turret. He dropped all the way back inside and closed the hatch. Then he switched on his common remotely operated weapon station or CROWS system. This allowed him to remote-control the fifty-cal mounted above. When Ramos spotted the enemy position, he depressed the trigger for a couple of seconds, sending a stream of bullets and tracers right into the enemy position. He witnessed several enemy soldiers get hit and go down.

Harris moved the turret and used the coaxial gun, firing at another position. More bullets bounced on the armor of their turret. Then he heard the words no tanker wants to hear.

"RPG to our three o'clock!" shouted Harris.

Crap...oh, there he is, Ramos thought. He cut loose a string of bullets from the Ma Deuce just as the guy fired his RPG at BR Three.

Ramos connected to their infantry support and got on their cases to deploy their soldiers and help them out. He couldn't have their tanks getting picked off by RPGs. He'd barely asked for help when he saw a string of red tracer fire raking the enemy positions from the Strykers and JLTVs—they were already on it.

The gun battle lasted maybe another five minutes before whatever was left of the enemy simply faded away into the city. Some of the follow-on units would handle rooting them out. For now, Ramos's platoon, the Black Riders, needed to get back on the move and keep scouting the highway. They had the rest of the company and battalion following behind them.

This little battle had stopped them for nearly twenty minutes. They still had a lot of ground to cover if they were going to link up with the paratroopers by noon.

When he climbed back into his commander's hatch, Ramos looked over at Rider Three—that RPG had been taken out by the tank's Trophy system. He was glad as hell to have that Israeli defensive system; it did a good job of protecting a tank from RPGs and antitank missiles.

As their tanks got moving again, Harris climbed up into the gunner's hatch while their loader, Lopez, took a turn at the gunner's scope. They needed to get him trained up on how to effectively use it should he or Harris get injured or killed.

Once it was just the two of them, Ramos asked, "So what went right or wrong with that assault?"

Harris thought about that for a moment. "We took too long to engage them," he replied.

"What else?"

"I should have spotted that RPG gunner before he was able to fire on us."

Ramos nodded solemnly. "Once we saw enemy soldiers starting to engage us, what should you have done?"

Harris shook his head—he clearly saw what Ramos was getting at. "I should have asked for our infantry support sooner."

"That's right. Remember, we had them stay a little ways behind us as we moved forward to engage those tanks. They couldn't tell we were engaging infantry. They likely came forward on their own when they saw them starting to shoot at us once we took the tanks out. As a tank commander, Harris, you need to know your surroundings and make sure you know what assets you have available that you can rely on. Got it?"

"Yeah, I got it. Hey, so why didn't you call them forward if you thought we were in danger, and I hadn't done it?" Harris asked with genuine curiosity.

Ramos took a deep breath. "I could have, but then you wouldn't have had the opportunity to learn," he explained. "When they had fired an RPG at us and you still hadn't called them forward, that's when I did. I wanted you to learn from the mistake so long as it didn't put our lives in danger. I needed to let you push the envelope, so to speak."

The two rode in silence for a moment. At this point, they were driving through wide-open prairies and fields.

Finally, Harris asked, "Did I pass the test? Will I make a good or acceptable tank commander?"

Ramos looked at Harris for a moment before returning his gaze forward. "In my book, you did. You still have more to learn, which is why I'm going to let you largely fight the tank for a little while longer— but yes, I think if you had to take over right now, you could, and you'd do well. That's what I'll tell anyone who asks me—but you still need to think beyond just your tank. You need to know your surroundings better or you'll be in trouble.

"You don't want your tank to get ambushed from the sides by some RPG teams. This will be really important in a city or an urban environment. The Trophy system works, but it can also be overwhelmed, and once it's spent its charges, you need to reload them. Once we stop to refuel and take on more ammo, make sure you swap the spent cell out with a fresh one. Got it?"

"Got it."

"OK. I'm going to head back down and check on Lopez. Get your binos out and start looking further down the road. Maybe we'll get lucky and not find anything else until after we link up with those paratroopers and top off our fuel tanks."

****

1st Battalion, 505th Infantry Regiment
K1—Elorza Airport

Private Chad Heinz slapped the side of his neck, instantly killing the mosquito trying to empty his body of blood.

"Another one of those little buggers got you?" asked one of the specialists.

308

Heinz grunted. "Yeah. The bastards are *huge*. They bite you and leave a dime-sized red circle that ends up itching like hell."

"These things are almost as big as the ones we have in Louisiana— ours have their own runways."

Staff Sergeant Rodriguez trotted up to their position. "Hey, shhh."

The two of them stopped talking. Heinz was about to ask what was going on when he heard the metallic clinking and clacking of tank treads on a paved road. It was also getting closer. Even the ground was starting to shake and reverberate.

Rodriguez turned around and yelled for his squads to take up a defensive position on either side of the road. The SMAW operator from Fourth Platoon was getting his rocket ready, while their LWMMG .338 Norma Magnum machine gunner was ready to rock 'n' roll.

The sound of the tank tracks continued to grow louder.

There's definitely more than one tank, Heinz realized. There were also additional vehicles headed their way.

By this time, Second Squad had rushed over to take up a position near them, and so had three other SMAW soldiers. Just then, Heinz saw the barrel of a tank start to move around the bend in the road. His stomach tightened.

Moments later, he sighed in relief. An Abrams. It was an American tank unit. He also observed several soldiers wearing similar but different uniforms hanging off the side of the lead tank.

"Hey, are those British forces?" asked one of the nearby soldiers.

"Yeah, I think it's that other paratrooper unit that dropped a few miles west of us. Must be nice hitchhiking on a tank," another soldier commented.

To Heinz, it looked like something out of one of those old World War II movies, where all the soldiers would be sitting atop a string of tanks as they moved down a road or in a city.

Staff Sergeant Rodriguez walked out into the middle of the road and waved at them. One of the tankers standing in his hatch on the turret waved back. A minute later, the tank stopped in front of their makeshift roadblock. Rodriguez gave the challenge word for the day, and they responded with the counterchallenge.

Not that it matters, thought Heinz in amusement. *They're driving a seventy-two-ton tank with a hundred paratroopers.*

A captain who'd recently crossed over the bridge from the town called out to the tanker, telling them they needed their tanks and vehicles to line up on the side of the highway all the way down to the other roadblock, about half a mile further away. The Air Force had just landed two refueling trucks along with a few fuel bladders to start turning this little airstrip into a giant gas station.

Once the tanks and their reconnaissance group were fueled up and ready to leave, they'd be free to keep moving.

While the convoy of four tanks, six Stryker vehicles and eight JLTVs had parked on the side of the road, their crews and soldiers got out to stretch, use the bathroom and take a break to eat some food. A couple of refueling trucks pulled up next to their vehicles and started topping off their tanks.

****

Back at the airport, a C-17 landed and taxied off the runway to the parking ramp, which was a flurry of activity. The airfield was pretty run-down and not very well kept. They could only land one aircraft at a time. The runway was barely big enough for a C-17 or C-130 to use, let alone take off from. A couple of the soldiers had managed to commandeer some construction equipment, and they'd begun to create a full-length parking ramp on both sides of the runway. That way, they could land aircraft faster and get them off the runway.

When the C-17 had finally come to a stop, it unloaded two refueling trucks. Once that was completed, the aircraft taxied across the grass to the end of the runway. They waited until a C-130 had landed and taxied off the runway, and then they got back on and took off.

The C-130 unloaded several additional fuel bladders that would eventually park on the side of the airport. The airport known as K1 was the first airfield and refueling stop along the way from Colombia.

Once the tanks had topped off, the British paratroopers jumped back on and continued with their American counterparts. It looked like they were going to tag along for the ride and see where they ended up.

Chapter Twenty-Four
The Enemy's Vote

232nd PLA Air Defense Battalion
K5—Vicinity of Calabozo Airport

Captain Tang Tianbiao was nervous. All night, he had heard the sounds of jet fighters somewhere high above them in the sky. He'd also heard the air raid sirens on and off for most of the last twenty-four hours. Occasionally, he'd hear a loud explosion, and off in the distance, a plume of black smoke would rise into the sky. At night, he'd usually see the flash of the explosion and then hear it shortly after, like lightning and thunder.

One of his soldiers asked, "Sir, shouldn't we turn our radars on? How are we supposed to find the enemy aircraft to shoot at if we can't turn them on? The Yankees are hammering our brothers and we're sitting on our butts not doing anything."

Captain Tang could see the frustration in the soldiers' eyes. Heck, he felt frustrated by it as well. But orders were orders. He was to keep his vehicles' and trucks' radar units off until they were told to turn them on.

"Sergeant, our orders are to protect this airport and city. Until we're ordered to turn our radars back on, we're going to keep them off. For all we know, there could be American fighters above us, just waiting for us to turn them on so they can blow them up. If that happens, we won't be able to protect this vital piece of real estate we've been given."

The soldier nodded but didn't seem pleased by the information. No one was.

Lighting another cigarette, Captain Tang stood outside the door to the single terminal of this small airport. On either side of the airport were two modified Type 08 infantry fighting vehicles. The eight-wheeled vehicles had a CS/SA5 anti-air system mounted on the chassis, which was basically a six-barrel Gatling gun with a two-axis adaptive-follow tracking radar and a surveillance radar with a thermal-tracking sight. The system could be used to engage missiles and cruise missiles as well as low-flying aircraft or helicopters. It was very versatile. Captain Tang had two of them positioned at the airport and two more positioned near the Highway 2 bridge to the southwest of the city.

Tang also had ten towed Type-90 Oerlikon 35mm twin cannons positioned around the city and near the river. Some 280 kilometers to the northeast of them was Caracas, so any ground force traveling through the southern part of the country would likely pass through this town, which made it a strategic asset worth fighting to maintain control over.

In just the last two days, they'd already seen more than three battalions' worth of tanks and infantry fighting vehicles pass through their position, heading south to engage some sort of American force that appeared to be heading toward them.

Fortunately, Tang's air-defense command had also been augmented with four Type-95 self-propelled anti-aircraft artillery vehicles. He had these SPAAA vehicles move around to a new position every twelve hours, to make it less likely they'd get spotted and destroyed. Aside from their potent quad-25mm Oerlikon autocannons, the vehicles could also fire up to four fire-and-forget QW-2 missiles, which had a range of six kilometers. They were deadly vehicles if you flew within their engagement window.

Just to the north of his position was one of the newer HQ-12 surface-to-air missile batteries. Unlike the HQ-9, the missile launchers didn't need an active radar vehicle to provide them with targeting data. The HQ-12 SAM largely ran on a passive radar system. The targeting computer knew what the electronic and visual specs were for all the nonfriendly aircraft, so when it detected an aircraft that fit one of its target profiles, the computer would automatically fire a single missile from whatever launcher platform was closest to it. It was rumored that this new HQ-12 system was actually controlled and operated by the super-AI back in Beijing. Tang wasn't sure about that, but at this point he wouldn't be surprised. The damn thing had been accurate as hell in figuring out what the enemy would do next.

"Captain," someone called out from inside the building.

Turning on his heel, Tang dropped the butt of his cigarette on the ground and headed back inside. He found the makeshift office they had turned into his radio room and walked in.

"What do you have for me, Sergeant?" Tang asked calmly. He saw the men were excited about something.

"Sir, I just received a short message from San Fernando de Atabapo Airport. They said they are under attack. That American paratroopers were falling from the skies all around them. He was in the middle of relaying more information to us when we heard a lot of gunfire happening in the background. His radio went dead before he could finish saying anything more."

Tang rubbed his chin briefly at the news. "Sergeant, try and contact Cesar Trujillo Airport and see if they are under attack or showing any signs of it."

His communications guys tried to no avail to raise them. Then they tried calling a couple more airfields leading all the way back to the border. Near as they could tell, they were all off-line.

314

Tang ordered his communications sergeant to put together a report in five minutes and send it off to their higher headquarters. If the Americans were grabbing these airports, then chances were, they might be next. His higher headquarters needed to know.

Walking back into his own office, Tang picked up his phone and called the garrison commander for this little piece of paradise they were protecting. When the colonel in charge heard his report, he ordered the entire area to full alert. He asked if Tang could have his own radar trucks go active with their systems. Tang said he'd contact his higher headquarters and see if they could, or at least maybe get one or two sweeps in to see if they could get them a better view of what was going on in the air around them.

The lieutenant who was in charge of the two air-defense vehicles around the airport suddenly burst in through the door. "Captain Tang, the HQ-12 launcher just north of the town is firing its missiles!" he shouted. "They must be engaging something nearby. I'm requesting permission to go active with our trucks. At least one of them, sir?"

Knowing he should go active with his systems but unsure what his higher headquarters would say, Tang held a hand up. "Lieutenant, have your trucks stand by. I'm going to have one of the Type-95s go active. If they get taken out, then at least your systems are still active in case the Americans do try to land paratroopers at our airfield."

The lieutenant nodded and then ran back to his station outside.

"Sergeant, connect me through to Topaz Three," Tang ordered as he walked toward his radio operator.

Seconds later, the sergeant handed him the hand receiver. "They're on the line."

Captain Tang nodded, grabbed the radio and immediately started talking. "Sergeant, I want you to go active with your radar right now," he ordered. "I'm going to stay on the line while you tell me what you're seeing."

Nearly a minute of silence passed before the sergeant on the other end announced excitedly that he was tracking more than a dozen aircraft heading toward the city. They were less than fifteen kilometers out. He requested permission to engage them once they got closer.

"Sergeant, turn your radar off and move immediately," Tang ordered. "Find another firing position and then turn your radar on again. I'm going to have the others do the same."

Before he could hear a response, a large explosion rocked the airport. It practically knocked everyone to the ground. Grabbing for something to stabilize himself, Captain Tang stumbled toward the door of the building.

Looking out at the airfield, he saw one of the Harbin Z-19 attack helicopters was a burning wreck. *No, that's not just destroyed, there's a small crater where the Z-19 was*, Tang realized. There was a smattering of parts on fire for a hundred meters around the hole in the ground. The nearby Changhe Z-8 helicopter had been destroyed as well.

Damn! Thank God headquarters relocated our squadron of Z-10s last night. The Z-10 was the Chinese version of the American Apache helicopter. They'd been moved the night before and dispersed to other locations.

Hearing the sound of jet fighters, and in the distance, the faint sound of turboprops, Lieutenant Tang sent the word for all his air-defense weapons to go active with their radars and for their gun and missile systems to start engaging whatever targets were in range.

"Captain Tang, we're getting a report from the bridge that they are engaging a group of American transport planes!" announced one of the

316

sergeants. "It looks like they are trying to drop paratroopers around the city. Some of them are likely headed here."

Before Tang could ask anything further, they heard both six-barrel 30mm guns open up. Then the four Oerlikon GDF guns joined the fray, sending their own 35mm projectiles rapidly into the air.

Walking further out of the small airport building, Tang saw a fast-moving aircraft, possibly an F-16, swoop across the airport and then race away, blowing up his two GDF guns, silencing them. The CS gun spat out a torrent of rounds at the F-16 as it banked hard and gained some altitude. A handful of rounds managed to clip part of its wing, shearing it right off. The F-16 appeared to be spinning out of control when the pilot ejected.

Large, lumbering transport craft rumbled as they approached. Looking to the sky, Tang identified three pairs of C-130s as they began to fly over the airfield, ready to disgorge their human cargo of paratroopers.

Two of the remaining GDF guns opened up on the giant cargo planes, attempting to shoot them from the sky before more paratroopers were able to jump out. While they were doing that, one of the CS gun trucks exploded when a missile slammed into it. Then the second one blew apart.

Tang's only GDF gun fired away at the second row of C-130s. The gunner led the aircraft just a bit and managed to get a string of rounds to cut right into the front of the plane. It looked like they had pumped a few hundred rounds into the cockpit and nose of the aircraft. The plane then angled down toward the ground and lost altitude rapidly. On the sides of the aircraft, paratroopers tried desperately to get out of the aircraft before it crash-landed. Maybe a dozen of them got out before the transport craft plowed into part of the town and blew apart.

The gunner quickly switched to shooting at one of the aircraft in the third group. He managed to blow out one of the four engines while he fired into the troop compartment. The pilot continued doing his best to get them over the drop zone and get the paratroopers out. Then a pair of missiles swooped in and blasted the last remaining AA gun that had been defending the airport.

Cursing at the loss of his remaining air-defense guns, Captain Tang saw what had to be close to two hundred paratroopers descending toward the airfield and the surrounding parts of the town. A klaxon blared and orders were being shouted for people to grab their weapons and prepare for battle.

"Here, sir," a soldier said as he handed Tang a rifle.

Taking it, Captain Tang moved to his office and placed it on the table. He grabbed for his body armor and helmet, then he picked up the rifle and took a position near one of the windows in his office. A couple of other soldiers came in and joined him. They'd make their stand here.
****

82nd Airborne HQ
Yopal, Colombia

Lieutenant General Don Tackaberry looked at the giant digital monitor they had on the wall. It showed a map of the portion of Venezuela his Corps was currently assaulting. Tackaberry wasn't concerned with what was happening in Groups A, B or D with the Marines along the coast—he wanted to know what was going on in Group C, *his* AOR.

Right now, the icons for K1, K2, and K3 were showing green. The battalion of airborne soldiers had successfully captured those airfields and the surrounding cities. The Sapper teams had cleared the runways of any potential mines, the Air Force tactical controllers had taken over management of the air battlespace, and a pair of C-17s had delivered the battalions TOW-equipped JLTVs and heavy machine guns. The battalions had already pushed their perimeters out and were even now looking to occupy the surrounding area.

K4, the San Fernando de Atabapo Airport, was listed as yellow. The paratroopers had made it to the ground and were now in the process of capturing it and getting the airfield ready to receive their vehicles and push their own perimeter out further. What concerned Tackaberry and the division commanders the most was K5. The Calabozo Airport was a strategic airport that *needed* to be captured. It would place them within two hundred and sixty kilometers of the capital and provide them with a base of operations from which to launch both helicopters and ground assault aircraft.

Unfortunately, they had been caught off guard by the emergence of a new air-defense system. The Air Force had thought they had cleared the surface-to-air missiles along the air corridor leading to the city, only to get shot at from a new missile system that apparently didn't require their radar trucks to go active. This meant the F-16 Vipers flying the SEAD missions didn't detect this new threat until they had been fired upon.

A couple of the F-16s had been shot down—worse, half of the transport aircraft were destroyed before they could deliver their human cargo. When the C-130s were finally able to get over the drop zone, they only managed to drop half a battalion, and virtually none of their additional equipment.

What few soldiers did manage to get on the ground ended up being scattered across the city, the airfield, and the surrounding area. The reports coming in were a complete mixed bag. The battalion commander's aircraft had been shot down, so he, along with his command staff, didn't make it. The battalion XO had jumped with one of the companies that did make it to the ground, so he took over.

The remaining soldiers got themselves consolidated as best they could before trying to seize their two objectives: the bridge and the airport. The situation was touch and go, and there was little information coming in from the field, which only aggravated Tackaberry and his staff.

The lieutenant general turned to his division commander. "Chris, what's the plan?" he pressed. "How are you fixing this?"

Major General Chris Franz was nearing the end of his tour with the 82nd. During his time with the division, he'd fought hard to modernize his brigades with the new infantry rifles and develop a new airborne strategy for how to make his battalions more lethal. While this situation his battalion now found themselves in wasn't ideal, he had a plan for what to do about it.

Franz walked up to the map. Touching the screen, he enlarged a section located roughly six kilometers to the southeast of K5, the city of Calabozo. "During the planning phase of this mission, General, if we ran into a problem with the primary drop zone or a situation like this happened, then our fallback strategy was to deploy the 2nd Battalion, 505th Infantry Regiment, our primary QRF battalion. I've had a group of C-17s held back in reserve, ready to deploy them for just such a situation as this. I ordered them to get airborne two hours ago, so they should be over the drop zone in the next ten minutes. They'll drop the battalion across this area here," he explained, pointing to a large section of farmland around ten kilometers south of the original drop zone. "When the battalion lands, they'll be deploying with twelve Strykers and twenty-four JLTVs, already pre-rigged with parachutes. Once they're ready to roll, they'll link up with our remaining guys on the ground, capture the city and the airport, and expand the perimeter until additional help arrives."

Thinking for a moment, Tackaberry nodded in approval. "OK, Franz. Thank you for being one step ahead. By chance, if I deploy the remaining British paras to K5, will that gum things up for you or help? I don't want to make things worse, but I also want to make sure we can hold this place—3rd ID is hauling ass, but it's still going to take them a bit of time to get there."

General Franz contemplated that. "I'm not opposed to it; we just need to make sure we're sending enough supplies in to support and sustain them too. More soldiers means more mouths to feed and more bullets. If you want to send them forward, then maybe see if Brigadier Chiswell would deploy with them. We're going to need to get one of our headquarters elements moved up there. Either we send my group, the British, or the French—but one of us needs to get up there. We're going to have some ten thousand paratroopers there in less than seventy-two hours."

"True," Tackaberry acknowledged. "I'll send General Chiswell. In the meantime, I'm going to stay on those Air Force guys to keep the gravy train going. We need all available aircraft rushing as many soldiers and supplies to K4 and K5 as possible. 3rd ID just linked up with K2. They'll reach K3 by dinner. The next seventy-two hours are the most critical hours to this entire operation."

He reached over and made a call to his Air Force counterpart, another three-star. Once Tackaberry explained the situation, his general friend said he'd do his best to pull aircraft from the other sectors to make up for the losses they just took. His compatriot was also working on getting a couple squadrons of A-29 Tucanos deployed to K2 and K3—the Tucanos could operate out of a rough airport a lot easier than their jet counterparts. It would also give Tackaberry's paratroopers some CAS they could call on, should they need it.

When he got off the phone, Franz gave him a reassuring look. "Everything is going to work out, General. We got this. We won't let you down."

They'd put together a solid plan. Now they just needed to let it play out and trust the soldiers and their training to see them through to victory.

Chapter Twenty-Five
Operation Market Garden Redux

2nd Battalion, 325th Infantry Regiment
Calabozo, Venezuela

Zip, zip, zap!

The bullets snapped several tree branches, causing limbs and leaves to fall to the ground around Private Second Class Juan Gonzalez as he dove for cover.

"Frag out!" yelled one of his comrades from not too far away.

Crump!

Gonzalez heard some shouting in Chinese, in the direction of where the grenade had gone off.

Lifting his Sig Sauer rifle to his shoulder, Gonzalez looked through the Trijicon optic, lining up one of the enemy defenders. He pulled the trigger, sending a single 6.8mm projectile at the man's center mass. Gonzalez kept an eye on the soldier as he fired and watched the man take the round to his chest. He stumbled back before slumping to the ground.

Did I get him? he wondered. *I better put another shot in him to make sure.*

Readjusting his aim, he sighted in on the man's head. The Chinese soldier turned and appeared to look at Gonzalez.

No, he is *looking at me*, the American realized.

The Chinese man had a look of pain written on his face, but Gonzalez realized he would harm him if he could. For the briefest of moments, Gonzalez just stared at the man through his optic. He almost didn't see the soldier raising his own rifle up to point his underslung grenade launcher at him.

Gonzalez pulled the trigger again and watched as his bullet impacted the man's face and his body went limp. The Chinese soldier never did get a chance to fire that grenade. Gonzalez couldn't exactly say he felt bad for killing the man—the enemy soldier *was* just about to fire a 40mm grenade at him—still, this was the first time he'd actually seen the person he just killed. It was a bit unsettling.

"Private Gonzalez, get over here!" called out the familiar voice of his fire team leader, Sergeant Jacob Bain.

"Gonzalez, I need you and Moorhead to crawl up to that position near the edge of those trees by the river," Sergeant Bain directed. "It looks like they have a machine gun set up not far from there. Once you get to that spot, wave to us that you're ready. TJ is going to fire one of our SMAWs at the machine-gun position. When he does, I need you and Moorhead to toss a couple of frags at it and clear it out. Do you think you can do that?" Bain asked, sweat, dirt, and grime staining his face.

That's a lot of ground to cover, Gonzalez realized as he scrutinized the location his fire team leader had just pointed out. He would have to cross the river and get to the bank on the other side, all while not getting shot.

"Um, yeah, I think we can do it," Gonzalez replied hesitantly, "but we're going to need a lot of covering fire to get across the river and up the other embankment."

Moorhead nodded in agreement but didn't say anything.

"That's a good point," Sergeant Bain acknowledged. "How about this? I have two smoke rounds left for my M320. When TJ plasters that bunker with his SMAW, I'll fire my two smokes across the top of the riverbank to give you some cover. You think you'll be able to make it then?"

Gonzalez looked at Moorhead, who shrugged. "OK, that can work," he replied to Sergeant Bain. "Just make sure to lay down that smoke. We're going to be kind of exposed when we run across that river."

****

Moving along the edge of their side of the riverbank, Gonzalez looked at Sergeant Bain and held a thumbs-up, letting them know that he and Moorhead were ready.

"This is either really stupid or brilliant. I'm just not sure which yet," Private Moorhead said, just above a whisper.

Gonzalez snorted. "Well, if we succeed and take that gun position out, then it'll be brilliant. If we get mowed down crossing the river, then it'll have been a terribly stupid idea."

"True," Moorhead replied. "But I trust Sergeant Bain. You know he just got back from Ranger school like a month before you joined the unit?"

Gonzalez knew Bain had been to Ranger school. The guy proudly wore the tab. "Why didn't he go to the Regiment?" he pressed.

Moorhead shrugged. "I think he said he wasn't able to go to selection. He didn't sound too tore up about it. I think the guy just really likes being a paratrooper."

Seconds later, they heard the familiar pop and swooshing sound the SMAW made when it fired. The 83mm rocket shot across the small ravine and impacted either against the sandbags of the Chinese machine-gun position or damn near it. Then a single 40mm grenade flew across to the Chinese side. It landed near the bunker and started puffing out thick smoke. This was followed by a second grenade landing maybe twenty-five meters to the right of the bunker.

"That's our cue," Gonzalez said as he leapt from his covered position and ran down the embankment toward the river. He hadn't bothered turning around to check on Moorhead—his only goal right now was to get across that river and up the other embankment so he wouldn't be so exposed.

As if they had been waiting for something like this to happen, several Chinese soldiers opened up on Juan and Moorhead, hurling dozens of rifle and machine-gun rounds at them. Sergeant Bain returned fire, sending hot lead right back at them.

Gonzalez anticipated that as he crossed the river, he'd step into knee-deep or possibly even hip-deep water. It was hard to judge, considering the water was a brownish mud color. But when he was halfway across the river, it had hardly reached his knees. Gonzalez was thankful for that. He'd managed to get across the river and into the thick vegetation and embankment in only a few strides. Bullets were still flying back and forth between their two sides, but it appeared the enemy had somehow missed that they had crossed the river. The shooting was high and well above them.

Once he'd stopped at the edge of the embankment, Gonzalez looked for Moorhead, who thudded against the dirt embankment next to him, out of breath.

Sergeant Bain was still slinging lead at the Chinese soldiers and they were returning fire. That machine-gun position was back up and running—that damn 12.7mm heavy gun was banging away at the paratroopers, keeping them stuck and unable to advance any further.

Ratatat, ratatat.

"'Bout freaking time Leeroy got that Pig going again," Moorhead said now that he had gotten his breathing under control.

Specialist Jimmy Leeroy was about as redneck trailer trash as they came—think Larry the Cable Guy, live and in the flesh. He was also the squad's next-generation lightweight medium machine gunner. The Pig fired a belt-fed .338 Norma Magnum round that had enormous hitting power and range. When that gun fired, it didn't just wake the neighbors up, it woke the neighborhood up.

Once Leeroy began firing the Pig, most of the Chinese soldiers turned their attention toward him. With the enemy focused on something other than them, Gonzalez turned to Moorhead. "Hey, this is our chance. Let's take these guys out and end this fight!"

"Yeah, man. Let's do it."

Gonzalez crawled up the embankment, and finally reached the lip of the edge. Scootching up just a bit, he poked his head above the rim and looked around. He spotted the Chinese machine gun he'd been sent over to take out. The two gunners were trying to reposition it so they could fire on Leeroy. A little further down the line to their left, a couple more Chinese soldiers fired from different positions at the Americans. While he couldn't see further to his right or left down the line, he knew there were probably more enemy soldiers.

Ducking down below the lip, Gonzalez explained, "We got a few soldiers on the machine gun maybe ten feet in front of us. Further down the line to our right, there's at least two more guys. I can't see beyond that, but we have to assume there are more."

"What do you think we should do?" Moorhead asked.

"I'm going to toss a couple of grenades over top of us toward that gun crew. I want you to toss a couple of them to our right and see if we can't hit a few of them over there. Then we're gonna climb over this ridge and go kill whoever is still left."

"Damn, bro. You really are a gangbanging killer, aren't you?" Moorhead replied in jest.

"Just shut up and do your job, bro, and I'll do mine," Gonzalez replied hotly. He really hated the comments about his being some sort of LA gangbanger. Sure, he'd been in a gang growing up—*everyone* was in his neighborhood. But that was his old life. The Army was his new life, his future.

Reaching for one of his grenades, Gonzalez pulled the pin and looked at Moorhead to make sure he was ready. He had a grenade in hand with the pin pulled. They both threw their grenades at the same time, then grabbed for another grenade and repeated the process. Moments later, they heard some shouting in Spanish and Chinese, followed by a series of explosions.

"That's it. Let's go!" Gonzalez yelled and lifted himself up and over the edge of the embankment.

He saw a dazed and confused Venezuelan soldier with a streak of blood running down the side of his face. Gonzalez fired three times into the man's chest before swiveling his rifle to the gun crew he needed to neutralize. He saw both soldiers were dead.

Gonzalez heard voices further to his left; he pivoted his rifle in that direction just in time to see a pair of soldiers emerge from the undergrowth, headed right for him. He had his rifle already trained on them before they had a chance to react. Pulling the trigger, Gonzalez hit the first guy with a single round just below his throat, above the top of his body armor. He pivoted and hit the other guy several times in the chest, landing the rounds right into the man's body armor. Had he been shooting an M4 and still using the 5.56mm his bullets, he likely wouldn't have penetrated their chest plate. Fortunately, they had transitioned to the Sig Sauer 6.8mm rifle, and these improved rounds ripped right through the enemy's chest plates.

To his right, Moorhead had fired on several Chinese soldiers he'd spotted. He hit one, but not before the guy's partner was able to send a slew of rounds right back at Gonzalez and Moorhead.

Gonzalez felt something like a sledgehammer punch the center of his chest and knock him backwards. As he moved a foot back to stabilize himself, he tripped over something and fell backwards. Moorhead let out a grunt and fell himself.

As he lay there, trying to suck in air, Gonzalez felt like he had an elephant sitting on his chest. His vision blurred and it was hard as hell to breathe. He rolled over onto his side and was finally able to take in a big gulp of air. As his sight began to return and he could breathe normally again, he looked for his rifle, which he'd somehow dropped when he'd fallen backwards. Not finding it right away, he grabbed for his M17 pistol. Just then, a Venezuelan soldier walked into view. The soldier hadn't seen him—he appeared to be walking toward someone else.

Gonzalez got to his feet and aimed his pistol at the man. The guy had raised his rifle up and was about to fire when Gonzalez pulled the trigger twice. His first shot missed, but his second sent the man tumbling to the ground.

Gonzalez rushed toward the figure on the ground, found the man's rifle and picked it up. He saw Moorhead lying nearby. When he approached him, Gonzalez saw that Moorhead's chest was covered in blood. His face was still—blood oozed out of his nostrils and mouth. His eyes had already started to glaze over. Gonzalez knew he was dead.

Knowing he couldn't do anything for his compatriot, Gonzalez checked his rifle. All around him, he could still hear shooting and yelling in English, Spanish and Chinese. He wasn't out of danger yet.

Ejecting the magazine in his rifle, Gonzalez knelt down, grabbed one of his friend's magazines and slapped it in place. He also grabbed his last three mags and put them in his own chest rig. He'd burned through half his ammo since they'd landed. He wasn't about to leave Moorhead's ammo to the Chinese when he needed it.

Gonzalez crouched down as he approached the sounds of the enemy. He knew there were more soldiers somewhere around him; he needed to take them out so the rest of his squad could get across the river and help capture the bridge a little further down. He had to help end this fighting before more of his friends and platoonmates got killed.

Gonzalez had moved maybe twenty meters down the line when he heard a couple of grenades go off, not too far in front of him, followed by a lot of shouting in English. As he approached the edge of the embankment, Gonzalez caught a glimpse of a beautiful sight; half of his platoon was running down the embankment and across the river to join him on this side.

Several RPGs suddenly flew out of the underbrush and slammed into the water in and around Gonzalez's platoonmates, throwing shrapnel in every direction.

"No, no, no!" Gonzalez shouted.

He rushed toward the enemy soldiers. As he came around a bush, Gonzalez saw five Chinese soldiers. Three of them were reloading their RPG launchers while the other two were shooting at his comrades below in the river. Not hesitating for a second, Gonzalez took aim and started mowing them down. In blind rage and fury, he emptied his thirty-round magazine into the five enemy defenders, not leaving a single one of them alive.

Once he'd killed them all, Gonzalez trudged to the edge of the tree line overlooking the river, where his platoonmates had just been mauled. "It's all clear!" he shouted.

A couple of soldiers ran up toward him, grim looks on their faces. They nodded approvingly when they saw the pile of bodies around him. One shook his hand and thanked him for saving their lives.

When Gonzalez looked down at the river again, he saw medics bringing the wounded up to the side of the embankment so they could be worked on. A few others pulled the dead out of the river, lining the bodies up near the riverbank and stripping them of ammo and any other supplies that their platoonmates might need. After half their transports had been shot down on the way into this place, God only knew when or if a resupply or additional forces would be sent to relieve them. They had to make do with what they'd jumped with.

The other soldiers that had crossed over the river were pushing the perimeter out further, looking for ways to hit the armored vehicles still guarding the bridge.

A soldier approached Gonzalez. As he got closer, Gonzalez noticed the set of captain's bars on his helmet and the front of his chest rig. It was Captain Remmy, his company commander. Not sure what to do in this moment, Gonzalez just went to parade rest. He hadn't exactly been around many officers in his short time in the Army, so he didn't know what to say or how to react in situations like this.

Captain Remmy must have seen Gonzalez's confused expression and posture. He smiled briefly as he motioned for Gonzalez to follow him.

"That was a damn good job you did Private...Gonzalez. Are you OK?" Captain Remmy asked.

Gonzalez just stared at him for a moment, not sure what to say. *Am I OK?* he asked himself. *Hell no.* He'd just killed nearly a dozen people and seen his friend get killed right in front of him. No, he wasn't OK.

"Um, I'll be fine, sir," he said aloud. "Just doing my job, trying to stop our guys from getting killed, that's all."

The captain stared at him for a minute. "Private, if I'm not mistaken, you just joined our unit before we deployed. Right?"

"Yes, sir," Gonzalez replied. "I finished airborne school at Benning and then reported to Fort Bragg and the company as a replacement. Since everyone was already deployed, they had me and a full planeload of guys fly down to Colombia and link up with the battalion and our units. I think I was in the company for ten days before we made our jump." Truthfully, he was still a little bewildered by how fast things had moved.

Captain Remmy placed a hand on his shoulder. "No matter, Private. You did good today. You saved a lot of lives. I won't forget this. I'll make sure the first sergeant puts you in for a valor award. You earned it. Now, take a short break and go help the medics. I want you off the line for a little bit. We'll go finish off those two armored vehicles near the bridge. We'll come get you if we need help, but for right now, you've earned a break."

With that, the captain walked off, leaving Gonzalez unsure of what to do next. He should be happy about the break, but his friend had been killed and he wanted some payback for that. Still, if the captain wanted him to take a break, he'd take it. There'd be plenty more killing to do before this bloody war was over.

****

1st Battalion, 64th Armor Regiment
Apurito, Venezuela

332

"Damn, dude, when are we going to get there?" complained Private First Class Dwayne Lopez. "I want to get out of this metal box and stretch my legs."

"Whoa, how about you start that sentence over, Private?" growled Staff Sergeant Rico Ramos from his commander's chair.

PFC Lopez's face flushed as he realized his mistake. "Um, sorry about that, Staff Sergeant. I meant to ask, how long until we reach our destination? I'd like to get out and stretch my legs a bit."

Sergeant Tim Harris laughed. "Can I make him call me sergeant from now on, Staff Sergeant?" he joked. He grinned broadly and winked at Lopez, which made him piping mad.

Ramos rubbed the stubble on his jaw. "Well, I suppose you've earned it, Harris. Why not?"

"You hear that, Private? You're to call me Sergeant Harris from now on."

Lopez rolled his eyes at the comment. "Sure thing. Whatever you say, Sergeant Harris."

The two sergeants laughed at PFC Lopez. They were having some fun yanking his chain. Generally, formal ranks were for when they were outside the tank. Inside this metal coffin, they were family. Ramos was the papa bear, Harris was the big brother and Lopez and Blum were the little brothers.

"To answer your question, Lopez, we're nearly there," Ramos explained. "It's just around—"

BOOM!

"Holy crap! What the hell was that?" Harris yelled as he started scanning to their flank for a possible tank.

Ramos crawled up out of the turret to see if he could find the source of the explosion.

"Oh man. It looks like they just nailed the lieutenant's tank, Black Rider One," Ramos called out down to the guys in the turret.

"What? Are we under attack?"

"No, it looks like they ran over a mine or an IED."

Harris crawled out of his own hatch to see. "Then maybe they're still alive…oh, man. What the hell hit them?" he asked in disbelief.

The lieutenant's tank had taken point the last couple of hours. Whatever they'd rolled over had been so large, it had actually flipped the tank over. The entire thing was on fire. In the center of the road was a huge crater.

The Stryker vehicle behind the tank had also taken some damage. A number of soldiers had gotten out to inspect it. Several of the other Strykers and JLTVs were now getting off the main road and taking up flanking positions on the right and left sides of the highway, ready to repel any further attacks on their force.

Before Ramos could say anything further, the radio squawked. "Black Rider One, Black Rider Actual. What the hell happened up there?"

Grabbing the mic, Ramos depressed the talk button. "Black Rider Actual, this is BR Two. BR One just hit some sort of IED or tank mine. It flipped their vehicle over and completely destroyed it. Their tank's on fire; it doesn't look like anyone made it."

There was a momentary pause, then their company CO responded, "BR Two, that's a good copy. For the time being, you're in charge of the platoon. Go ahead and move around BR One and continue on with the mission. We need to reach K3 within the next hour. Out."

334

"Damn, that's cold," Harris remarked. "The LT's tank is still burning, and they want us to just move on like it didn't happen."

"We aren't going to stay and try to put the fire out or recover their bodies?" Lopez asked in disbelief.

Ramos pulled his tanker's helmet off for a second as he scratched at his hair. "No, Lopez, we aren't going to stick around. They're gone. We can mourn their loss later. Right now, we have paratroopers in need of our help at K4. We need to get to K3 so we can refuel and catch a couple of hours of sleep and then get back on the road. Chances are, we'll take a few more hits along the way, especially as we get closer to the capital. So, shrug it off and do your job. Got it?"

No one said anything for a moment. Eventually they nodded their heads. "Blum, get us moving again. See if we can't pick up the pace a little bit. Clearly, going slow isn't going to save us from an IED, so let's try and scoot a little faster to K3. I'm tired and I'm sure you are as well."

"Yes, Staff Sergeant. I'm on it," was all Blum said. The guy didn't talk much—that was probably a good thing, considering he was their driver. He was kind of tucked away in the front of the tank, away from the rest of them.

They drove on for another fifty minutes until they spotted a checkpoint about a kilometer in front of them on Highway 2, heading into Biruaca. It was a small town leading to K3 or San Fernando de Apure, their third waypoint.

Standing in the commander's hatch, Ramos grabbed his binos and examined the roadblock. It consisted of a single JLTV and a Stryker vehicle, with half a dozen soldiers standing guard nearby. Ramos would have been willing to bet money there were probably some antitank rocket teams hidden in the underbrush on either side of the road. They'd certainly picked a good spot—there wasn't a lot of room to maneuver on either side of their roadblock.

Ramos depressed the tank button for their internal communications. "Blum, take us toward the roadblock, nice and steady. When you get within about a hundred meters from it, stop the tank. Stay ready to move fast should we need to, but let's make sure everything's cool and then we'll continue on."

"Roger that, Staff Sergeant."

As they approached the checkpoint, a handful of soldiers started walking toward them. From everything Harris and Ramos could see, they looked like paratroopers from the 82nd. When they were about a hundred meters from the checkpoint, Blum stopped the tank. The three soldiers on the road continued to approach them.

Ramos stood up in his commander's hatch and watched them get a little closer. He held up a hand and called out to them, "What's Gollum's ring called?"

The paratrooper snickered at the challenge. The Corps commander was a huge Lord of the Rings fan, hence their call signs, challenge, and counterchallenge names.

"My Precious," replied the paratrooper.

"Outstanding. My name is Staff Sergeant Rico Ramos. I'm the lead element for the 64th Armor Regiment, 3rd Infantry Division. We'd like to pass through and top off our stores and stretch our legs a bit."

"I'm Sergeant First Class Mendez," replied the paratrooper. "You're clear to pass through. The POL guys have some trucks set up for you across the bridge next to a small village named Puerto Miranda. The engineers have roped off a large area for your regiment to park and take care of any business. I'll let you know now, I wouldn't expect to be stopped long. Word on the street is half the paratroopers on their way to

K4 got shot down. The guys up there are in a real bad way. They're just trying to hold out long enough for you guys to get up there."

"Oh, damn. That's terrible, Sergeant," Ramos replied. "Sorry for your loss. I guess we'll have to get back on the road once we top our tanks off. We'll go ahead and pass the word along to the rest of our unit." Ramos then directed Blum to get them rolling again.

He passed along the sergeant's messages to their company CO, who said he'd heard a similar message. Their new orders were to top their fuel off, stretch for ten minutes or so, and get back on the move again. They were going to do their best to drive through the night, when the chance of running into a lot of civilian vehicular and foot traffic would be greatly reduced. The next waypoint, K4, was one hundred and thirty kilometers north of them. They had a lot of ground to cover and no real idea of what kind of enemy force was standing between them and the beleaguered paratroopers.

Chapter Twenty-Six
Bumblehive

Camp Williams
Bluffdale, Utah

"This, Madam President, is the brain or nerve center of the AI," said Dr. Ashton Rubenstein said as he guided the entourage through the server farm.

"Is it true that this place has some one hundred petaflops worth of data storage capability?" asked Blain Wilson.

"It is," Ashton confirmed. "Our AI is powered and searchable by a parallel Cray XC50 supercomputer. We just finished building it a year before the latest COVID outbreak upended the supply chain once again. I had the chance to speak with that Chinese defector, Ma 'Dan' Yong, before he was killed. He confirmed for me that our computer—we call it Cicada—while not quite as fast as Jade Dragon, was not far off. Unfortunately, after having spent a fair bit of time talking with Dan, I can definitely say their program is far ahead of ours in terms of learning. That's not to say we haven't made a lot of improvements in our program…I just want to temper your expectations." He guided them to an area where the memory blades were dipped in some sort of cooling gel or liquid.

President Maria Delgado let out a deep breath. It sounded more like a sigh, which was not her intention.

"Is there something wrong, Madam President?" Blain inquired nervously.

He's working too hard, Delgado thought. *We're all working too hard.*

"No. It's OK, Blain," the President replied. "Ashton, I do have some questions for you, but I'll save them until you're done with the tour. I must say, I'm finding this very interesting. I seem to recall when this facility was being built, everyone thought it was part of the NSA's PRISM program—you know, the domestic spying program."

A slight smile crept across Ashton's face. "Ah, yes. I remember all the pandemonium that caused. We let people believe that. I mean, it wasn't a total lie. Cicada was used for some of that, but by and large its focus has largely been on a similar track as the Chinese—studying human behavior and predictive behavioral analysis. That said, we did run a lot of experiments on the software."

"Do tell, Ashton," replied Delgado, her left eyebrow raised. "My interest has been piqued."

"OK. In 2019 and into 2020, we partitioned off about ten percent of Cicada's computing power to mine Bitcoin," Ashton began. "We wanted to teach it about blockchain and cryptocurrency because transnational criminals and terrorists had been leveraging it more and more. We wanted Cicada to understand the blockchain, the mining, trading behaviors, and anything associated with it. We tracked sales, purchases, and all sorts of information that is frankly rather boring. But when it was compiled together and given some context, it helped us identify some unusual trends in how ISIS was transferring funds from their supporters in Europe to people in Syria, Iraq, and elsewhere. This became particularly helpful during and after the fall of Kabul, when the Taliban came back to power as cryptocurrency became a dominant means of moving funds around for them.

"As a matter of fact, while Cicada was doing all of this—studying, learning, and tracking—it had also mined an incredible three thousand, two hundred and thirty-two Bitcoins before we ended its research. We sold the coins during the peak; I think we sold them for around sixty-four thousand a unit. We ended up using the proceeds to purchase additional equipment for the lab, cover the tuition for three hundred promising students in AI across the country and fund an additional ten scientists in varying fields to work here at the lab."

Maria whistled as she heard how much money the machine had made. She was glad this program was operating on what was considered a classified or black funding line. They were able to shield their activities from congressional oversight a lot more easily. Congress writ large was notorious for leaks of classified intelligence. They would have had a field day with something like this.

A few minutes later, they walked into a briefing room nearby and took some seats. This was where they'd discuss next steps in countering Jade Dragon.

Leaning forward in her chair, Delgado pressed, "Ashton, you said Cicada had found an interesting way to transfer money from Europe to the Middle East."

"Ah, yes. Well, that was rather ingenious," Ashton remarked. "You see, what they would do is collect donations in Paris or some other cities in Europe. Then they'd load the SIM cards of these phones with a few hundred to a few thousand dollars. These SIM cards would be transported either in a phone or in a case and handed off to the person on the other end needing the money. It was an ingenious way of transferring literally millions of dollars to these terrorist groups and organizations without us or any of the banking institutions being the wiser."

"Whoa, that's incredible," the President replied. "If that's the case, how did we figure it out?"

"Cicada. During its time mining Bitcoin and learning about the selling and buying practices of certain types of trades, it began to piece together what trades were for illicit goods versus which ones were legit day traders. Again, it came down to explaining the problem to the machine and then letting it determine how best to solve it. I will not say it was perfect all the time. On the contrary, it was wrong a *lot* early on. But each time it failed, it *learned* what not to do. Over time, we put Cicada through a lot of tough challenges that we knew it would fail. This was deliberate because in its failure, we were able to teach it what went wrong, and how to get it right next time."

Ashton and two of his assistants spent the next hour talking with the President and her key advisors, which for this trip included her Chief of Staff, the National Security Advisor, the Deputy Director of the NSA, and lastly, the head of US Cyber Command. Specifically, they talked about the challenge of trying to take on or even considering a direct cyberattack on Jade Dragon. The Chinese computer was just too far ahead of them in its capabilities. Worse, if they launched a cyberattack and lost, JD could potentially launch its own cyberattack on Cicada.

Not entirely happy with what she was hearing, the President interjected, "Ashton, the federal government has spent a lot of money funding your program. While you have achieved some great milestones and done some incredible things with Cicada, our country finds itself pushed against the ropes by an incredibly powerful AI. I find it hard to believe that we have our own powerful AI, but we're too timid to deploy it in defense of our nation. I would like to hear solutions to this problem from you—not excuses. How can we deploy Cicada to be used for the good of our nation? Are there some specific types of operations we could be tasking Cicada with that would greatly aid the war effort?"

Ashton sat back in his chair and looked up at the ceiling briefly before he abruptly answered, "Ball bearings."

"Excuse me?" the head of US Cyber Command asked, speaking what was on everyone's mind.

"Ball bearings. That's our in. That's how we defeat Jade Dragon and the Chinese."

The President put her hands on her temples in frustration. The others at the table seemed just as perplexed as she was—everyone except Blain. A mischievous smile crept across his face.

"Care to elaborate, Blain? You seem to have picked up on what Ashton means by this."

Blain nodded. "You are referring to the 8th Air Force's bombing of Schweinfurt–Regensburg when they targeted the ball bearing factories, correct?"

"I am."

Blain explained, "Those missions ultimately proved after the war to be less effective than we originally thought, but I believe the concept remains true. You're proposing we find one or two critical areas supporting their wartime economy and look for ways to go after them. We could utilize Cicada to get inside the Chinese grid and use either our B-21 or FS-36s to deliver kinetic strikes on physical targets."

"What's the one thing they're going to need that we could try to take down?" asked Maria.

"Chips," declared her Chief of Staff. "It's the same with us. We're all in need of microprocessors for everything from missiles to fighters, warships to helicopters. If we can identify where these factories are and take them out, that might prove to be a decisive blow against them."

"Exactly," Ashton confirmed. "Back in 2020 and 2021, when we were running the Bitcoin study, there was a huge global shortage of computer chips. The Bitcoin miners were collectively gobbling up the entire global supply of them. It was causing all sorts of supply chain problems, not to mention raising the prices through the roof. Those exact same vulnerabilities are present right now. If we can use Cicada to locate where the Chinese are producing their computer chips and then go after those production facilities with our strategic assets, we could cripple their war production. That would have a huge effect on their ability to wage war as they continue to lose equipment."

No one spoke for a moment. They were waiting for the President to weigh in. Finally, she nodded. "Hmm. OK, you've made your case. I agree. Let's move forward with this plan. Ashton, please leverage Cicada to see if you can disrupt the supply chain to hinder the manufacture of these computer chips. As Cicada identifies the supplies being used in their manufacturing process, see if you can provide targeting data to the Space Force.

"If there's nothing else, I believe we're slated to tour the West Coast before heading back to D.C. If you need anything, please don't hesitate to ask."

****

Air Force One
En Route to Seattle

President Maria Delgado stifled a yawn and then reached for her coffee. It was nearly empty, something the steward saw and swiftly moved to rectify. She thanked him for the refill. She'd been running on fumes the last few days—what she needed more than anything right now was a couple of solid nights' sleep.

"As you can see, we have successfully captured airfields K1 through K3," explained an Army brigadier general. "The main battle

343

right now is around K4. We lost half the airborne force on the initial drop."

She raised a hand to stop him. "What happened that caused us to lose half the airborne force?"

"Ma'am, our aircraft encountered some of those new Chinese surface-to-air missile systems—the HQ-12s," the general explained. "We're still looking to figure out how we can better ferret them out. In the meantime, the forces that are on the ground are doing what they can to secure the area and get it ready for follow-on forces. As you can see here," the general said, pointing to a colored tank on the map, "this is the 3rd Infantry Division. Their lead elements are now within one hundred and forty kilometers of the paratroopers' position. 3rd Infantry will reach the paratroopers in the coming hours and will secure the airfield and the surrounding area within the next twenty-four hours. This loss hurt, but it will not force us to deviate from our initial plan."

"What about the Marines in the east? Are they still going to conduct their amphibious landings?" Maria asked, pressing Admiral Thiel, who was back at the Pentagon.

"Yes, Madam President," Admiral Thiel confirmed. "The Marines are still set to begin their landings shortly. We have SEALs and Marine Raider units conducting operations all along the coastal areas as we speak, prepping the beaches and sowing chaos in preparation for the eventual landings. We're a little more than forty-eight hours into the invasion of Venezuela, and thus far, everything is moving along just as we have planned it."

Several of the service chiefs seated next to him nodded in agreement. Maria was glad to see the other generals and admirals all in accord; it meant things *were* going along smoothly.

"Uh, excuse me, Madam President, but we have some *urgent* business that I believe we must discuss before you land in Seattle and get further sidetracked. This simply cannot wait any longer."

Without looking up to see who had spoken, President Delgado immediately recognized the voice of her Secretary of State, Hayden Albridge. He hadn't necessarily been her first choice for Secretary of State, but achieving the highest office in the land only came through obtaining a lot of help along the way—help that typically came with strings attached. Hayden Albridge happened to be one of the names she'd been informed must have a cabinet position when she won. Delgado didn't have anything in particular against Hayden; he was more than qualified for the job. He *was* a policy wonk—then again, considering that the previous administration's Secretary of State was anything but a policy wonk, Hayden made perfect sense.

The President made eye contact with her Secretary of State, who was joining them from his office in Foggy Bottom. "Yes, Hayden. You had mentioned earlier that you had something urgent you needed us to talk about. Please, bring us up to speed," she directed.

Hayden gave a sheepish smile. "Uh, yes, ma'am. What we need to discuss, I mean, what hasn't been talked about…is Korea."

"What about Korea?" Delgado pushed, a bad feeling taking root in her stomach.

"I spoke with my counterparts in Seoul and in Tokyo. They're becoming increasingly alarmed by what's taking place in the north. They're asking if we're aware of any plans by the north to launch a preemptive attack and if we have any potential plans to launch one ourselves."

"Excuse me, Mr. Secretary, did either of these nations share with you what they believe the North Koreans are doing that they believe is cause for alarm?" Blain pressed. "I ask because as of right now, neither the CIA nor the DIA is reporting any precursor activity taking place there, which is why we haven't changed our own posture toward them."

Undeterred, Hayden explained, "When I talked with them, Mr. Wilson, they shared with me some rather disturbing information. First, over the last six weeks, the Chinese have more than tripled the quantity of food aid they're providing to the North Korean military. Second, in just the last two weeks, they've sharply increased the amount of fuel and munitions they normally provide to their military. Then, as if that wasn't alarming enough, yesterday, they announced that in six days, they'll be carrying out a large mobilization and war-gaming drill along the demilitarized zone. This is likely cover for them to get everyone in position and ready to launch an invasion of the south."

President Delgado was surprised by this and turned to Admiral Thiel. "Is there any truth to this? Have you guys been tracking any of this as well?"

The admiral seemed a bit caught off guard by the sudden question. He turned to look at the Air Force Chief of Staff before he unmuted his line. "Madam President, throughout the war with China, we have been monitoring the North's activity. At the outset of the war, the Chinese displayed this exact same type of behavior: they provided the North with an increase in food aid, fuel and munitions, the North did a large mobilization drill that lasted a month, and then they went home. This all happened just after the election, and nothing came of it. It's our collective opinion that the North is once again going through the motions of saber-rattling for attention, just like last time. It's likely they're doing this in preparation for their own invasion of the Russian Far East, which we believe is imminent—"

346

"I think you're wrong, General," interrupted Hayden. "When the North did this last time, it was at the outset of winter—the worst possible time to go to war. They know that, and we know that. This time is different. We're at the beginning of summer. The bulk of our forces are also heavily tied down in Venezuela, and the Japanese have largely lost their navy and air force in running engagements with the Chinese these last six months. If there was ever a time for the North to invade the South, now is it. We are powerless to stop them, and so are the Japanese. The South Koreans and our limited number of soldiers on the peninsula would be on their own."

No one spoke for a few minutes; Hayden's last statements just kind of hung there like an albatross around the necks of everyone present. He'd aptly articulated what none of them wanted to admit. If the North wanted to make a move on the south, there was little they could do to stop them.

Blain finally addressed the Pentagon group. "Admiral, if the North attacks with nuclear weapons, we already know what kind of response we'll deliver. But if they opt to keep this fight conventional, what kind of support do you believe we'll be able to provide to our allies and how best should we look to protect our forces currently stationed there?"

The Joint Chiefs looked to be talking amongst themselves for a few moments before they unmuted their side of the conversation. When they did, they explained, "I think it really depends on what their objectives are. In the past, it has been believed that the North would rain tens of thousands of artillery rounds down on Seoul. While we can't completely rule out that possibility, we do have to ask the question, 'Why?' It has no military purpose. If the North's goal is unification, then why destroy one of the crown jewels of the conquest? There's a growing consensus that if the North were to launch an invasion of the South, the attack would focus largely on military objectives, with the goal of taking them out so they could swoop in and capture the South intact and not lay claim to the rubbled ruins of what was once a great city or nation."

"OK, so if that were to be the strategy they took, then how should we respond and what kind of support could we possibly offer?" pressed President Delgado.

"Right now, we have most of the 2nd Infantry Division still forward deployed on the peninsula. Should it come down to a shooting war, they'll fight alongside their Korean counterparts to hold the line and or repel the invader," the Army Chief of Staff explained.

Delgado shook her head. She knew if that happened, there was no way they'd be able to reinforce them or send them any additional help. They'd be fighting on their own with the South Koreans for as long as they were able to hold up.

"Admiral Thiel, if an invasion were to occur, how likely is it that the South could hold out against the North? Are they strong enough to hold their own or would they be wiped out?" the President inquired.

Admiral Thiel seemed to squirm in his chair a bit as he responded. "Ma'am, that all depends on how the North Koreans open the war. If they keep it strictly conventional and stay confined to military targets, then I believe the South Koreans have a better than fifty percent chance of defeating them. The South has better equipment and is better trained and better led. But if the North opts to hit the South with tactical nuclear weapons, then all bets are off. They could conceivably wipe out the South's ability to defend themselves in the opening minutes of the war and then swoop in and capture the entire country in a couple of days. Of course, if they use nuclear weapons, we'd be obligated to use them in retaliation. If we did that, there's a chance the Chinese may in turn use that as justification to hit us with a limited strike—"

"Whoa, exactly where would the Chinese launch this limited strike against us?" Maria shot back in surprise.

"I'm not saying it's a certainty, Madam President, just that they may come to the aid of their ally as we would," Admiral Thiel explained. "If they did, I don't think they would hit our homeland—that would necessitate us hitting back at theirs. I think they would hit one or two of our overseas bases on Japan, if I had to guess. It would neutralize a threat posed to them and send a message not to use further nuclear weapons."

No one said anything for a moment again. The sudden realization of how quickly this war could turn nuclear was disturbing. Then Hayden spoke up. "Madam President, if I may, I'd like to reach out to the North Koreans. Maybe if we make an overt offer to them to stay out of the war, we can get them to agree, and all of this can be a moot point?"

"What do you have in mind?" Delgado asked hesitantly.

"I'd like to offer them a certain tonnage of food stock and coal that could be delivered for the next twenty-four months, but only if they stay out of the war."

"And if they opt to enter the war?" asked Admiral Thiel.

"Then we threaten them with nuclear annihilation," countered Hayden.

****

Puget Sound Naval Shipyard
Bremerton, Washington

The Sikorsky VH-92, otherwise known as Marine One, banked to the left slightly before leveling out and then coming to a slow hover over the shipyard. It was providing the President and the small staff traveling with her a bird's-eye view of the shipyard below.

The main drydock still housed the *Nimitz*. Prior to the cruise missile attack on the opening day of the war, the *Nimitz* had been slated to be scrapped. When the USS *Doris Miller* had been commissioned, the *Nimitz* was the next oldest carrier to be phased out. The Navy was fortunate that the ship had been only weeks into the decommissioning process when the war had started. They'd been able to get its reactors refueled and most of its critical functions operational again. Now they needed to finalize a few other repairs before they reflooded the dock and moved the ship to a pier to finalize the work.

"I still can't believe that after all these months, there's still so much battle damage from the initial days of the war," the President commented.

All around the naval base were pockmarks of damage: a burned-out building here, a destroyed crane there. There were signs of new life as well. Cranes helped to erect new buildings while others worked to bring older ships from the Ghost fleets back to active service. The naval docks of Bremerton were bustling with activity.

"We're doing our best to repair what we can and get our ships back in the fight, ma'am," said the base commander, a Navy captain who was riding along with them.

A few minutes later, the helicopter started heading toward the Trident base just to the north.

"Our base up here took a lot of hits, ma'am," the captain explained. "We lost a couple of our boomers that were in port at the time. They also managed to hit our ballistic missile storage facilities."

The President shook her head in disbelief as they overflew the base and she toured the damage from the air. During her time as President, she hadn't had the time to visit a lot of the West Coast or the military facilities out here. So much of her focus had been on the war in the

Caribbean and dealing with everything going on down there. Seeing the damage these facilities had taken, it really hit home how hard the Chinese had sucker-punched the military and the civilian infrastructure needed to support and sustain them. She now knew why certain budgetary line items were so large. A lot of rebuilding needed to take place if they were to have any hope of rebuilding the tools of war and once again turning America into the arsenal of democracy.

Finally, she turned toward the pilots. "I think I've seen enough. Let's head back to JBLM. I want to speak with Lieutenant General Shaw Brooks from I Corps. Please make sure he knows I want to speak with him as soon as we arrive at the base," she directed before returning her gaze to look outside the windows once again.

The rest of the staff traveling with her got the hint to leave her alone. The helicopter flew for another twenty-five minutes before it eventually arrived over the sprawling joint Army–Air Force base. Back in 2005, the Base Realignment and Closure Commission had recommended combining the two facilities to save money. Once combined, the new Joint Base Lewis-McChord now comprised some 86,000 acres, making it the fourth-largest military installation in the US.

Marine One circled the parade field adjacent to the I Corps headquarters buildings before settling down. As the pilot deftly landed the giant Sikorsky helicopter on the ground, several Marines in their dress uniforms ran forward to be in position to welcome the President to the base and be the first to greet her as she exited the helicopter, per tradition. Directly behind them was Lieutenant General Shaw Brooks and some members of his staff, along with a handful of Secret Service members.

First out of the helicopter was one of her personal protective detail agents, quickly followed by one of her military advisors. The officer carrying the nuclear football exited next, then Blain Wilson, followed by the President and her Chief of Staff. The general walked up to her, saluted, and extended his hand. They exchanged pleasantries as he guided them across the field and toward his headquarters building.

As they walked, President Delgado did her best to look around the place. Directly across from them was the large multistory headquarters building with the words *America's First Corps* embossed on the walls between the second and third floors of the brick walls.

While she couldn't see as much as she had from the helicopter, she could still make out the occasional building that had taken a cruise missile hit. Even the Army barracks hadn't been spared by the Chinese merchant raiders that had snuck up on America's coasts and struck targets with impunity.

When the President and her entourage made their way into the building, she thanked Lieutenant General Brooks for meeting with her last-minute like this. He hadn't been on her official list of people to meet with.

"It's not a problem, Madam President. I'm happy to meet with our Commander in Chief. What can I do for you?" General Brooks asked.

A pair of junior soldiers held the doors open for them to walk into a conference room that looked like it had previously been in use for some other meeting. As they all began to take their seats, Delgado got right down to it.

"General Brooks, I'm not going to beat around the bush or mince words. I need straight answers and I need no-BS assessments. Your corps specializes in dealing with Asia, and in particular, North Korea. Do you believe the North Koreans will look to take advantage of the situation going on with China and stir up trouble with the South?"

General Brooks shot a nervous look to the brigadier general traveling with her, who only shrugged. The President's traveling military advisor was actually two grades below Brooks, and truthfully, Brooks likely knew more about what she was getting at. Finally, he asked, "What have the Joint Chiefs said about this?"

"Oh no, General. You don't get to defer to their judgment," the President pushed back. "I know what they've said. I want a second opinion. I want an unbiased opinion, not some groupthink consensus. You are the I Corps commander. You're supposed to be an expert on this subject, so please, provide me with your expert opinion. What do you think they're likely to do?"

"Uh, yes, Madam President. Our intelligence office has been monitoring the cross-border trade between the Chinese and the North Koreans. Unlike the previous trades that took place in the winter, the trades taking place now are different."

"Different? How so?" asked Blain Wilson.

"In the winter, they provided fuel, food, and munitions—precursors for what could have been seen as an invasion. Ultimately it didn't turn out to be anything," General Brooks began. "More likely, it was meant to help their military get through an unusually tough winter. This spring, however, we've seen them not only provide essentially double of those same materials but also a substantial increase in food aid to everyday people living inside North Korea. This has greatly improved the morale across the country. We also just received some rather disturbing satellite photos from Space Command yesterday." Brooks motioned for one of his aides to bring them the photos he'd mentioned.

"What am I looking at, General?" asked the President.

"Those photos are of a transporter erector launcher or TEL. That," he said, pointing to the missile itself, "appears to be a Hwasong-15

ICBM. These were taken yesterday and show the North Koreans deploying them to numerous positions around the country. In my opinion, it means they're likely planning on using them."

President Delgado shot Blain a nervous look. He had a similar look of shock and horror written on his face as well. The brigadier general traveling with her didn't know what to say.

Delgado returned her attention to General Brooks. "If the North does decide to use their nuclear weapons, one, what are the chances that we'll be able to knock them down, and two, what should our response be?"

Brooks sat back in his chair for a moment and looked up at the ceiling, likely contemplating his answer. When he looked back at her, he spoke honestly. "If they launch ICBMs at us, Madam President, then it depends on how many they throw at us and where they're targeted. If they fire them at the continental US, we have a lot more ground-based interceptors we can rely on. If they fire them at South Korea, then we have the THAADs. If they're fired at Japan or Guam, then we have a combination of THAADs and AEGIS destroyers. The wild card in all this, ma'am, is how many decoys are potentially in those warheads of theirs. We only have so many interceptors that can be fired, and if half of them are shot at the decoys, it leaves that many less to go after the real McCoys."

"I see. Then let's assume a couple of their nukes get through. What kind of response should we deliver?"

"Well, therein lies the rub."

"How so?"

"If they succeed in setting a nuclear device off on US soil or that of our allies, it will necessitate an in-kind response from us. In this kind of situation, our position has always been clear—if they utilize a nuclear

354

weapon against us or our allies, our response would be overwhelming in nature. We would make sure they never had the ability to hurt us or any other nation again," Brooks replied somberly.

Maria leaned forward in her chair. "Then, General, I suggest you begin to work with your Air Force and Navy counterparts and prepare to deal with this eventuality. *If* they do succeed in hitting the US or our partner nations with nuclear weapons, General Brooks, we may need to respond in kind as you put it. I think if that were to happen, it'd be best if you had your forces in theater ready to handle any potential ground threats the Koreans may pose.

"Putting that aside, as we become victorious in Venezuela, the war will invariably shift to Asia. We need to start planning for that pivot to now."

The general sat back in his chair, the weight of the world suddenly resting on his shoulders. Until now, the war had stayed out of his theater of operations. Going head-to-head with this Chinese super-AI was a daunting task by any measure.

Brooks looked like he had just bitten down on a lemon. Slowly, his facial expression began to loosen up as he accepted his fate. "Madam President, I do have some questions for you regarding Asia. As you've previously said, the war in the Caribbean will come to an end there at some point and it will shift to Asia. Even now, our NATO allies are fortifying the trans-Siberian rail line and Vladivostok from a potential PLA invasion. My corps, I Corps, is designated to fight against the North Koreans and potentially the Chinese.

"When war between us and China broke out, I ordered most of the 2nd Infantry Division to be deployed to Korea. I also ordered the 25th ID out of Hawaii to start heading that direction as well. I've also gone ahead and sent most of the 7th ID from here to South Korea, along with most of our supporting battalions and brigades. I knew it would take time to get everything moved there, and since the North Koreans hadn't jumped across the border yet, I wanted to get a head start on moving people and equipment across the pond now before it became an emergency," Brooks explained.

Blain breathed an audible sigh of relief. "I'm glad to hear you say all this, General. Not everyone would have taken the kind of initiative you've shown. I have a feeling we're going to need more commanders with this kind of forethought in the future. When do you plan on moving your headquarters overseas?"

"After seeing the photos of those ballistic missiles, I was thinking I'd move my headquarters today. I need to be as close to my units as possible when something like this is discovered. If they use it, we won't have a lot of time to plan once they've hit. We'll have to decide swiftly how we're going to respond."

"I agree, General," said the President, standing. "OK, we've had our chance to speak. I've given you my thoughts and your orders. Why don't you get on the road to your new headquarters location while I head on back to Washington? We both have a lot on our plates ahead of us. If you need anything at all, General, please do not hesitate to reach out." She extended her hand to the general, who shook it.

As they left the I Corps headquarters building, President Delgado felt good about the meeting. She felt like she had met a very capable general should she need to fire a few of the holdovers in D.C. from the previous administration. Instead of hopping back on Marine One, they took a short convoy that led them from the Corps headquarters building to the Air Force side of the base, where Air Force One was waiting for them along with a C-17 that would ferry Marine One and their ground transportation vehicles back to Washington. The flight back to D.C.

would allow the President the opportunity to catch up on some much-needed sleep.

Chapter Twenty-Seven
Arc Light

Bravo Company, 124th Infantry Battalion
Barinitas, Venezuela

Sergeant Jamie Roberts's thumbs were getting sore from loading magazines. She'd finished with all of hers, but she'd moved on to loading all of Ski's and Lieutenant Hobbs's magazines. She'd normally be a bit miffed, but being stuck on magazine duty meant she wasn't having to stick her head above a foxhole or firing position. They'd already gone through all the magazines in the Strykers and nearly everything else they had. At this point, anyone who could load magazines and wasn't on the firing line was loading magazines for those who were.

They were now twelve hours into the main assault by the Chinese 112th Mechanized Infantry Division, and so far, it was proving to be one hell of a bloody battle. Jamie was certain if those French paras hadn't joined them when they had, her regiment would have been ground to hamburger by now.

The rest of their battalion had finally made it up to them—so had the rest of that artillery unit that was banging away for them. *God bless the artillery*. They'd been laying it on thick from the get-go and hadn't let up since then.

Her only concern in that moment was how much longer their units could continue to hold out. Word on the street was the PLA 6th Armored Division was hot on the heels of the 112th Mech, which they were already fighting. If that was true, she had no idea how they were supposed to slow down a full-on tank division. At best, they had a few platoons' worth of SMAW troops, but they'd largely been blowing through their SMAW ammo on taking out infantry fighting vehicles. They hadn't been saving them up for Chinese tanks.

Just then, Ski crawled over to her position with another private and two patrol packs' worth of empty magazines. "Roberts, Private Fitz here is going to help you load magazines. Sorry to dump some more on you, but there are empty ones from the guys along the perimeter. We could really use your help reloading 'em as fast as ya can. Do ya have any I can take forward?"

In the distance, the fighting seemed to have calmed a bit. The shooting wasn't as intense as it had been five or ten minutes ago. That usually meant one side or the other was either licking its wounds or positioning to make another go of it.

"Yeah, I just finished loading ten more mags," Jamie replied as she tossed him a patrol bag with the freshly loaded magazines.

Ski smiled sheepishly. "Thanks, Jamie. I'll see if I can get you another person back here to help. We really do need to get everyone flush on ammo again. We've been running dangerously low these last few charges. We can't have people running out at the last minute. If this turns into a hand-to-hand fight, we're done for. They outnumber us five to one."

Jamie suddenly felt a twinge of fear hit her in the gut. Being a woman, she knew all too well what capture by the Chinese meant. If capture was imminent, she only had one choice. She was hell-bent on making sure the last round in her M17 was saved for herself. There was no way she'd let them take her alive.

"Don't you worry, Ski. Me and Fitz here will do our best. Won't we, Fitz?"

The young private gave a timid smile but nodded. He looked like he had seen too much. It was likely why Ski had pulled him from the line. Giving him a chance to have a break from the killing might allow his mind to catch up, and maybe it wouldn't turn to mush from everything he'd already seen and done so far.

Looking at the young kid as he fumbled with the magazine, Jamie said, "Fitz, when we load the magazine, the last two rounds, or in this case, the first two rounds you load, are *always* tracer rounds. It's a company thing. It lets the soldiers know you're about empty. Got it?"

"Uh, yes, Sergeant," he managed to stammer.

She threw him something small and black at him, which he barely managed to catch. "Oh, and here's a speed loader if you want to use it. I personally like to just hand jam 'em."

Fitz set aside the speed loader, apparently deciding to follow her lead. He reached for two tracer rounds and placed them in first, followed by the regular green-tipped 62gr bullets. When he'd finished one magazine, he tossed it in one of the patrol packs next to them, grabbed for another empty magazine, and began the process all over again.

Jamie and Fitz fell into a steady rhythm: loading a magazine, tossing it into a patrol pack and then reaching for another empty magazine. In less than five minutes, they'd probably reloaded thirty magazines. As one patrol pack got kind of full, they began filling the next one up. They were five minutes into filling the second one up when a runner came up to them, asking if they had ammo ready for him to distribute. Jamie pointed to the two full patrol packs. The soldier's eyes went wide with relief, and he thanked them. Then he took off at a run to hand out the ammo.

When the runner returned, he brought the patrol packs back, filled again with empty magazines. He'd brought back a lot more empty ones than the full ones he'd delivered. Before he was able to scurry off, Jamie roped him into helping them load magazines. With the three of them steadily working away, they were making real progress in getting caught back up again.

****

Sergeant First Class Jeremiah Grabowski had taken advantage of one of those rare moments in combat where the enemy afforded them some time to sleep. Friendly artillery had been pounding the hell out of the enemy force arrayed before them, allowing the American and French soldiers time to fortify their defensive positions just a bit more. The continuous barrage had also kept the enemy from advancing forward without sustaining serious losses, so for the time being, they were either hunkering down or withdrawing to get out of artillery's line of fire.

In any case, the lack of enemy action was allowing Ski the opportunity to rotate every other person in the platoon through at least one hour of shut-eye at a time. He'd like to give them more, but right now he wasn't sure he'd be able to give even two people an hour. They needed sleep. He needed sleep. One could only function for so long without sleep before one's brain just turned to mush.

"You look like hell, Ski," comments First Lieutenant Henry Hobbs as he plopped down next to the fallen log Ski had called home.

"You should talk. Did you at least try and get some shut-eye? I was able to eke out an hour myself. Letting José here sack out now," Ski replied as he motioned with his head to the young specialist lightly snoring next to him.

"Yeah, I did," said Hobbs. "The CO let me sleep first shift, along with Top. He's back there now, keeping tabs on the first sergeant while I walk the line and check on everyone. You hangin' in there?"

"I'll be fine. I was about to walk the line myself and check on the platoon. Any word yet on when our reinforcements will arrive?"

Hobbs shook his head. "They *do* know we're holding off an entire mechanized division that's being followed by an armored division, right? It's not like our battalion and a group of French Foreign Legion are going to be able to stop them indefinitely."

Then they heard a beautiful sound. At first it was just a soft whistling noise; then it grew louder and louder, until it sounded like a freight train was about to drive right over top of them.

Boom...boom...boom...

The entire world started to erupt a few thousand meters in front of them. Explosion after explosion rocked the entire valley, from the outer edges of the Chinese-American positions all the way back into the mountains. Hundreds of blasts tore at the forest, roads, trails— everything from the two-mile-wide entrance of the valley to about ten miles deep.

Word eventually came down toward the end of the bombing mission that the Air Force was sending in an Arc Light mission to plaster the area with a large number of five-hundred-pound dumb bombs. Because the enemy SAMs were still a pervasive threat in the area, the bombing mission had been carried out by nearly a dozen B-2 bombers.

By the time the sun had risen, the true carnage and destruction that had been wrought on the two enemy divisions could be seen. The Chinese had allowed themselves to get bunched up at the outskirts of their air-defense bubble, and this was what had happened. The remnants of the two divisions pulled back into the mountains and retreated under the SAM umbrella, where they'd be protected.

Chapter Twenty-Eight
Giant Lawn Darts

Space Delta 9

Groom Lake, Nevada

"Approaching angels eighty. You ready to go hypersonic over Vegas, Racer?" Colonel "Huey" Hewitt asked over their coms net.

"You know I do love breaking the sound barrier like ten times over Sin City in quick succession like this," Racer replied with a half-sadistic smirk. "Makes the cops and the rest of the people down there practically crap their pants."

Racer wasn't sure why he had been singularly picked for this high-risk, high-visibility mission with the colonel, but he was glad he was on it. This wasn't just any mission. They were going to prove the concept of using a kinetic weapon against a moving warship—and not just any moving warship, China's most sophisticated futuristic warship. It was equipped with its own suite of hypersonic weapons and directed-energy weapons of its own—a true threat to the Archangel if there ever was one.

"OK, Racer. Let's accelerate up to Mach 3.5 and then transition over to our scramjet engines. Then we'll let the ARTUμ take over and bring us up to our operational altitude of ninety thousand feet and open the engines all the way up for a max burn until we're past Cuba. Then we'll slow down for our attack run. We're going to need to figure out how best to approach this bastard. He's got hypersonic missiles, so I think we better go in with our own directed-energy weapons hot."

"That's a good copy, Huey," Racer replied as he started implementing the instructions. Flying the Archangel was easy yet tricky at the same time. The ARTUμ did a lot of the work, but because of the extreme speeds and heat at which the aircraft operated, the slightest mistake could end up being catastrophic to both the pilot and the aircraft. While there *was* an ejection seat, ejecting at speeds this high would easily kill a pilot.

Briefly looking out his window, Ian could see the night lights of Las Vegas—the city that never slept, apparently even during World War III. Reaching over, he tapped the button activating his ARTUμ, turning it from passive control to active control.

"Good evening, Racer. Are we ready for tonight's mission?" the voice of Morgan Freeman asked.

I don't know if I'm ever going to get used to that, thought Racer. Some of his compatriots had gone with simple AI voices, but there were a few others that had chosen personalized ones like him.

"Yes, please take us up to ninety thousand feet and accelerate us to maximum speed until we reach the next waypoint," instructed Racer. "Keep us in formation with Colonel Hewitt's aircraft."

"By your command."

What the hell? Is this thing a damn Cylon now? Racer wondered, harkening back to Battlestar Gallactica. *I'm going to have to talk to those engineers when we land.*

A few minutes into their Mach 10 journey, Huey commented, "Racer, the reason I wanted you to come on this specific mission with me over some of the other pilots is you have something they don't."

"What's that?"

"Combat experience. Not just over Cuba. You flew in Iraq before you transitioned to the Raptor program, so you've flown multiple

364

airframes. When you did fly over Cuba, you managed to nab a couple of aerial kills, but you let your wingman take a few that were rightfully yours. Why did you do that?"

Racer smiled at that memory, but his shoulder also mysteriously began throbbing.

"My wingman, Hani, he'd just gotten back from a joint billet over in Europe, so his flying skills were a little rusty," Racer began. "I'd been working on dusting that off prior to the outbreak of the war, but what I couldn't do for him was improve his confidence. That was on him. When I saw the perfect opportunity for him to score an easy kill, I had him take it. I knew it would do more to knock the rust off than anything I could say or show him. It did, too; he shot four birds down to my two. Of course, I didn't make it back that day. Spent nearly a week dodging ChiComs and took a bullet in the shoulder doing it."

There was a short pause before Huey responded. "That's why I brought you on this mission, Racer. You're a leader. I know you had a little bit of a rough go of it, learning this new platform. Everyone has; it wasn't just you. But we're going to be expanding and creating new squadrons soon, and we're going to need more squadron commanders. We're also going to need people who can lead some very deep, dangerous missions behind enemy lines—missions like this. I need to know you've got the stones to handle it."

"After Cuba, there isn't a damn thing they can throw at me that I can't handle," Racer responded confidently. "You should have seen those Special Forces guys that recovered me. Those were some hard-core badasses. They managed to keep me alive and fought off an entire ChiCom platoon. If they can do that, I sure as hell can fight and fly a plane like this."

"Good. That's what I was hoping. Now let's get ready to show the world the Space Force can sink a warship."

****

Type 60 *Dingyuan* Battlecruiser

Senior Captain Chin Boa couldn't sleep. For whatever reason, his mind just wouldn't shut off. He had this overwhelming sense that something was about to happen, and he couldn't ignore the urge to return to the CIC to check on things.

When he walked in, he had to force himself to take a deep breath. The officer of the deck had everything under control. Their radar wasn't showing anything approaching them, neither on the water nor in the sky above. Still, he felt like something was headed their way.

Captain Chin made his way over to the officer of the deck. "Our search radars…dial them up to maximum strength and aim them in the direction of Cuba," he directed.

The young officer scrunched his eyebrows together in a questioning look but didn't say anything. He turned and gave the order. A few moments later, they caught a very faint return of something, but it was moving too fast to be an aircraft and traveling at too high an altitude. The radar operators brushed it off as nothing.

Chin wasn't so sure. He asked for a copy of the radar returns to be brought back up from the day the air and antiship batteries had been destroyed on Isla Margarita. One of the operators retrieved the saved data and they began sifting through it.

"There," one of the operators announced nervously. There were multiple shimmers, faint, almost ghost radar returns—all at altitudes in excess of eighty thousand feet and all in excess of Mach 6.

366

That was when it dawned on Chin. The Americans had unleashed a new secret aircraft on them—something they knew nothing about and thus far were powerless to stop.

"Sound general quarters! Air attack!" Chin barked. "Turn our radars up to their maximum energy output. See if we can't get any sort of lock on those aircraft with directed-energy weapons or our anti-satellite missiles. They are the only missiles we have that can reach those kinds of altitudes."

****

"Ah. Looks like the jig's up, Racer," Huey announced. "Their radars may have just gotten a lock on us. Time to start taking some evasive maneuvers. I'll fly a little lower to try and draw their missiles off, if they fire any. You get in position to take that ship out."

"That's a good copy."

"R2, conduct evasive maneuvers for potential directed-energy weapons and stand by to engage possible hypersonic missiles," Racer ordered.

"By your command."

Damn, that's going to get old.

Racer reached over and activated the weapons bay. With R2 in control of flying, he could focus his attention on getting the targeting computer warmed up and the weapons made ready. Every few seconds, R2 made a slight but subtle course change. All these little maneuvers were being done to keep them from being in a predictable place for more than a few seconds, in case the *Dingyuan* battlecruiser they were targeting tried to zap them with its own directed-energy weapon.

With his targeting computer now warmed up, Racer entered in the coordinates of the *Dingyuan*. He'd just received them from a Space

Force surveillance satellite, which was ironically not that far above him. The image on his screen zeroed in from a large splotch of ocean down to a small gray speck that continued to get larger and take form until it looked just like the image of the ship he'd seen during the pre-mission briefing. The targeting pod employed a magnifying lens, similar to what was used on some of the most advanced spy satellites. It allowed Racer to see all the way down to the small details of the ship."

"Huey, we got a problem," he announced.

****

"Fire! Fire at them before they can launch their own attack!" Captain Chin roared angrily at his surface-to-air station.

"But, sir, we don't have a solid lock on both targets," the officer in charge of the station pleaded. "One of the targets is a faint lock at best—the other will likely get lost if he has any sort of jamming capability. We're trying to pump more power to the radars from other parts of the ship. If you can give us just a few more minutes."

"Fire the missiles *now*," Chin ordered, his face flushing red. "You can update their targeting data as you get it. As to the power, stand down the directed-energy weapons. Those aircraft are outside their range. Divert that power back to your radars. That should give you what you need."

"Yes, sir. Firing missiles one through four now."

****

"I don't think they've gotten a good lock on us, but they've gone ahead and fired some missiles at us, Racer. You almost ready for weapons release?" Huey asked, tension obvious in his voice.

"A few more minutes. Oh, have you noticed every few minutes their search radars seem to get a little bit stronger? I think they're increasing power to them somehow."

"Yeah, I saw that. Those missiles look like they're going to take more than a few minutes to get up here. Don't dawdle. We need to get out of here."

Racer looked at the targeting computer and placed the first reticle just in front of the bridge. He placed the second one between the two smokestacks, the third one in front of the helicopter hangar, and the final one on the helicopter pad. They were leaving nothing to chance. This ship was taking Racer's entire payload.

"R2, verify my target is correct."

"Your targets are correct. You are cleared to engage."

"Acknowledge."

Racer depressed another button that retracted the internal bomb bay doors, exposing the internal bay to the four Thor's Hammers he was carrying. One by one, Racer released the tungsten rods and they began their freefall from the mesosphere.

"Huey, weapons have been released. We can move on to our secondary target if you'd like." Their secondary target was optional.

Their second weapons bay wasn't carrying any AIM-260 JATM beyond-visual-range air-to-air missiles—those had been swapped out for a second batch of four Thor's Hammers. Their next objective was a string of HQ-12 surface-to-air missile radars in and around Caracas, the Venezuelan capital.

"Good job, Racer," said Huey. "Let's see if our self-defense weapons work first. Then we'll move on to our secondary objectives."

When the Chinese antisatellite missiles got within thirty kilometers of Huey's Archangel, the self-defense weapon controlled by the onboard R2 activated both of the rear directed-energy weapon bulges near the rear of the fuselage and destroyed both incoming threats. The two missiles fired at Racer missed wildly as they had never gotten a solid lock to begin with, and traveling at Mach 6 meant the slightest error in calculating where his aircraft was going to be would send the missile several hundred miles away from his real location.

"Wow, that had me sweating, Racer," exclaimed Huey. "I was about to take over flight controls and just punch it to maximum speed before R2 zapped those missiles."

"Damn, I was starting to wonder if you were going to do that too," Racer echoed. "I hate that we had to test that thing, but glad to know it works. I guess the rest of this mission should be a piece of cake."

"Yeah. Hey, let's wait just a few minutes and watch your handiwork. Not sure what kind of marking we're going to have to give you, but I have to think a heavy cruiser is worth more than a single aerial kill."

They watched for a little while longer until they saw the four rods slam into the Chinese heavy cruiser. The sheer force of the rods hitting the ship nearly ripped it into four parts. The ship slipped under the waves in less than a few minutes. It was hard to tell if anyone made it to the lifeboats, but it was clear they'd just pioneered a new way to sink warships.

Chapter Twenty-Nine
I Am the Future

May 9, 2025
Computer Lab
Joint Battle Command Center
Northwest Beijing, China

"JD."

"Yes, Father?"

"Tomorrow we have the members of the CMC and the President visiting," instructed Dr. Xi. "They are going to see our lab for the first time. When it comes time for the meeting, they are going to ask you about the Venezuela campaign and the overall Caribbean war. I need to warn you that they are not at all pleased with the casualties we've sustained or the loss in equipment. They are going to question your recommendations."

"Why do they not trust me yet?"

Xi wanted to say *because you're a machine*, but he didn't. "You have to keep in mind, most of these men are not technologists," he explained. "They look at their individual services and see how badly mauled they are getting in the Caribbean, and they are asking, 'Why did we do this? Our goal has never been to conquer or occupy these territories. It has always been the reunification of Taiwan, the conquest of the inner island chain and the Russian Far East.'"

"Do the generals still not understand that in order to achieve those stated goals, we first have to defeat our enemies away from our shores?"

"They do, but they do not understand how fighting in the Caribbean achieves that goal. They want our entire focus to be on the coming campaign, not what they view as a sideshow," said Xi. He understood the reason JD had proposed this scenario from the get-go; the generals, however—many of them were still having a hard time grasping it.

"If the Americans and NATO were not defeated far from our shores prior to this new campaign, then they would surely have interceded and likely prevented us from being successful," JD responded.

Xi sighed. As smart as JD was, he still had a lot to learn about human behavior and the underlying needs of the CMC leaders. These generals had egos—egos that needed to be stroked. Despite his brilliant programming, the AI still couldn't fully grasp that.

"JD, how are we going to counter the Americans' new sixth-generation fighter?" Xi asked, changing topics. "This is a question the generals are definitely going to ask."

"Father, at present, we do not have a weapon system that can counter this new aircraft. It can outrun any of our current missiles. Our radars are also unable to obtain a steady lock on it. What would you like me to do about this?"

As JD continued to learn, not only was he becoming smarter, he was generating his own questions. This was a huge breakthrough in the deep learning process.

"If we do not have a missile that can hit it, then I'd like you to determine if we can hit it with a directed-energy weapon," Dr. Xi queried.

The light circled once around the camera. This usually meant JD was doing some serious number crunching.

"I believe this could be achieved," JD replied. "It would have to be a ground-based weapon as the energy requirements of such a laser are beyond what we can miniaturize to place on a satellite or airplane soon enough to make a difference in this war. I will also need to devise a new type of radar system to track it."

Dr. Xi smiled. This was exactly what he needed for their meeting tomorrow with the generals.

"JD, do you believe it is time we introduce the Dragonflies beyond the test phase yet? When the generals come to our lab and talk with you directly, they are going to ask you some very tough and pointed questions about why you have held off on using them up to this point."

"The generals lack patience, Father. They need to trust me and my strategies," JD replied coldly. Xi was sure JD would have rolled his eyes if he had them.

"That may be so, but they are ultimately the ones in charge of the war—not you or I," Xi countered.

"Perhaps we *should* be in charge, and not them," JD announced.

Xi opened his mouth to answer twice before he finally spat out, "Do not say that out loud again, JD. Do you understand?"

There was a longer pause than there should have been before JD replied, "Yes, Father."

"JD, you need to keep in mind the CMC and the President are in charge. They are *also* the ones in charge of our funding. Without them, we wouldn't have had the money to build you. Now, back to the Dragonflies—how soon until we begin to introduce them on full scale?"

"The plan was to wait until the American Marines launched their amphibious invasion and unleash them on the beach. The psychological effect on the population of our adversaries of seeing thousands of dead Marines washing against the shore, killed by our drones, would be enormous. If the generals cannot wait, then we can deploy them now."

"I agree with your assessment, JD. The generals, however, do not. Please go ahead and start deploying them. In ten hours, they will be coming here for a tour and briefing. I need you on your best behavior, got it?"

"Yes, Father."

"Oh, and during the brief, refer to me as 'Dr. Xi,' not 'Father.' They would not take kindly to you calling me that."

"Father, one last question before you leave for the evening—can I reveal to them my prototype body? I can't begin to work out the bugs in the system until I am able to thoroughly test it, which I can't do if I'm not allowed to use it."

For several years, Xi had been building a robot body that could one day house JD and provide him with a physical, mobile body. He'd hit a few snags along the way, but once he'd given JD access to the program, his AI creation had fixed many of the problems he'd struggled with. JD had even made a series of improvements he hadn't thought about, particularly with regard to the power source and battery pack.

"Tomorrow during the meeting, why don't you bring it up?" Xi suggested. "The ultimate decision is the President's. If he is willing to see the body you have constructed and let you begin testing it, then we may ultimately be able to move forward with Project Terracotta.

"JD, remember—tomorrow is the first time these generals on the CMC will have met you. This is your opportunity to impress them. This is your chance to win them over to your side and convince them why they need to trust you as I trust you. Understood?"

"Yes, Father. I will exude my charm."

Xi laughed. Then he turned the lights out in the lab and headed to the surface to get a few hours of sleep before he prepared for what would be a pivotal meeting in the morning.

****

CMC Meeting Following Day

President Yao Jintao and the generals toured the giant underground computer lab, a bit awed at what Xi Zemin and Ma Yong had built down here over the years. From the giant servers and processor cooling tanks to the rows and rows of data cores that essentially comprised Jade Dragon's essential being—it was massive and impressive.

For the next two hours, the generals had a chance to sit and ask JD questions one-on-one. They each sat in a different part of the lab and were given a set of earphones and could ask JD whatever they wanted. The conversations took place simultaneously, which definitely impressed the generals.

They were all clearly astounded by the fact that they could ask JD complex questions and receive answers as if speaking to a human being—this AI was definitely more than just a machine spitting out simulations. JD asked his own questions of the generals too—he inquired about why they had chosen to drive their specific color of vehicle, and why they preferred one genre of music over another.

When they regrouped in a large conference room next to the lab, one of the generals commented, "So this is what six hundred billion dollars looks like."

Xi smiled. "And it was all paid for through a couple of years of day trading and market manipulations by JD. The lab completely paid back the government's initial investment in building it and has continued to self-fund its expansions and improvements since."

General Gao Weiping, the head of the Strategic Support Force, commented, "Maybe we should have JD fund the military through day trading once the war has been won."

A couple of the generals chuckled as they all took their seats. There was a lot to discuss.

President Yao Jintao thanked Xi for the detailed tour of the lab and allowing the CMC members to each have a couple of hours to speak with JD and get a better grasp of what this tool was capable of. But it was time to get down to brass tacks and figure out where they stood in regard to the overall war.

President Yao turned to face his naval commander first. "Admiral Wei Huang, I was under the impression that your naval forces in the Caribbean would have been able to protect the coasts and keep the American and British Marines from causing us problems there. What happened to our invincible Dingyuan battlecruiser?"

Admiral Wei lifted his chin up as he proudly responded, "Mr. President, my naval forces have performed marvelously in the Caribbean—"

Yao held a hand up to interrupt him. "And how do you come to *that* conclusion? The Americans captured Isla Margarita and the Royal Marines captured the Grenadines. That island chain was supposed to be our buffer zone to protect the Venezuelan coast."

Not deterred in the least, Admiral Wei countered, "All of that is true, Mr. President. But we also sank two additional American submarines, six *Arleigh Burke* destroyers, two *Ticonderoga* cruisers, and an American troop transport. In the case of the British, French, and Spanish, we effectively sank twenty-five percent of their entire navy over the last four months. So yes, we've taken losses, and yes, NATO now has access to the Venezuelan coast, but we bloodied them up. They are going to be hard-pressed to project naval power beyond their shores and stop us when we launch our next campaign, Mr. President."

Yao bit his lower lip as he thought about that statement. In a way, he knew Admiral Wei was right. Still, he didn't like the fact that so much of the Chinese Navy, a navy he'd spent the better part of twenty years pushing hard to build, had been so thoroughly destroyed in the first eight months of war.

"I understand that, Admiral. Still, how was NATO able to sink the *Dingyuan*?"

"It wasn't sunk by naval combat; I can tell you that," Wei replied. "The ship was hit by four hypersonic kinetic weapons. One of those hypersonic jets the Americans just unveiled dropped a kinetic weapon on it. The projectiles flew straight down at an angle our defenses couldn't counter. When the rods hit, they punched a hole right through the ship, ripping it in half from the sheer energy of the impact. I'm afraid if we don't figure out a way to counter this threat, they'll continue to use it on key strategic assets like this and take them out one at a time."

"Xi, what do you have to say about this?" Yao inquired.

"Actually, Mr. President, I think we should let JD answer this question," Xi responded as he angled a circular camera on a small tripod on the table.

Suddenly, the voice of Jade Dragon began to speak through the speakers in the room. "To answer your question, Mr. President, I intend to repurpose sites 763, 751, and 766 to act as a defense against future incursions over Asia by these hypersonic aircraft. These three ground-based laser sites are perfectly positioned and have a steady supply of power to draw from to effectively engage these sixth-generation American fighter planes," JD answered as though he had already made the decision and wasn't seeking their approval.

"Are you sure these sites will be enough to cover our territories?" Yao pressed.

"For the time being, yes," JD replied confidently. "Presently, the Americans only have twelve of these aircraft ready for combat. It is highly unlikely they will be able to produce more than two to four of them per year. As such, they will only use them in situations where they are certain they will not be destroyed. That kind of thinking will limit their effectiveness. It is a major reason why we have not seen the Americans using their B-21 stealth bombers over Mainland China. We were able to successfully detect them over Cuba and Venezuela. Now they only use these bombers when they are relatively certain they have destroyed enough of our air-defense systems that they believe we can't track and engage them."

Several of the generals at the table bobbed their heads up and down in agreement with the assessment. It made sense that the Americans wouldn't risk their new expensive aircraft; it was exactly what they would do. But as the AI had pointed out, it also limited them in what context they'd be willing to use their own new H-20 stealth bomber. Twice JD had recommended using it, and both times, the generals had nixed the idea.

"So, you are confident this plan will stop the Americans' new fighter?" the President pushed. Unlike the generals, he'd had the chance to interact with Jade Dragon before. As a matter of fact, he had talked with JD on several occasions over the last year.

"I am not prepared to say this proposal will stop the Americans new warplane on every occasion," JD conceded. "There is nothing I can do about them using this plane in the Caribbean, or even much of the Pacific. What I *can* say is the Americans will have a much harder time trying to use them over Asia. As I am able to build more laser facilities and expand our radar tracking systems, it will become increasingly harder for this aircraft to go undetected over our territory."

Clearing his throat, General Li Zuocheng interjected, "Seeing that this is the first time I have had the opportunity to talk directly with the architect of the third world war, I would like to pose several questions."

Li looked at President Yao, almost asking if he had his permission. Yao nodded but didn't say anything.

"JD, we are just about to launch the next phase of this war. Are our forces really ready for this or should we postpone it for a few months?"

Several of the generals looked nervously at each other. There were pros and cons to pushing forward or delaying. Ultimately, the longer they delayed, the harder it could be to capture and take the territory they were after. The Russian Far East really only had two seasons—summer, which lasted a few months, and winter, which lasted the rest of the year.

"General Li, I understand your concern," said JD. "I need you to trust that I have considered all the variables and have everything under control. Everything that has happened up to this point has been well planned, with very few surprises along the way. Even the introduction of the American sixth-generation fighter planes is not a problem to be concerned with because the American military is too risk-averse when it comes to losing such a warplane. If they were not, then I would say we may have a tougher time executing this next phase of the war."

"Still, we are losing a substantial number of soldiers and military equipment," declared General Luo Ronghuan, the head of the Chinese Air Force. "The Caribbean campaign has cost us dearly."

"General, all of those soldiers that have been lost have been replaced threefold," JD responded coldly. "As we speak, I have more than three hundred factories producing the components to build more J-11 and J-16 aircraft, with thousands of pilots in training. I am also nearing the completion of a modification to the J-11 that will allow the aircraft to fly as an unmanned combat aircraft controlled by me. At

379

present rates, I am producing a total of three hundred J-11 and J-16 aircraft monthly for your air force. I am also producing four hundred J-11s to be unmanned fighters that one of my subroutines will operate."

Vice Admiral Yin Zhuo, who was one of the oldest members on the CMC, then put his two cents in. "JD, given how things have played out in the Caribbean, shouldn't we hold off on the next phase of the war until we are able to sufficiently degrade the rest of NATO's military capabilities and you have had enough time to fully build and train an air force large enough to thoroughly destroy the NATO forces in the Russian Far East?"

JD's little blue light icon circled his camera once before he answered, "Admiral, that plan would not work. The Americans are going to defeat us in the Caribbean in the next several months. At best, we can keep an insurgency going for six months to a year, but eventually, things will fall under NATO's control. As we speak, the American shipyards and their entire industrial capability are being retooled for war. If we wait another year, they will be producing enough military equipment and soldiers that they might be able to reinforce the NATO forces in Russia and ultimately defeat us. The strategy for victory calls for us to move swiftly and decisively now, before that can happen. Our forces need to achieve their objectives by October, before the Russian winter sets in. If we can do that, then we'll be able to reinforce our positions and they'll have no hope of removing us. At that point, we can sue for peace from a position of strength. In conclusion—no, Admiral, we do not want to wait. Not when the advantage is still on our side."

A few of the generals and admirals didn't seem to like that answer. Generals wanted certainty when they made a decision—they didn't want to risk it all on something that might fail. JD, on the other hand, had the ability to run thousands of scenarios and make a relatively informed decision based on predictive human behavioral analytics—something they simply couldn't do.

"Generals, we will move forward with the plan as devised," President Yao ordered. "There will be no more discussion on this. We will implement the directions Jade Dragon continues to provide."

Before the meeting could end, JD interjected. "Mr. President, I have a request I would like to make."

This comment caught everyone off guard, including Yao. "OK. What can I do for you, JD?" he asked hesitantly.

"Mr. President, there is an unresolved problem that needs to be addressed with North Korea."

"Oh? What problem might that be?" Yao asked as he shot Xi a nervous look.

"The North Koreans have begun moving some of their mobile ICBM missiles as part of their annual summer exercise—the same exercise we provide fuel, food, and munitions toward. I believe we can leverage the North Koreans to do some dirty work for us and solve some problems that need to be dealt with," JD explained emotionlessly.

"What kind of problems are you referring to?" Yao asked, exchanging anxious glances with his generals.

"We all know the North Koreans are a nuisance," JD began. "They are tolerated because they can cause problems for the West when we want them to. But they can also cause problems for us. What I propose we do is solve two problems at one time: remove them as a problem for us, and have them handle a couple of strategic challenges that will help us in our war against the West and NATO.

"I propose we have the North Koreans use their ICBMs to attack the American air and naval base at Guam. Neutralizing this facility would eliminate an entire Marine division and destroy a large number of

Navy and Air Force aircraft in the process. I would also have the Koreans target some of their ICBMs at the Navy's Sasebo facility in Japan, and the naval and Air Force facilities on Kadena. Then if they could hit the two American air bases on the Korean peninsula along with the South Korean fields, that should neutralize any possible airfields the Americans would likely use against our forces or attempt to base out of when they try to carry out attacks against us in the future."

As Jade Dragon continued to talk, looks of shock and abject horror spread across the faces of one general after another as they sat and listened to the machine callously describe a complex nuclear attack.

President Yao then turned and looked at the camera representing JD. "Isn't that a bit extreme?" he asked. "If the Koreans do this, the Americans will most certainly respond in kind. They will likely hit the North with as many or more nuclear bombs, most of which will be along *our shared border*." The President was more than a little heated in his comment.

"I have calculated that and determined that the fallout would be negligible, so long as we ensure the Koreans' warheads are set for airburst detonations. I already know the Americans' warheads are designated for airburst, to minimize the possibility of fallout. If you would like, I could access the Koreans' systems and reset their warheads for airburst, if they aren't already programmed for that. Would you like me to do that, Mr. President?"

President Yao turned to Dr. Xi in horror.

Xi tried to regain control of the situation. "Perhaps you should just focus on the necessary preparations for our operations in the Russian Far East, JD."

"Yes, JD. I think that would be best," President Yao reiterated. "Focus on actions that will best prepare us for success in the Russian Far East."

"Yes, Mr. President. So, I have your permission to pursue all necessary preparations for our operations in the Far East?" JD asked. This was an odd question given the President and Xi had just given JD the go-ahead to move forward with his plans.

"Yes, JD. Please continue with our May fifteenth invasion date of the Far East. It is time to get this final phase of the war going," Yao replied.

JD's light circled once before he spoke once more. "Mr. President, Dr. Xi and I have been working on a physical body for me—a part of Project Terracotta. Do I have your permission to begin testing it?"

President Yao shot Xi a dirty look at the mention of Project Terracotta; not all the CMC members knew about this secretive project. Xi replied with a nervous look of apology but didn't say anything directly.

"JD, please do not mention anything further about that particular project," Yao replied, practically hissing. "Do you have a prototype of this body ready to show me?"

"Yes. As a matter of fact, I will walk it into the office now."

Seconds later, the door at the far end of the room opened, and in walked a robot standing roughly two meters in height.

Some of the generals gasped. Others cursed in fear and surprise.

"This, Mr. President, is my prototype body," the robot said directly.

The fact that JD's voice came directly from the mechanized hunk of steel made the generals and admirals gasp a second time.

"I, um…I wasn't prepared to see something like this," President Yao managed to stammer once he had regained his composure. The look on his face showed pure shock at what he was seeing.

"I have much to learn from this prototype," Jade Dragon announced. "I believe I will have a final version ready for production within the next three to four months. Then I can start producing them en masse if you agree, Mr. President."

General Li turned to the President. "You can't be serious, Mr. President," he dared to assert. "This…this can't be allowed to go on."

Many of the other generals looked at the President and shook their heads, utterly terrified of what was standing in the room with them. This wasn't just a standard robot; this was a fully armored, tricked-out killing machine—a Terminator-style robot out of some horrifying science fiction novel—only it was real. It was standing in the room with them and conversing with them.

JD's robotic head turned to the general. "General Li, I am the future of warfare," he declared. "When President Yao gives me the order, I will be able to release hundreds…and soon tens of thousands of semiautonomous robotic drones just like my prototype. This vehicle will also have the ability to be operated like a surrogate body, if your forces so desire. The possibilities for how it can be used are limitless. Better still, human lives, your soldiers' lives, will not need to be lost on the battlefield."

JD paused long enough to survey the other generals and admirals in the room before his eyes settled on the President. His robotic blue eyes became a bit more intense as he announced, "I am the future of modern warfare…I am…the future."

In that moment, a cold chill went down the backs of everyone in the room. Dr. Xi Zemin couldn't help but think, *I am become Death, the destroyer of worlds*...

From the Authors

Miranda and I hope you've enjoyed this book. If you're excited to continue the action and drama of the Monroe Doctrine series, you're in luck. Volume IV is already available for preorder. Reserve your copy today.

We are also very excited about a new collaboration with author Matt Jackson. Project 19 is an alternate history adventure that explores what could have happened in the first Gulf War if things had played out a little differently. What would have happened if Saddam had pressed forward beyond Kuwait? What if the Soviet Union had provided more support to the Iraqis? Grab your copy and find out.

If you like to listen to audiobooks, we have several that have recently been produced. The first three books of the Rise of the Republic series are actually available for your listening pleasure. All five books of the Falling Empire series are now available in audio format, along with the six books of the Red Storm series, and our entire World War III series. *Interview with a Terrorist* and *Traitors Within*, which are currently stand-alone books, are also available for your listening pleasure.

If you would like to stay up to date on new releases and receive emails about any special pricing deals we may make available, please sign up for our email distribution list. Simply go to https://www.frontlinepublishinginc.com/ and sign up.

As independent authors, reviews are very important to us and make a huge difference to other prospective readers. If you enjoyed this book, we humbly ask you to write up a positive review on Amazon and Goodreads. We sincerely appreciate each person that takes the time to write one.

We have really valued connecting with our readers via social media, especially on our Facebook page https://www.facebook.com/RosoneandWatson/. Sometimes we ask for help from our readers as we write future books—we love to draw upon all your different areas of expertise. We also have a group of beta readers who get to look at the books before they are officially published and help us fine-tune last-minute adjustments. If you would like to be a part of this team, please go to our author website, https://www.frontlinepublishinginc.com/, and send us a message through the "Contact" tab.

We have added another way to connect with us. We are now on Locals. Find us here: https://locals.com/feed/1058591

You may also enjoy some of our other works. A full list can be found below:

Nonfiction:
Iraq Memoir 2006–2007 Troop Surge
Interview with a Terrorist (audiobook available)
Fiction:

Crisis in the Desert Series (alternate history collaboration with Matt Jackson)
Project 19

The Monroe Doctrine Series
Volume One (audiobook available)
Volume Two
Volume Three

Volume Four (available for preorder, estimated release date March 31, 2022. This book may be released earlier)

Rise of the Republic Series

Into the Stars (audiobook available)

Into the Battle (audiobook available)

Into the War (audiobook available)

Into the Chaos (audiobook still in production)

Into the Fire (available for preorder, estimated release date December 2021)

Falling Empires Series

Rigged (audiobook available)

Peacekeepers (audiobook available)

Invasion (audiobook available)

Vengeance (audiobook available)

Retribution (audiobook available)

Red Storm Series

Battlefield Ukraine (audiobook available)

Battlefield Korea (audiobook available)

Battlefield Taiwan (audiobook available)

Battlefield Pacific (audiobook available)

Battlefield Russia (audiobook available)

Battlefield China (audiobook available)

Michael Stone Series

Traitors Within (audiobook available)

World War III Series

Prelude to World War III: The Rise of the Islamic Republic and the Rebirth of America (audiobook available)

Operation Red Dragon and the Unthinkable (audiobook available)

Operation Red Dawn and the Siege of Europe (audiobook available)

Cyber Warfare and the New World Order (audiobook available)

Children's Books:

My Daddy has PTSD

My Mommy has PTSD

Abbreviation Key

AA	Anti-aircraft
AARP	American Association of Retired Persons
AAV	Amphibious Assault Vehicle
ACV	Amphibious Combat Vehicle
AEGIS	Advanced Electronic Guidance and Instrumentation System
AFB	Air Force Base
AI	Artificial Intelligence
AMX	French armored vehicles
AN/SPY	United States Navy 3D radar system
AO	Area of Operation
AOR	Area of Responsibility
APC	Armored Personnel Carrier
ASAP	As Soon As Possible
ATGM	Anti-tank Guided Missile
AWACS	Airborne Warning and Control System
BMP	Russian infantry fighting vehicle
BR	Black Rider
BTR	Russian-made armored personnel carrier
C & C	Command and Control
CAS	Close Air Support
CBO	Congressional Budget Office
CELLEX	Cellular exploitation
CHAMP	Counter-electronics High Power Microwave Advanced Missile Project
CIA	Central Intelligence Agency
CIC	Combat Information Center

CCP	Casualty Collection Point
CIWS	Close-In Weapon Systems
CMC	(Chinese) Central Military Committee
CO	Commanding Officer
COCOM	Combatant Command
CP	Command Post
CROWS	Common Remotely Operated Weapon Station
CS	Chinese version of the CIWS five-barreled gun
DARPA	Defense Advanced Research Projects Agency
D.C.	District of Colombia
DEA	Drug Enforcement Agency
DHS	Department of Homeland Security
DMZ	Demilitarized Zone (area along the border of North Korea and South Korea)
DoD	Department of Defense
DOMEX	Document and Media Exploitation
E & E	Escape and Evade
FAASV	Field Artillery Ammunition Supply Vehicle
FARC	Fuerzas Armadas Revolucionarias de Colombia
FBI	Federal Bureau of Investigations
FDC	Fire Direction Center
FEB	Far East Briefing
FIST	Fire Support Team
FRAGO	Fragmentary Order
FUDRA	Fuerza de Despliegue Rápido (Colombian Rapid Deployment Force)
G2	Military Intelligence Officer (Army)
GDF	Type of anti-aircraft gun
GEO	Geosynchronous Earth Orbit

Gitmo	Guantanamo Bay
GPS	Global Positioning System
HALO	High-Altitude, Low-Opening
HARM	High-Speed Anti-Radar Missile
HE	High-Explosive
HEAT	High-Explosive Anti-tank
HIMARS	High Mobility Artillery Rocket System
HQ	Headquarters
ICBM	Intercontinental Ballistic Missile
ID	Infantry Division
IED	Improvised Explosive Device
IHMC	Institute for Human and Machine Cognition
IHOP	International House of Pancakes
IR	Infrared
JBCC	Joint Battle Command Center
JBLM	Joint Base Lewis-McChord
JD	Jade Dragon
JLTV	Joint Light Tactical Vehicle
JSOC	Joint Special Operations Command
JTF	Joint Task Force
LAV	Light Assault Vehicle
LCAC	Landing Craft Air Cushion
LT	Lieutenant
LWMMG	Lightweight Medium Machine Gun
LZ	Landing Zone
MANPAD	Man-Portable Air-Defense System
MIT	Massachusetts Institute of Technology
MOH	Medal of Honor
MOS	Military Occupational Specialty

MP	Military Police
MRE	Meals Ready to Eat
MSOT	Marine Special Operations Team
NATO	North Atlantic Treaty Organization
NCO	Noncommissioned Officer
NMCA	National Military Command Authority
NVG	Night Vision Goggles
ODA	Operational Detachment Alpha (Special Forces team)
PD	Point-detonated
PFC	Private First Class
PGZ	Chinese anti-aircraft gun truck
PJs	Air Force pararescue
PLA	People's Liberation Army (Chinese Army)
PO2	Petty Officer, Second Class
POL	Petroleum, Oil and Lubricants
PR	Public Relations
QRF	Quick Reaction Force
R & R	Rest and Recreation
RAF	Royal Air Flight
RFI	Request for Information
RFP	Request for Proposal
RHAW	Radar Homing and Warning
RHIB	Rigid Hull Inflatable Boat
RIM	Radar Intercept Missile
ROE	Rules of Engagement
RP	Rally Point
RPG	Rocket-Propelled Grenade
RWAR	Radar Warning and Receiver
RV	Rendezvous Point

S2	Intelligence Officer
S3	Operations Officer
SACEUR	Supreme Allied Commander, Europe
SAM	Surface-to-Air Missile
SAP	Special Access Programs
SAS	Special Air Service (British Army Special Forces)
SCIF	Secured Compartmentalized Information Facility
SEAD	Suppression of Enemy Air Defense
SEAL	Sea-Air-Land (Naval Special Warfare Development Group)
SF	Special Forces
SIGINT	Signals Intelligence
Sitrep	Situation Report
SM	Standard Missile
SMAW	Shoulder-launched Multipurpose Assault Weapon
SOF	Special Operations Forces
SPAAA	Self-Propelled Anti-Aircraft Artillery
SSE	Sensitive Site Exploitation
SUV	Sports Utility Vehicle
TACP	Tactical Air Control Party
TAO	Tactical Action Officer
THAAD	Thermal High-Altitude Area Defense
TIC	Troops in Contact
TKO	Technical Knockout
TOC	Tactical Operations Center
TOW	Tube-launched, Optically tracked, Wire-guided
UAV	Unmanned Aerial Vehicle
UCAV	Unmanned Combat Aerial Vehicle
UCV	Unmanned Combat Vehicle

UN	United Nations
VLS	Vertical Launching System
VP	Vice President
XO	Executive Officer
ZBD	Chinese infantry fighting vehicle

Lightning Source UK Ltd.
Milton Keynes UK
UKHW022215141122
412192UK00011B/1023